Edward Ryder, Elizabeth Gurney Fry

Elizabeth Fry

Life and labors of the eminent philantropist, preacher, and prison reformer

Edward Ryder, Elizabeth Gurney Fry

Elizabeth Fry
Life and labors of the eminent philantropist, preacher, and prison reformer

ISBN/EAN: 9783337295363

Printed in Europe, USA, Canada, Australia, Japan

Cover: Foto ©Raphael Reischuk / pixelio.de

More available books at **www.hansebooks.com**

ELIZABETH FRY:

LIFE AND LABORS OF THE EMINENT PHILANTHROPIST, PREACHER AND PRISON-REFORMER.

COMPILED FROM HER JOURNAL AND OTHER SOURCES

BY EDWARD RYDER.

389 pages, 8vo., WITH FULL LENGTH PORTRAIT.

THIS work is designed to supply a deficiency in English and American Literature by presenting within moderate compass, a true *Life*, rather than a *Sketch*, of the great Quaker Philanthropist, whose name is one of the purest stars of English History, and whose tireless efforts to extend the mantle of Christian Charity until it should reach the *feet* of toiling, enslaved humanity, deserve the thanks of all who need mercy, and the admiration of those who do not. The aim has been to preserve what is of universal and permanent interest in her eventful life, at the same time avoiding such fullness of detail as would discourage general perusal. If the proper medium be secured, such a record cannot fail to be a living power for good and a pleasure to those who read. Any true life of Elizabeth Fry must be largely autobiographical.

TESTIMONIALS

From REV. W. S. CLAPP, Pastor of the Baptist Church, Carmel, N. Y.

CARMEL, N. Y., July 24, 1883.

FRIEND EDWARD RYDER,

My Dear Brother :—I sincerely thank you for sending me a copy of your book on the "Life and Labors of Elizabeth Fry." I have read it with the greatest interest. The philanthropy of her nature together with the almost angelic purity of her spiritual affections, her self-consecration to Prison and Hospital work, and the helping hand she held out with a wise discrimination to every form and degree of human suffering she encountered, gave harmonious strength and effectiveness to her life and labors, and made a place for her in the front rank of the moral heroes of history. The charm of her character and the spirit of her work qualified her for exercising a great personal influence among all classes. I could wish that your book might be found in every Christian family.

With much esteem, yours faithfully,

W. S. CLAPP.

From Mrs. J. R. Nichols, State Lecturer for Indiana W. C. T. U.

INDIANAPOLIS, IND., Oct. 18, 1883.

I cannot tell you how pleased I am with the "Life of Elizabeth Fry." It seems to fill a long felt want in the way of practical help in our woman's work for woman. I do not think any book could have been issued at the present time that would have been so welcome to the women of our country who are engaged in reform work. You have cleared away all the superfluous matter in the other lives, and given us the kernel of the whole thing in such a way that it will be of immense practical use. Then it is up with the advanced ideas of the Friends at the present time, who are very liberal, especially here in the West. I took a copy on my last trip, and as I met some Friends of standing, I showed it to them. They were eager to have a copy and declared that such a book ought to be introduced all over the West and would be exceedingly popular.

From Jos. B. Clark, Sec. American Home Missionary Society.

NEW YORK, Nov. 22, 1883.

I have examined with great pleasure the "Life and Labors of Elizabeth Fry," by Mr. Edward Ryder. The materials, drawn chiefly from her own Journal and Letters, have been arranged with more than usual literary skill. The labor was evidently one of love on the part of Mr. Ryder, and the result is a striking picture of a noble and useful life.   Jos. B. CLARK.

From Wm. M. F. Round, Cor. Sec. of the N. Y. Prison Association.

Dear Sir:—Whatever calls the attention of the public to the noble and self-sacrificing efforts of Elizabeth Fry will be likely to help the cause of Prison Reform. Your book is timely and seems to me to sum up with excellent judgment the strong points in Mrs. Fry's career.   WM. M. F. ROUND.

"It is a grand book."—*Mrs. H. E. Brown, Editor Advocate and Guardian.*

"The book is of great interest and the style is admirable."—
Amendment Herald.

"There is something in it to touch every case."—*Mrs. M. Thomas.*

"There is no woman in modern history, living or dead, that I admire so much."—*Miss Jennie Collins.*

We cordially recommend the "Life and Labors of Elizabeth Fry" as a biography of great interest and value. The brightness of her character and gifts, and the remarkable success which attended her labors for human improvement, must ever make her story an inspiration to the lovers of Humanity.

JOHN G. WHITTIER.
BENSON J. LOSSING, L.L.D.
THOMAS ARMITAGE, D.D.
S. D. BURCHARD, D.D., President Rutger's Female College.
OLIVER JOHNSON.
DIO LEWIS.
A. C. ARNOLD, New York Bible Society.
THOS. E. VERMILYE, D.D., 15 West 56th Street, New York.
THEO. L. CUYLER, D.D., 176 Oxford Street, Brooklyn.
REBECCA COLLINS, Honorary President N. Y. W. C. T. U.
D. W. COUCH, Pastor Beekman Hill M. E. Church.
GEORGE HUGHES, Editor *Guide to Holiness.*
HELEN E. BROWN, Editor *Advocate and Guardian.*
WM. M. TAYLOR, D.D., 5 West 35th Street, New York.
HOWARD CROSBY, D.D., 116 East 19th Street, New York.
JULIA COLMAN, Supt. Literature Department National W. C. T. U.
JOS. B. CLARK, Secretary Home Missionary Society.
FRANCES E. WILLARD, President National W. C. T. U.
ALFRED H. LOVE, President Universal Peace Union.

FROM THE N. Y. INDEPENDENT, FEB. 14, 1884.

The world needs no introduction to Elizabeth Fry. Hers is a name that is sure to live in the Christlike connection of charity with criminals as He connected divine love with sinners. Our readers will be glad to learn that a new life has been published, under the title *Elizabeth Fry: Life and Labors of the Eminent Philanthropist, Preacher and Prison Reformer*, by Edward Ryder. This memoir is not an attempt to rewrite the life on the basis of new and original studies and researches, but to present a portrait of Mrs. Fry and a representation of her career compiled from the accepted sources, but unembarrassed by the prolixities, the needless details, and now cold questions of the two full octavos published in 1847. Elizabeth Fry was endowed with all the resources and attractions of the fullest womanhood. She was the mother of eleven children, and at one time in her life saw around her twenty-five grandchildren. Her Quakerism, though genuine, was of that mild type in which Christian character shines at its brightest. It was not till 1817 that her work in the Prison Reform was fully begun. The principles of that reform were essentially the separation of the sexes, the classification of criminals, the supervision of women by women, and the introduction of useful employment, an important feature of her work which the New York reformers at Albany, in their zeal to buy favor with criminal classes out of prison, are just now attempting to win a little cheap popularity by suppressing. Mrs. Fry, as is well known, extended her labors through the continent of Europe, and next after Howard has written her name on the roll of honor in this reformation. In biographic interest, and in fullness, weight and quality of life, she greatly surpassed Howard. As a biography, the Life gains by the condensation applied to it by Mr. Ryder, whose brevity kindles in it a new inspiration, and gives more effect to the beauty of holiness and to the power of saintliness, and a new exhibition of the deep and strong sympathy which exists between the holiest and the purest natures and those lowest down in the degradation of sin.

FROM THE N. Y. OBSERVER, FEB. 21, 1884.

....The portrait, adorning the volume just published, presents a combination of majesty and loveliness very rarely seen in the human form and face. And then the character and work revealed in her daily walk with God and man, preserves the same noble features, so that it is quite probable no woman of modern times has more completely exhibited what a woman ought to be by what she was. Eulogies while she was living, were as many and frequent as they have been since her death, and her praise is still constant on the lips of those who have read of her virtues and her deeds.

....One of the most happy tributes was paid to her in the German Almanac for the beautiful and the good: "Though faithful to her duty as a wife and mother, into the night of the prison Elizabeth Fry brings the radiance of love, brings comfort to the sufferer, dries the tear of repentance, and causes a ray of hope to descend into the heart of the sinner. She teaches her that has strayed, again to find the path of virtue, comes as an angel of God into the abode of crime, and preserves for Jesus' kingdom that which appeared to be lost."

From The Christian Union, Feb. 21, 1884.

Elizabeth Fry: Life and Labors of the Eminent Philanthropist, Preacher, and Prison Reformer, is the title of a volume of nearly four hundred pages, which has been carefully compiled from her journals and published writings concerning her, by Edward Ryder, of Brewster, Putnam County, N. Y. The design of the book is to put within the reach of all classes of readers a knowledge of the saintly woman and her deeds, for the benefit of the young especially. No woman appears more prominently in the annals of philanthropy, in the Christian ministry, and as a model in domestic life, than Elizabeth Fry: no preacher or reformer has ever won more love and admiration from the good of all lands than this noble and devout woman, who, for more than thirty years, was a powerful preacher of righteousness in words and example, not only before some of the most enlightened and exalted persons in England and on the Continent, but the inmates of prisons and almshouses. She was a member of the Society of Friends, or Quakers. Her life was a perpetual evangel: her creed was the Golden Rule: her utterance was always a healing chrism, consecrated by the great High Priest: and her commission bore the seal of the loving Father of us all. In person, Elizabeth Fry was one of the most beautiful women of her times: she was tall and stately, fair in complexion, and her whole countenance beamed with intelligence and love. She was ever queenly in grace and spirit. Possessed of wealth, and social in her nature, she entertained many people of all ranks in life with uniform dignity and simplicity. Her home was her imperial kingdom, wherein she ruled right royally. In 1842, she entertained the King of Prussia (brother of Emperor William, of Germany) at breakfast. After presenting to him her ten children, with their husbands and wives, and her twenty-five grandchildren, they partook of the repast, when she offered a most impressive prayer for him, his family, and his country.

That prince of cynics, John Randolph, who was in England in 1822, said to a friend: "Two days ago I saw the greatest curiosity in London—aye, and in England, too, sir—compared to which Westminster Abbey, the Tower, Somerset House, the British Museum, nay Parliament itself, sink into utter insignificance! I have seen, sir, Elizabeth Fry in Newgate, and have witnessed there the miraculous effects of true Christianity upon the most depraved of human beings! And yet the wretched outcasts have been tamed and subdued by the Christian eloquence of Elizabeth Fry! I have seen them weep repentant tears while she addressed them; I have heard their groans of despair, sir! Nothing but religion can effect this miracle; for what can be a greater miracle than the conversion of a degraded sinful woman taken from the very dregs of society?" An account of all the important events in the career of Elizabeth Fry may be found in this volume, lucidly expressed. It is full of spiritual aliment; and it is exceedingly attractive as a narrative of a grand life.

ELIZABETH FRY:

LIFE AND LABORS

OF THE

EMINENT PHILANTROPIST, PREACHER, AND PRISON REFORMER.

COMPILED FROM HER JOURNAL AND OTHER SOURCES.

BY EDWARD RYDER.

"Verily I say unto you, Wheresoever this Gospel shall be preached in the whole world, there shall also this which this woman hath done be told for a memorial of her."
—*Matt.* 26:13.

THIRD EDITION.

NEW YORK :

PUBLISHED BY E. WALKER'S SON, 14 DEY ST.,

FOR THE AUTHOR.

1884.

"Mr. Harvey, two days ago I saw the greatest curiosity in London—aye and in England too, sir,—compared to which Westminster Abbey, the Tower, Somerset House, the British Museum, nay Parliament itself, sink into utter insignificance! I have seen, sir, Elizabeth Fry in Newgate, and have witnessed miraculous effects of true Christianity upon the most depraved of human beings."

—*John Randolph.*

"We shall not look upon her like again! and must try to preserve the impression of her majesty of goodness which it is a great privilege to have beheld."

—*Baroness Bunsen.*

"To see her was to love her; to hear her was to feel as if a guardian angel had bid you follow that teaching which could alone subdue the temptations and evils of this life, and secure a redeemer's love in eternity."

—*Captain K. B. Martin.*

"May you continue, my dear madam, to be the honored instrument of great and rare benefits to almost the most pitiable of your fellow-creatures."

— *William Wilberforce.*

"Of all my contemporaries none has exercised a like influence on my heart and life."

—*Thomas Fliedner.*

"Though faithful to her duty as a wife and mother, into the night of the prison Elizabeth Fry brings the radiance of love, brings comfort to the sufferer, dries the tear of repentance, and causes a ray of hope to descend into the heart of the sinner. She teaches her that has strayed again to find the path of virtue, comes as an angel of God into the abode of crime, and preserves for Jesus' kingdom that which appeared to be lost."
—*German "Almanac for the Beautiful and Good."*

"Your name has long been to us 'A Word of Beauty.'"
—*German Pastor.*

"TO MRS. FRY.

Presented by HANNAH MORE
As a token of veneration,
Of her heroic zeal,
Christian charity,
And persevering kindness
To the most forlorn
Of human beings.
They were naked and she
Clothed them;
In prison and she visited them;
Ignorant and she taught them,
For *His* sake,
In *His* name, and by *His* word
Who went about doing good."
—*H. More, in copy of "Practical Piety."*

PREFACE.

My aim has been not to preserve everything she said and did, but to present a Life Portrait of Elizabeth Fry and her unique career. This can best be done by letting herself be the chief speaker, since she has spoken so admirably:—next those who knew her well. Of the latter we have many witnesses, but the principal are her two daughters, Katherine Fry and Rachel E. Cresswell, both still living at this date, who in 1847, two years after her death, published a "Memoir of the Life of Elizabeth Fry," in two octavo volumes of 525 and 552 pages. This was extensively read at that time, when the name of Elizabeth Fry was in all mouths; but it necessarily contained much of transitory interest to the rapidly changing world of men, who are too busy to dwell long on what does not closely concern them. The work was not reprinted and has long been out of the market, and only to be found among those who purchased at the time of its publication. An abridgement of it was afterwards published, with some additional notes and recollections by Susanna Corder, a teacher of Friends' schools, who was well acquainted with Mrs. Fry, and a member of the same religious Society.

This work of 667 pages is still to be obtained at Friends book stores, and seems to have been undertaken partly with a view to furnishing members of that Society with a "Life of Elizabeth Fry," relieved of both a portion of matter passing from public interest, and of the unquakerly style in which the original Memoir was written—one of the daughters, Mrs. Cresswell, and apparently the larger writer, having become a member of the Episcopal church, and not conforming to the peculiarities of her mother. Mrs. Fry, also left on record some observations looking toward greater liberty than her Society were then ready to adopt, though they are now approaching the standard to which her catholic spirit and wide experience at length brought her sympathetic mind.

In reading first this Abridgement, obtained for a circulating library in a community partly made up of Friends, I was struck with the large number of highly interesting facts and incidents it contained, as well as with the delightful spirit which it exhibited—a spirit which I felt ought to bring a contagion of heavenly-mindedness into the soul of each reader—and I found a regret arising that such choice seed of the Kingdom of Heaven was not scattered broadcast through all lands. I therefore resolved, as I trust under the inspiration of Him whose eyes run to and fro in the earth, seeking where good may be accomplished and His children made happy, to undertake a further pruning of decaying branches from this noble olive tree, leaving only such as will bear fruit for all times and places, and then to essay its introduction not only into the parks of those who are rich in knowledge and spiritual wisdom, but also in the little gardens of the poor where Elizabeth Fry was so fond of sowing seeds of kindness and love, hoping they might spring up unto everlasting life.

The part I have had to perform is mainly that of an artisan whose material is already furnished to his hand, requiring only careful selection and judicious arrangement to give effect to the simple beauty which the subject itself contains. I have ventured to add the connecting thread of a few observations in passing, and occasional comments on portions which seemed to invite further illustration, or criticism.

Pawling, Duchess County, N. Y.   E. RYDER.

Feb. 1, 1883.

CONTENTS.

ELIZABETH FRY.

CHAPTER FIRST.

EARLY LIFE.

ELIZABETH FRY was born in Norwich, England, on the 21st of May, 1780. She was the third daughter of John Gurney of Earlham, a liberal-spirited Quaker, "a man of ready talent, of bright discerning mind, singularly warm-hearted and affectionate, very benevolent, and in manners courteous and popular;" and of Catherine Bell, daughter of Daniel Bell, a London Merchant, and great-grand-daughter of Robert Barclay, the well-known and able expounder of Quakerism.

From this excellent stock eleven children, seven daughters and four sons, grew to maturity, and several of them became active and useful members of the Society of Friends, including Elizabeth Fry, Joseph John Gurney and Priscilla Gurney, whose memoirs have been given to the public.

From the "Memoir of the Life of Elizabeth Fry," edited by two of her daughters, the following extracts relating to her early life are taken:

"In the year 1786, Mr. and Mrs. Gurney removed to Earlham Hall, a seat of the Bacon family, about two miles from Norwich. Mr. Gurney subsequently purchased an adjoining property, thus adding to the range and variety afforded to his large young party, by that pleasant home.   Earlham has peculiar charms from its diversified scenery.   The house is large, old, and irregular; placed in the centre of a well-wooded park.   The River Wensum, a clear winding stream, flows by it.   Its banks, overhung by an avenue of ancient timber trees, formed a favorite resort of the young people; there, in the summer evenings, they would often meet to walk, read, or sketch.   On the south front of the house extends a noble lawn, flanked by groves of trees growing from a carpet of wild flowers, moss, and long grass.   Every nook, every green path at Earlham, tells a tale of the past and recalls to those who remember the time when they were peopled by that joyous party, the many loved ones of the number, who, having shared with one another the pleasures of youth, the cares of maturer age, and above all, the hope of immortality, are now together at rest!

"Of the twelve children of Mr. and Mrs. Gurney, nine were born before their removal to Earlham; one of them died in infancy.   The three youngest sons were born after their settlement there.

"The mode of life at Bramerton was continued with little alteration at Earlham, till Nov. 1792, when it pleased God to remove from this large family, the kind mistress,—the loving wife,—the devoted mother.   She died after an illness of three weeks, leaving eleven children, the eldest scarcely seventeen, the youngest not two years old.   During a period of comparative leisure, Elizabeth Fry occupied herself in perusing her early journals.   She thought it well to destroy all that were written before the year 1797, and to substitute the following sketch of their contents, assisted by her own recollections.

"'*Dagenham, Eighth Month,* 23d, 1828.—My earliest recollections are, I should think, soon after 1 was two years old; my father at that time had two houses, one in Norwich, and one at Bramerton, a sweet country place, situated on a Common,

near a pretty village; here, I believe, many of my early
tastes were formed, though we left it to reside at Earlham
when I was about five years old. The impressions then received remain lively on my recollection; the delight in the
beauty and wild scenery in parts of the Common, the trees,
the flowers, and the little rills that abounded on it, the farm
houses, the village school and the different poor people and
their cottages; particularly a poor woman with one arm,
whom we called one-armed Betty; another neighbor, Green-
grass, and her strawberry beds round a little pond; our
gardener, who lived near a large piece of water, and used to
bring fish from it; here, I think, my great love for the
country, the beauties of nature, and attention to the poor,
began. My mother was most dear to me, and the walks she
took with me in the old-fashioned garden, are as fresh with
me, as if only just passed; and her telling me about Adam
and Eve being driven out of Paradise: I always considered
it must be just like our garden at Bramerton. I remember
that my spirits were not strong: that I frequently cried if
looked at, and used to say that my eyes were weak; but I
remember much pleasure and little suffering or particular
tendency to naughtiness, up to this period. Fear about this
time began to show itself, of people and things: I remember being so much afraid of a gun, that I gave up an expedition of pleasure with my father and mother because there
was a gun in the carriage. I was also exceedingly afraid of
the dark, and suffered so acutely from being left alone without a light after I went to bed, that I believe my nervous
system was injured in consequence of it; also, I had so great
a dread of bathing, (to which I was obliged at times to submit) that at the first sight of the sea, when we were as a
family going to stay by it, it would make me cry; indeed,
fear was so strong a principle in my mind as greatly to mar
the natural pleasure of childhood. I am now of opinion,
that it would have been much more subdued, and great suffering spared, by its having been still more yielded to; by

having a light left in my room; not being long left alone; and never forced to bathe; for I do not at all doubt that it partly arose from that nervous susceptible constitution, that has at times, throughout my life, caused me such real and deep suffering. I know not what would have been the consequence, had I had any other than a most careful and wise mother, and judicious nurses, or had I been alarmed, as too many children are, by false threats of what might happen.

" 'I had, as well as a fearful, rather a reserved mind, for I never remember telling of my many painful fears, though I must often have shown them by weeping when left in the dark, and on other occasions: this reserve made me little understood, and thought very little of, except by my mother and one or two others. I was considered and called very stupid and obstinate. I certainly did not like learning, nor did I, I believe, attend to my lessons, partly from a delicate state of health, that produced languor of mind as well as body; but, I think, having the name of being stupid, really tended to make me so, and discouraged my efforts to learn. I remember having a poor, not to say low, opinion of myself, and used to think I was so very inferior to my sisters, Catherine and Rachel. I believe I had not a name only for being obstinate, for my nature then had a strong tendency that way; and I was disposed to a spirit of contradiction, always ready to see things a little differently from others, and not willing to yield my sentiments to theirs.

" 'My natural affections were very strong from my early childhood, at times almost overwhelmingly so; such was the love for my mother, that the thought that she might die and leave me used to make me weep after I went to bed, and for the rest of the family, notwithstanding my fearful nature, my childlike wish was, that two large walls might crush us all together, that we might die at once, and thus avoid the misery of each other's death. I seldom, if I could help it, left my mother's side; I watched her when asleep in the day with exquisite anxiety, and used to go gently to her bedside to listen, from the awful fear that she did not breathe ; in short, I may truly say, it amounted to deep reverence that I felt for my father and mother. I never remember, as a little child, but once being punished by my mother; and she then mistook tears of sorrow for tears of naughtiness, a thing that deeply impressed me, and I have never forgotten the pain it gave me. Although I do not imply that I had no faults, far from it, as some of the faults of my childhood are very lively in my recollection; yet, from my extreme love and fear, many of these faults were known almost only to myself. My imagination was lively, and I once remember, and only once, telling a real untruth with one of my sisters and one of my brothers. We saw a bright light one morning, which we represented far above the reality, and upon the real thing being shown us that we had seen, we made it out not to be it. My remembrance is of the pleasure of my childhood being almost spoiled through fear, and my religious impressions, such as I had, were accompanied by gloom; on this account I think the utmost care is needed in representing religious truth to children, that fearful views of it should be most carefully avoided, lest it should give a distaste for that which is most precious. First show them the love and mercy of God in Christ Jesus, and the sweetness and blessedness of His service ; and such things in Scripture, for instance, as Abraham's sacrifice, should be carefully explained to them. I think I suffered much in my youth from the most tender nervous system; I certainly felt symptoms of ill health before my mother died, that I thought of speaking to her about, but never did, partly because I did not know how to explain them; but they ended afterwards in very severe attacks of illness. I have always thought being forced to bathe was one cause of this, and I mention it because I believe it a dangerous thing to do to children. What care is needful not to force children to learn too much, as it not only injures them, but gives a distaste to intellectual pursuits. Instruction should be adapted to their condition, and communicated in an easy and agreeable way.

"How great is the importance of a wise mother, directing the tastes of her children in very early life, and judiciously influencing their affections. I remember with pleasure my mother's bed for wild flowers, which, with delight, I used, as a child to attend to with her; it gave me such pleasure in observing their beauties and varieties; that though I never have had time to become a botanist, few can imagine, in my weary journeys, how I have been pleased and refreshed, by observing and enjoying the wild flowers on my way. Again, she collected shells, and had a cabinet, and bought one for Rachel and myself, where we placed our curiosities; and I may truly say, in the midst even of deep trouble, and often most weighty engagements of a religious and philanthropic nature, I have derived advantage, refreshment and pleasure, from my taste for these things, seeking collections of them, and various natural curiosities, although, as with the flowers, I have not studied them scientifically.

"'My mother also encouraged my most close friendship with my sister Rachel, and we had our pretty light closet, our books, our pictures, our curiosities, our tea things, all to ourselves; and as far as I can recollect, we unitedly partook of these pleasures without any of the little jealousies or the quarrels of childhood.

"'My mother, as far as she knew, really trained us up in the fear and love of the Lord. My deep impression is, that she was a devoted follower of the Lord Jesus; but that her understanding was not fully enlightened as to the fulness of Gospel truths: she taught us as far as she knew, and I now remember the solemn religious feelings I had whilst sitting in silence with her, after reading the Scripture, and a Psalm before we went to bed. I have no doubt that her prayers were not in vain in the Lord. She died when I was twelve years old; the remembrance of her illness and death is sad, even to the present day.'

"Among the vast changes of the last century, there was no change greater than that which took place in the education of women.

"Addison and his coadjutors were among the foremost to teach the women of modern England, that they possessed powers of mind and capabilities of usefulness.

"Many, as they sipped their coffee with the Spectator of the morning in their hand, were awakened to the consciousness of a higher destiny for woman, than the labor of the tapestry frame, or pursuits of an entirely frivolous nature. A taste for reading became more or less general. The heavy wisdom of Johnson, the lighter wit of Swift, the satire of Pope, the pathos of Gray, and the close painting of Goldsmith, found among women not only those who could enjoy, but who could appreciate their different excellencies. Mrs. Montague, Mrs. Carter, Mrs. Chapone, with a group of gifted friends and associates, proved to the world the possibility of high literary attainments existing with every feminine grace and virtue. The stimulus was given, but like all other changes in society, the opposite extreme was reached before the right and reasonable was discovered. Infidelity was making slow though sure advances upon the continent. Rosseau and Voltaire were but types of the state of feeling and principles in France. The effects gradually extended to our own country, and England has to blush for the perversion of female talent, the evil influence of which was only counteracted by its showing as a beacon light, to warn others from shipwreck. Science, and philosophy, so called, advanced and flourished, but by their side flourished the Upas tree of infidelity, poisoning with its noxious breath the flowers and the fruits otherwise so pleasant to the eye, and so good for the use of man. The writings of Hannah More were well calculated to enlighten and improve her sex; she spoke as woman can alone speak to women; but she was then only rising into celebrity, and as an author was little known.

"Norwich had not escaped the general contagion. On the contrary, at the period of which we speak, it was noted for the charm, the talent, and the skepticism of the society of the town and neighborhood. The death of Mrs. Gurney had left her seven daughters unprotected by a mother's care to pursue the difficult path of early womanhood.

"They appear to have been rich in attraction and talent, lively and original, possessing a peculiar freshness of character, with singular purity of purpose and warmth of affection. But their faith was obscure, and their principles necessarily unfixed and wavering. They appreciated the beauty and excellence of religion; but it was more natural than revealed religion with they were acquainted.

"There was something of mysticism amongst the Quakers of that day, and by no means the clear and general acknowledgment of the doctrine of the '*Trinity* in *Unity*,' as revealed in the New Testament, which is now to be met with amongst the greater part of the Society of Friends. To the present time, that expression as designating the Deity is not in use among them, from its not being found in the Bible. The family of Mr. Gurney, thus left to their own resources, unaccustomed to the study of the Scriptures, and with no other source of information from which to learn, for a time were permitted to 'stumble upon the dark mountains seeking rest and finding none.'

"These remarks apply especially to the three older daughters, as they gradually advanced in life. The four younger ones, sheltered in the school room, were comparatively spared the difficulties through which their sisters were pioneering the way. Mr. Gurney's occupations, both public and private, and his naturally trustful disposition, prevented his seeing all the dangers to which they were exposed. They formed many acquaintances, and some friendships, with persons greatly gifted by nature, but fearfully tainted with the prevailing errors of the day. Great pain and bitter disappointment resulted from these connexions; but demanding only an allusion here, as they indirectly affected Elizabeth through the suffering of others, and the experience gained to herself.

"To the gayeties of the world, in the usual acceptation of the term, they were but little exposed. Music and dancing are not allowed by Friends; though a scruple as to the former is by no means universal. Mr. Gurney had no objection to music: they all had a taste for it, though almost uncultivated; some of them sang delightfully. The sweet and thrilling pathos of their native warblings is still remembered with pleasure by those who heard them, especially the duets of Rachel and Elizabeth. They danced occasionally in the large ante-room leading to the drawing-room, but with little of the spirit of display so often manifested on these occasions. It was more an effusion of young joyous hearts, who thus sought and found an outlet for their mirth. When her health permitted it, no one of the party entered with more zest into these amusements than Elizabeth. Her figure tall, and at that time slight and graceful, was peculiarly fitted for dancing. She was also an excellent horse-woman, and rode fearlessly and well; but she suffered much from delicacy of constitution, and was liable to severe nervous attacks which often impeded her joining her sisters in their different objects and pursuits. In countenance, she is described as having been as a young person very sweet and pleasing, with a profusion of soft flaxen hair, though perhaps not so glowing as some of her sisters.

"She had much native grace, and to many people was very attractive. Elizabeth was not studious by nature, and was, as a child, though gentle and quiet in temper, selfwilled and determined. In a letter, written before she was three years old, her mother thus mentions her;—'My dove-like Betsey scarcely ever offends, and is, in every sense of the word, truly engaging.' Her dislike to learning proved a serious disadvantage to her after she lost her mother; her education, consequently being defective and unfinished. In natural talent, she was quick and penetrating, and had a depth of originality very uncommon. As she grew older, enterprise and benevolence were two prominent features in her character. In contemplating her peculiar gifts, it is wonderful to observe the adaptation of her natural qualities to her future career; and how, through the transforming power of divine grace, each one became subservient to the highest purposes. Her natural timidity changed to the opposite virtue of courage, but with such holy moderation and nice discretion, as never failed to direct it aright. The touch of obstinacy she displayed as a child, became that finely tempered decision and firmness which enabled her to execute her projects for the good of her fellow creatures. That which in childhood was something not unlike cunning, ripened into the most uncommon penetration, long-sightedness, and skill in influencing the minds of those around her. Her disinclination to the common methods of learning appeared to be connected with much original thought, and a mind acting on its own resources; for she certainly always possessed more genius, and ready, quick comprehension, than application or argument.

"Such were the circumstances, and such the character of Elizabeth Gurney and her sisters, after the death of their mother: and years passed on, with few changes, but such as necessarily came with the lapse of time, and their advance in age. But He who had purposes of mercy towards them, In His own way, and in His own good time, was preparing for them emancipation from their doubts, and light for their darkness. Wonderful is it to mark how, by little and little, through various instruments, through mental conflicts, through bitter experience, He gradually led them, each one, into the meridian light of day—the glorious liberty of the children of God.

"At a time when religion in a more gloomy form might not have gained a hearing, when the graver countenance of rebuke would probably have been unheeded, a gentleman

became acquainted with the Earlham family, of high principle and cultivated mind. With him the sisters formed a
strong and lasting friendship. He addressed himself to
their understandings on the grand doctrines of Christianity;
he referred them to the written word as the rule of life; he
lent them, and read with them, books of a religious tendency. He treated religion, as such, with reverence; and although himself a Roman Catholic, he abstained from every
controversial topic, nor ever used his influence, directly or
indirectly, in favor of his own church. There was another
individual who proved an important instrument in leading
the sisters to sound views of religion, though, when first acquainted with them, herself wandering in the wilderness of
doubt, if not of error. This was Marianne Galton, afterward
Mrs. Schimmel Penninck. Being a highly educated person,
of great mental power, and accustomed to exercise her abilities in the use of her reason and an honest search after
truth, she acquired considerable influence over them. As
the truth of revelation opened upon her own understanding,
and her heart became influenced by it, they shared in her
advance, and profited by her experience. There were other
individuals with whom they associated, whose influence was
desirable, but less powerful, than that of either Miss Galton
or Mr. Pitchford.

"They appear also to have derived advantage, at times,
from the religious visits of Friends to Earlham. The family of Mr. Gurney were in the habit of attending no place of
worship but the Friends' meeting. The attendance of Elizabeth was continually impeded by want of health, and it is
difficult to know when the habit of absenting herself might
have been broken through, but for her uncle, Joseph Gurney, who urged the duty upon her and encouraged her to
make the attempt. He was a decided Friend, and had much
influence with her, both then and during her subsequent life.
She was ready indeed to essay anything that might tend to
satisfy her conscience, or meet the cravings of her heart for

a something which as yet she had not obtained. There is occasionally to be met with in the character of fallen man a longing after perfection—after that which can alone satisfy the immortal spirit: this she experienced in no common measure. Her journal is replete with desires after 'virtue' and 'truth.' She seeks and finds God in His works, but as yet she had not found Him as He stands revealed in the page of inspiration."

I shall now present such selections from the Journal as seem best adapted to give a clear and life-like portrait of Elizabeth Fry's mind, character and career. Happily the materials are so abundant as chiefly to require an exercise of judgment in omitting those which may, with least injury, be sacrificed to the demands of brevity.

"My mind is in so dark a state that I see everything through a black medium."

"I see everything darkly—I can comprehend nothing—I doubt upon everything."

"*April.*—Without passions of any kind how different I should be. I would not give them up, but I should like to have them under subjection; but it appears to me, as I feel, impossible to govern them; my mind is not strong enough, as I at times think they do no harm to others. But am I sure they will hurt no one? I believe by not governing myself in little things I may by degrees become a despicable character, and a curse to society; therefore my doing wrong is of consequence to others as well as to myself."

"*April 25th.*—I feel by experience how much entering into the world hurts me; worldly company I think materially injures; it excites a false stimulus, such as a love of pomp, pride, vanity, jealousy, and ambition; it leads to think about dress and such trifles, and when out of it we fly to novels and scandal, or something of that kind, for entertainment.

I have lately been given up a good deal to worldly passions. By what I have felt I can easily imagine how soon I should be quite led away.

"29th.—I met the Prince,* it showed me the folly of the world; my mind feels very flat after this storm of pleasure.

"*May* 16th.—There is a sort of luxury in giving way to the feelings! I love to feel for the sorrows of others, to pour wine and oil into the wounds of the afflicted: there is a luxury in feeling the heart glow, whether it be with joy or sorrow. I think the different periods of life may well be compared to the different seasons.

"I love to think of every thing, to look at mankind; I love to 'look through Nature up to Nature's God.' I have no more religion than that, and in the little I have I am not the least devotional; but when I admire the beauties of Nature I cannot help thinking of the Source from whence such beauties flow. I feel it a support; I believe firmly that all is guided for the best by an invisible Power, therefore I do not feel the evils of life so much. I love to feel good, I do what I can to be kind to everybody. I have many faults which I hope in time to overcome.

"*Monday, May* 21st.—I am seventeen to-day. Am I a happier or a better creature than I was this time twelvemonth? I know I am happier; I think I am better. I hope I shall be much better this day year than I am now. I hope to be quite an altered person, to have more knowledge, to have my mind in greater order; and my heart too—that wants to be put in order as much, if not more, than any part of me, it is in such a fly-away state; but I think if ever I were settled on one subject it would never, no never fly away any more; it would rest quietly and happily on the heart that was open to receive it; it will then be more con-

---

*H. R. H. William Frederick, afterwards Duke of Gloucester, then quartered, with his regiment, at Norwich.

stant; it is not my fault it now flies away, it is owing to circumstances.

"*Monday, June.*—I am at this present time in an odd state; I am like a ship put to sea without a pilot: I feel my heart and mind so overburdened. I want some one to lean upon.

(Written on a bright summer's morning.)

"Is there not a ray of perfection midst the sweets of this morning? I do think there is something perfect from which all good flows.

"*June 20th.*—If I have long to live in this world may I bear misfortunes with fortitude; do what I can to alleviate the sorrows of others; exert what power I have to increase happiness; try to govern my passions by reason, and adhere strictly to what I think right.

"*July 7th.*—I have seen several things in myself and others I have never before remarked; but I have not tried to improve myself; I have given way to my passions and let them have command over me. I have known my faults and have not corrected them, and now I am determined I will once more try, with redoubled ardor, to overcome my wicked inclinations. I must not flirt; I must not be out of temper with the children; I must not contradict without a cause; I must not mump when my sisters are liked and I am not; I must not allow myself to be angry; I must not exaggerate, which I am inclined to; I must not give way to luxury; I must not be idle in mind; I must try to give way to every good feeling and overcome every bad. I will see what I can do: if I had but perseverance, I could do all that I wish; I will try. I have lately been too satirical, so as to hurt sometimes; remember, it is a fault to hurt others.

"*8th.*—A much better day, though many faults.

"*10th.*—Some poor people were here; I do not think I gave them what I did with a good heart. I am inclined to give away; but for a week past, owing to not having much money, I have been mean and extravagant. Shameful!

Whilst I live may I be generous ; it is my nature, and I will not overcome so good a feeling. I am inclined to be extravagant and that leads to meanness, for those who will throw away a good deal are apt to mind giving a little.

"11th.—I am in a most idle mind, and inclined to have an indolent, dissipated day; but I will try to overcome it and see how far I can. I am well; oh most inestimable of comforts! Happy, happy I, to be so well! how good, how virtuous ought I to be! May what I have suffered be a lesson to me, to feel for those who are ill, and alleviate their sorrows as far as lies in my power; let it teach me never to forget the blessings I enjoy. I ought never to be unhappy. Look back at this time last year; how ill I was, how miserable! yet I was supported through it. God will support through the suffering he inflicts. If I were devotional, I should fall on my knees and be most grateful for the blessings I enjoy ;—a good father, one whom I dearly love, sisters formed after my own heart, friends whom I admire, and good health which gives a relish to all. Company to dinner; I must beware of being a flirt, it is an abominable character; I hope I shall never be one, and yet I fear I am one now a little. Be careful not to talk at random. Beware, and see how well I can get through this day, without one foolish action. If I do pass this day without one foolish action, it is the first I ever passed so. If I pass a day with only a few foolish actions I may think it a good one.

"25th.—This book is quite a little friend to my heart; it is next to communicating my feelings to another person. I would not but write in it for something, for it is most comfortable to read it over and see the different workings of my heart and soul.

"30th.—Pride and vanity are too much the incentives to most of the actions of men. They produce a love of admiration, and in thinking of the opinions of others we are too apt to forget the monitor within. We should first look to ourselves, and try to make ourselves virtuous, and then pleasing. Those who are truly virtuous not only do themselves good, but they add to the good of all. All have a portion entrusted to them for the general good, and those who cherish and preserve it are blessings to society at large; and those who do not, become a curse. It is wonderfully ordered, how in acting for our own good we promote the good of others. My idea of religion is, not for it to unfit us for the duties of this life, like a nun who leaves them for prayer and thanksgiving, but I think it should stimulate and capacitate us to perform these duties properly. Seeing my father low this evening, I have done all I could to make him comfortable; I feel it one of my first duties; I hope he will always find in me a most true and affectionate daughter.

"*August 1st.*—I have done little to-day, I am so very idle. Instead of improving I fear I go back. My inclinations lead me to be an idle, flirting, worldly girl. I see what would be acting right, but I have neither activity nor perseverance in what I think right. I am like one setting out on a journey; if I set out on the wrong road, and do not try to recover the right one before I have gone far, I shall most likely lose my way FOREVER, and every step I take the more difficult shall I find it to return; therefore the temptation will be greater to go on, till I get to destruction. On the contrary, if now, whilst I am innocent of any great faults, I turn into the right path, I shall soon feel more and more contented every step I take. Trifles occupy me far too much, such as dress, &c., &c. I find it easier to acknowledge my vices than my follies.

"*6th.*—I have a cross to-night. I had very much set my mind on going to the oratorio, the Prince is to be there, and by all accounts it will be quite a grand sight, and there will be the finest music; but if my father does not like me to go much as I wish it I will give it up with pleasure, if it be in my power, without a murmur. I went to the oratorio; I enjoyed it but spoke sadly at random; what a bad habit!

"*Aug. 12th.*—I do not know if I shall not soon be rather

religious, because I have thought lately what a support it is through life; it seems so delightful to depend on a superior Power for all that is good; it is at least always having the bosom of a friend open to us, to rest all our cares and sorrows upon; and what must be our feelings to imagine that friend perfect, and guiding all and everything as it should be guided. I think anybody who had real faith could never be unhappy; it appears the only certain source of support and comfort in this life, and what is best of all it draws to virtue, and if the idea be ever so ill-founded that leads to that great object, why should we shun it? Religion has been misused and corrupted: that is no reason why religion itself is not good.

"15th.—For a few days past I have been in a worldly state, dissipated, a want of thought, idle, relaxed and stupid, all outside, no inside. I feel I am a contemptible fine lady. May I be preserved from continuing so, is the ardent prayer of my *good* man, but my *evil* man tells me I shall pray in vain. I will try. I fear for myself. I feel in the course of a little time I shall be all outside frippery, vain, proud, conceited. I could use improper words at myself, but my *good* man will not let me. But I am good in something; it is wicked to despair of myself; it is the way to make me what I desire not to be. I hope I shall always be virtuous; can I be really wicked? I may be so, if I do not overcome my first weak inclinations. I wish I had more solidity and less fluidity in my disposition. I feel my own weakness and insufficiency to bear the evils and rubs of life. I must try by every stimulus in my power to strengthen myself both bodily and mentally; it can only be done by activity and perseverance."

How beautiful is this deliberate stepping forward of the young and ardent spirit into the doorway of eternal

happiness! "I will try what prayer can do," said Elizabeth
Gurney; and she was so well satisfied with the result that
prayer became her staff in life and her pillow in death.

Soon after this time a Quaker preacher from America,
named William Savery, visited Norwich, and his ministry
had the effect of fanning the secretly burning embers of piety into an open flame. This important event is thus described by one of Elizabeth's sisters:—

"On that day we seven sisters sat, as usual, in a row under the gallery (the speakers' seat,) at Meeting; I sat by
Betsey. William Savery was there—we liked having Yearly Meeting Friends come to preach; it was a little change.
Betsey was generally rather restless at Meeting; and on
this day I remember her very smart boots were a great
amusement to me; they were purple, laced with scarlet At
last William Savery began to preach. His voice and manner were arresting, and we all liked the sound. Her attention became fixed. At last I saw her begin to weep, and she
became a good deal agitated. As soon as meeting was over
I have a remembrance of her making her way to the men's
side of the meeting, and, having found my father, she asked
him if she might dine with Mr. Savery, at the Grove, (the
residence of an uncle,) to which he soon consented. though
rather surprised by the request. We went home as usual,
and, for a wonder, wished to go again in the afternoon. I
have not the same clear remembrance of this meeting, but
the next scene that has fastened itself on my memory is our
return home in the carriage. Betsey sat in the middle and
astonished us all by the great feeling she showed. She wept
most of the way home. The next morning William Savery
came to breakfast, prophesying of the high and important
calling she would be led into. What she went through in
her own mind I cannot say, but the results were most pow-

erful, and most evident. From that day her love of pleasure and of the world seemed gone."

The description from the inner side is as follows:

"*Sunday, February 4th*, 1798.—This morning I went to meeting, though but poorly, because I wished to hear an American Friend named William Savery. Much passed there of a very interesting nature. I have had a faint light spread over my mind, at least I think it is something of that kind, owing to having been much with, and heard much excellence from one who appears to me a true Christian. It has caused me to feel a little religion. My imagination has been worked upon, and I fear all that I felt will go off. I *fear* it now, though at first I was frightened that a plain Quaker should have made so deep an impression on me; but how truly prejudiced in one to think that because good came from a Quaker I should be led away by enthusiasm and folly. But I hope I am now free from such fears. I wish the state of enthusiasm I am in may last, for to-day I have felt *that there is a God;* I have been devotional, and my mind has been led away from the follies that it is mostly wrapt up in. We had much serious conversation; in short, what he said and what I felt was like a refreshing shower falling upon earth that had been dried up for ages. It has not made me unhappy: I have felt ever since humble. I have longed for virtue. I hope to be truly virtuous; to let sophistry fly from my mind; not to be enthusiastic and foolish, but only to be so far religious as will lead to virtue. There seems nothing so little understood as religion.

"*6th.*—My mind has by degrees flown from religion. I rode to Norwich and had a very serious ride there; but meeting and being looked at with apparent admiration by some officers brought on vanity, and I came home as full of the world as I went to town full of heaven.

"*Sunday,* 11*th.*—It is very different to this day week (a

day never to be forgotten while memory lasts). I have been to meeting this morning. To-day I felt all my old irreligious feelings. My object shall be to search, to try to do right, and if I am mistaken it is not my fault; but the state I am now in makes it difficult to act. What little religion I have felt has been owing to my giving way quietly and humbly to my feelings. But the more I reason upon it the more I get into a labyrinth of uncertainty, and my mind is so much inclined to both scepticism and enthusiasm that if I argue and doubt I shall be a total sceptic; if on the contrary I give way to my feelings, and, as it were, wait for religion, I may be led away. But I hope that will not be the case; at all events, religion true and uncorrupted is of all comforts the greatest; it is the first stimulus to virtue; it is a support under every affliction. I am sure it is better to be so in an enthusiastic degree than not to be so at all, for it is a delightful enthusiasm."

Soon after this she visited London, and spent seven weeks in the Metropolis. She mingled freely in the gaieties of city life, went to balls, theaters, social gatherings, etc., and at other times attended the meetings of her own sober, religious society. It was a crucial test for her of the rival claims of the World and Religion. She tried both, and freely and heartily chose the latter. In after life she esteemed this experience of great value to her. She again met her American evangelist at this time, and thus records her impressions and progress:

"*March 17th*, 1798.—May I never forget the impression William Savery has made on my mind! As much as I can say is, I thank God for having sent at least a glimmering of light, through him, into my heart, which I hope with care, and keeping it from the many draughts and winds of this life, may not be blown out, but become a large, brilliant flame that will direct to that haven where will be joy without sorrow, and all will be comfort. I have faith! how much is that to gain! Not all the pleasures in this world can equal that heavenly treasure. May I grow more and more virtuous, follow the path I should go in, and not fear to acknowledge the God whom I worship. I will try, and I do hope to do what is right. . . . May I never lose the little religion I now have; but if I cannot feel religion and devotion I must not despair: for if I am truly warm and earnest in the cause, it will come one day. My idea is that true humility and lowliness of heart is the first grand step towards true religion. I fear and tremble for myself, but I must humbly look to the Author of all that is good and great, and, I may say, humbly pray, that He may take me as a sheep strayed from His flock, and once more let me enter the fold of His glory. I feel there is a God and Immortality; happy, happy thought! May it never leave me, and if it should may I remember I have *felt* that there is a God and Immortality."

"*April* 21*st.*—I am glad I do not feel Earlham at all dull after the bustle of London; on the contrary a better relish for the sweet innocence and beauties of Nature. I hope I may say I do look 'through Nature up to Nature's God.' I go every day to see poor Rob, (a servant in declining health living in a cottage in the Park,) who I think will not live. I once talked to him about dying, and asked him if he would like me to read to him in the Testament. I told him I felt such faith in the blessings of immortality that I pitied not his state. It is an odd speech to make to a dying man. I hope to be able to comfort him in his dying hours.

"I gave some things to some poor people to-day; but it is not there I am particularly virtuous, as I am only following my natural disposition. I should be far more so if I never spoke against any person, which I do too often. I think I am improved since I was last at home, my mind is not so fly-away. I hope it will never be so again. We are all governed by our feelings. Now the reason why religion is far more likely to keep you in the path of virtue than any theoretical plan is that you feel it, and your heart is wrapt up in it; it acts as a furnace on your character; it refines it; it purifies it; whereas principles of your own making are without kindling to make the fire hot enough to answer its purpose. I think a dream I have had so odd I will write it down. Before I mention my dream I will give an account of the state of my mind from the time I was fourteen years old. I had very sceptical, or deistical principles. I seldom or never thought of religion, and altogether I was a negatively good character: having naturally good dispositions I had not much to combat with; I gave way freely to the weaknesses of youth. I was flirting, idle, rather proud and vain, till the time I was seventeen, when I found I wanted a better, a greater stimulus to virtue than I had, as I was wrapt up in trifles. I felt my mind capable of better things, but I could not exert it, till several of my friends, without knowing my state wished I would read books on Christianit; but I said, till I felt the want of religion myself I would not read books of that kind, but if ever I did would judge clearly for myself by reading the New Testament, and when I had seen for myself I would *then* see what others said. About this time I believe I never missed a week, or a few nights, without dreaming I was nearly being washed away by the sea, sometimes in one way, sometimes in another; and I felt all the terror of being drowned, or hope of being saved. At last I dreamed it so often that I told many of the family what a strange dream I had, and how near I was being lost. After I had gone on in this way for some months William Savery came to Norwich. I had begun to read the New Testament with reflections of my own, and he suddenly, as it were, opened my eyes to see religion; but · again they almost closed. I went on dreaming the dream,

The day when I felt that I had really and truly got true and real faith, that night I dreamed the sea was coming as usual to wash me away, but I was beyond its reach; beyond its powers to wash me away. Since that night I do not remember to have dreamed the dream.

Odd! It did not strike me at the time so odd; but now it does. All I can say is, I admire it, I am glad I have had it, and I have a sort of faith in it; it ought, I think, to make my faith steady. It may be the work of chance, but I do not think it is, for it is so odd not having dreamed it since. What a blessed thought, to think it comes from Heaven. May I be capable of acting as I ought to act; not being drowned in the ocean of the world, but permitted to mount above its waves, and remain a steady and faithful servant of the God whom I worship. I may take this dream in what light I like, but I must be careful of superstition, as many, many a.e the minds that are led away by it; believe only in what I can comprehend or feel. Don't, don't be led away by enthusiasm; but don't fear. I feel myself under the protection of One who alone is able to guide me in the path in which I ought to go.

"29th.—The human mind is apt to fly from one extreme to another: and why not mine like others? I certainly seem to be on the road to a degree of enthusiasm, but I own myself at a loss how to act. If I act as they would wish me, I should not humbly give way to the feelings of religion; I should dwell on philosophy, and depend more on my own reason than anything else. On the contrary, if I give way to religious feelings to which I am inclined, (and I own I believe much in inspiration,) I feel confident that I should find true humility and humble waiting on the Almighty, the only way of feeling an inward sense of the beauties and the comforts of religion. It spreads a sweet veil over the evils of life; it is to me the first of feelings. I own my dream rather leads me to believe in and try to follow the path I would go in. But I should think my wisest plan of conduct would be warmly to encourage my feelings of devotion, and to keep as nearly as I can to what I think right, and the doctrines of the Testament—not at present to make sects the subject of my meditations, but to do as I think right, and not alter my opinions from conformity to any one, gay or plain.

"*May 8th.*—This morning, being alone, I think it a good opportunity to look into myself, to see my present state, and to regulate myself. At this time the first object of my mind is religion. It is the most constant subject of my thoughts and of my feelings. I am not yet on what I call a steady foundation. The next feeling that at this present fills my heart is benevolence and affection to many, but great want of charity, want of humility, want of activity. My inclinations lead me I hope to virtue; my passions are I hope in a pretty good state; I want to set myself in order, for much time is lost and many evils committed by not having some regular plan of conduct. I make these rules for myself:—

First,—Never lose any time;—I do not think that lost which is spent in amusement or recreation. some time every day; but always be in the habit of being employed.

Second,—Never err the least in truth.

Third,—Never say any ill thing of a person when I can say a good thing;—not only *speak* charitably, but *feel* so.

Fourth,—Never be irritable, or unkind to any body.

Fifth,—Never indulge myself in luxuries that are not necessary.

Sixth,—Do all things with consideration, and when my path to act right is most difficult, feel confidence in that Power which alone is able to assist me, and exert my own powers as far as they go.

"*19th.*—Altogether I think I have had a satisfactory day I had a good lesson of French, and read much in Epictetus. Saw poor Rob, and enjoyed the beauties of nature which now shine forth; each day some new beauty arrives. I love the beauty of the country; it does the mind good. I love it more than I used to do. I love retirement and quiet much more since my journey to London. How little I thought six months ago I should be so much altered; I am since then, I hope, altered much for the better. My heart may rise in thankfulness to that Omnipotent Power that has allowed my eyes to be opened, in some measure, to see the light of truth, and to feel the comfort of religion. I hope to be capable of giving up my all, if it be required of me, to serve the almighty with my whole heart.

"21st. (May.)—To-day is my birth-day. I am eighteen years old! How many things have happened since I was fourteen; the last year has been the happiest I have experienced for some time.

"23rd.—I have just been reading a letter from my father in which he makes me the offer of going to London. What a temptation! But I believe it much better for me to be where I am, quietly and soberly to keep a proper medium of feelings, and not be extravagant any way.

"24th.—I wrote to my father this morning. I must be most careful not to be led by others, for I know at this time I have so great a liking for plain Friends, that, my affections being so much engaged, my mind may be also by them. I hope, as I now find myself in so wavering a state, that I may judge without prejudice of Barclay's Apology.

"27th.—I must be careful of allowing false scruples to enter my mind. I have not yet been long enough a religionist to be a sectarian. I hope by degrees to obtain true faith; but I expect I shall lose what I gain if I am led to actions that I may repent of; rememeber, and never forget my own enthusiastic, feeling nature. It requires caution and extreme prudence to go on as I should do. In the afternoon I went to old St. Peter's and heard a good sermon. The common people seemed very much occupied and wrapt up in the service, which I was pleased to see. Afterwards

I went to the Cathedral; then I came home and read to the Normans and little Castleton.

"*29th.*—I feel weak in mind and body. If I go on approving revealed religion, I must be extremely careful of taking the idle fancies of the brain for anything so far superior. I believe many mistake mere meteors for that heavenly light which few receive. Many may have it in a degree, but I should suppose few have it so as to teach others with authority.

"*June 1st.*—I have been a great part of this morning with poor Rob, who seems now dying. I read a chapter in the Testament to him—the one upon death—and I sat with him for some time afterwards. Poor fellow! I never saw death, or any of its symptoms before; sad to see it truly is. I said a few words to him, and expressed to him how happy we should be in the expectation of immortality and everlasting bliss. Father of mercies, wilt Thou bless him and take him unto Thee? Though my mind is flat this morning, and not favored with Thy Spirit in devotion, yet I exert what I have, and hope it will prove acceptable in Thy sight. Almighty God, Thy will be done, and not ours. May I always be resigned to what Thou hast ordered for me. I humbly thank Thee for allowing my eyes to be opened, so as even to feel faith, hope and love towards Thee. First and last of everything infinite, and not to be comprehended except by Thy Spirit which Thou allowest to enlighten our hearts."

The above is the first of those written prayers which abound in this devoted Christian's Journal, increasing in frequency and fervency to the close. It is worthy of remark, how gradually the devotional spirit became developed in her mind. At about the age of seventeen she wrote, "I love to 'look through nature up to nature's God.' I have no more religion than that; and in the little that I have *I am not the least devotional.*" Two or three months later

she says, "If I were devotional I should fall on my knees
and be most grateful for the blessings I enjoy." This was
in July. In January following, "I should think it almost
impossible to keep strictly to principles without religion;
I should think those feelings impossible to obtain, for even
if I thought all the Bible was true, I do not think I could
make myself feel it: I think I never saw any person who
appeared so totally destitute of it. I fear I am by degrees
falling away from the path of virtue and truth." When,
a month afterwards, the Holy Spirit was first sensibly shed
upon her through the preaching of the Gospel, causing
tears of joy to flow, she wrote, "I wish the state of enthusiasm I am in may last, for to-day I have felt *that there is a
God;* I have been devotional, and my mind has been led
away from the follies that it is mostly wrapped up in."
Four months thereafter, when watching over and trying to
administer the sacrament of Divine love, hope and faith to
a poor dying man, the spirit expressed itself as above.
Thus the light and warmth of religion very gradually increased in her mind and heart through the exercise of the
grace which was given.

"*12th.*—This evening I have got myself rather in a scrape;
I have been helping them beg my father to go to the
Guild-dinner, and I don't know whether it was quite what I
approve of, or think good for myself; but I shall consider,
and do not intend to go, if I disapprove of it. How strange
and odd! I really think I shall turn plain Friend. All I say
is, search deeply; do nothing rashly, and then I hope to do
right. They all, I think, now see it. Keep up to the duties I feel in my heart, let the path be ever so difficult. Err
not at all if I can avoid it Be humble and constant. I do

not like to appear a character I am not certain of being. For a few days past I have at times felt much religion for *me;* humility and comfort belong to it. I often think very seriously about myself. A few months ago if I had seen any one act as I now do, I should have thought him a fool; but the strongest proof I can have that I am acting right at the present time is that I am certainly a better and I think a happier character. But I often doubt myself when I consider my enthusiastic and changeable feelings. Religion is no common enthusiasm, because it is pure; it is a constant friend, protector, supporter and guardian; it is what we cannot do well without in this world. What can prove its excellence so much as its producing virtue and happiness? How much more solid a character I am since I first got hold of religion! I would not part with what I have for anything. It is a faith that never will leave my mind, I hope most earnestly. I do not believe it will, but I desire always to be a strictly religious character."

In the next entry we have an intimation of her future work.

"13*th.*—I have some thoughts of by degrees increasing my plan for Sunday evening; and of having several poor children at least to read in the Testament and religious books for an hour. I have begun with Billy, but I hope to continue and increase one by one. I should think it a good plan; but I must not even begin that hastily. It might increase morality among the lower classes if the Scriptures were oftener and better read to them. I believe I cannot exert myself too much: there is nothing gives me such satisfaction as instructing the lower classes of people."

During this summer—1798—John Gurney and his seven daughters traveled into Wales. They met with various classes of people, Quakers and others. The following extract shows the drawing of Elizabeth's mind toward the more serious part of her own religious Society:

"*Dawlish, August 3rd.*—This morning Kitty came in for us to read the Testament together, which I enjoyed; I read my favorite chapter, the 15th of Corinthians, to them. Oh! how earnestly I hope that we may all know what truth is and follow its dictates. I still continue my belief that I shall turn plain Quaker. I used to think, and do now, how how very little dress matters, but I find it almost impossible to keep up to the principles of Friends without altering my dress and speech. I felt it the other day at Weymouth. If I had been plain I should not have been *tempted* to go to the play, which, at all events I would not do. Plainness appears to be a sort of protection to the principles of Christianity, in the present state of the world. I have just received a letter from Anna Savery, and have been answering it, and have written rather a religious letter which I mean to show them, though it is to me a cross, as I say in it I think I am a Quaker at heart. I hope it will not hurt them; but it is better to be on clear grounds with my best friends upon that which so nearly interests me. I know it hurts Rachel and John the most. Rachel has the seeds of Quakerism in her heart, that, if cultivated, would grow indeed, I have no doubt. I should never be surprised to see us all Quakers.

"*Plymouth Dock,* 8th.— . . . . Am I right or not? An officer has come for us to hear a very famous Marine Band; and I do not go, because I have some idea it is wrong even to give countenance to a thing that inflames men's minds to destroy each other. It is truly giving encouragement, as far as lies in my power, to what I most highly disapprove; therefore I think I am right to stay at home.

"*Aberystwith,* 23rd.—Is dancing wrong? I have just been dancing; I think there are many dangers attending it;

it may lead to vanity and other things. The more the pleasures of life are given up, the less we love the world, and our hearts will be set upon better things; not but that we are allowed, I believe, to enjoy the blessings Heaven has sent us. We have power of mind to distinguish the good from the bad; for under the cloak of pleasure infinite evils are carried on. The danger of dancing, I find is throwing me off my center. At times, when dancing, I know that I have not reason left, but that I do things which in calm moments I must repent of.

"28th.—My mind is in an uncomfortable state this morning; for I am astonished to find that I have felt a scruple at music, at least I could not otherwise account for my feelings; but my mind is rather uneasy after spending time in it. These cannot be sensations of my own making, or a contrivance of my own forming, for I have such happiness when I overcome my worldly self; and when I give way to it I am uneasy. Not but what I think feelings are sometimes dangerous to give way to; but how odd, yet how true, that much human reason must be given up. I don't know what to think of it, but I must act somehow, and in some way,— yet do nothing rashly, or hastily, but try to humiliate myself to true religion, and endeavor to look to God who alone can teach me and lead me aright; have faith, hope, and if little things are to follow to protect greater ones, I must, yes, I must do it. I feel certainly happier in being a Quaker, but my reason contradicts it. Now my fears are these: lately I have had Quakerism placed before me in a very interesting and delightful light: and is it unlikely that inclination may put on the appearance of duty? Now my inclination may, before long, lead me some other way; that is a sad foundation to build the fortress upon which must defend me through life. But I think I am wrong in one thing, though it is right to doubt myself; yet do I not make myself more uneasy for fear I should be a ridiculous object to the world and some of my dear friends? I believe I can give myself a

little advice—not to promote anything leading to unquaker-
ism; but try if it make me happy or not, and then take
greater steps if I like."

The above is a very curious passage, showing, with dra-
matic clearness the struggle of conflicting ideas, inclinations
and tastes, in a conscientious mind, thoroughly bent on doing
its whole duty, and brought, by association, under the influence of opposite currents of opinion and differing modes
of practice. Judging at this distance, after the innocent,
and may we not say heavenly, charms of music have finally
overcome the prejudice against it, even among the sober
Quakers, except in a few instances, we can see that the case
was not judged on its own intrinsic merits, when it was decided to give up a source of pure and refined pleasure, because it was thought by certain serious people to militate
against the Christian life. Still, it is not necessary to conclude that she made a mistake, unless it had been better
then and thereto inaugurate a reform, and insist on holding
to all that was good in itself, notwithstanding the opposi-
tion. This, it is not probable a sensitive girl of eighteen
was strong enough to do, without a conflict greater than
she could bear, or without producing discords in the society
with which it was best for her to remain associated. Why,
therefore, might not the Spirit of Divine Wisdom truly have
impressed her mind to yield this and other points, as a
practical measure of harmony? But we can only say that
such *may* have been the case. When we trace the history
of this eventful life further, and see that, to her great sorrow, her own children refused to follow her in the narrow
path which she felt it right for her to choose, we are in-

clined to question whether a bolder and more steadfast ad-
herance to abstract truth and reason might not have produced better results. Of this we are perhaps incompetent
to judge: but we can safely assert that, although circumstances may justify a temporary conformity to existing customs, we should not make our special duties a law for
others, or even for ourselves in other relations and circumstances. The law of expediency, or relative duty, has necessarily a large share in the control of human conduct. A
very considerable part of the religious practices of men are
dictated by it. But since God Himself has wisely adapted
His laws to the the varying conditions of mankind, we ought
not to consider ourselves bound to anything which our
fathers found requisite for themselves, unless an unchang-
ing principle also enjoins it upon us. All societies, as now
organized, have their peculiarities which it may be well for
their members to abide by until some further development
renders these customs inappropriate. When He who "di-
videth unto every man severally as He will" put Elizabeth
Gurney, beautiful and engaging, with the head of a sage
and the heart of an angel, into a plain Quaker dress, and
persuaded her to give up music and other social amusements, to say "thee" and "thou," and to preach the gospel,
and labor for the salvation of lost souls, it is evident that
He considered Quakerism a good harness for her to work
in; and so the results proved it to be. But it would not
follow that others—not even her own children—were bound
by all the restrictions which she felt to be necessary. This
she herself freely acknowledged at a later period in life,
after much sorrow had brought its increase of wisdom.

The following entry which illustrates both her sincerity and good-sense, throws further light on the subject and may help others to understand the source of many of their convictions about religion and religious duty.

"*Jan.* 29, 1799.—I am in a doubtful state of mind. I think my mind is timid and my affections strong, which may be partly the cause of my being so much inclined to Quakerism. In the first place my affections were worked upon in receiving the first doctrines of religion through a Quaker; therefore it is likely they would put on that garb in my mind. In the next place my timidity may make me uncomfortable in erring from principles that I am so much inclined to adopt. So far I should be on my guard, and I hope not to forget what I have just mentioned. But yet, I think the only true standard I have to direct myself by is that which experience proves to give me the most happiness by enabling me to be the most virtuous. I believe there is something in the mind, or in the heart, that shows its approbation when we do right. I give myself this advice: Do not fear truth, let it be ever so contrary to inclination and feeling."

Her severest trial seems to have been in giving up the social amusements, music, singing and dancing, which appear to have been much, and, we should think, rationally enjoyed, in her large family of seven sisters and four brothers. The regret was not on her own account, for she would have preferred to lay these doves and lambs on the altar of conscience before she did, but she felt the grief it would cause in the dear home circle. Here are some of her touching reflections:

"27*th.*—This evening I have been doing exercises, and

singing with them; my mind feels very clear to night and my body much better. I have been thinking about singing; I hope in that, as in everything else, to do what is right. I cannot say I feel it is wrong to sing to my own family; it is sweet and right to give them pleasure. I do not approve of singing in company, as it leads to vanity and dissipation of mind; but that I believe I have no occasion to do, as dear Rachel does not request it, for she does not like it herself. I should be sorry quite to give up singing as the gift of nature, and on her account; as long as it does not lead me from what is right I need not fear.

" *October 5th.*—In the evening a fiddler came and we all had a dance. I had a toothache and so far from its making me merry it made me grave. I do not feel satisfaction in dancing.

" *6th.*—This morning I awoke not comfortable; the subject of dancing came strongly before my mind. Totally declining it as a matter of pleasure I do not mind; only as I am situated with the others I find it difficult. The question is if these may not be scruples of my own forming that I may one day repent of. The bottom of my heart is inclined to Quakerism, but I know what imagination can do. I believe the formation of my mind is such that it requires the bonds and ties of Quakerism to fit it for immortality. I feel it a very great blessing being so little in the company of superior fascinating Quakers, because it makes me act freely, and look to the only true Judge for what is right for me to do. The next question is, am I sufficiently clear that dancing is wrong to give it up? because I know much precaution is necessary. I believe I may, if I like, make one more trial, and judge again how I feel; but I must reflect upon it, determining to give it up if I think right. I wish to make it a subject of very serious reflection hoping as usual to do right. It will hurt them much I fear, but time I believe will take off that, if they see me happier and better for it. Let me redouble my kindness to them. Catherine

seems to wish I would give up correspondence with Anna
Savery, which I think I may do. This day·has been very
comfortable in most respects, though I have not done much.
I have finished my letter to dear cousin Priscilla, and that
to Mrs. ———; but I cannot feel quite easy to send it without first speaking to my father; for I do believe it is my
duty to make him my friend in all things; though I think
it probable he will discourage me in writing to my friend
Sophy; yet never keep anything from him; but let me be
an open, true, kind, and dutiful daughter to him whilst life
is in my body.

"12th.—I have many great faults, but I have some dispositions which I should be most thankful for. I believe I
feel much for my fellow-creatures; though I think I mostly
see into the minds of those I associate with, and am apt to
satirize their weakness; yet I don't remember ever being any
time with one who was not extremely disgusting but I felt
a sort of love for them, and I do hope I would sacrifice my
life for the good of mankind. My mind is too much like a
looking-glass;—objects of all kinds are easily reflected in it,
whilst present, but when they go their reflection is gone
also. I have a faint idea of many things, a strong idea of a
few; therefore my mind is cultivated badly. I have many
straggling, but not many connected ideas. I have the materials to form good in my mind, but I am not a sufficiently
good artificer to unite them properly together, and make a
good consistence; for in some parts I am too hard, in others
too soft. I hope and believe the Great Artificer is now at
work; that if I join my power to the only one able to conduct me aright, I may one day be better than I am.

"17th.—My journal has not gone on well of late; partly
owing to my going out, and having people in the room, now
there is a fire. I dislike going out; what my mind wants is
peace and quiet. The other night as I was alone in a carriage, a fine starlight night, I thought,—What is it I want?
how I overflow with the blessings of this world! I have

true friends—as many as I wish for—good health, a happy home, with all that riches can give, and yet all these are nothing without a satisfied conscience. At times I feel satisfied, but I have not reason to feel so often. . . . . This afternoon I have much to correct, I feel proud, vain and disagreeable; not touched with the sweet humility of Christianity; nor is my heart enlightened by its happy doctrines. I have two things heavily weighing on my mind—dancing and singing. So sweet and so pretty do they seem; but as surely as I do either, so surely does a dark cloud come over my mind. It is not only my giving up these things, but I am making others miserable, and laying a restraint upon their pleasures. In the next place am I sure I am going upon a good foundation? If I am doing right God will protect me and them also. If I am doing wrong what foundation do I stand upon? None: then all to me is nothing. Let me try to take my thoughts from this world, and look to the only true Judge. I believe singing to be so natural that I may try it a little longer: but I do think dancing may be given up. What particularly led me to this state was our having company, and I thought I must sing. I sang a little but did not stay with them during the playing. My mind continued in a state of agitation, and I did not sleep until some time after I was in bed.

"19th.—My mind feels more this morning, if anything than it did last night. Can such feelings be my own putting on? They seem to affect my whole frame, mental and bodily. They cannot be of myself, for if I were to give worlds I could not remove them. They truly make me shake. When I look forwards I think I can see, if I have strength to do as they direct I shall be another person: sorrow I believe will be removed to be replaced by joy. Then let me now act! My best method of conduct will be to tell Rachel how I am situated in mind, and then ask her what she would advise: and be very kind and tell her the true state of the case. Is it worth while to continue in so small a pleasure for so much

pain? The pleasure is nothing to me, but it is a grand step
to take in life.—I have been and spoken to Rachel, saying I
think I must give up singing. It is astonishing the total
change that has taken place. From misery I am now come
to joy. I felt ill before; I now feel well—thankful should
I be for being directed, and pray to keep up always to that
direction. After having spoken to my darling Rachel, where
I fear I said too much, I rode to Norwich after some poor
people: I went to see many and added my mite to their
comfort. Nothing, I think, could exceed the kindness of my
dear Rachel. Though I have no one here to encourage me
in Quakerism, I believe I must be one before I am content.

"*7th. December.*—I have had a letter to say my dear
friend William Savery is safely arrived in America. Kitty
and I have been having a long talk together this evening
upon sects; we both seem to think them almost necessary.
It is long since I have what I may truly call written in my
journal. Writing in my journal is to me expressing the feelings of my heart during the day. I have partly given it up,
from the coldness of the weather and not having a snug fire
to sit by. I wish now, as I have opportunity, to look a little
into the present situation of my heart. That is the advantage of writing a true journal—it leads the mind to look inward. Of late I do not think I have been sufficiently active,
but have rather given way to a dilatory spirit. I have been
reading Watts' Logic: it tells me how ill-regulated my
thoughts are—they truly ramble! Regularity of thought
and deed is what I much want; I appear to myself to have
almost a confusion of ideas, which leads to a confusion of
actions. I want order. I believe it difficult to obtain, but
yet with perseverance attainable. The first way to obtain it
appears to me to try to prevent my thoughts from rambling,
and to keep them as steadily as possible to the object in view.
True religion is what I seldom feel, nor do I sufficiently try
after it, by really seeking devotion. I do not warmly seek
it, I am sure, nor do I live in the fear of an All-wise Being

who watches over us. I seldom look deep enough, but dwell too much on the surface of things and let my ideas float. Such is my state. I can't tell how I feel exactly:—at times all seems to me mystery; ' When I look at the heavens, the work of Thy fingers, the moon and stars which Thou hast ordained, what is man that Thou art mindful of him, or the son of man that Thou visitest him?' Thou must exist, O God! for the heavens declare Thy glory, and the firmament showeth Thy handiwork.

"8th.—Since dinner I have read much logic and enjoyed it; it is interesting to me, and may, I think, with attention, do me good. Reading Watts impresses deeply on my mind how very careful I should be of judging; how much I should consider before I speak, or form an opinion; how careful I should be not to let my mind be tinged throughout with one reigning subject, to try not to associate ideas; but judge of things according to the evidence they give to my mind of their own worth. My mind is like a pair of scales that are not inclined to balance equally; at least when I begin to form a judgment, and try to hold the balance equally, as soon as I perceive that one scale is at all heavier than the other, I am apt at once to let it fall on that side, forgetting what remains in the other scale, which, though lighter, should not be forgotten. For instance, I look at a character; at first I try to judge calmly and truly; but if I see more vir-tues than vices I am apt soon to like that character so much that I like its weaknesses also, and forget they are weakness-es. The same if evil may preponderate, I forget the virtues.

"30th.—I went to meeting in the morning and afternoon, both times rather dark; but I have been a little permitted to see my own state, which is the greatest favor I can ask for at present; to know what I should do and to be assisted in my duties: for it is hard, very hard to act right, at least I find it so. But there is the comfortable consideration that God is merciful and full of compassion; He is tender over His children. I had a satisfactory time with my girls and boys.

"*January 4th*, 1799.—Most of this morning I spent in
Norwich seeing after the poor; I do little for them, and I
do not like it should appear that I do much. I must be
most guarded, and tell those who know I do charity that I
am only my father's agent. A plan, at least a duty that I
have felt for some time, I will now mention. I have been
trying to overcome fear. My method has been to stay in the
dark, and at night go into those rooms not generally inhabited. There is a strange propensity in the human mind to
fear in the dark; there is a sort of dread of something su-
pernatural. I tried to overcome that by considering that as
far as I believe in ghosts, so far I must believe in a state after death, and it must confirm my belief in the Spirit of
God; therefore if I try to act right I have no need to fear
the directions of Infinite Wisdom. I do not turn away such
things as some do : I believe nothing impossible to God,
and He may have used spirits as agents for purposes beyond
our conceptions. I know they can only come when He
pleases, therefore we need not fear them. But my most
predominant fear is that of thieves, and I find *that* still more
difficult to overcome; but faith would cure that also, for
God can equally protect us from man as from spirit.

"*8th*,—My father not appearing to like all my present
doings, has been rather a cloud over my mind this day : there
are few, if any, in the world I love so well; I am not easy
to do what he would not like, for I think I could sacrifice
almost anything for him, I owe him so much. I love him
so well.

" I have been reading Watts on Judgment this afternoon; it has led me into thought, and particularly upon the
evidence I have to believe in religion. The first thing that
strikes me is the perception we all have of being under a
power superior to human. I seldom feel this so much as
when unwell; to see how pain can visit me and how it is
taken away. Work forever, we could not create life. There
must be a cause to produce an effect. The next thing that

strikes me is good and evil, virtue and vice, happiness and unhappiness—these are acknowledged to be linked together: virtue produces good, vice evil; of course the Power that allows this shows approbation of virtue. Thirdly, Christianity seems also to have its clear evidences, even to my human reason. My mind has not been convinced by books; but what little faith I have has been confirmed by reading holy writers themselves.

"14th.—I hope I have from experience gained a little. I am much of a Friend in my principles at this time, but do not outwardly appear much so; I say 'thee' to people, and do not dress very gay; but yet I say 'Mr,' and 'Mrs.,' wear a turban, &c., &c. I have one remark to make; every step I have taken toward Quakerism has given me satisfaction.

"18th.—I feel I must not despair: I consider I first brought sceptical opinions upon myself, and it is only what is due to me that they should now hurt me. I hope I do not much murmur at the decrees of the Almighty: and can I expect who am so faulty, to be blessed with entire faith? Let me once more try and pray, that the evil roots in my own mind may be eradicated. I had altogether, a pretty good day; rather too much vanity at being mistress at home, and having to entertain many guests.

"24th.—What feeling so cheering to the human mind as religion! what thankfulness should I feel to God! I have great reason to believe Almighty God is directing my mind to the haven of peace; at least I feel that I am guided by a Power not my own. How dark was my mind for some days! How heavy! I saw duties to be performed that even struck me as foolish. I took courage and tried to follow the directions of this voice. I felt enlightened, even happy. Again I erred, again I was in a cloud. I once more tried, and again I felt brightened.

"25th.—This time last year I was with my dear friend, William Savery, at Westminster Meeting. I can only thankfully admire, when I look back to that time, the gentle lead-ings my soul has had from the state of great darkness I was in. How suddenly did the light of Christianity burst upon my mind! I have reason to believe in religion from my own experience; and what foundation so solid to build my hopes upon? May I gain from the little experience I have been blessed with. May I encourage the voice of truth: and may I be a steady and virtuous combatant in the service of God. Such I think I may truly say is my most ardent prayer. But God who is omnipresent knows my thoughts, knows my wishes, and my many, many feelings. May I conclude with saying 'cleanse Thou me from secret faults.'

"*28th.*—We had company most part of the day. I have an odd feeling. Uncle Joseph and many gay ones were here; I had a sort of sympathy with him. I feel to have been so much off my guard that if tempted I should have done wrong. I now hear them singing. How much my natural heart does love to sing. But if I give way to the ecstacy that singing sometimes produces in my mind, it carries me far beyond the center; it increases all the wild passions and works on enthusiasm. Many say and think it leads to religion; it may lead to emotions of religion, but true religion appears to me to be in a deeper recess of the heart, where no earthly passion can produce it.

"*March 1st.*—There is going to be a dance—what am I to do? As far as I can see I believe, if I find it very necessary to their pleasure, I may do it, but not for my own gratification. Remember don't be vain; if it be possible dance little.

"I began to dance in a state next to pain of mind; when I had danced four dances, I was trying to pluck up courage to tell Rachel I wished to give it up for the evening: it seemed as if she looked into my mind, for she came up to me-that minute, in the most tender manner, and begged me to leave off, saying she would contrive without me; I suppose she saw in my countenance the state of my mind. I am not half kind enough to her; I often make sharp remarks to her, and in reality there are none of my sisters to whom I owe so much. I must think of her as my nurse; she would suffer much to comfort me; may she, O God! be blessed; wouldst Thou, oh wouldst Thou, let her see her right path, whatever that may be, and wilt Thou enable her to keep up to her duty, in whatever line it may lead. Let this evening be a lesson to me not to be unkind to her any more. I think I should feel more satisfaction in not dancing; but such things must be left very much to the time. How very much do I wish for their happiness! That they may be blessed in every way is what I pray for to the Great Director. But all is guided in wisdom, and I believe as a family we have much to be thankful for, both for bodily and mental blessings."

The conclusion of the struggle is shown in the following:—

"*March 4th.*—I hope the day has passed without many faults. John is just come in to ask me to dance in such a kind way,—oh dear me! I am now acting clearly differently from them all. Remember this, as I have this night refused to dance with my dearest brother, I must out of kindness to him not be tempted by any one else. Have mercy O God! have mercy upon me! and let me act right, I humbly pray Thee. Wilt Thou love my dearest, most dear, brothers and sisters—wilt Thou protect us! Dear John! I feel much for him; such as these are home strokes; but I had far rather have them, if indeed governed by Supreme Wisdom, for then I need not fear. I know that *not* dancing will not lead me to do wrong, and I fear dancing does. Though the task is hard on their account I hope I do not mind the pain myself. I feel for them, but if they see in time that I am happier for it, I think they will no longer lament over me. I will go to them as soon as they have done, try to be cheerful, and to show them that I love them, for I do most truly, particularly

John. I think I might talk a little with John and tell him
how I stand, for it is much my wisest plan to keep truly intimate with them all—make them my first friends. I do not
think I ever love them so well as at such times as these. I
should fully express my love for them, and how nearly it
touches my heart acting differently to what they like. These
are truly great steps for me to take in life, but I may expect
support under them."

How charming is such a spirit! and she had her reward in
the conversion of several of her highly endowed brothers
and sisters to earnest fellowship in her own faith; she being
the pioneer in the movement. Her eldest sister, Catherine,
and some other members of the family attached themselves
to the National Church. They always, however, remained
firmly devoted to each other, and presented a lovely example
of unity of heart amid diversities of opinion.

Soon after this Elizabeth adopted the numerical style of
dates. This peculiarity of the Quakers originated from the
impression that it was unbecoming in Christians to engraft
idolatrous names upon their language, or to accept usages
originating in the worship of false gods. To this scruple the
only answer necessary is that given by Paul to those who refused meat which had once been offered to idols, feeling that
they thus became partakers of idolatry. "Whatsoever is sold
in the shambles eat, asking no questions for conscience
sake: for the earth is the Lord's and the fullness thereof."
1 Cor. x. 25, 26. Words, like meat, cannot be defiled by
having been wrongly applied. The sin lies in the mind
which uses a harmless instrument to express a wrong sentiment. We might just as well refuse to convert the spear
into a pruning-hook, as to reject the word Monday because

the Moon was worshipped on that day by our ancestors, or decline to say "you" to a single person now, because the practice originated in a purpose to flatter persons of rank. Words derive their meaning altogether from usage, and are merely the coin by which we exchange thought. The sturdiest patriot would not refuse a gold piece because it bore the image and superscription of Cæsar—at least, after Cæsar was dead and his kingdom destroyed.

However, such devotion, though logically erring, is pleasant to witness, and we may admire the faithfulness to conviction while we accustom ourselves to translate "First day" into Sunday, &c,, and "First Month" into January, through the remainder of this frank and altogether admirable heart-history.

"*Fourth Month* 6th.—I have not done a great deal to-day, and yet I hope I have not been idle : I try to do right now and then, but by no means constantly. I could not recover the feeling of being hurt at rejecting, I suppose, the voice of my mind last night, when I sang so much. They were not, I believe feelings of my own making, for it was my wish to enjoy singing without thinking it wrong.

"7th.—I have hopes the day may come when Norwich Meeting will prosper and be enlivened again from a state of cloudiness. In the afternoon I went with them to hear a person preach at the Baptist Meeting. I felt afraid of setting my own opinions up and being uncharitable. It did not seem to suit me like our silent method of worship, and the prayers and sermon did not make their way into the heart as those of our Friends do ; but it is likely I should feel that, as I have much love for my own Society. Uncle Joseph was here in the evening and he seemed rather surprised at my going to hear Kinghorn. I had an interesting time with my young flock. I fear I might say rather too much to them; Mayst Thou, O Father! preserve them, for without Thy aid my efforts are ineffectual. Mayst Thou make me an instrument in leading them to true virtue, and may the day come when Thou wilt call them to everlasting joy.

"22nd.—I have read a good deal in Lavater's journal, and have felt sympathy with him. I like the book, as it reminds me of my duty. I hope that I shall have more steady reliance upon God; more regularity of mind; less volatility of thought. To have my heart pure in the sight of Thee who knowest and seest all my weaknesses, all my defects, God have mercy on me, I pray Thee! Mayst Thou find in me a faithful servant, abounding in good works. May my whole heart truly say, 'Thy will be done!' May I ever, with all my heart say the Lord's prayer. Thou knowest my wishes, O God! Thou knowest them!

"*Fifth Month*, 1st.—Even acting right will sometimes bring dissensions in a family, as it says in the Testament. We must not be discouraged even when that is our lot; for whatever may be our situation, if we strictly adhere to what we believe to be our duty, we need not fear, but rest steadily upon Him who can and will support us. I often observe how much weakness of body seems to humble the mind. Illness is of great benefit to us as I have found from experience, if we try to make good use of it: it leads us to see our own weakness and debility, and to look to a stronger for support. So I believe it may be with the mind; dark and gloomy states are allowed to come upon it that we may know our own insufficiency, and place our dependence upon a Higher Power."

Here is a little dip into politics.

"16th.—I have not done much to day, partly owing to taking a walk to Melton, and company this afternoon. I am sorry to say imperceptibly my mind gets wrapped up in the Election. I must take care or I think I shall be off my guard, and I do think, if I become so warm in it, I shall find it better to go off out of the way; and may perhaps go to London Yearly Meeting. But why not try to command my mind at home? I intend to try, but in such cases as this it is difficult to act a negative character; for even such a body as I am might, I believe, get many votes amongst the poor: but yet I feel as if it were giving to the poor with an expectation of return from them to ask their votes. Still if the cause be such as may be of use in tending to abolish the war, (for every member in the House carries some weight) is it not right to be anxious to get any one who opposes war into it. 'Many a little makes a mickle.'

"27th.—At last the long-wished-for, expected day has arrived; it has been one of real bustle. Before we went to Norwich I was much affected to hear of the death of poor Betty Pettet, and it moved me. Let death come in any way, how very affecting it is! We went to Norwich and there entered its tumults. I have not been so very, very much interested; I might have acted pretty well if pride, vanity and shame had not crept in. We lost the Election which is certainly a very great blank, but we soon get over such matters, and it convinces me the less public matters are entered into the better: they do not suit us. Keep to our sphere and do not go out of its bounds.

"Seventh Month, 12th.—This day was not idle, but not religious. I was most part of the morning at Norwich; in the afternoon I settled accounts; and in the evening cut out clothes for the poor. I don't think I have looked into the Testament, or written my journal to-day. It leads me to remember what Uncle Joseph said to me the other day, after relating or reading to me the history of Mary who anointed our Saviour with the precious ointment, and His disciples said she might have sold it and given to the poor; but Christ said, 'The poor ye have always with you, but me ye have not always.' Now I thought, as Uncle Joseph remarked, I might this evening have spent too much time about the poor that should have been spent about better things.

"*Ninth Month*, 13*th*.—This morning I awoke with a cloud over my mind, and so I must expect both to wake and sleep, if I do not try more completely to do the will of God. I dare not take resolutions, as I know now I cannot keep up to them.

"17*th*.—I feel a comfortable state of mind, not so inclined to be off my guard as sometimes. I know it is not owing to myself, but being so should be a cause of gratitude.

"This evening I did a thing I felt I had to repent of; but it has at least made me clear upon the subject. As they were singing and playing they begged me to sing, and I did it; but I felt far more pain than pleasure from doing it. A really uneasy mind was my portion the rest of the evening.

"18*th*.—This morning I went to meeting and fully felt my weakness; but I have found myself to-day and yesterday a little under the influence of religion which is a blessed thing. I had much palpitation at the Meeting of Discipline, because I saw some things so clearly, but being mentioned by others, I thought I might get off giving an opinion. I was proposed to be a representative, and said I had no objection, on my own part, because though I know how weak I am, yet even the weak should not fear to exert the little power they have; and I do feel interested for the Society, and for the most part approve its principles highly.

"*Tenth Month*, 1*st*.—I feel in a state of much mental weakness, real and true discouragement; I have little faith and little hope, and am almost fallen so as not to be able to rise. But if there be a God and a Saviour I need not fear; for though I know and find my state of corruption, yet I believe the warmest wish of my heart is to do the will of God and act right: I do most truly hunger and thirst after righteousness. I find one thing very hard to overcome, which is pride and vanity in outward religious matters. True religion I believe will not admit of pride and vanity. Another

temptation is that I have too much formed in my own mind
what I think I am to be; which may outwardly encourage
me in a path that nothing but the dictates of conscience
should lead me into.   I am really weak in faith and in works.
I believe, at least I have a hope, that if I exert the little
power I now have given me, the day will come when I shall
feel the power of God within me.

"13th.—Narrow is the path that leadeth unto life eternal,
and few there be that find it.   There are many called, but
few chosen—for though we are blessed with being called,
yet if we follow not when we are called, and that strictly,
we do not deserve to be called the children of God, for, as
it says in Revelations, 'He that overcometh shall inherit all
things, and I will be his God and he shall be my son.'

"*Eleventh Month*, 17th, *First day*.—In the evening, with
my children, I had, in some respects, a very comfortable
time; it was at least my wish to act right with them.   In
part of one of the chapters I seemed carried through to explain something to them in a way I hardly ever did before.
It was striking the difference in my power this evening and
this day week.   This day week I tried and tried to explain,
and the more I tried the more I seemed to blunder; and this
evening I was determined not to attempt it unless I felt capable; and *that* I did, suddenly and unexpectedly to myself.
I had a flow of ideas come one after another, in a sweet and
refreshing way.   The rest of the evening was principally
spent with Hannah Scarnell talking about my poor mother,
who died this day seven years.

"26th.—Towards the latter part of yesterday evening I
had some uncomfortable mental feelings, and this morning
they really amounted to pain of mind.   I believe they
were deep and inward temptations of the imagination.   Silent waiting upon God seemed my only resource, and it was
difficult to do so.   It was like a trial in my mind between
the two powers.   My imagination I think was partly set at
work by being nervous, rather more so than usual; and it

requires spiritual strength to overcome the painful workings of nervous imagination. There are few temptations, I believe, so hard to overcome, as those that try to put on the appearance of duties. They are willing to represent the Spirit of truth in our hearts. At such times, before I act try quietly to wait upon God; look to Him for help: and when things at all appear in the light of duties, the thought of which produces agony to the soul, it requires much deliberation before we act.

"*Twelfth Month*, 11*th*.—In the afternoon I was rather industrious. I was uncertain whether to go to the Grove or not, but at last I fixed to do so. In going there I observed the sweet states I had experienced for being obedient. My path seemed clear, and my heart acknowledged 'I have sought and have found, I have knocked and it has been opened unto me.' It also appeared to me in how beautiful a manner things work together for good. After all this again myself got the victory, and I came home with a degree of remorse for saying more upon some subjects than I should have said. How great a virtue is silence, properly attended to!"

CHAPTER SECOND.

MARRIAGE AND THE MINISTRY.

We have now seen Elizabeth Gurney, at the age of nine-teen, developed into an earnest, pious and sensible Quaker-ess, lovely in person, agreeable in manners, and full of ben-evolent impulses and aspirations, already conscious of a call to the highest work of which man is capable, and steadily engaged in the preparatory offices of teaching the young and giving help to the needy. In addition to her Sabbath evening class in the Testament, she had for some time kept a charity day school for poor children, at her father's resi-dence. This school enlarged until it numbered eighty-six pupils, all of which she taught and governed with a tact pe culiar to herself. She also visited the sick, reading and con-versing with them as opportunity offered. All this appears to have been done, less from sense of duty, than from the kindly impulses of her own heart.

"At this time, Elizabeth Gurney wore the cap and close handkerchief of Friends, and with the dress had adopted their other peculiarities. This added to her comfort and spared her many difficulties. Of the truth of their princi-ples she had long been convinced, and had deliberately chos-en Quakerism as the future religious profession of her life.

"Her mind, being thus established on matters of the first

importance, was better prepared to entertain a subject which now claimed her consideration—proposals of marriage from Mr. Joseph Fry, at that time engaged with his brother, Mr. William Fry, in extensive business in London. Her timid, sensitive nature shrank at first from so momentous a question, and for a time she seemed unable, or unwilling to encounter the responsibility. Gradually, with individual preference, her mind opened to the suitability of the connection. Her habits and education had rendered affluence almost essential to her comfort; whilst entering Mr. Fry's family and the prospect of residing among Friends offered great and strong inducements to her feelings. Her anxious desire to be rightly guided in her decision is marked by the following letter to her cousin Joseph Gurney Bevan." (Memoir.)

The following minute of self-examination is given before the letter referred to as it precedes it in date.

" *Twelfth* Month, 12th. (1799)—I believe the true state of my mind is as follows. I have, almost ever since I have been a little under the influence of religion, thought marriage . at *this* time was not a good thing for me; as it might lead my interests and affections from that source in which they should be centered; and also if I have any active duties to perform in the church, if I really follow, as far as I am able the voice of Truth in my heart, are they not rather incompatible with the duties of a wife and mother? And is it not safest to wait and see what is the probable course I shall take in this life, before I enter into any engagement that affects my future career? So I think, and so I have thought: But to look on the other side. If Truth appears to tell me I may marry, I should leave the rest, and hope, whatsoever my duties are, I shall be able to perform them; but it is now, at this time the prayer of my heart that if I ever should be a mother I may rest with my children, and really find my duties lead me to them and my husband; and if my duty ever leads me from my family, that it may be in single life. I must leave all to the wisdom of a superior Power, and, in humble confidence, pray for assistance, both now and forevermore, in performing the Divine will."

Clapham, Fourth Month, 1800.

"My dearest Cousin:—

It is not pleasant to me having a subject that now is of no small importance to me unknown to thee, for I feel thee to be, and love thee as my kind friend. Some time ago Joseph Fry, youngest son of William Storrs Fry of London, paid us a visit at Earlham and made me an offer of marriage. Since our stay in the neighborhood he has renewed his addresses. I have had many doubts, many risings and fallings about the affair. My most anxious wish is that I may not hinder my spiritual welfare, which I have so much feared as to make me often doubt if marriage were a desirable thing for me at this time, or even the thoughts of it. But as I wish (at least I think I wish) in this as in other things to do the will of God, I hope I shall be shown the path right for me to walk in. I do not think I could have refused him, with a proper authority at this time. If I am to marry before very long it overturns my theories, and may teach me that the ways of the Lord are unsearchable; and that I am not to draw out a path of right for myself; but to look to the One who only knows what is really good for me. But the idea of leaving my station at home is to me surprising, as I had not thought that would have been the case, and perhaps it may not now happen, but it does not seem improbable. How anxiously do I desire I may, through all, strive after the knowledge of God, and one day, if it be right, obtain it. Excuse this hasty scrawl and believe me, my dear cousin, thy very affectionate

E. GURNEY."

"*Earlham, Fifth Month,* 30*th.*—I have written lately many melancholy journals, and I seem rather inclined this morning gratefully to mention the calm and sweet state I feel in. Even if the feelings be only for this time, it is a blessing to have them. My feelings towards Joseph are so calm and pleasant, and I can look forward with so much cheerfulness to a connection with him.

"*Sixth Month,* 6*th.*—I felt rather nervous and weak this morning. I wrote to Eliza Fry, and worked and talked. I might talk too much. I received a letter I liked from Joseph, and answered it this afternoon. I felt unwilling to represent my own faults to him, although I told him how faulty I was; yet it is much more unpleasant to acknowledge any real fault committed than the natural inclination to faults.

"*Eighth Month* 13*th.*—This morning the Fellows were here; nothing particular happened until evening when all my poor children came. It was rather a melancholy time to me. After having enjoyed themselves playing about I took them to the summer-house and bade them farewell; there were about eighty-six of them; many of them wept; I felt rather coldly when with them, but when they went away I shed my tears also; and then my desires took the turn of anxiously longing for the spiritual welfare of us all, as a family."

I now quote at some length from the Memoir, chapter fifth.

"The marriage of Joseph Fry and Elizabeth Gurney took place on the 19th of August, 1800, at the Friends' Meeting house in Norwich; her own description of the day is:—

"'I awoke in a sort of terror at the prospect before me, but soon gained quietness and something of cheerfulness. After dressing we set off for Meeting; I was altogether comfortable. The Meeting was crowded: I felt serious and looking in measure to the only sure place for support. It was to me a truly solemn time; I felt every word; and not only felt but in my *manner* of speaking expressed how I felt; Joseph also spoke well. Most solemn it truly was. After we sat silent some little time Sarah Chandler knelt down in prayer; my heart prayed with her. I believe words are inadequate to describe the feelings on such an occasion; I wept good part of the time, and my beloved father seemed as much overcome as I was. The day passed off well, and I think I was very comfortably supported under it, although cold hands and a beating heart were often my lot.'

"Leaving the home of her childhood was a great effort to her. Driving through Norwich for the last time as a residence 'the very stones of the street seemed dear' to her. On the 31st of the same month she says:—

"'We arrived at Plashet about three o'clock; it was strange to me. I was much pleased with the place, and admired the kindness of its inhabitants.'

"Her home, however, was for some years, to be in scenes far less congenial to her early habits than Plashet House, in Essex, then the residence of her husband's parents. It was a much more prevailing custom in that day than it is now, for the junior partner to reside in the house of business, in conformity with which Mr. and Mrs. Joseph Fry prepared to establish themselves in St. Mildred's Court, in the city of London. The house was large, airy, commodious, and what in the city is a still more rare advantage, quiet; and continued to be an occasional residence of different members of the family till it was pulled down in consequence of alterations in London.

"Elizabeth Fry was by her marriage, brought into completely new circumstances; her husband's family had been members of the Society of Friends since an early period after its foundation. In this it resembled her own; but, unlike her own parents, her father and mother-in-law were 'plain and consistent Friends;' she was surrounded by a large circle of new connections and acquaintance who differed from her own early associates, in being, almost exclusively, strict Friends. Thus she found herself the 'gay instead of the plain and scrupulous one of the family.' This for a time brought her into occasional difficulty and trial, from the incongruity of the parties assembled at her house, formed of her own family and nearest connections whom she so tenderly loved, and those with whom she was in strict religious communion, but whose habits and sentiments differed from theirs; and she feared for herself, lest in the desire to please all she should in any degree swerve from the line of conduct which she believed right for herself.

"George Dilwyn from Philadelphia, a Friend engaged in religious service in London, became their guest on the 7th of November, only a week after the young married pair had arrived at their home; he remained with them upwards of a month, and his company appears to have been useful and agreeable to them, although his presence brought the bride into difficulty on a point which at the present time seems almost inconceivable—that of reading the Holy Scriptures aloud after breakfast. Family devotion among all persuasions was much less common at that period than it is now; and the habit of assembling the household at a stated hour daily for domestic worship was almost unknown. Mr. and Mrs. Fry's servants were not partakers of this privilege, except on Sunday evenings, until some years after their marriage."

"*Eleventh Month, 7th.*—George Dilwyn came to-day; I feel almost overcome with my own weakness, when with such people.

"*11th.*—After breakfast I believed it better to propose reading the Bible, but I felt it, particularly as my brother William was here; not liking the appearance of young people like us, appearing to profess more than they who had lived here before us. However I put off, and put off, till both William and Joseph went down; I then felt uneasy under it, and when Joseph came back I told him, as I did before, what I wished. He, at last, sat down, having told George Dilwyn my desire. I began to read the 46th Psalm, but was so overcome that I could hardly read, and gave it to Joseph to finish.

"12*th*.—I rather felt this morning it would have been right for me to read the Bible again, and stop George Dilwyn and Joseph reading something else. Now stopping G. D., was a difficult thing; for a person like me to remind him! however I did not fully do as I thought right, for I did not openly tell G. D., we were going to read, but spoke to my husband so as for him to hear; then he read, I knowing I had not done my best.

"14*th*.—I again felt some difficulty at reading the Bible; however I got through well. George Dilwyn encouraged me by saying he thought I portioned the reading well. After a little bustling we set off for Hampstead. I was there told by ——— he thought my manners had too much of the courtier in them, which I knew to be the case, for my disposition leads me to hurt no one that I can avoid: and I do sometimes but just keep to truth with people from a natural yielding to them in such things as please them. I think doing so in moderation is pleasant and useful in society. It is amongst those things that produce the harmony of society for the truth must not be spoken out at all times, at least not the whole truth. I will give an instance of what I mean. Suppose any one was to show me the color of a room that I thought pretty, I should say so, although I thought others more so, and omit saying that. Perhaps I am wrong; I do not know if I be not; but it will not always do to tell our minds. This I have observed (and I am sorry for it) that I feel it hard, when duty dictates, to do what I think may hurt others. I believe this feeling of mine originates in self-love, from the dislike of being myself the cause of pain and uneasiness."

The above is a fine illustration of character. Through her entire want of self-esteem she takes to herself discredit for that disposition which won her almost universal favor an enabled her to accomplish very difficult reforms without making an enemy—a disposition wanting which many well-meaning, but not wholly well-feeling, people often do as much harm as good in trying to do what they conceive to be their duty. I said, without making an enemy. Perhaps she made one, and that through inattention, as she thought, to the principle above noted, not always to speak what is in our mind. In her humane zeal to save a poor weak girl from the gallows for passing counterfeit money at the persuasion of her lover, she offended the Secretary of State, Lord Sidmouth, by reflecting on the conduct of certain bank officers, concerned in the case, and the inhuman Judge let the unhappy girl die, and closed his ears thereafter to appeals from her intercessor. It may have been an indiscretion, though it seems born of the Spirit which cried "Woe unto you Scribes and Pharisees, hypocrites!" and which brought the wrath of those murderers on the head of Him who could not brook wrongs to the poor.

"15th.—George Dilwyn said for our encouragement this morning, that he had seen, since he had been with us, the efficacy of reading in the Bible the first thing,—he thought it a good beginning for the day."

The next step, so delicately pointed to by the guiding Finger of Light in her mind, she found equally difficult to take, and did not take, until long afterwards, perhaps in consequence of her shrinking from the first gentle command.

"9th. (December)—Anna Savery drank tea here; we had

not sat long after tea before we fell into silence. During the time 1 first felt a sort of anxiety for the welfare of us young travelers, and it came strongly across my mind openly to express it. This put me into an agitation not easily to be described; and I continued in this state, which was a truly painful one, nearly feeling it my duty to pray aloud for us; oh how hard it did seem! I tried to run from it, but I found the most safety in trying to wait upon God; hoping if it were imagination, to overcome it; if it were a duty that I might be obedient. Towards the latter end I felt *more* inclined towards obedience. But what an obstacle is my not holding my will in subservience to that of my Maker; for perhaps, after all, it was only a trial of my obedience that would not have been called for, but to show me how far I was from a resigned state of heart. I felt oppressed the rest of the evening.

"10*th.*—I woke in a burdened state of mind; I thought it better to relieve it to my dear husband and found comfort in doing so; he warned me against imagination. I must try to trust in the Lord, and I hope to find safety. I felt quite in a state of agitation till we went to Meeting; it made me feel almost ill in body, both last night and this morning. However my mind was sweetly calmed in Meeting, and I felt vastly relieved from my terrors, and a little love and trusting in the Heavenly Master. I was *almost* ready to do whatever might be right for me. Oh! may I give up to what is called for at my hand; and may I not be deceived, but follow the true Shepherd, for my feet seem much in-inclined to wander!"

That fatal "*almost!*" How many have been wrecked upon it! "*Almost* thou persuadest me to be a Christian." The Jews were almost ready to go into the Promised Land, but turned back, alarmed by their false spies. So it is with all of us. Even faithful Elizabeth Fry was no exception.

Had she been able to yield to the simple impulses of her heart when she felt longings for the welfare of herself and Anna Savery, and, asked God to bless and guide them, as she would have asked her earthly parent for aid had she needed it, her entrance upon the open work of the ministry would have been easy and natural. Battles she would have had still to fight, but victory would have been given to faithful obedience. She was, however, not ripe for it, as the event proved. She turned back because she was still in bonds, spiritually. She was trying to do God's work as a servant, rather than as a child—under compulsion, instead of from love. She still needed the baptism of the Holy Ghost and of fire which would bring the Spirit of Christ into her very soul, before a true and efficacious gospel ministry could flow from it. After nine years of incessant and often bewildering struggle with life, in a crowded city home, and the birth of six children, and when her beloved father lay dead in the home of her childhood, having breathed out his soul, after a severe struggle with conscience, in a lively hope of Heaven—then, at last, the subdued flame of piety burst forth in prayer and thanksgiving in the sight of men.

If we could only be faithful to the first, or even the second call, how much sorrow would be spared. But because we are then only half converted, because we have Christ before our eyes, instead of in our hearts, because, though the spirit is willing the flesh is yet weak, we slumber while the crucial hour of fate is passing; and after twice rousing us, and again silently looking upon our prostration, the Lord says to us, "Sleep on now and take your rest;—he is at hand that doth betray me." The traitor is indeed at hand in all our hearts when either the fear of man or the love of gain effectually closes our eyes and ears to Christ's appeal.

The minute in her Journal succeeding that last given shows that the Spirit was now to some extent withdrawn.

"14th.—I attended both Meetings as usual, and as usual, came from them flat and discouraged. To attend our place of worship, and there spend almost all the time in worldly thoughts is I fear too great a mark of how my time is mostly spent; indeed my life appears, at this time, to be spent to little more purpose than eating, drinking, sleeping and clothing myself. But if we analyze the employment of most, what do they more than, in some way attend to the bodily wants of themselves or others? What is our work, the good we do for the poor, &c., &c., but for the body?

"*Third Month*, 15th. (1801).—I felt really better this morning (alluding to a previous indisposition) and went to Meeting, but all my small efforts to quiet my thoughts were ineffectual; the same in the afternoon; it is very serious. Really when I awake in the morning I feel a flatness; when I find my great object of the day no longer appears to be even to wish to do the will of my Creator. But I am as one who has, in some measure, lost his pilot and is tossed about by the waves of the world. But I trust that there is yet a power that will prevent my drowning. I draw some consolation from my dreams of old, for how often was I near drowning, and yet at last saved.

"25th.—I feel almost overcome with the multiplicity of visitings and goings out.

"15th. (*June*)—If I can with truth acknowledge it to be my first wish to do my best, although I may not feel the sensible gratification of doing my duty, I may yet be really doing it. If I do all I can, I have no occasion to fear sooner or later meeting with my reward. I was rather disappointed at our having company: indeed we have now little time alone. It is quite a serious thing, our being so constantly liable to interruptions as we are. I do not think since we

married we have had one-fourth of our meals alone. I long
for more retirement, but it appears out of our power to procure it ; and therefore it is best to be as patient under interruptions as we can, but I think it a serious disadvantage to
young people setting out in life.

"15th. (August)—I have had an interesting talk with my
dear sister Rachel : She appears to me to have perceived
that which will direct her steps. But how hard it is deeply,
strictly, and for a long time together, to have our first object to serve our Creator—for at first there is a natural glee,
as for something new, and then we feel we have to pass
through lukewarmness which is a dangerous state; I believe
one where many are lost. May I be carried through it !

Her maternal trials and pleasures, succeeded each other
apace, adding what all mothers understand to the anxieties
as well as charms of a busy life.

"Tenth Month, 1st.—My present feelings for the babe,
are so acute as to render me at times unhappy from an over
anxiety about her, such a one as I never felt before for any
one. Now it appears to me this over anxiety arises from
extreme love, weak spirits and state of health, and not being
under the influence of principle that would lead me to overcome these natural feelings, as far as they tend to my
misery. For if I were under the influence of principle, I
might trust that my dear infant indeed was under the care
and protection of an infinitely wise and just Providence that
permits her little sufferings for some good end that I knew
not of. How anxiously do I hope this poor dear baby may
be held by me in resignation to the Divine will. Oh ! that
I might feel dependence on that Almighty arm about her,
and about other things. Beyond everything else I wish to
do my duty, idle and relaxed as I am in performing it.

"Fourth Month, 19th,(1802)—Oh! may my obedience
keep pace with my knowledge, at this time; my knowledge
of good appears small ; my longings to be better are only

known by a Superior Power, who I trust will, in time, have
mercy on me. I have this day prayed that in this day of
darkness I may not prove an obstruction in the way of
others ; truly a South Land is my portion,—I only long for
the wells of living water."

The birth of her second child is thus recorded:

"*Fourth Month*, 12*th*.—My heart abounded with joy and
gratitude when my dear little girl was born, perfect and
lovely. Words are not equal to express my feelings, for I
was most mercifully dealt with, my soul was so quiet, and
so much supported.

"*Plashet, Fifth Month*, 21*st*.—I have been long prevented
from writing in my journal by a severe attack of indisposition. It is difficult exactly to express what I have gone
through, but it has been, now and then, a time of close trial ;
my feelings being such, at times, as to be doubtful whether
life or death would be my portion. One night I was, I believe, very seriously ill : I never remember feeling so forcibly
how hard a trial it was in prospect, to part with life. Much
as my mind, as well as body, was tried in this emergency,
still I felt forcibly an inward support, and it reminded me
of that text of Scripture, 'Can a woman forget her sucking
child ? Yea, they may forget, yet will I not forget thee.'
And then I told those around me that I was so ill I could
almost forget my child ; but that I felt the existence of a
Power that could *never* forget. I have gone through much
since, in various ways, from real bodily weakness, and also
the trials of a nervous imagination. No one knows, but those
who have felt them how hard those are to bear, for they lead
the mind to look for trouble, and it requires much exertion
not to be led away by them. Nothing I believe allays them
so much as the quieting influence of religion, and that leads
us to endeavor after quietness under them, not looking beyond the present. But they are a regular bodily disorder

that I believe no mental exertion can cure or overcome ; but we must endeavor not to give way to them."

From this time onward the light gradually grew brighter, and she again became engaged in various good works, as opportunity was afforded. She was slowly coming back toward the Land of Promise, which to her was the active work of benevolence, and the Ministry of the Gospel as th highest part of that work.

"*Plashet, Second Month, 5th.* (1805)—Since I last wrote I have been much occupied with many things, rather more than usual about the poor. I have been desirous that attending to them as I do may not prove a snare to me : for I think acting charitably leads us often to receive more credit than we deserve, or at least to fancy so. It is one of those things that give my nature pleasure; therefore I believe I am no further praiseworthy than that I give way to a natural inclination. Attending the afflicted is one of those things that so remarkably bring their reward with them that we may rest in a sort of self-satisfaction which is dangerous ; but I often feel the blessing of being so situated as to be able to assist the afflicted, and sometimes a little to relieve their distresses.

"*11th.*—We ought to make it an object in conversation and in conduct to endeavor to oblige those we are with, and rather to make the pleasure of others our object than our own. I am clear it is great virtue to be able constantly to yield in little things : it begets the same spirit in others and renders life happy.

"*Fifth Month, 7th.*—Yesterday my sister Eliza Fry was here ; we were saying something about the children's dress ; and she remarked that for the sake of others, (she meant the fear of not setting a good example) she would not do so and so. I said it struck me that those who do their duty with integrity are serving others as well as themselves, and do more real good to the cause of religion than in looking much outwardly either to what others do or think. I think that conscience will sometimes lead us to feel for others and not act so as materially to hurt a weak brother; but I believe we should seldom find that we hurt those whose opinion would be worth caring for, if we kept close to the witness in our own hearts. If I were going to do a thing I should endeavor to find whether it appeared to me in any way wrong, and whether I should feel easy to do it, looking secretly for help where it is to be found, and there I believe I should leave it; and if it led me to act rather differently from some I should probably be doing more good to society than in any conformity merely on account of others; for if I should be preserved in the way of obedience in other things it would in time show from whence such actions sprung: and I think this very spirit of conforming in trifles to the opinion of others leads into forms that may one day prove a stumbling block to the progress of our Society; whereas if we attend to the principle that brought us together it will lead us out of forms and not into them."

The above observation has been abundantly verified not only in the Society of Friends but in all others. The true principle, as referred to, is that laid down by Christ when He said "The light of the body is the eye; if therefore thine eye be single thy whole body shall be full of light." It was expressed by George Fox in words that became a kind of watch-word, "Mind the Light." Had these injunctions been generally heeded sectarianism would have been a thing unknown.

"Seventh Month, 3rd.—It appears to me that we who desire to be the servants of Christ must expect to do a part of our Master's work, which no doubt is to bear with the weaknesses and infirmities of human nature, and if we be favored to feel them and not sink under them, we may be enabled in time to help others bear their burdens; and it appears to me that all Christian travelers must expect to pass through, in their measure, the temptations and trials their Master did on earth.

"*Mildred's Court*, 19th.—Yesterday and the day before I have been driven from one thing to another, and from one person to another, as is usual in this place. I have feared my attention being quite diverted from good. But I have also thought that *doing our duty is most effectually serving the Lord.* May I therefore endeavor to do mine and not be impatient at my numerous interruptions, but strive to center my mind in a humble desire to do the will of my Creator, which will, through all, create a degree of quietness.

"26th.—I have observed how much better things are done, and how much more satisfaction they produce, when done in that quiet, seeking state of mind. How greatly I desire that all I do may be done to the glory of God rather than to my own self-satisfaction."

In the month of May 1808, for the first time since the decease of their mother, death entered the large and highly favored family of John Gurney and removed the wife of Elizabeth Fry's eldest brother John. This event became the occasion of some important changes. In his affliction he sought the advice of the Rev. Edward Edwards, whose influence among the brothers and sisters, all of whom were awakened to the importance of a religious life, was such as to lead several of them to a judgment favoring the Church of England. Others chose the hereditary faith of the Friends, Elizabeth having been the first to assume a decided stand. They became nearly equally divided on these extreme right and left wings of Protestanism; and yet they preserved a remarkable unity of spirit and purpose; thus setting a most beautiful example of Christian charity. Two of the brothers, Samuel and Joseph John, and two of the sisters, Elizabeth and Priscilla, were Friends—three of them being ministers. The brothers John and Daniel, with Catharine, the eldest of the family, who remained unmarried, Louisa, who married Samuel Hoare, Esq., Richenda, wife of Rev. Francis Cunningham, and Hannah who became the wife of Sir T. Fowell Buxton, joined the Episcopal Church; while Rachel the second sister also unmarried, remained without decided preference. In referring to this divergence Mrs. Fry's daughters, who were similarly divided,—the eldest, Katharine, remaining a Friend, and the second Rachel, who united with her in editing their mother's Memoir, becoming an Episcopalian—remark: "It was not without pain that she who had so decidedly chosen the path of Friends, saw others so dear to her as decidedly choosing another way, and uniting themselves with the Church of England; but as each one became established in his own course, some one way and some the other, a wonderful union and communion sprang up among them; so that their bond in natural things was not stronger than that which united them as devoted worshipers of the same Lord."

"*Eighth Month*, 20*th*. (1808).—1 have been married eight years yesterday. Various trials of faith and patience have been permitted me; my course has been very different to what I had expected; and instead of being, as I had hoped, a useful instrument in the Church Militant, here I am, a care-worn wife and mother, outwardly, nearly devoted to the things of this life. Though at times this difference in my destination has been trying to me, yet I believe those trials (which have certainly been very pinching) that I have had to go through, have been very useful, and brought me to a feeling sense of what I am; and at the same time have taught me where power is, and in what we are to glory; not in ourselves, nor in anything we can be, or do, but we are alone to desire that He may be glorified, either through us, or others,—in our being something, or nothing, as He may see best for us. I have seen, particularly in our spiritual allotments, that it is not in man that walketh to direct his steps. It is our place only to be as passive clay in His holy hands, simply desiring that He would make us what He would have us to be. But the way in which this great work is to be effected we must leave to Him who has been the Author and we may trust will be the Finisher of the work: and we must not be surprised to find it going on differently to what our frail hearts would desire.

"I may also acknowledge that, through all my trials, there does appear to have been a particular blessing attending me, both as to the fatness of the land and the dew of Heaven; for, though I have been at times deeply tried, inwardly and outwardly, yet I have always found the delivering Arm has been near at hand, and the trials have appeared blessed to me. The little efforts, or small acts of duty, I have ever performed have often seemed remarkably blessed to me; and where others have been concerned, it has also, I think, been apparent to them that the effort on my part has been blessed to both parties. Also what shall I say when I look at my husband and my five lovely babes? How have I been favored to recover from illness, and to get through them without material injury in any way. I also observe how any little care towards my servants appears to have been blessed, and what faithful and kind friends to me I have found them. Indeed I cannot enumerate my blessings; but I may truly say, that of all the blessings I have

received, and still receive, there is none to compare with believing that I am not yet forsaken, but, notwithstanding all
my deviations, in mercy cared for. And, if all the rest be
taken from me, far above all I desire that, if I should be led
through paths which I know not of, which may try my weak
faith and nature, I may not lose faith in Thee; but may in-
increasingly love Thee, delight to follow after Thee, and be
singly Thine, giving all things up to Thee who hast hitherto been my only merciful Protector and Preserver."

The death of her father-in-law, soon after the date of the
above extract, caused the removal of Joseph Fry's family
from London to the country home at Plashet, in Essex,
which for the next twenty years formed their principal residence; a portion of the season being passed at Mildred's
Court, London. About a year after their removal to Plashet,
Elizabeth's father died; and it was on this occasion that her
spirit was so powerfully wrought upon that she gave brief
expression to her feelings, in obedience to an impulse of the
Spirit, which was regarded as an entrance upon the work of
the Ministry.

This event is best described in her own words.

"*Earlham*, 30*th*. (1809)—I hardly know how to express
myself: I have indeed passed through wonders. On the
26th, as we were sitting quietly together, (after my dear sister Richenda had left us, and my soul had bowed on my beloved father's account, of whom we had daily very poor reports,) an express arrived bringing Chenda back, saying our
most dear father was so ill that they did not expect his life
would be spared. Words fall short to describe what I felt,
he was so tenderly near and dear to me. We soon believed
it best to set off for this place, on some accounts under
great discouragement, principally from my own bodily weak-

ness, and also the fever in the house; but it did not appear as if we could omit it, feeling as we did; therefore, after a tender parting with my beloved flock, my dearest Joseph, Chenda and I with the baby set off. We arrived at Mildred's Court the first night, where our dear sister left us, in hopes of seeing our dear parent alive. In very great weakness I set off next morning, and had at times great discouragements; but many hours were comforting and sweet. Hearing on the road, at different stages that my dearest father was living, we proceeded till we arrived at Earlham about twelve o'clock that night. We got out of the carriage and once more saw him who has been so inexpressibly dear to me through life, since I knew what love was; he was asleep but death was strongly marked on his sweet and to me beautiful face. Whilst in his room all was sweetness, nothing bitter, though how I feel his loss is hard to express: but indeed I have abundant cause to rejoice on his account; after very deep probation his mind was so strikingly visited and consoled at last in passing through the valley of the shadow of death. He frequently expressed that he feared no evil, but believed that through the mercy of God in Christ he should be received in glory. His deep humility, and the tender loving state he was in, were most valuable to those around him. He encouraged us, his children, to hold on our way; and sweetly expressed his belief that our love of good (in the degree we had it) had been a stimulus and help to him.

The next morning he died quite easily. I was not with him, but on entering the room, soon after it was over, my soul was bowed within me, in love, not only for the deceased, but also for the living, and in humble thankfulness; so that I could hardly help uttering (which I did) my thanksgiving and praise, and also what I felt for the living as well as the dead. I cannot understand it, but the power given was wonderful to myself and the cross none; my heart was so full that I could hardly hinder utterance.

"*Eleventh Month, 3rd.*—We attended our beloved
father's funeral. Before I went I was so deeply-impressed
at times with love for all, and thanksgiving that I doubted
whether it might not possibly be my place to express it
there; but I did, the evening before, humbly crave not to
be permitted to do so unless rightly called to it. Fear of
man appeared greatly taken away. I sat the meeting
under a solemn quietness, though there was preaching
that neither disturbed nor enlivened me much. The same
words still powerfully impressed me that had done ever
since I first entered the room where the corpse lay. Upon
going to the grave this still continued. Under this solemn,
quiet calm, the fear of man appeared so much removed
that I believe my sole desire was that the will of God
might be done in me. Though it was unpleasant to me
what man might say, yet I most feared it was a temptation, owing to my state of sorrow; but that I fully believe
was not the case, as something of the kind had been on my
mind so long; but it had appeared more ripe the last few
weeks, and even months; I had so often had to 'rejoice in
the Lord, and glory in the God of my salvation,' that it
had made me desire that others might partake, and know
how good He had been to my soul, and be encouraged to
walk in those paths which I had found to be paths of
pleasantness and peace. However, after a solemn waiting,
my dear uncle Joseph spoke, greatly to my encouragement
and comfort, and the removal of some of my fears. I remained till dearest John began to move to go away:
when it appeared as if it could not be omitted, and I fell
on my knees and began, not knowing how I should go on,
with these words, 'Great and marvelous are Thy works,
Lord God Almighty! just and true are Thy ways, Thou King
of Saints! Be pleased to receive our thanksgiving.' And
there I seemed stopped, though I thought that I should
have had to express that I gave thanks on my beloved
father's account. But not feeling the power continue I

arose directly. A quiet, calm and invigorated state, mental and bodily, were my portion afterwards, and altogether a sweet day, but a very painful night, discouraged on every side—I could believe by him who tries to deceive. The discouragement appeared to arise principally from what others would think; and nature flinched and sank; but I was enabled this morning to commit myself in prayer."

It should perhaps here be mentioned that the Friends do not consider it unsuitable for even nearest relatives of the deceased to express their minds, under a proper impulse, at funerals. Rarely, perhaps, are ministers first called forth on such occasions; and yet the deep and lively emotions might aid in weakening the bond of timidity by which nearly all are embarrassed on a first exposure. Probably few have a greater natural dread of such a trial than Elizabeth Fry who possessed a peculiarly sensitive organization; and yet when the proper time came the promised grace was found sufficient for her. The river was parted and she went through on dry ground.

"*Plashet, Eleventh Month*, 16*th*.—We arrived here on Third-day evening. Though plunged into feeling before I arrived, I felt flat on meeting my tenderly beloved little flock. I was enabled, coming along to crave help, in the first place to be made willing either to do, or to suffer whatever was the Divine will concerning me. I also desired that I might not be so occupied with my present state of mind, as to its religious duties, as in any degree to omit close attention to all daily duties my beloved husband, children, servants, poor, &c.; but if I should be permitted to enter the humiliating path that has appeared to be opening before me, to look well at home and not discredit the cause I desire to advocate. Last First-day morning I had a deeply trying

Meeting, on account of the words, 'Be of good courage and He will strengthen your hearts, all ye that hope in the Lord,' which had impressed me toward Norwich Meeting before I went into it; and after I had sat there a little time they came with double force, and continued resting on my mind, until my fright was extreme, and it appeared almost as if I must, if I did my duty, utter them. I hope I did not wholly revolt, but I did cry in my heart for that time to be excused, that like Samuel, I might apply to some Eli, to know what the voice was that I heard. My beloved Uncle Joseph I thought was the person. On this sort of excuse, or covenant, as I may call it, a calmness was granted the rest of the meeting; but not the reward of peace. As soon as the Meeting was over I went to my dear Uncle and begged him to come to Earlham to see me. The conflict I had passed through was so great as to shake my body, as well as mind, and I had reason to fear and to believe I should have been happier and much more relieved in mind, if I had given up to this little service. I have felt since like one in debt to that Meeting. My dear Uncle came, and only confirmed me, by his kind advice, to walk by faith, and not by sight. He strongly advised a simple following of what arose, and expressed his experience of the benefit of giving up to it, and the confusion of not doing so. How have I desired, since, not to stand in the fear of man; but I believe it is the soul's enemy seeking whom he may devour; for terrible as it was, as then presented to me and as it often had been before, yet when some ability was granted to get through, that same enemy would have had me glory on that account. May I not give way either to one feeling or the other, but strive to look to the preserving power of God.

" *Twelfth Month*, 4th.—When I have given up, in the morning only to make an indifferent remark to the servants on our reading, sweet peace has been my portion: but when it has been presented to me and I have not followed, far different has been the case. In Meeting it is such an awful matter, for the sake of others as well as myself. If it be Thy work in me, be pleased, O Lord, to grant faith and power sufficient for the needful time. I long to serve Thee and to do Thy commandments, and I believe if I be faithful in the little Thou wilt be pleased to make me ruler over more.

"*9th.*—Soon after sitting down in Meeting on Fourth-day, (the Friends hold a meeting in the middle of the week) I was enabled to feel encouraged by these words, 'Though the enemy come in like a flood, the Spirit of the Lord will lift up a standard against him.' This appeared my experience, for soon the storm was quieted and a degree even of ease was my portion. About eleven o'clock these same words that had done so in Norwich meeting came feelingly over me—'Be of good courage and I will strengthen your hearts, all ye that hope in the Lord.' And that which had hitherto appeared impossible to human nature seemed not only possible, but I believe I was willing simply desiring that in the new and awful undertaking I might not lose my faith and that the Divine will might be done in me. Under this sense, and feeling as if I could not omit, I uttered them. Though clearness still continued, nature, in a great measure, seemed to sink under the effort afterwards, and low feelings and imaginations to have much dominion, which, in mercy, were soon relieved, and I have gone on sweetly and easily since, even rejoicing.

"*22nd.*—Again, on Fourth-day, I have dared to open my mouth in public: I am ready to say What has come to me? —even in supplication, that the work might be carried on in myself and others, and that we might be preserved from evil. My weight of deep feeling on the subject I believe exceeded any other time. I was, I may say, brought into a wrestling state, that the work of the ministry in me might, if right, be carried on, if not, stopped short. I feel, of myself, no power for such a work; I may say, wholly unable; yet when the feeling and power continue, so that I dare not omit it, then what can I do?

"*23rd.*—Giving up to make a little remark after reading to the servants, has brought sweet peace: indeed, so far, it has appeared to me that prompt obedience has brought me the most peace. The prospect of the meetings next week, more particularly the Quarterly Meeting, already makes me tremble. I can hardly say why, but it is very awful to be thus publicly exposed, in a work that I feel so little fitted for; yet I believe it is not my own doing, nor at my own command.

"*Plashet, First Month,* 1*st,* 1810.—It is rather awful to me entering a new year, more particularly when I look at the alterations the last has made—most striking the last three months, or a little more. First a child born; second the loss of nurse; third my beloved father's death; fourth my being opened in meetings. My heart says, What can I render for having been so remarkably and mercifully carried through these various dispensations of Providence? I think I never knew the Divine Arm so eminently extended for my comfort, help and deliverance; and though of late I may have had to pass through the valley of the shadow of death, yet it has not lasted long at a time, and Oh, the incomings of love, joy and peace that have, at other periods, arisen for my confirmation and consideration! But the manna of yesterday I find will not do for to-day.

"*11th.*—It has been strongly impressed upon me how very little it matters, when we look at the short time we remain here, what we appear to others; and how far too much we look at the things of this life.

"What does it signify what we are thought of here, so long as we are not found wanting towards our Heavenly Father? Why should we so much try to keep back something, and not be willing to offer ourselves up to Him, body, soul and spirit, to do with us what may seem best unto Him, and to make us what He would have us to be? O Lord! enable me to be more and more singly, simply and purely obedient to thy service!

"19th.—Yesterday was an awful, and to me instructive day at Plaistow Meeting. I had not sat very long before I was brought into much feeling desire that the darkness in some minds might be enlightened. However no clearness of expression came with it; but under a very solemn covering of the spirit of supplication, a few words offering, I, after a time, gave way to utter them. But that which appeared greatly in the cross to me was having some words presented to speak in testimony afterwards, which I did, I believe, purely because I desired to serve my Master, and not to look too much to the opinion of my fellow-servants; and there was to me a remarkable solemnity, and something like an owning, or accepting of this poor little offering. I have desired, and have been in a little degree enabled to feel on that sure foundation, that although the winds may blow, and the rain may descend, yet whilst I keep on this Rock they will not be able utterly to cast me down. What a mercy amidst the storm to feel, ever so slightly, something of a sure foundation! Thus much I know, that, even if I be mistaken in this awful undertaking, my desire is to serve Him in it whom my soul, I may truly say, loves and delights to please. O Lord! I pray Thee preserve Thy poor handmaid in the hour of temptation, and enable me to follow Thee in the way of Thy requirings even if they lead me into suffering and unto death.

"31st.—My little —— has been very naughty; his will I find is very strong; oh that my hands may be strengthened rightly to subdue it. O Lord! I pray for help in these important duties! I may truly say I had rather my dear lambs should not live than live eventually to dishonor Thy great cause; rather may they be taken in innocency: but if Thou seest meet, O Lord! preserve them from great evils, and be pleased in Thy abundant mercy to be with them, as Thou hast been, I believe, with their poor unworthy parents; visit them and revisit them, until Thou hast made them what Thou wouldst have them to be. Oh that I could like Hannah, bring them to Thee, to be made use of as instruments in thy Holy Temple! I ask nothing for them in comparison of Thy love; and above all blessings, that they may be vessels in Thy house. This blessing I crave for them, that they may be employed in Thy service, for indeed I can bow and say, What honor, what joy so great as, in ever so small a measure, to serve Thee, O Lord!

"*Mildred's Court, Sixth Month, 1st.*—Yesterday I attended the funeral of our beloved Anna Reynolds, whose death has been deeply felt by me. We had, I think I may truly say, a glorious time; for the power of the Most High appeared to overshadow us. A belief of her being in safety has bowed my soul prostrate, in humble thankfulness, and renewedly led me to desire to prove my gratitude for such unspeakable mercy as has been shown my near and beloved relations by my love and entire dedication. I uttered a few words in supplication, at the ground; my uncle Joseph, my cousin Pricilla, and many others, beautifully ministered. After Meeting, I might truly say, my cup ran over, such sweetness covered my mind. After a solemn time in the family, with dear cousin Pricilla and Ann Crowley, I ventured on my knees, praying that His Holy Hand would not spare, nor his eye pity, until He made us what He would have us to be: only I craved that He would not forsake us, but let us be made in some small measure sensible that He was with us, and that it was His rod and His staff that we depended upon. Through heights and through depths, through riches and through poverty may it alone be my will to do the will of the Father!"

The foregoing selections, covering a period of seven months, are sufficient to show the workings of this deeply earnest mind and heart under the impulse of the Spirit to participate in the exercises of the Church. Slow as it may seem the progress of Elizabeth Fry was more rapid than is usual with this class of ministers, for she was endowed by nature with fertile conception and ready utterance, and, her heart being fully enlisted, so soon as the embarrassment of her new position wore off, she became a very ready speaker. Her nature being emotional and full of benevolent impulses, her words appealed to the better feelings of those she addressed, while her prayers, being the sincere utterance of her heart, rather than her intellect, carried the hearts of others to the Throne of grace. In little more than a year from its commencement, her ministry was formally "acknowledged" by the Society as being acceptable. This simple mode of ordination—or laying on of hands in a figurative sense—entitles those receiving it to pass freely through the different branches of the Society and to appoint special meetings if they feel it right to do so; after having obtained the consent of their own Monthly or Quarterly Meetings thus to labor in the work of the Gospel abroad.

Referring to this official acknowledgment Elizabeth Fry says:

"This mark of their unity is sweet, and I think strengthening, and I believe it will have advantages as well as trials attending it. I feel and find it is not by the approbation, any more than the disapprobation, of man that we stand or fall; but it once more leads me only to desire that I may simply and singly follow my Master in the way of His requirements, whatsoever they may be. I think this will make a way for me in some things which have long been on my mind."

The following incidents illustrating her care for the needy in her own neighborhood are related by her daughters.

"In establishing herself at Plashet Mrs. Fry had formed various plans for her poorer neighbors which she gradually brought into action. One of her early endeavors was to establish a girls' school for the Parish of East Ham. of which Plashet is a hamlet. Immediately opposite the gate of Plashet House there stood a dilapidated dwelling, picturesque from its gable end and large projecting porch. It was inhabited by an aged man and his still more aged sister. They had seen better days, and eked out a narrow income with the help of a brother's labors in a small garden, and the sale of rabbits of which they kept a vast quantity. Like persons fallen in life they were reserved; the sister almost inaccessible: but by degrees Mrs. Fry won her way to the old lady's heart. She might be seen seated in an upper chamber on one side of a fire-place lined with blue Dutch tiles opposite the invalid who, propped by cushions, leaned back in an easy chair, in a short white dressing-gown over a quilted petticoat, her thin wrinkled hands resting on her knees, and her emaciated refined countenance brightening under the gentle cheering influence of her guest, as she endeavored to raise her hopes and stimulate her desires after that country where it shall no more be said 'I am sick.' Annexed to this old building was a spacious and comparatively modern room which appeared suitable for a school-room, and Mrs. Fry's persuasions succeeded in obtaining the consent of the old people to use it as such.

"A young woman named Harriet Howell, who was much occupied at that time in organizing schools on the Lancasterian system, came to Plashet. The excellent clergyman of East Ham, Mr. Aulezark, with his lady united with her in the object. A school of about seventy girls was established, and although afterwards removed to a more central situation, continues to the present day.

"The bodily wants of the poor, especially in cases of sickness or accident, claimed her careful attention. There was a depot of calico and flannels always ready, besides other garments, and a roomy closet well supplied with drugs. In very hard winters she had soup boiled in an out-house in such quantities as to supply hundreds of poor people with a nourishing meal. Nor was her interest confined to the English poor in East Ham. About half a mile from Plashet, on the high road between Stratford and Ilford, the passer-by will find two long rows of houses with one larger one in the center, if possible more dingy than the rest. At that time they were squalid and dirty; the windows generally stuffed with old rags, or pasted over with brown paper, and the few remaining panes of glass refusing to perform their intended office, from the accumulated dust of years; puddles of thick black water before the doors; children without shoes or stockings; mothers whose matted locks escaped from the remnants of caps which looked as though they never could have been white; pigs on terms of evident familiarity with the family; poultry sharing the children's potatoes—all bespoke an Irish colony.

"It was a pleasant thing to observe the influence obtained by Mrs. Fry over these wild but warm-hearted people. She had in her nature a touch of poetry, and a quick sense of the droll; the Irish character furnished matter for both. Their powers of deep love and bitter grief excited her sympathy; almost against her judgment she would grant the linen shirt and the boughs of evergreen to array the departed and ornament the bed of death.

"One clear frosty morning Mrs. Fry called her elder children to accompany her on a visit to one of these cottages. A poor woman, the mother of a young family had died there; she had been well conducted as a wife and mother, and had long shown a desire for religious instruction; the priest, a kind-hearted, pains-taking man, liberal in his views and anxious for the good of his flock, thought well of the poor woman, had frequently visited her in her illness, and was in that as in many other cases, very grateful to Mrs.

Fry for the relief and nourishment she had bestowed, which it was not in his power to give.

"On the bed of death lay extended the young mother, her features, which were almost beautiful, stiffened into the semblance of marble. Her little children were on the floor, her husband in the corner leaning on a round table, with his face buried in his hands. A paper cross lay on the breast of the corpse; the sun shone into the room and mocked the dreary scene. The apartment was close from the fumes of tobacco and the many guests of the wake which had been held during the night, contrasting strangely with the fresh air which blew in through the half-opened doorway. Mrs. Fry spoke soothingly to the husband; she reminded him of his wife's desires for his good and for that of his children; she slightly alluded to theuselessness of the cross as a symbol, but urged the attention of those present to the great doctrine of which it was intended to remind them. Again she offered solace to the mourner, promised assistance for his little ones, and left the room.

"Some of the scenes in Irish Row were very different, 'Madam Fry,' as she was called by them, being so popular as to cause some inconveniences and many absurdities. She enjoyed giving pleasure; it was an impulse as well as a duty with her to do good. Gathering her garments round her she would thread her way through children and pigs, up broken stair-cases and by narrow passages, to the apartments she sought; there she would listen to their tales of want or woe, or of their difficulties with their children, or of the evil conduct of their husbands. She persuaded many of them to adopt more orderly habits, giving some presents of clothing as encouragement; she induced some to send their children to school, and with the consent of the priest, circulated the Bible amongst them. On one occasion, when the weather was extremely cold and great distress prevailed, being at the time too delicate herself to walk, she went alone in the carriage literally piled with flannel petticoats for Irish Row, the rest of the party walking to meet her, to assist in the delightful task of distribution. She made relieving the poor a pleasure to her children by the cheerful spirit in which she did it; she employed them as almoners when very young, but expected a minute account of their giving and their reasons for it. After the establishment of the Tract Society she always kept a large supply of such as she approved for distribution. It was her desire never to relieve the bodily wants of any one without endeavoring in some way, more or less directly, to benefit their souls. She was a warm advocate for vaccination, and very successful in performing the operation; she had acquired this art from Dr. Willan, one of its earliest advocates and most skilful practitioners. At intervals she made a sort of investigation of the state of the parish, with a view to vaccinating the children. The result was that small-pox was scarcely known in the villages over which her influence extended.

"In a green lane near Plashet, it has been the annual custom of the gipsies to pitch their tents for a few days in their way to Fairlop fair. The sickness of a gipsy child inducing the mother to apply for relief, led Mrs. Fry to visit their camp; from that time, from year to year, she cared for them when they came into her neighborhood. Clothing for the children and a little medical advice she invariably bestowed; but she did far more than that—she sought to influence their minds aright; she pleaded with them on the bitter fruits of sin, and furnished them with Bibles and books the most likely to arouse their attention. But though thus abounding in labors for the good of all around her, she was liable to deep inward discouragements, undoubtedly increased by her sensitive nature and delicate frame, but arising chiefly from her intense desire in nothing to offend Him whom her soul loved, and whom she so entirely desired to serve.

"In September, Mrs. Fry visited Earlham. On the 10th

of that month, 1811, was held the first meeting of the Norwich Bible Society: it was very largely and generally attended. Mrs. Fry, who was warmly interested in the Bible society from its commencement to the close of her life, was present, with her brother Joseph John Gurney, and other members of the family. Mr. Gurney, then in the prime of early manhood, on this occasion first took his stand in public life as an advocate for the general circulation of that sacred volume which he had chosen as the guide of his youth and which has proved the stay of his advancing years."

The following extracts from the Journal are beautifully illustrative:

"*Earlham, Ninth Month,* 10*th.*—I think a more deeply exercised state—which has at times bordered on distress of soul—I hardly ever remember than I feel this morning on going to meeting; in the first place with the Edwardses and my own family in their various states; in the next place, my prospect of going into the men's Monthly Meeting; and in the last, an idea having passed my mind, whether I may not have, amongst their very large companies who are very likely to be here, consisting of many clergyman and others, to say something, either before meals, or at some other time. The words that (I believe) have arisen for my encouragement are these: 'The Lord is my shepherd, I shall not want? Yes I will try not fear, for if God be with me who can be against me?'

"12*th.*—What can I render for all His benefits? In the first place, I went to the Meeting for worship with the Edwardses: I had not long been there before I felt something of a power accompanying me, and words arose, but my exercise of mind was so great that it seemed like being 'baptized for the dead;' though not that I know of from any particular fear of man. I was helped (I believe I may say) as to power, tongue and utterance. That Meeting might be said to end well.

"Yesterday was a day indeed; one that may be called a mark of the times. We first attended a General Meeting of the Bible Society where it was sweet to observe so many of various sentiments all uniting in the one great object—from the good Bishop of Norwich (Bathurst), for so I believe he may be called, to the dissenting minister and young Quaker (my brother Joseph). We afterwards, about thirty-four of us, dined here; I think there were six clergyman of the Establishment, three dissenting ministers, and Richard Philips, beside numbers of others. A very little before the cloth was removed such a power came over me of love, I believe I may say life, that I thought I must ask for silence after Edward Edwards had said grace, and then supplicate the Father of mercies for His blessing, both of the fatness of the earth and the dew of Heaven, upon those who thus desired to promote His cause by spreading the knowledge of the Holy Scriptures; and that He would bless their endeavors, that the knowledge of God and His glory might cover the earth as the waters cover the sea; and also for the preservation of all present, that through the assistance of His grace we might so follow Him and our blessed Lord in time that we might eventually enter into a glorious eternity where the wicked cease from troubling and the weary are at rest. The power and solemnity were very great. Richard Philips asked for silence; I soon knelt down: it was like having our High Priest amongst us. Independently of this power His poor instruments are nothing; and with His power how much is effected. I understood many were in tears; I believe all were bowed down spiritually. Soon after I took my seat; the Baptist minister said, 'This is an act of worship;' adding that it reminded him of that which the disciples said. 'Did not our heart burn within us while He talked with us by the way?' A clergyman said, 'We want no wine for there is that amongst us which does instead.' A Lutheran minister remarked that although he could not always understand the words, being a foreigner, he felt the spirit of prayer, and went on to enlarge in a striking manner. Another clergyman spoke to this effect: How the Almighty visited us, and neither sex nor anything else stood in the way of His grace. I do not exactly remember the words of any one, but it was a most striking circumstance for so many, of such different opinions, thus all to be united in one spirit; and for a poor woman to be made the means, amongst so many great, wise, and I believe good men, of showing forth the praise of the great 'I Am.'"

One of the secretaries of the Bible Society, Mr. Joseph Hughes, thus describes this occasion :—

"On the Monday after my return, I proceeded with my excellent colleagues for Norwich where a numerous and respectable meeting was held on Wednesday in a very spacious and commodious hall. The mayor presided; the Bishop spoke with great decision and equal liberality; and the result of the whole was the establishment of the Norfolk and Norwich Bible Society. About seven hundred pounds was subscribed, and one happy, amiable sentiment appeared to pervade the company. My colleagues and myself adjourned to Earlham, two miles from Norwich where we had passed the previous day, and where we witnessed emanations of piety, generosity and affection in a degree that does not often meet the eye of mortals. Our hosts and hostesses were the Gurneys, chiefly Quakers, who, together with their guests amounted to thirty-four. A clergyman, at the instance of one of the family, and I presume with the most cordial concurrence of the rest, read a portion of the Scriptures morning and evening, and twice we had prayers; I should have said thrice, for after dinner, on the day of the meeting, the pause encouraged by the Society of Friends, was succeeded by a devout address to the Deity, by a female minister, Elizabeth Fry, whose manner was impressive, and whose words were so appropriate that none present can ever forget the incident, or ever advert to it without emotions alike powerful and pleasing. The first emotion was surprise; the second awe; the third pious fervor. As soon as we were re-adjusted at the table, I thought it might be serviceable to offer a remark that proved the coincidence of my heart with the devotional exercise in which we had been engaged; this had the desired effect. Mr. Owen and others suggested accordant sentiments, and we seemed generally to feel like the disciples whose hearts burned within them as they walked to Emmaus."

Elizabeth Fry's engagements in the Gospel ministry thus received the approbation, not only of her own Society, but also of ministers belonging to several other denominations, whose testimony is the more valuable because it was both cordial and spontaneous.

CHAPTER THIRD.

Ministers in the Society of Friends, both men and women, are usually called to a very active life. In addition to their ordinary avocations, which they are expected to leave only when summoned temporarily to higher duties, and to the regular semi-weekly, monthly, quarterly, and yearly gatherings; they frequently make excursions of various lengths to neighboring communities of their own, or other people, following as nearly as they can the intimations of the good Shepherd, as to where His thirsty flocks most need attention. Elizabeth Fry soon became engaged in this missionary labor, for which she was admirably adapted, as well as in services within and about her own home. A few of the most important of these earlier engagements will now be noticed. The first is dated February, 1812, about four and a half months after the events last related.

"3rd.—The prospect I have had for some months of going into Norfolk to attend the Monthly and Quarterly Meetings is now brought home to me, as I must apply to my next Monthly Meeting for permission. It is no doubt a sacrifice of natural feeling to leave the comforts of home and my beloved husband and children; and to my weak nervous habits, the going about, and alone (for so I feel it in

one sense, without my husband) is, I have found from experience, a trial greater than I imagined; and my health
suffers much I think, from my habits being necessarily so
different. This consideration of its being a cross to my
nature I desire not to weigh in the scale; though no doubt,
for the sake of others as well as myself, my health being so
shaken is a serious thing. What I desire-to consider most
deeply is this:—Have I authority for leaving my home and
evident duties? What leads me to believe I have? for I
need not doubt that when away, and at times greatly tried,
this query is likely to arise. The prospect has come in that
quiet, yet I think powerful way, that I have never been able
to believe I should get rid of it; indeed hitherto I have
hardly felt anything but a calm cheerfulness about it, and
very little anxiety. It seems to me as if in this journey I
must be stripped of outward dependences, and my watch-
word appears to be, —'My soul, wait thou ONLY upon God;
for my expectation is from Him.'

"20th.—My sister, Elizabeth Fry, means to go with me
into Norfolk: my Uncle Joseph is likely to go another way:
it appears as if I could not mind much who is to go with
me. But I feel disposed to a very single dependence, and
if I be rightly put forth to this service, may He who puts
me forth be with me; if I have to minister food to others
may it be that which is convenient for them, and which will
tend to their lasting nourishment. I have often thought
that in this little prospect I must go like David, when he
went to slay the giant. I am ashamed of the comparison;
but I only mean it in this respect, I go not trusting in any
power or strength of my own; I feel I dare look to no helper
outwardly. I feel young and a stripling, without armor, yet
I trust the Lord will be with me, and make the sling and
stone effectual, if He please to make use of His poor child
to slay the giant in any one.

"Earlham, Third Month, 14th.—Have I not renewed
reason for faith, hope and confidence in the principle which

I desire to follow? In the night I had to acknowledge that the work must be Thine, O Lord! and that it is to me wonderful. My fears and causes of discouragement were many, for some little time before I set off my own poor health, and my little ones; then my lowness and stupidity. In the first place my health and the dear children's improved so much, and I inwardly so brightened, that I left home very comfortably. As I went on my way such abundant hope arose that light, rather than darkness appeared to surround me. I have now attended the Monthly Meetings and three other Meetings. I have also had frequent opportunities of a religious nature in families; the most remarkable were one in a clergyman's family, in supplication for him and his house, and another where he had to supplicate for my help. May I ever remember how utterly unfit I am in myself for all these works: unto me alone belongs abasedness. I can take nothing to myself. As Thou hast seen meet, O Lord! Thou who art strength in weakness, thus to make use of Thy poor handmaid as an instrument in Thy service, be pleased to keep her from the evil, both in reality and appearance, that she may never, in any way, bring reproach upon Thy cause."

After her return she thus balances the account:—

"May I now be enabled to attend to my own vineyards, and after having been made instrumental thus to warn and encourage others may I not become a cast away myself. I hardly understand what Friends mean by reward for such services, for I do not feel the work mine, and no reward is due. As for reward, is it not enough to feel a Power better than ourselves influencing and strengthening us to do the work that we humbly trust is His own? for what honor, favor, or blessing so great as being engaged in the service of Him whom we love, in whatever way it may be, whether performing one duty or another, and having a little evidence granted us that we are doing His will, or endeavoring to do it? I peculiarly feel, in ministerial duties, that I have no part, because the whole appears a gift,—the willing heart, the power, and everything attending it; the poor creature has only to remain as passive as possible, willing to be operated upon.

"*Plashet, Third Month,* 28th.—I will first mention how it was with me in the Norwich Quarterly Meeting. I went, looking to Him who has hitherto helped me; my beloved uncle Joseph said a few words, as a seal to what I had expressed, and it was, I believe, a peculiarly solemn and favored time: much blessed in a few words of supplication at the Grove before dinner. In the adjourned meeting I felt it safest to go to the Men's Meeting,* where I had to bid them farewell in the Lord, after I had been helped with a few words of tender love and encouragement. Sarah Bowley said a little, and then my dear sister Elizabeth Fry arose and said, 'She hoped what had passed that day would not be attended to as a tale that was told, but as everlasting truths;' which appeared to bring great solemnity and sweetness with it. In the Women's meeting we also had a very solemn time at parting, in which I bade them farewell, desiring that we might all ascend, step by step, that ladder which reaches from earth to heaven. Before we set off I had, after reading, in heart-felt and heart-tendering supplication, to pray for the preservation of the family, and our support in the day of trial, and amidst all the various turnings and overturnings of the Holy Hand upon us. Here I once more am, surrounded by outward blessings, and well in health; yet I hardly know how to return thanks, or to rejoice in Him who has helped me; being poor, low, stripped, the tears come into my eyes. Though cast down I love the Lord above all, and desire, through the saving, redeeming power of Him who came to save that which was lost, and has, I believe proved a Saviour to me, in part, that

---

*Men and women hold their meetings for discipline separately

I may draw nearer and nearer to the most high God, and become in all things more completely His."

"*Six Month*, 16*th*.—It now appears too late to give much account of the Yearly Meeting. The prospect of going into the Men's meeting, naturally was so awful, nay, almost dreadful, that as I sat at breakfast, fears arose lest my understanding should fail. However, though in great measure taken from me on first sitting down in meeting, yet after a time the concern arose with tranquillity, and with a powerful, though small voice—at least with power sufficient to enable me to cast my burden upon the meeting. This brought, I thought, great solemnity; I appeared to have the full unity of Friends: dear Rebecca Bevan went with me. I felt myself much helped when there: matter, tongue and utterance were all given, in testimony and supplication. I think the calm frame I enjoyed upon returning to the Women's Meeting must almost be a foretaste of that rest which the soul pants after.

"*Sixth Month*.—My press of engagements has been very great. . . . I think my temper requires great watchfulness; for the exercises of my mind, my very numerous interests, and the irritability excited by my bodily infirmities, cause me to be in so tender and touchy a state that the 'grasshopper becomes a burden.' In this as in all my infirmities, I have but one hope; it is in the power of Him who has in mercy answered my prayers, and helped me in many of my difficulties, and I humbly trust yet will arise for my deliverance. As to the ministry, I have been raised up and at times cast down, but my heart and attention have been mostly turned to rigidly performing my practical duties in life, which is my object by night and by day. I have felt as if I could rest in nothing short of serving Him whom my soul loves; but I desire to watch, and am fully aware that with regard to myself I have nothing to trust to but mercy; but, leaving myself, I long, whilst permitted to remain in mortality, not to be a drone, but to do everything to the glory of God. I think I desire to do all things well more for the cause's sake, than for the sake of my own soul; as my conviction of the mercy and loving kindness of Him who loveth us and who is touched with a feeling of our infirmities, is so great that whilst my heart is seeking to serve Him, (full as I am of defects), I am ready to trust that that mercy which has hitherto compassed me about will be with me to the end of time, and continue with me through eternity. The fear of punishment hardly ever arises, or has arisen in my mind; it is more the certain knowledge that I have of the blessedness of serving our Master, and the very strong excitement of love and gratitude, and desire for the promotion of the blessed cause upon earth. Through all my tried states I have one unspeakable blessing to acknowledge, and that is an increase of faith."

Elizabeth Fry was peculiarily fitted to minister at the bed of sickness, and where sickness had done its work, and the hearts of bereaved friends needed the voice of sympathy and wise counsel. She was often engaged in this most sacred service, frequently among her own very large circle of friends and relatives, and also among the poor. The following extracts, part taken from the Journal, and part from the biographical notes, illustrate this portion of her work, and show how careful she was to do nothing ceremoniously, or when it was uncalled for by her inward Guide.

"*Ninth Month*, 2nd.—This morning our poor servant who has for some weeks kept his bed very seriously ill, died. I feel that I have cause for humble gratitude in having been at the awful time strengthened by faith, and I believe I may say, having experienced the Divine presence near. I have often sat and watched by his bed-side, desiring to know

whether I had anything to do, or say, as to his soul's welfare.
I found neither feeling, faith nor ability to say or do much
more than endeavor to turn his mind to his Maker; but I
think never more than once, in anything of the anointing
power.   Yesterday I found him much worse, a struggle upon
him that appeared breaking the thread of life, and his sufferings great, mentally and bodily.   The first thing I found
in myself was that a willing mind was granted me, and in sitting by him the power and spirit of supplication and intercession for him arose, to which I gave way.   It immediately
appeared to bring a solemn tranquillity; his pains and rest-
lessness were quieted; his understanding I believe was
quite clear : he thanked me and said, 'God bless you ma'am,'
as if he felt much comfort in what had passed.   Faith, love,
and calmness were the covering of my mind.   He had I believe only one or two more slight struggles after I left him.
After that I was sent for and found that the conflict appeared over, and he breathed his last in about a quarter of
an hour.   There was peculiar sweetness, and great silence
and solemnity in the room.   I had to acknowledge that I
believed the mercy of our Heavenly Father was then extended towards him, and to express a desire that it might,
in the same awful moment, be extended toward us, feeling
how greatly we stood in need of mercy.   The rest of the day
passed off as well as I could expect.   I feared lest the servants and others should attribute that praise to me with
which I had nothing to do, for I could not have prayed or
found an answer to prayer without an anointing from the
Most High.   It led me to feel it a blessing to be entrusted
with this sacred and precious gift; for though ministers
may have much to pass through and many crosses to take
up for their own good and that of others, yet it is a marvelous gift when the pure life stirs, operates and brings down
strongholds.   My nerves were rather shaken, so as to make
me naturally fearful at times the rest of the day.   I have a
great desire that this event may be blessed to the household,

more particularly the servants, that it may humble and bow. their spirits; that they may live more in love, and grow in the knowledge of God and of our Lord and Saviour Jesus Christ."

"The funeral of the servant was fixed for the following Sunday; as the time approached Mrs. Fry felt an earnest desire arise in her heart that the occasion might be one of benefit to others, as several of his friends were to be present; some from the immediate neighborhood. She proposed that in the evening all the assembled guests should be invited to attend the family reading, with her own household; but before the hour arrived for the performance of a duty which was to her exceedingly weighty she was summoned to visit Eliza, the newly married wife of her cousin, James Sheppard, who was rapidly sinking into the grave. The afflicted husband and sister were deeply needing the skillful tenderness with which she could meet such exigencies. At Meeting in the morning her heart had been strengthened and apparently prepared for the duties of the day. By the bed of languishing we find her waiting for that unction without which she was sensible that her services could avail nothing; and on the same evening, in her own dwelling, when surrounded by about forty, besides her own children, she speaks in exhortation and prayer. Her address was closely suited to the state of some persons present, and unflinchingly did she impress upon them that 'the way of the transgressor is hard.' The occasion was long remembered by individuals who were there, and who attributed their permanent improvement to the solemn truths they then heard, and for the first time effectively received into their hearts. Her own Journal of the day, written the following morning, portrays the workings of her own mind."

"*Plashet, Ninth Month, Second-day.*—Yesterday was rather a remarkable day. I rose very low and fearful: my spirit appeared overwhelmed within me, partly I think from some serious outward matters, but principally from such an extreme fear of my approaching confinement, feeling nothing in myself to meet it, and knowing that it must come unless death prevent. I went to Meeting, but was almost too low to know whether I should go or not; however being helped in testimony to show the blessedness of those who hope in the Lord and not in themselves appeared to do me good, as if I had to minister to myself as well as others. I had a trust that my help was in the Lord, and that therefore I should experience my heart to be strengthened. A message came requesting my immediate attendance on poor dear Eliza Sheppard, who appeared near her end. Of course I went. These visits are very awful; to sit by that which we believe to be a death-bed; to be looked to by the afflicted and others, as a minister from whom something is expected, and the fear, at such a time of the activity of the creature arising and doing that which it has no business to do. After sitting sometime quiet, part of which she appeared to sleep, and part to be awake, a solemn silence covered us; the words of supplication arose in due time, when I believed her to be engaged in the same manner by putting her hands together; I knelt down and felt greatly helped, but had not so much to pray for her alone as for all of us there present with her. I had a few words also to say in taking leave. The visit appeared sweet to her by her smiles, and her whispering to her sister expressing this. . . . I think I found myself strengthened rather than weakened by the day's work, mentally and bodily, though my own great weakness soon returned upon me, and it appeared striking that such an one should have been so engaged; but painful as these feelings of depression are to bear, I know 'it is well,' as it keeps me humble; at least I hope so,—lowly and abased. Oh, saith my soul, after thus ministering to others, may I not become a cast-away myself, and neither in trouble nor rejoicing bring discredit on the cause that I love, or on His name whom I desire to serve."

In 1814, she made a short visit to her native county, which is thus described:

"*Eleventh Month*, 12*th*.—I am likely to set off early to-morrow without my husband to go into Norfolk. This prospect I feel pleasant and painful; pleasant, the idea of being at Earlham; painful, leaving home and more particularly my husband. May I be enabled there faithfully to do my duty, in whatever way I may be led, in meeting or out of meeting; may the time spent there be to our mutual comfort and edification, and may those left be cared for and preserved, soul and body, by Him who careth for us; this I humbly trust will be the case. Amen.

"*Plashet*, 25*th*.—I returned safely home to my beloved family on Second-day evening, the 22nd, I trust I may say in thankfulness of heart, finding all well, and going on altogether very comfortably. I returned by Ipswich accompanied by my sister Priscilla and my brother Joseph, and spent all First-day there; but I was unusually low, almost distressed, on account of little Betsey, as I heard she was unwell, and knew not the extent of it; so that my natural impatience to get home was great; but I felt kept there, and as if I could not go away; and thus deeply tried in myself was greatly helped from one service to another, during the day, being variously and often engaged. It was a day of natural tribulations, as far as fears went; and may I not say almost of spiritual abounding? So it is; and so I often have found it, that I have to be brought to the dust of the earth before I am greatly helped. Out of the depths we are raised to the heights."

The death of her brother John Gurney, which occurred in 1814, and which first broke the circle of eleven affectionate brothers and sisters, proved a very tender occasion. Arriving just before his death, she was warmly greeted

with the words "My dear sister come and kiss me." As the
seven sisters all stood round his bed, he expressed great
satisfaction, saying, it was delightful, how they loved one
another. Elizabeth then knelt and offered thanks for such
"unspeakable blessings." He then said "What a sweet
prayer!" and afterwards, "I never passed so happy a morning; how delightful being together and loving one another
as we do!" One of the sisters sang hymns which he enjoyed, and as the day advanced he remarked, "What a
beautiful day this has been?"

On the day of the funeral Elizabeth writes:—

"My heart feels very full; my body I believe has trem-
bled ever since I rose, to meet the party now assembled
and likely to assemble here. My own corrupt dispositions
I found showed themselves yesterday, which I believe tended
to lay me very low; may I not say the feeling of my heart is
that I am lying prostrate in the dust? I have been greatly
tendered in spirit with love to those here whom I believe to
love the *Lord;* united to them in a manner inexpressible, in
my inmost heart—all barriers being broken down. Yet I
feel it needful to be very watchful, very careful; to be faithful
to the testimony that I apprehend myself called upon to
bear, not only for my own sake, but also for the sake of the
younger ones about me. Lord be pleased to help me, to
guide me, to counsel me, that from my own will and prejudice I wound not a beloved brother or sister in Christ; but
so keep me in Thy fear, in Thy love, and under a sense of
Thy presence, that I may act in these most awful and important duties according to Thy most holy and blessed will.
. . . . Let Thy good presence be with us that the feeble be strengthened, the discouraged animated by hope, the
lukewarm stimulated, and the backslider turned from the

error of his ways,—even so if consistent with Thy holy will. If Thou seest meet to make use of Thy unworthy children to speak in Thy name, be unto them tongue and utterance, wisdom and power, that through Thy grace, and the help of Thy Spirit sinners may be converted unto Thee. Amen, Amen."

"*Plashet*, 22nd.—My beloved brother's funeral was a very solemn and humbling day to me. Whilst we sat at Earlham, round the body, my uncle Joseph, my sisters Catherine, Rachel, Priscilla, and I each had something to say; also Edward Edwards. I had to finish the sitting with these words 'There are different gifts but the same Spirit. And there are differences of administration, but the same Lord. And there are diversities of operations, but it is the same God which worketh all in all. But let us earnestly covet the best gifts.' It certainly was a striking occasion. Were we not all in a measure leavened into one spirit? It was a very solemn time at the ground, and I trust an instructive one, very affecting to our natural feelings thus to leave the body of one so tenderly beloved to moulder with the dust. Upon my return I heard of the sudden death of my long-loved cousin, Joseph Gurney Bevan. My spirit was much overwhelmed within me, but there was a stay underneath; blessed be the name of the Lord! I bade them all farewell at Earlham in near unity. Oh may my children love as we love—this has been the prayer of my heart!"

But with all her gifts, her motherly kindess, her humility, her adroitness in dealing with different characters, Elizabeth Fry found it nowhere so difficult to act in the capacity of a minister with success, as in her own immediate family. This was due to various causes. Perhaps in the first place it was altogether natural, from the necessary familiarity on the one hand and the necessity of enforcing authority on

the other.   The profound law which secures diversity in
unity is also apt to make some children branch off from the
parent stock in spiritual as well as natural likings.   In addition to these things considerable variety of opinion existing in the large family of uncles and aunts, several of whom
belonged to the Church of England and were persons of estimable character, had its effect on the young minds.   Still
again, it appears from various passages both in the Journal
and the later editor's notes that Elizabeth Fry's husband
did not wholly sympathize with her at all times in her religious zeal although a member of the same society.   We are
even led to suspect, from the care taken to avoid explicit
statements, and the profound grief of the devoted wife and
mother, that there was a more serious want than the lack of
denominational zeal.   Something of this gathering cloud
which overshadowed many of the later years of her life, may
be seen in the following extracts, one from the Journal, and
one from the abridged Life of Elizabeth Fry, edited by Susanna Corder.

"*Plashet, Eleventh Month, 2nd,* (1814).—My beloved
husband and girls returned from France on Second-day;
my heart was rather overwhelmed in receiving them again.
I also had to feel the spirit in which some persons took my
having allowed them to go, making what appeared to be
unkind remarks.   Oh how I do see rocks on every hand!
thus almost all persons who appear to pride themselves
upon their consistency are apt to judge others; whilst
some who no doubt yield to temptations greatly suffer and
weaken themselves by it.   How weak, how frail are we on
every hand!   My heart was much overwhelmed seeing the
infirmities of others and feeling my own ; I sat and wept in

meeting yesterday. I long, for myself, to have a more prompt obedience to the manifestation of light in my soul. When I have time to *pro* and *con* the matter, to try the fleece wet and dry, I do pretty well, seldom for instance leaving a Meeting condemned for disobedience so much as for want of maintaining a faithful exercise. But at home where things quickly arise in my mind, before meals, or in our pause after reading, it appears as if I could not give up to them without trying the thing again and again. I question whether I should not do better if I more simply, in these things, walked by faith—whether I should not prosper better, or make more progress Zionward;—but to go to the root of the matter, may my will become more subjected to the Divine will. How do I long for the time when I may know the Almighty to be my all in all, my Lord and my God, that He may be continually served by me, both day and night, in small things and in great."

Remarks of Mrs. Corder, on the above.

"Elizabeth Fry exercised a watchful care, never, unless *duty* required it, to oppose the wishes of her husband; and it could not reasonably be expected that she would prevent his taking his two elder girls on this excursion. But her solicitude on account of her family became increasingly great. She found as her children advanced in age, and the corrupt propensities of the natural mind developed themselves, that she often failed in her attempts to control the unyielding will and to subdue the vain inclination—and from external circumstances she did not receive the cooperation requisite rightly to govern their volatile temperament: but earnest were her efforts to guide them into the way of peace, and fervent her prayers that they might be gathered to the fold of the good Shepherd."

It is proper here to add some editorial remarks of her daughters made in this connection.

"Mrs. Fry was always very jealous over herself, lest her avocations as the head of the family should be neglected from her time and attention being so greatly occupied by those duties which she believed herself called to perform in the church; but she was even more alive to the danger of carrying on the business of life in dependence upon her own strength."

"It would not be true to say that Mrs. Fry naturally cared much for outward appearance, or that she took pleasure in domestic concern. She loved a simple liberality and unostentatious comfort. Her element was hospitality, and, whilst Christian moderation was observed, her taste was gratified by an open, generous mode of living; but she would not have chosen for her own pleasure the oversight of either house or table; and when in later life circumstances rendered care and economy a duty, it was a great relief to her to be able to depute the charge of household affairs to one of her daughters. She was always most correct in account-keeping; the distinct heads of house, garden, farm, charity, with many others, marked the painstaking care with which she performed her self-imposed task.

"As mistress of a family, if she erred it was upon the side of indulgence; scarcely liking to exert that power over the wills and feelings of others which is so conducive to their good, and so infinitely in favor of those governed, as well as those in the more arduous position of governing others; but she was aware of this herself, and a 'firm hand with a household,' was among the maxims she impressed upon her daughters as they advanced in life.

"During the infancy of her children she was singularly devoted to them by night as well as day. She attended to their minutest ailments, and was distressed by their sufferings; in health and happiness they refreshed her by their smiles. She had the gentlest touch with little children, literally and figuratively. She would win their hearts if they had never seen her before, almost at the first glance, and by the first sound of her musical voice. As her children grew older her love was undiminished, but her facility was less than before the sinfulness of the human heart had developed itself in positive evil; this especially applies to the elder ones. She had not a talent for education if that word be used for imparting knowledge; probably because her own had been interrupted and unfinished; nor did she appreciate, till the experience of life taught her, the necessity of exerting minute, continued and personal influence over the minds of children. She had to learn that if the golden harvest of success is to be reaped, the husbandman must exert both industry and skill. The genial sun to ripen, and the refreshing shower to moisten the ground, are indeed needful; but the soil must have been turned up, and the seed sown by the labor of man."

Pretty good results, however, seem to have been finally obtained; and it must always remain a question for individual judgment how much of the work belongs to man, and how much must be left to nature and grace.

"*Mildred's Court, First Month*, 16*th*, 1815.—We came here for a little change of air on account of our poor babe, who has been and continues seriously ill. Instead of her sweet smile her countenance mostly marks distress; the cause appears greatly hidden; my mind and heart are oppressed and my body fatigued, partly from losing so much sleep. I have felt my infirmity during this affliction, and also having betrayed it to others, which I have, I apprehended, to judge by my touchy feelings; but I trust I repent. Oh what am I? very poor, very unworthy, very weak; but through all I trust that the Lord will be my stay; and even when brought thus low I have known a little of being at seasons clothed with that righteousness which cometh from God. I found it was well so feelingly to have been brought to a knowledge of what I am *in myself*, as I could more fully testify from whence the good comes, when brought in measure under its calming, enlivening, and loving influence. Preserve me, O Lord, from hurting the little ones, more particularly those before whom I have to walk; and permit me yet to encourage their progress Zionward.

25th.—A time of anxiety about things temporal has lately been my portion, but much deliverance has so far been granted; my sweet baby is much better: though other matters are still pressing, yet it appears, as to things temporal, that prayer has been heard and answered. From one cause or another how much my heart, mind and time have, for more than a year past, been engaged with the cares of this life; alas! may the pure seed not be choked."

Two short religious visits were made during the year 1815, and before its close she who had ministered consolation to others was called to bear a new and severe trial of her own strength in the loss of a child. The event is thus described in her Journal.

"Plashet, Eleventh Month.—It has pleased Almighty and Infinite Wisdom to take from us our most dear and tenderly beloved child, little Betsey—between four and five years old. She was a very precious child, of much wisdom for her years, and I can hardly help believing much grace; liable to the frailty of childhood. At times she would differ with the little one and rather loved her own way; but she was very easy to lead, though not one to be driven. She had most tender affections, a good understanding, for her years a remarkably staid and solid mind. Her love was very strong and her little attentions great to those she loved, and remarkable in her kindness to servants, poor people, and to all animals, she had much feeling for them. But what was more, the bent of her mind was remarkably

toward serious things. It was a subject she loved to dwell upon. She would often talk about 'Almighty,' and almost everything that had connection with Him. On Third-day, after some suffering of body from great sickness she appeared wonderfully relieved, and I may say raised in spirit. She began by telling me how many hymns and stories she knew, with her countenance greatly animated, a flush on her cheeks, and her eyes very bright, a smile of inexpressible content, almost joy. I think she first said with a powerful voice,

'How glorious is our Heavenly King,
  Who reigns above the skies;'

and then expressed how beautiful it was, and how the little children that die stand before Him; but she did not remember all the words of the hymn, nor could I help her. She then mentioned other hymns, and many sweet things; she spoke with delight of how she could nurse the little ones and take care of them, etc., her heart appeared inexpressibly to overflow with love. . . . In her death there appeared abundant cause for thanksgiving; prayer appeared indeed to be answered, as very little if any suffering seemed to attend her, and no struggle at last; but her breath grew more and more seldom and gentle, till she ceased to breathe. During the day, being from time to time strengthened in prayer, in heart, and in word, I found myself only led to ask for her that she might be forever with her God, whether she remained much longer in time or not, but that, if it pleased Infinite Wisdom, her sufferings might be mitigated, and as far as it was needful for her to suffer, that she might be sustained. This was marvelously answered, beyond anything we could expect. I desire never to forget this favor but, if it please Infinite Wisdom, to be preserved from repining or unduly giving way to lamentation for losing so sweet, so kind a child. . . My loss has touched me in a

manner almost inexpressible; to awake and find my much
and so tenderly beloved little girl so totally fled from my
view, so many pleasant pictures marred. As far as I am
concerned, I view it as a separation from a sweet source of
comfort and enjoyment, but surely not a real evil. Abundant comforts are left me, if it please my kind and Heavenly Father to give me power to enjoy them, and continually in heart to return Him thanks on account of His unutterable loving-kindness to my tenderly beloved little one,
who had so sweet and easy a life and so tranquil a death;
and that in her young and tender years her heart had been
animated with love and desires after Himself, and also that
for our sakes she should so often have expressed it in her
childish, innocent way.

In reference to this event, Richenda Gurney, writing to
her sister Rachel, at Rome, said ;—

" I never witnessed stronger faith, more submission, more
evidences of the power of grace in any one, than in our beloved sister at this time; I felt it a mercy to be a humble sharer in the rich portion granted her in that hour of
need; never was I more impressed with the blessedness
which is experienced by those who have served the Lord
Jesus, who have preferred Him above all things, who have
been willing to take up their daily cross and follow Him.
He is not a hard Master; He never leaves nor forsakes His
own, and will show Himself strong in behalf of those whose
hearts are perfect towards Him. After a few minutes we
retired with our dear sister to the next room. She was desirous that children and servants, (especially the nurses,)
and all her friends who had been present should come to
her. When thus surrounded as she lay upon the sofa, she
poured out her heart in thanksgiving and prayer, in a manner deeply affecting and edifying. For myself I felt it

highly valuable, and would not but have been there for a great deal. Whilst memory lasts, I think and hope I never shall forget the scene or the impression it made."

The trials of the mother and minister are touchingly portrayed in the following entry in her Journal within less than a month after the death of her child.

"*Plashet, Twelfth Month, 2nd.*—I am brought into some conflict this morning respecting my attending the Dorsetshire Quarterly Meeting. I had looked to it before the illness of our dear lamb, and not feeling clear of it, and yet not much light shining upon it, my poor soul is tried within me; for under my present circumstances I appear much to want the help of faith to leave my other sweet lambs. But ought I not rather to feel renewed stimulus, seeing how short time is, to do what comes to hand, and after all that I have experienced should I not rather trust than be afraid:—for was the hand of Providence ever more marked, even as it related to outward things? I believe I am fully resigned to go if it be the Lord's will: for I do believe, for all my many and great infirmities, my flinching nature, my want of faith and patience, yet it remains my first desire to do or to suffer according to the Divine will. If consistent with Thy holy will, dearest Lord, if I ought to go, be pleased to throw a little light upon the subject; and if not, somehow make it manifest; and if Thou shouldst think fit to call Thy poor child into Thy service, be pleased to be with her in it, and bless her labors of love where her lot may be cast, that others may be made sensible how good a God Thou art, how great is Thy tender mercy and loving kindness, and that these may be encouraged yet to serve Thee more with the whole heart; also be pleased, dearest Lord, if Thou shouldst order it that I go, to keep my beloved husband, children and household in my absence, that no harm may

come to them, spiritually or bodily. Thou hast in abundant
mercy regarded the weak estate of Thy handmaid, and hitherto answered her cry, and even met her in her weakness; that
if not asking in her own will she could supplicate Thee that
their poor bodies, as well as their souls, may be preserved
from (much) harm in her absence; but, dearest Lord, let
me not go if my right place be at home; but if Thou callest
me out, be pleased to grant a little faith, and a little
strength, that I may go forth in Thy power, trusting in
Thee, as it relates to them, as well as to myself. Be
pleased also, if I be called from home at such a time, not to
let it try or weaken the faith of others; but rather may it
tend to confirm and strengthen it.

"*Plashet*, 11th.—Truly I went forth weeping; and my
sweet Louisa being poorly, much increased my anxiety; and
it is difficult to say the fears and doubts that crept in, on my
way to Shaftsbury, though through mercy the enemy's
power appeared limited, and my fears gained no dominion
over me; but they were soon quieted, and I had mostly
quiet, comfortable nights, though it was wading through
deep waters and in great weakness; yet help was from season to season administered.

"*Plashet*, 14th.—It is the opinion of medical men that
the scarlet fever, in a mild form, is the complaint in the
house. It is most probable that it will again appear
amongst us, but that I desire to leave. They also think
our dear Rachel has a very serious hip complaint, but this
I also feel disposed not to be very anxious about. With
regard to my tenderly beloved little Betsey, she is in my
most near and affectionate remembrance, by night and by
day. When I feel her loss, and view her little (to me) beautiful body in Barking burying-ground, my heart is pained
within me; but when, with the eye of faith, I can view her
in an everlasting resting-place in Christ Jesus, where indeed
no evil can come nigh her dwelling, then I can rest, even
with sweet consolation; and I do truly desire that when

her loss is so present with me, as it is at times, that I cannot help my natural spirits being much overwhelmed, that I may be preserved from anything like repining, or undue sorrow, or in any degree depreciating the many blessings continued; particularly so many sweet dear children being left us: for through all I feel receiving them a blessing, having their life preserved a blessing, and in the sweet lamb who is taken, I have felt a blessing in her being taken away; such an evidence of faith has been granted that it is in mercy, and at the time such a feeling of joy on her account. It is now softened down into a very tender sorrow; the remembrance of her is inexpressibly sweet, and I trust that the whole event has done me good, as I peculiarly feel it an encouragement to suffer whatever is appointed me; that being (if it may ever be my blessed allotment) made perfect through suffering, I may be prepared to join the purified spirits of those that have gone before me; and having felt so very deeply, I am almost ready to think has a little prepared my neck for the yoke of suffering."

Her tenth child was born on the 18th of May, 1816. In June her children went to Pakefield, for the benefit of sea air, and remained for a time in the family of her brother-in-law, Francis Cunningham, "an active and devoted clergyman." "She deeply felt their being thrown among those who were not Friends, but the advantages of the wise care and oversight of her sister Rachel Gurney, and the privilege of associating with the brother who invited them to be his guests, overcame her objections, and she agreed to an arrangement which appears to have given the complexion to their future lives, and more or less directly to have influenced every member of the family." *

* I have received a letter, bearing date August 22, 1882, from the son

Afterwards her two eldest boys went to Earlham to pursue their education under the care of their aunts, and her daughters to North Runcton, in the family of her brother Daniel Gurney. "Whilst conscious of the literary advantages enjoyed by her children, she feared the probable effect of their circumstances, and of the influences to which they were subjected."* The following extract exhibits her feelings and spirit under these conditions.

"*Seventh Month, 4th.*—I have been at Pakefield with my beloved brother and sister: my soul has travailed much in the deeps on many accounts; more particularly while with them that in keeping to our scruples respecting prayer, &c., &c., the right thing might be hurt in no mind. Words fall very short of expression of how much my spirit is overwhelmed within me for us all. Our situation is very peculiar, surrounded as we are with those of various senti-

whose birth is last recorded, and who still resides at Plashet, giving the following particulars of Elizabeth Fry's family and descendents. Eight of her eleven children are still living. Of these only two are members of the Society of Friends, the others belonging to the Church of England. "The grandchildren, great grandchildren, and great great do., amount to 139 souls." He adds: "With respect to the Life of my mother as originally published by my sisters Katherine Fry and Rachel E. Cresswell, in 2 vols.—it has long been out of print, and is very difficult to obtain. I think I know an old Friend who would part with one he has for two pounds, as money would be of more use to him than the book. . . . There is a large engraving after Richmond's picture, about 30 inches high, full length, but it is difficult to obtain a copy, and would cost about three pounds. This was taken when she was about 63 years old. . . . If I can be of any further service to you in the collection of matter for your book I shall be very happy to help you, and remain

"Yours truly,
"S. GURNEY FRY."

* S. Corder.

ments, and yet I humbly trust each seeking the right way.
To have a clergyman for a brother is very different to having one for a friend; a much closer tie, and a still stronger call, for the sake of preserving sweet unity of spirit, to meet him as far as we can, to offend as little as possible by our scruples, and yet for the sake of others, as well as ourselves, faithfully to maintain our ground, and to keep very close to that which can alone direct aright."

The benefit of having families somewhat divided in religious opinion and practice, is well illustrated by the above extract. When our own brothers and sisters, equally sincere and intelligent with ourselves, see paths of duty differing from our own, we are induced to hope, that there may be nothing harmful in these diversities. And yet our weakness often lies very close to our strength. What we have found good for ourselves we naturally think must be good for others, and especially our children. Elizabeth Fry afterwards suffered acutely because her children, as they grew up, with these various examples before them, indulged a growing disinclination to the peculiar customs of Friends, and generally chose other associations. But as she herself mingled more with Christians holding different views, her liberality continued to increase, as it might not have done had her own religious society been more flourishing, and had her wishes been granted in respect to her own family.

"*Mildred's Court, Twelfth Month*, 13*th.* (1816)—I returned yesterday from attending poor dear Joseph's funeral at Norwich, the son of my uncle Joseph Gurney. I have gone through a good deal, what with mourning with the mourners, the ministry, &c., &c. I think I was in this respect, at the funeral helped by the Spirit and the power that we cannot command; though I left Earlham with a burdened mind, not having any apparently suitable opportunity for relief, hurrying away, to my feelings prematurely, of which I find even the remembrance painful. My sweet dear girls and boys I much feel again leaving, seeing their critical age and state. What I feel for the children I cannot describe. Oh! may they be sheltered under the great Almighty wing so as not to go greatly astray."

This chapter may fitly be concluded by her advices to her girls and boys when at school.

"Plashet, Ninth Month, 27th, 1816.

"MY MUCH LOVED GIRLS,

"Your letters received last evening gave us much pleasure. I anxiously hope that you will now do your utmost in whatever respects your education, not only on your own account, but for our sakes. I look forward to your return with so much comfort, as useful and valuable helpers to me, which you will be all the more if you get forward yourselves. I see quite a field of useful service and enjoyment for you, should we be favored to meet under comfortable circumstances in the spring. I mean that you should have a certain department to fill in the house, amongst the children and the poor, as well as your own studies and enjoyments; I think there has not often been a brighter opening for two girls. Plashet is after all such a home; it now looks sweetly, and your little room is almost a temptation to me to take it for a sitting-room for myself, it is so pretty and so snug; it is newly furnished and looks very pleasant indeed. The poor and the schools I think will be glad to have you home, for help is wanted in these things. Indeed if your hearts are but turned the right way, you may I believe be made instruments of much good; and I shall be glad to have the day come that I may introduce you into prisons and hospitals. 'Therefore gird up the loins of your

mind and be sober.'   This appears to me your present business—to give all diligence to your present duties; and I
cannot help believing, if this be the case, that the day will
come when you will be brought into much usefulness."

To each of her sons at school she gave " Rules for a Boy
at Boarding School," from which the following extracts are
made:

" Be regular; strict in attending to religious duties; and
do not allow other boys around thee to prevent thy having
some portion of time for reading, at least a text of Scripture, meditation, prayer, and if it appears to be a duty, flinch
not from bowing the knee before them as a mark of thy al-
legiance to the King of Kings and Lord of Lords. . ...
Strongly as I advise thy faithfully maintaining thy principles and doing thy duty, I would have thee very careful of
either judging or reproving others; for it takes a long time
to get the beam out of our own eye, before we can see
clearly to take the mote out of our brother's eye.   There is
for one young in years much greater safety in preaching to
others by example than in word. . . .   Maintain truth
and strict integrity upon all points.   Be not double-minded
in any degree; but faithfully maintain, not only the upright
principles on religious grounds, but also the brightest honor.
I like to see it in small things and in great, for it marks the
upright man."

CHAPTER IV.

We now approach the work of Christian benevolence, which gave the name of Elizabeth Fry to fame. The first accounts of this enterprise take us back to the year 1813.

"*Mildred's Court, Second Month,* 15th.—My fear for myself the last few days is, lest I should be exalted by the evident unity of my dear friends whom I greatly value; and also my natural health and spirits being good; and being engaged in some laudable pursuits, more particularly seeing after the prisoners in Newgate. Oh how deeply, how very deeply, I fear the temptation of ever being exalted, or self-conceited! I cannot preserve myself from this temptation any more than being unduly cast down or crushed by others. Be pleased, O Lord! to preserve me; for the deep inward prayer of my heart is that I may ever walk humbly before Thee, and also before all mankind. Let me never, in any way, take that glory to myself which alone belongs unto Thee, if in Thy mercy Thou shouldst ever enable one so unworthy either to do good or to communicate.

"16th.—Yesterday we were some hours at Newgate with the poor female felons, attending to their outward necessities. We had been twice previously. Before we went away dear Anna Buxton offered a few words in supplication, and, very unexpectedly to myself, I did also. I heard weeping and I thought they appeared much tendered: a very solemn quiet was observed: it was a striking scene, the poor people on their knees around, in their deplorable condition."

"Thus simply and incidentally," observe her daughters, from whose account I shall now make some extracts, "is recorded Elizabeth Fry's first entrance upon the scene of her future labors, evidently without any idea of the importance of its ultimate results.

["From early youth her spirit had often been attracted, in painful sympathy, toward those who, by yielding themselves to the bondage of sin, had become the victims of human justice. Before she was fifteen years of age, the House of Correction at Norwich excited her feelings of deep interest, and by repeated and earnest persuasion she induced her father to allow her to visit it. She referred, many years afterwards, to the impressions which had then been received, and mentioned to a dear and venerable father in the truth amongst us, that it had laid the foundation for her engagements in prison."—*S. Corder.*]

"In January of this year, four members of the Society of Friends, all well known to Elizabeth Fry, had visited some persons in Newgate who were about to be executed. Although no mention is made of the circumstance in the journal, it has always been understood that the representations of these Friends, particularly those of William Foster, one of the number, first induced her personally to inspect the state of the women, with the view of alleviating their sufferings occasioned by the inclemency of the season.

"At that time all the female prisoners in Newgate were confined in that part now known as the untried side. The larger portion of the Quadrangle was then used as a state prison. The partition wall was not of sufficient height to prevent the state prisoners from overlooking the narrow yard and the windows of the two wards and two cells of which the women's division consisted. These four rooms comprised about one hundred and ninety superficial yards, into which, at the time of these visits, nearly three hundred women, with their numerous children, were crowded: tried and untried, misdemeanants and felons, without classification, without employment, and with no other superintendence than that given by a man and his son who had charge of them by night and by day. In the same rooms, in rags and dirt, destitute of sufficient clothing, (for which there was no provision,) sleeping without bedding, on the floor, the boards of which were in part raised to supply a sort of pillow, they lived, cooked and washed.

"With the proceeds of their clamorous begging, when any stranger appeared amongst them, the prisoners purchased liquors from a regular tap in the prison. Spirits were openly drunk, and the ear was assailed by the most terrible language. Beyond that which was necessary for safe custody, there was little restraint over their communication with the world without.

"Although military sentinels were posted on the leads of the prison, such was the lawlessness prevailing, that Mr. Newman, the governor, entered this portion of it with reluctancy. Fearful that their watches would be snatched from their sides, he advised the ladies (though without avail) to leave them in his house.

"Into this scene Elizabeth Fry entered, accompanied only by Anna Buxton. The sorrowful and neglected condition of these depraved women and their miserable children, dwelling in such a vortex of corruption, deeply sank into her heart, although at this time nothing more was done than to supply the most destitute with clothes. She carried back to her home and into the midst of other avocation and interests a lively remembrance of all that she had witnessed at Newgate, which within four years induced that systematic effort for ameliorating the condition of these poor outcasts, so signally blessed by Him who said 'That joy shall be in Heaven over one sinner that repenteth, more than over ninety and nine just persons that need no repentance.'

"Not only did a considerable space of time elapse, after Elizabeth Fry's first visits to Newgate, before she renewed them, but in the interim many events occurred of deep import to herself. He 'who sits as a Refiner and a Purifier of silver,' saw fit to exercise her in the school of affliction before raising her up for the remarkable work which she had to do. Long and distressing indisposition, the death of her brother John Gurney, that of her paternal friend Joseph Gurney Bevan, the loss of a most tenderly beloved child, considerable decrease of property, separation for a time from all her elder children, were among the means used by Him who cannot err to teach her the utter instability of every human possession, to draw her heart more entirely to Himself, and to prepare her for His service."

I again quote from Mrs. Corder's volume at a later date, —page 233.

"Three years had now elapsed since Elizabeth Fry had first visited Newgate; but her spirit had from time to time been led into deep and solemn feeling on account of the degraded inmates of that prison; and a conviction became gradually impressed on her mind that she was required by Him to whose service she had been enabled to dedicate herself as an unquenched coal on His sacred altar, to labor, as He might see meet to open the way and to direct her steps, for the moral reformation and above all for the spiritual conversion and help of the most depraved and miserable of her sex. Nothing but the constraining love of Christ could have induced this tender and delicate woman thus to surrender domestic comfort and personal ease, and even to risk her own reputation, to follow what she believed to be the call of her Divine Master, leading her into labors most ardu-

ous and painful, from which her nature recoiled with dread.
Yet was the unction of holy love so abundantly poured out
upon her spirit that she willingly yielded to the appointment of that compassionate Saviour who, through her instrumentality, was thus graciously extending His hand of
mercy, in order to rescue from the pit of destruction those
who were sunk in vice and wretchedness."

"*Mildred's Court, Second Month*, 24*th*, (1817).—I have
lately been much occupied in forming a school in Newgate
for the children of the poor prisoners, as well as the young
criminals, which has brought much peace and satisfaction
with it; but my mind has also been deeply effected in attending a poor woman who was executed this morning. I
visited her twice. This event has brought me into much
feeling, attended with some distressingly nervous sensations
in the night, so that this has been a time of deep humiliation to me, thus witnessing the effect and consequences of
sin. This poor creature murdered her baby; and how inexpressibly awful now to have her own life taken away!
The whole affair has been truly afflicting to me; to see what
poor mortals may be driven to through sin and transgres-
sion, and how hard the heart becomes even to the most tender affections. How should we watch and pray that we fall
not by little and little, become hardened and commit greater
sins. I had to pray for these poor sinners this morning,
and also for the preservation of our household from the
evil there is in the world."

Extract from a letter to her sister, Rachel Gurney:—

"*Mildred's Court, Third Month*, 10*th* and 11*th*.—My
heart and mind and time are very much engaged in various
ways. Newgate is the principal object, and I think until I
make some attempt at amendment in the plans for the
women, I shall not feel easy; but if such efforts should
prove unsuccessful, I think that I should then have tried to

do my part and be easy. . . . The poor occupy me little more than at the door, as I cannot go after them, with my other engagements. The hanging at Newgate does not overcome me as it did at first, and I have only attended one woman since the first. I see and feel the necessity of caution in this respect, and mean to be on my guard about it, and run no undue risk with myself."

Mrs. Fry's method of reform seems to have been original with herself. In commencing her experiment, she requested to be left alone with the prisoners. After asking their attention she read the parable of the Lord of the vineyard, and made some remarks upon the subject which called forth expressions from a few of them. Some asked who Christ was, and others feared that their day of salvation was passed. She then "addressed herself to the mothers, and pointed out to them the grievous consequences to their children of living in such a scene of depravity, and proposed to establish a school for them, to which they acceded with tears of joy. She desired them to consider the plan, for without their steady co-operation she would not undertake it—leaving it to them to select a governess from among themselves."

"On her next visit they had chosen as school-mistress a young woman named Mary Conner, recently committed for stealing a watch. She proved eminently qualified for the task, and became one of the first fruits of Christian labor in that place; she was assiduous in her duties, and was never known to infringe one of the rules. A free pardon was granted her about fifteen months afterwards; but this proved an unavailing gift, for a cough which had attacked her a short time previously, ended in consumption."

Elizabeth Fry was soon surrounded by a company of earnest co-workers, and received liberal aid and encouragement from the authorities and officers of the prison, although they at first looked upon the experiment as hopeless and even visionary. An unoccupied cell was assigned for the school-room; and Mrs. Fry accompanied by Mary Sanderson and the teacher elect, opened the school for children and persons under twenty-five years of age. Many older ones earnestly entreated permission to share in the instructions, but the small size of the room forbade. Mary Sanderson, then visiting the prison for the first time, thus describes her impressions.

"The railing was crowded with half-naked women struggling together for the front situations, with the most boisterous violence, and begging with the utmost vociferation. I felt as if I were going into a den of wild beasts, and well recollect shuddering when the door closed upon me, and I was locked in with such a herd of novel and desperate companions."

In her evidence, subsequently given before the House of Commons, Mrs. Fry made this statement, "It was in our visits to the school, where some of us attended almost every day, that we were witnesses to the dreadful proceedings that went forward on the female side of the prison; the begging, swearing, gaming, fighting, singing, dancing, dressing-up in men's clothes,—scenes too bad to be described, so that we did not think it suitable to admit young persons with us."

One of the strong characteristics of Elizabeth Fry was now called into requisition. Her perseverance was equal to the heavy demand made upon it. She encouraged her friends and continued to enlist others in the enterprise until in April, 1817, "An Association for the Improvement of the Female Prisoners in Newgate" was formed, consisting of eleven members of the Society of Friends and the wife of a clergyman. Their object was stated to be, "To provide for the clothing, the instruction and the employment of the women; to introduce them to a knowledge of the Holy Scriptures, and to form in them, as much as possible, those habits of order, sobriety and industry which may render them peaceable, whilst in prison, and respectable when they leave it."

An interview was had with the prisoners, in presence of the sheriff and other officers of the prison. Elizabeth Fry asked them if they were willing "to abide by the rules which it would be indispensable to establish among them for the accomplishment of the object so much desired by them all. The women fully and unanimously assured her of their determination to obey them strictly. The sheriffs also addressed them, giving the plan the countenance of their approbation; and then turning to Elizabeth Fry and her companions, one of them said, 'Well ladies, you see your material.'

"How they used these 'materials' and the blessing permitted to attend their exertions is demonstrated by a letter received in 1820 from one of the prisoners then present."

To Mrs. Fry.

"*Paramatta, New South Wales, July* 10*th*, 1820.
"HONORED MADAM,—

"The duty I owe to you, likewise to the benevolent So-

ciety to which you have the honor to belong, compels me to
take up my pen to return to you my most sincere thanks for
the heavenly instruction I derived from you and the dear
friends during my confinement in Newgate.

"In the month of April 1817 how did that blessed prayer
of yours sink into my heart; and as you said so have I
found it, that when no eyes see and no ears hear, God both
sees and hears; and then it was that the arrow of conviction entered my hard heart; and in Newgate it was that poor
Harriet S———, like the prodigal son, came to herself, and
took with her words, and sought the Lord; and truly can I
say with David, 'Before I was afflicted I went astray, but
now have I learned Thy ways O Lord!' And although affliction cometh not forth of the dust yet how prone have I been
to forget God, my Maker, who can give songs in the night;
and happy is that soul that when affliction comes can say
with Eli, 'It is the Lord,' or with David, 'I was dumb and
opened not my mouth because Thou didst it;' and Job,
when stripped of every comfort, 'Blessed be the Lord who
took away as well as gave,'—and may the Lord grant every
one that is afflicted such an humble spirit as theirs. Believe me, my dear madam, I bless the day that brought me
inside of Newgate walls, for then it was that the rays of
Divine truth shone into my dark mind; and may the Holy
Spirit shine more and more upon my dark understanding,
that I may be enabled so to walk as one whose heart is set
to seek a city whose builder and maker is God. Believe me,
my dear madam, although I am a poor captive in a distant
land, I would not give up having communion with God one
single day for my liberty; for what is liberty of the body
compared with liberty of the soul! and soon will that time
come when death will release me from all the earthly fetters that hold me now, for I trust to be with Christ who
bought me with His precious blood. And now my dear
madam, these few sincere sentiments of mine I wish you to
make known to the world, that the world may see that your

labor in Newgate has not been in vain in the Lord. Please give my love to all the dear friends, and Dr. Cotton, Mr. Baker, Simpson and all, the keeper of Newgate, and all the afflicted prisoners; and although we may never meet on earth again I hope we shall all meet in the realms of bliss never to part again. Please give my love to Mrs. Stonnett and Mrs. Guy. "And believe me to remain

"Your humble servant,

"HARRIET S———."

The next step was to provide employment. This part of the history may best be given in the words of Sir T. F. Buxton, "whose exertions to benefit these 'outcasts of the people' were only excelled by hers of whom he wrote."

"It struck one of the ladies that Botany Bay might be supplied with stockings, and indeed all articles of clothing, of the prisoners' manufacture. She therefore called upon Messrs. Richard Dixon & Co., of Fenchurch Street, and candidly told them that she was desirous of depriving them of this branch of their trade, and stating her views begged their advice. They said at once that they should not in any way obstruct such laudable designs, and that no further trouble need be taken to provide work, for they would en-engage to do it. Nothing now remained but to prepare the room; and this difficulty was obviated by the sheriffs sending their carpenters. The former laundry speedily underwent the necessary alterations, was cleansed and whitewashed, and in a few days the Ladies' Committee assembled in it all the tried female prisoners. One of the ladies, Mrs. Fry, began by describing to them the comforts to be derived from industry and sobriety, the pleasure and profit of doing right, and contrasted the happiness and peace of those who are dedicated to a course of virtue and religion with that experienced in their former life, and its present consequences; and describing their awful guilt in the sight of God appealed to themselves, whether its wages, even here, were not utter misery and ruin. She then dwelt upon the motives which had brought the ladies into Newgate: they had left their homes and their families to mingle amongst those from whom all others fled, animated by an ardent and affectionate desire to rescue their fellow-creatures from evil, and to impart to them that knowledge which they, from their education and circumstances had been so happy as to receive.

"She then told them that the ladies did not come with any absolute and authoritative pretensions; that it was not intended they should command and the prisoners obey; but that it was to be understood all were to act in concert; that not a rule should be made, or a monitor appointed without their full and unanimous concurrence; that for this purpose each of the rules should be read and put to the vote; and she invited those who might feel any disinclination to any particular, freely to state their opinion. The following were then read:

RULES.

"1. That a matron be appointed for the general superintendence of the women.

"2. That the women be engaged in needlework, knitting, or any other suitable employment.

"3. That there be no begging, swearing, gaming, card-playing, or immoral conversation. That all novels, plays and other improper books be excluded; and that all bad words be avoided; and any default in these particulars be reported to the matron.

"4. That there be a yard-keeper chosen from among the women, to inform them when their friends come, to see that they leave their work with a monitor when they go to the grating, and that they do not spend any time there, ex-

cept with their friends. If any woman be found disobe-
dient in these respects, the yard-keeper is to report the case
to the matron.

"5. That the women be divided into classes of not more
than twelve, and that a monitor be appointed to each class.

"6. That monitors be chosen from among the most
orderly of the women that can read, to superintend the
work and conduct of the others.

"7. That the monitors not only overlook the women in
their own classes, but if they observe any others disobey-
ing the rules, that they inform the monitor of the class to
which such persons belong, who is immediately to report to
the matron, and the deviations to be set down on a slate.

"8. That any monitor breaking the rules shall be dis-
missed from her office and the most suitable in the class
selected to take her place.

"9. That the monitors be particularly careful to see that
the women come with clean hands and face to their work,
and that they are quiet during their employment.

"10. That at the ringing of the bell, at nine o'clock in
the morning, the women collect in the work-room to hear a
portion of Scripture read by one of the visitors, or the matron; and that the monitors afterwards conduct the classes
from thence to their respective wards in an orderly manner.

"11. That the women be again collected for reading at
six o'clock in the evening, when the work shall be given in
charge to the matron by the monitors.

"12. That the matron keep an exact account of the work
done by the women, and of their conduct.

"As each was proposed every hand was held up in
token of their approbation. In the same manner, and
with the same formalities, each of the monitors was proposed, and all were unanimously approved. When this
business was concluded one of the visitors read aloud the
twenty-first chapter of St. Matthew, the parable of the bar-
ren fig-tree seeming applicable to the state of the audience;

after a period of silence, according to the custom of the
Society of Friends, the monitors with their classes withdrew to their respective wards in the most orderly manner.

"During the first month the ladies were anxious that the
attempt should be secret, that it might meet with no interruption; at the end of that time, as the experiment had
been tried, and had exceeded even their expectation, it was
deemed expedient to apply to the Corporation of London.
It was considered that the school would be more permanent
if it were made a part of the prison system of the City, than
if it merely depended on individuals. In consequence a
short letter descriptive of the progress already made was
written to the sheriffs.

"The next day an answer was received proposing a meeting with the ladies at Newgate.

"In compliance with this appointment the Lord Mayor,
the sheriffs, and several of the Aldermen attended. The
prisoners were assembled together; and it being requested
that no alteration in their usual practice might take place,
one of the ladies read a chapter in the Bible, and then the
females proceeded to their various avocations. Their attention during the time of reading, their orderly and sober deportment, their decent dress, the absence of every thing like
tumult, noise or contention, the obedience and respect shown
by them, and the cheerfulness visible in their countenance
and manners, conspired to excite the astonishment and admiration of their visitors. Many of these knew Newgate,
had visited it a few months before, and had not forgotten
the painful impression made by a scene exhibiting perhaps
the very utmost limits of misery and guilt.

"The magistrates, to evince their sense of the importance
of the alterations which had been effected, immediately
adopted the whole plan as a part of the system of Newgate,
empowered the ladies to punish the refractory by short confinement, undertook part of the expense of the matron, and
loaded the ladies with thanks and benedictions.

"About six months after the establishment of the school for the children, and the manufactory for the tried side, the committee received a most urgent petition from the untried, entreating that the same might be done for them, and promising strict obedience. In consequence the ladies made the same arrangements, proposed the same rules, and admitted in the same manner as on the other side, the prisoners to participate in their formations. The experiment here has answered, but not to the same extent. They have had difficulty in procuring a sufficiency of work; the prisoners are not so disposed to work, flattering themselves with the prospect of speedy release; besides they are necessarily engaged in some degree in preparation for their trial. The result of the observations of the ladies has been, that where the prisoners, from whatever cause, did no work, they derived little if any moral advantage; where they did some work they received some benefit, and where they were fully engaged they were really and essentially improved."

The reform prospered steadily and continued to attract public attention, until people came from all parts of the country to witness what soon became one of the greatest curiosities of London. But we must pause to get an inside view of the mind which was the leading instrument in this beneficent enterprise.

"*Mildred's Court, Twelfth Month,* 17th.—A remarkable blessing still appears to accompany my prison concerns,—perhaps the greatest apparent blessing on my deeds that ever attended me. How have the spirits both of those in power and the poor afflicted prisoners appeared to be subjected, and how has the work gone on! Most assuredly the power and the glory are alone due to the Author and Finisher of every good work.

"*Mildred's Court,* 1818.—Lord be pleased to grant the

blessing of preservation which is above every blessing. It is very striking and wonderful to me to observe how some things have been verified that, in times of great lowness and unutterable distress, I have been led to believe would happen; in reading the 142nd Psalm these words particularly—'The righteous shall compass me about, for Thou shalt deal bountifully with me.' Has not this been, and is it not now, remarkably verified, by those filling almost the highest stations to the lowest; by persons of almost all denominations have I not been compassed about? My prison concerns have thus brought me, a poor and very unworthy creature, into public notice, and I may most humbly adopt this language of the 71st Psalm, 'I am as a wonder unto many, but Thou art my strong Refuge. Oh! let my mouth be filled with Thy praise, and with Thy honor all the day:' but, O Lord! merciful and gracious, Thou who knowest the heart and its wanderings, and also its pantings after Thyself, be pleased yet to manifest Thyself to be a God hearing and answering prayer. Thou hast, in times of deep adversity and great affliction, when the heart of Thy handmaid was ready to say Refuge failed her, Thou hast then been her Stronghold, her Rock and her Fortress; so that she has not been greatly moved nor overcome by her soul's enemy. Be pleased, most merciful and gracious Lord God Almighty, now to keep her in the day of prosperity, when the righteous compass her about, that she may be for a time even as a wonder to many. Keep her, O Lord, even as in Thine own Almighty hand, that no evil befall her, nor any plague come nigh her dwelling; and as Thou hast, so far in Thine abundant mercy and loving kindness delivered her soul from death, oh be pleased to keep her feet from falling! hold up her goings in Thy paths, that her footsteps slip not; and increasingly enable her, at all times, under all circumstances, in heights and in depths, in life and in death, to show forth Thy praise, to walk faithfully and circumspectly before Thee, obeying Thee in all things, in Thy fear

and in Thy love; abounding in the truth as it is in Jesus;
ever giving Thee, O Lord God on High, with Christ Jesus
our Lord, and Thy Holy Spirit our Comforter, one God,
blessed forever, the glory due unto Thee, now in time, and
in an endless eternity. Amen, amen."

Let us observe, as we go along, how well this prayer
was answered; with what perfect grace she was enabled to
keep her heart to its first love, and her feet in the path
of Divine appointment, while princes and nobles of the
earth were paying her the most flattering honors.

"During this winter she received many letters of inquiry
from different parts of the country in relation to the system
pursued in Newgate; ladies wished to form similar associations; magistrates wished to improve the state of prisoners
under their control, &c., &c., and all these required minute
and carefully considered replies. Some of the most distinguished and influential persons in the kingdom were anxious to witness for themselves what had been done in the
prisons, and a part of almost every day was spent in accompanying such parties thither. Many were asking for counsel, others for employment which they supposed Elizabeth
Fry could obtain for them; and almost constant applica-
tions from the poor who thought her purse as inexhaustible as her good will, 'humbly praying' for assistance. Her
benevolent feelings would hardly suffer any of these to
pass unheeded; and her daughters, the oldest of whom was
in her seventeenth year proved efficient helpers in answering the demands.

"During the former period it had been the practice for
convicts on the night preceding their departure for Botany
Bay, (where they were transported for certain crimes,) to
pull down and break or burn everything within their reach;
and to go off shouting with the most hardened effrontery.

But when the last went out they took an affectionate leave
of their companions, and expressed the utmost gratitude to
their benefactors, and the next day entered their conveyances
peaceably; and their departure, in the tears that were shed
and the mournful decorum that was observed, resembled a
funeral procession; and so orderly was their behavior that
it was deemed unnecessary to send more than half the usual
escort.　As a proof that moral and religious instruction
had produced some effect upon their minds, when these
poor creatures were going, those who remained entreated
that their share of the profits (a little fund they were allowed to collect for themselves, kept in a box under the
care of the Ladies Committee) might all be given to those
who were about to leave them.

"In ten months after the working system had been introduced the women had made nearly twenty thousand articles of clothing, and their knitting produced from sixty to
a hundred pairs of socks and stockings every month.
Their earnings averaged about eighteen pence per week for
each one."

"Elizabeth Fry was informed that some were still gaming in the prison.　She went alone, assembled the prisoners
and told them what she had heard,—that she feared it was
true, dwelt upon the sin of gaming, its evil effects upon their
minds, the interruption it caused, and the distaste it excited
for labor, told them how much the report had grieved her
and said 'She would consider it a proof of their regard if
they would have the candor and kindness to bring the cards
to her.'　She did not expect that they would do it, as it
would be betraying themselves.　But soon after she had retired to the ladies' room there was a gentle tap at the door,
and in came a trembling girl who, in a manner that indicated
real feeling, expressed her sorrow for having broken the
rules of so kind a friend, and presented her pack of cards.
She was soon followed by another and another, until Elizabeth Fry had received five packs which she burnt in their

presence; assuring them that so far from its being remembered against them she should 'remember it in another way,' A few days after this she took with her some presents of clothes, and calling the first one gave her a neat muslin handkerchief. To her surprise the girl said she hoped Elizabeth Fry would excuse her being so forward, but if she might say it she felt exceedingly disappointed. She had hoped that Elizabeth Fry would have given her a Bible with her own name written in it, which she would value beyond anything else and would always keep it and read it. This was irresistible. The treasure so much desired was brought, and Elizabeth Fry assured a friend that she never gave a Bible which was received with so much interest and satisfaction, nor one that she thought more likely to do good. This had been one of the worst of girls, and had behaved very badly upon her trial; but she conducted herself afterwards in so amiable a manner that she appeared 'almost without a flaw,' and it was hoped ' would become a valuable member of society.' " *

On the 27th of Feb. 1818, Mrs. Fry was called upon to give evidence before a Committee of the House of Commons, in the course of which she said, " Our habit is constantly to read the Scriptures to them twice a day—many of them are taught, some can read a little themselves. It has an astonishing effect; I never saw the Scriptures received in the same way. When I have sometimes gone and said it was my intention to read, they would flock up stairs after me, as if it were a great pleasure I had to offer them."

When asked by the Committee if the ladies confined themselves to the reading of the Scriptures without inculcating any peculiar doctrines Mrs. Fry replied,—"We con-

---

* Life by S. Corder.

sider from the situation we fill, as it respects the public, as well as the poor creatures themselves, that it would be highly indecorous to press any peculiar doctrine of any kind,—anything beyond the fundamental doctrines of Scripture."

It was mentioned to her that one of the prisoners had said it was "more terrible to be brought up before Mrs. Fry, than before the judge;" on which she remarked :—" I think I may say we have full power among them, though we use nothing but kindness. I have never proposed a punishment, and yet I think it is impossible, in a well regulated house, to have rules more strictly attended to than they are."

When asked if she thought any reformation could be effected without employment, she replied, "I should believe it impossible. We may instruct as we will, but if we allow them their time, and they have nothing to do, they naturally must return to their evil passions."

The report of the Parliamentary Committee contains the following sentence :—" The benevolent exertions of Mrs. Fry and her friends, in the female department of the prison, have indeed, by the establishment of a school, by providing work and encouraging industrious habits, produced a most gratifying change. But much must be ascribed to unremitting personal attention and influence."

The duties of this position, however, were by no means all of an agreeable kind. The severity of English law at this time, which made every degree of forgery, as well as many other secondary offenses punishable with death, rendered executions terribly frequent. It is estimated that had the laws been carried fully into effect, they would have required an average of more than four executions per day in Great Britain and Ireland. Almost every device was resorted to by the humane among the officers and courts to evade these sanguinary enactments.

Elizabeth Fry was among the earliest to express effectively her disapproval of these unchristian statutes. She felt the wrong with great keenness when unfortunate women, often misled by worse companions were compelled to answer for some not unpardonable act of dishonesty with their lives; and the more especially after her labors with them had brought repentance. A sad case of this kind occurred about the time we are speaking of, February, 1818, when two women were executed for forgery. At six o'clock in the morning, one of them addressed the following letter to Elizabeth Fry:

"HONORED MADAM:—

As the only way of expressing my gratitude to you for your very great attention to the care of my poor soul,—I feel I may have appeared more silent than perhaps some would have been on so melancholy an event; but believe me, my dear madam, I have felt most acutely the awful situation I have been in. The mercies of God are boundless, and I trust, through His grace this affliction is sanctified to me, and through the Saviour's blood my sins will be washed away. I have much to be thankful for; I feel such serenity of mind and fortitude. God of His infinite mercy grant I may feel as I do now in the last moments! Pray, madam, present my most grateful thanks to the worthy Dr. Cotton and Mr. Baker, and all our kind friends, the ladies, and Mrs. Guy. It was a feeling I had of my own unworthiness made me more diffident of speaking as was perhaps looked for. I once more return you my most grateful thanks. It is now past six o'clock. I have not one moment to spare. I must devote the remainder to the service of my offended God.

With respect your humble servant,
CHARLOTTE NEWMAN."

On the same day she received the following letter from William Wilberforce:

"Kensington Gore, 17th. Feb., 1818.

"MY DEAR MADAM:—

I think I need not assure you that I have not forgotten you this morning. In truth, having been awake very early, and, lying in peace and comfort and safety, the different situation of the poor women impressed itself strongly on my mind.

"I shall be glad, and Mrs. Wilberforce also, I assure you, to hear that your bodily health has not suffered from your mental anxiety, and I will try to get a sight of you when I can, to hear your account and remarks on the effects of the last few days, both on the poor objects themselves and the prison companions.

"With real esteem and regard, I am, my dear Madam

"Yours very sincerely,
"W. WILBERFORCE."

A still sadder case than the above is thus recorded on page 275 of Mrs. Corder's biography, abbreviated from the original account.

"During the spring of this year executions had become so frequent that they were made subjects for investigation and for public as well as private discussion. The sanguinary provisions of the penal code were beheld with a sentiment of disapprobation, and even abhorrence, before unfelt. The wretched tenants of the 'condemned cells,' after having received the sentence of death at the Old Bailey, awaited, with mingled hope and fear, the decision of the Council, by whom some were selected for mercy, leaving the others to suffer the extreme penalty of the law. No reasons were assigned by the Council for this distinction; each one therefore hoped to escape the dreadful doom.

"Among those who were waiting in this state of terrible suspense was a young woman named Harriet Skelton. There was something peculiarly touching in the case of this poor creature. 'A child might have read her character in her countenance—open, confiding, affectionate, possessing strong feelings, but neither hardened in depravity nor capable of cunning.' Under the influence of the man whom she loved she had been induced to pass some forged notes: 'thus adding another to the dismal list of those who, with the finest impulses of our nature, uncontrolled by religion, have been lured to their own destruction.' Skelton was ordered for execution. The sentence was unlooked for: 'her deportment in prison had been good, amenable to regulations, quiet and orderly. Some of her companions in guilt were heard to say that they supposed she was chosen for death because she was better prepared than the rest of them.' Elizabeth Fry was vehemently urged to exert herself on behalf of this unhappy woman. She made various attempts, one through the Duke of Gloucester who with other dwellers in palaces and lordly halls, visited the poor convict in Newgate; and 'his former companion in the dance' led the Duke through the gloom and darkness of that most gloomy of prisons—a new scene indeed to him and to many others who through life had been 'nursed on the downy lap of ease,' in luxurious abodes that strangely contrasted with the 'dark vaulted passages, the clanking fetters, the offensive smell, the grating sound as the heavy key was turned, the massive bolt drawn back, and the iron-

sheathed door forced reluctantly open'—unaccustomed, and
as if unwilling to admit such guests.

"The Duke of Gloucester made a noble effort to save
Skelton by an application to Lord Sidmouth. He also accompanied Elizabeth Fry to the Bank Directors. But all
entreaties were in vain. Lord Sidmouth was annoyed by
Elizabeth Fry's earnest solicitations, and highly offended at
some disclosures which involved a degree of censure on the
Bank Directors. There were, in the case, circumstances of
collusion, on the part of some who were concerned in bringing this unfortunate creature to the gallows, of which Elizabeth Fry might perhaps have spoken with a degree of freedom that exceeded the limits of strict prudence: but who
can read the tale without a strong and sympathetic interest
in her humane appeal for mercy? or without deep regret and
surprise that this appeal could have been regarded in the
light of an offence? And how does the emotion acquire intensity when we contemplate the dreadful severity of the
enactment which, within a few years afterwards, was,
through the aroused and resistless force of public opinion,
expunged from the statute book!

"The claims of *mercy* had rendered it very important to
Elizabeth Fry that she should have access to the Secretary
of State. She had been wont to intercede with Lord Sidmouth on behalf of those whom his decision might either
consign to an untimely and ignominious death, or award a
further term of earthly probation. But now her influence
with him was lost. She endeavored, by a personal interview, to remove the unfavorable impression which he had
imbibed, and to convince him that, although she might have
erred in judgment, her intentions had been upright, and
her desire sincere not to oppose his wishes. But all was in
vain: his heart was steeled against remonstrances and
nothing but pain resulted from the interview.

"Elizabeth Fry had been accompanied in this unsatisfactory visit by the excellent Countess Harcourt, one of the ladies of the court, and, under her special care and protection, had, on the same day, reluctantly, and with a heavy heart, to mingle in a very different scene, and to encounter objects of a remarkably opposite character. The aged Queen Charlotte, who, through a lengthened life, had appeared little moved by questions of a philanthropic character, her interest being much confined within the sphere of her court and its cold formalities and etiquette, had heard of the wonderful changes in Newgate and elsewhere, wrought through the instrumentality of Elizabeth Fry, and had become impressed by the evidences of an awakened and powerfully religious feeling, which had begun to operate on the minds of some persons of rank and influence who had witnessed the labors of this devoted woman; and on the occasion of a public examination of the children of some large metropolitan schools in the Egyptian Hall of the Mansion House, the Queen intimated her desire to be present, and requested that Elizabeth Fry would also attend on the occasion. This was an injunction that could not, with any degree of propriety, be disregarded; and accordingly, though as she says against her will, Elizabeth Fry, in company with the Countess Harcourt, repaired thither. It had been intended that she should be presented to the Queen in the drawing-room. This would have been much more select and agreeable. But, through some misunderstanding, Lady Harcourt and Elizabeth Fry were conducted to the Hall and placed on the side of the platform which was crowded with waving feathers, jewels, and orders; several of the bishops standing near her, the great Hall lined with spectators, and in its center hundreds of poor children from the different schools. Elizabeth Fry was an object of general attraction. After a time the Queen perceived her, and advanced to address her. It was a striking scene, and painted by an artist—the diminutive stature of the Queen, covered with diamonds, but her countenance lighted with an expression of pleasure and of the kindest benevolence—Elizabeth Fry's tall figure clad in her simple Quaker dress, her countenance a little flushed, but preserving her wonted calmness of look and serious dignity of manner. The spectators of this remarkable interview, with a murmur of applause, hailed the scene before them, as the mead of approval offered by royalty at the shrine of mercy and good works."

CHAPTER FIFTH.

In the spring of 1818, Elizabeth Fry and her family returned to their country residence at Plashet, where she again found time to note her experiences and reflections, occasionally, in her journal—not the least useful of her many employments. What a privilege it is to be introduced into the very "sanctum sanctorum" of the world's true nobility, and permitted to see the inmost workings and complexion of their minds in these confidential revelations of themselves to themselves, with us of the unknown and unborn future, and the friends who may remain after their death, for a possible audience.

"*Plashet, Fourth Month,* 29*th.*—May we more evidently *live,* in the best sense, even unto God. Since I last wrote I have led rather a remarkable life; so surprisingly followed after by the great, and others, in my Newgate concerns; in short the prison and myself are become quite a show, which is a very serious thing in many points. I believe that it certainly does much good to the cause, in spreading amongst all ranks of society a considerable interest in the subject; also a knowledge of Friends and their principles; but my own standing appears critical in many ways. In the first place the extreme importance of my walking strictly, and circumspectly amongst all men in all things, and not bringing discredit upon the cause of truth and righteousness. In the next place, after our readings there, the ministry is a most awful calling, thus publicly amongst men to be in season and out of season. I desire to live, (more particularly in these things,) in the fear of God rather than of man, and that neither good report nor evil report, the approbation nor the disapprobation of men, should move me the least, but my eye should be kept quite single to the great and good Shepherd and bishop of souls—this is my continual prayer for myself."

Though at a somewhat greater distance, her interest in Newgate and its concerns still continued unabated, and soon became extended from the prison itself to those, still more unfortunate, who were condemned to transportation to Australia. When the next ship load was being prepared, Mrs. Fry interested herself to have the removals to the ship made as privately as possible, and then set to work to arrange the convicts into classes, each having a monitor, with a Bible and school books at hand, to take the charge and keep the classes separate from each other. Then after much deliberation how to find them employment, the committee were told that patchwork and fancy work found a ready sale at New South Wales. A call was at once issued for little pieces of colored cotton cloth, and in a few days enough were sent from the different Manchester houses in London to supply the want. When the preparations were as complete as opportunity and means permitted, the Committee took a solemn leave of the one hundred and twenty-eight unhappy exiles whom they had so generously befriended. The scene is thus described:

"There was great uncertainty whether the poor convicts would see their benefactress again. She stood at the cabin door, attended by her friends and the captain; the women on the quarter deck facing them. The sailors, anxious to see what was going on, climbed into the rigging, upon the capstan, or mingled in the outskirts of the group. The silence was profound, when Mrs. Fry opened her Bible, and in a clear, audible voice, read a portion from it. The crews of the other vessels in the tier, attracted by the novelty of the scene, leaned over the ships on each side, and listened apparently with great attention.' She closed the Bible, and, after a short pause, knelt down on the deck and implored a blessing on this work of Christian charity from that God who, though one may plant and another water, can alone give the increase. Many of the women wept bitterly; all seemed touched. When she left the ship they followed her with their eyes and their blessings, until, her boat having passed within another tier of vessels, they could see her no more."

The following entry in July of this year shows that all was not sunshine, even when conscience approved and the world applauded.

"*Plashet, Seventh Month*, 1*st*.—Since I last wrote much has happened to me; some things have occurred of an important nature. My prison engagements have gone on well, and many have flocked after me, may I not say of almost all descriptions, from the greatest to the least; and we have had some remarkably favored times together in the prison. The Yearly Meeting was a very interesting one to me, and also encouraging. I felt the unity of Friends a comfort and support. I had to go into the Men's Meeting, which was a deep trial of faith; but it appeared called for at my hand, and peace attended giving up to it. The unity which the women expressed at my going, and the good reception I found amongst the men, were comforting to me; but it was a close, very close, exercise. Although I have had much support from many of my fellow mortals, and so much unity expressed with me, both in and out of our Society, yet I believe many Friends have great fears for me and mine; and some not Friends do not scruple to spread evil reports, as if vanity, or political motives, led me to neglect a large family. I desire patiently to bear it all, but the very critical view that is taken of my beloved children grieves me much."

"*8th.*—My heart is too full to express much; yesterday I had a very interesting day at Newgate with the Chancellor of the Exchequer, and many other persons of consequence : Much in the cross to myself I had to express a few words in supplication before them; but the effect was solemn and satisfactory. After this I felt peaceful and comforted. Sometimes I think, after such times, I am disposed to feel as if *that* day's work was *done*, and give way to cheerful conversation, without sufficiently waiting for the fresh manifestations of the Spirit, and abiding under the humiliations of the Cross."

The impression made upon the witnesses on some of these occasions is shown by an extract from a letter of Sir. James Mackintosh, then a member of Parliament, to his wife. He says—

"I dined on Saturday, June 3d, at Devonshire House. The company consisted of the Duke of Norfolk, Lords Lansdown, Lauderdale, Albemarle, Cowper, Hardwicke, Carnarvon, Sefton, Ossulston, Milton, Duncannon, &c. The subject was Mrs. Fry's exhortation to forty-five female convicts, at which Lord ——— had been present on Friday. He could hardly refrain from tears in speaking of it. He called it the deepest tragedy he had ever witnessed. What she read and expounded to the convicts, with almost miraculous effect was the fourth chapter to the Ephesians. Coke (of Norfolk) begged me to go with him next Friday.

I doubt whether, as that is the day of my motion, (For the revision of the Penal Laws,) I shall be able to go, and whether it be prudent to expose myself to the danger of being too much warmed by the scene, just before a speech in which I shall need all my discretion."

The year when this letter was written is not given, but a comparison of the month and day, June 3, when the circumstance was related, with that of an account written by the Hon. Mrs. Waldegrave for her mother, June 2nd, 1820, together with the identity of the subject—4th Ephesians— and the fact that Lord Albemarle is named in both instances makes it probable that we have a pretty full report of this remarkable meeting in the account which is here subjoined. It was sent the compiler of the " Life of Elizabeth Fry," with the accompanying note. If not the same event the coincidence is remarkable.

"Account of a visit to Newgate, June 2nd, 1820, written by the late Hon. Mrs. Waldegrave, for her mother, lady Elizabeth Whitbread, on whose death in 1846, it was sent to me.

"Elizabeth Waldegrave, Jun.
"4 *Harley Street, London, March 2nd,* 1852."
" *June,* 2*nd,* 1820.—We reached Newgate at half-past ten, and waited with the rest of the company in a small room up stairs ; in the way to it we passed through several wards in which the most perfect stillness prevailed; these were the former scenes of all the riot and confusion of which we had heard so much.
"After waiting a short time Mrs. Fry entered, saluting everybody in the most dignified manner. The female convicts, forty in number, came in upon a bell being rung, and

took their seats at one end of the room with perfect order—the monitors sitting on the first bench and the others in classes behind; each had her work, at which she employed, herself till Mrs. Fry began reading. They had ivory tickets round their necks with numbers on them.

"Mrs. Fry arranged a large old Bible on her desk and sat down—her voice was so gentle that we wondered we could hear what she said, but remarkably mild and sweet. She began by requesting their *attention*.—'I am desirous that your attention should be, as much as possible, undivided—notwithstanding our being subject to-day to the interruptions of company, it is equally important that your attention should be fixed on what I say—praying that the Holy Spirit may enlighten your understanding. I am going to read the 4th chapter of Paul's Epistle to the Ephesians.' They all laid aside their work, most of them fixing their eyes on the ground, and we could not observe that more than two or three looked about afterwards till she had done reading. She read the chapter slowly and impressively—the 6th, 28th and 32nd verses appeared to affect them deeply—every word that she uttered seemed to be written in her own heart. She then turned to the book of Psalms. After a moment's pause she turned back to the chapter she had been reading, and said, 'I was going to read a Psalm; but I thought I should be best satisfied to say a word on the chapter I have been reading. The greater part of it is so simple and clear that a very little endeavor on your part will enable you to understand it; but there is one expression which perhaps may be obscure. 'One Lord, one Faith, one Baptism.' If you look only at the external you might say, so many different opinions prevail, people are so divided as to what they think ought to be believed, how can they be said to have one faith? I have always viewed it very differently; 'One Lord,'—yea, and have not all Christians the same Lord, which is Christ? and while we acknowledge Him our Master, look to Him for our justification, follow his precepts, obey his commandments, love him, serve him, he is our Lord, he is the 'one Lord' of all who *thus* acknowledge him their *Head.*—Again, 'one Faith' —there is a diversity of opinions, but only one true and saving Faith, the Faith which lives in the heart, and becomes evident by its fruits; which lays hold of the promises; which actuates to all godliness, and produces the blessed effects of a holy life. This one true, saving faith is common to all Christians, how exceedingly soever they may seem to differ. So also 'one Baptism:' Christians may differ as to the manner of administering the Baptism of water; nay though some even dispense with that altogether, yet there is one spiritual baptism of the heart,—the Spirit of God sanctifying and renewing the heart, and creating it after God in righteousness and true holiness. In this manner we have all 'one Lord, one Faith, one Baptism; one God and Father of all, who is above all, and through all, and in you all. What a sweet bond of unity is this, where we are not only brethren in this world, but may hope to meet in Heaven, there to give glory to Him with one accord for ever and for evermore.'

"Mrs. Fry then read the 86th Psalm, at the end of which a brother Quaker said a few words of exhortation to all present to join in prayer on behalf of the poor sufferers contained in these walls, and not to be unmindful that all were sinners, all under one condemnation.

"She then knelt down and prayed so beautiful a prayer, —with such fervency, so rich a flow of ideas, such perfect command of Scripture language to clothe them in, that it is impossible to convey an idea of its beauty. The *chaunt*, in which the Quakers recite their prayers, gave it a very singular, but very impressive effect; for her voice is good, and when exerted, very strong and clear. This, after a few words from one of the company, concluded the service—the women retired in perfect order, each class separately, with its monitor from the front row; all making courtesies as they left the room. Mrs. Fry, in the course of some conversation with Lord Albemarle, said that she believed the coolness she had experienced from Lord Sidmouth, to have originated in too anxious a desire on her part to save the life of a condemned woman; which had induced her to speak to the Duke of Gloucester on the subject after Lord Sidmouth had refused to interfere; by which she believed she had given offence; that she thought they had been wrong and urged too far; that at first they had free communication with the Secretary of State's office, but that it had been closed for some time.

"She said that her success had surprised herself as much as it did others—That a very remarkable Providence had attended all her efforts—she had never seen the Bible received as it had been there. 'Ten years ago,' she said, 'when it occurred to me to make trial, I went with a young Friend into one of the wards in which the greatest riot and confusion prevailed. I went in with my Bible in my hand, and told them I was come to read the Scriptures. They all flocked round me, and I am convinced many had never heard them before. It seemed to be glad tidings to them. All were attentive. I had been warned to take off such things as could possibly be stolen but no attempt of the kind was made. If I dropped anything it was picked up and brought to me. I felt rather alarmed at first at the idea of being shut up with these poor creatures, but I was preserved through it.

"She said that some remarkable things had happened for her encouragement: one which occurred lately she related. 'A woman who was one of the lowest of the low—a thief, a drunkard, and in every way as bad as possible, was committed to Newgate. On the first day that she attended (the reading) I happened to read the parable of the prodigal son. She was much affected by it, and the next day I received a letter, in which she expressed her thankfulness to God that, through our instrumentality, a new way had been opened before her—that she was like the prodigal son, and it seemed as if God had seen her afar off—that she prayed to be enabled to hold fast the hope she felt—all in this strain. We made her our school mistress, and during the whole term of her imprisonment I never knew her to break one rule, or be guilty of the smallest impropriety of speech or behavior. When they quit Newgate we support them from our fund till they are otherwise provided for. In consequence of illness *she* remained for some time dependent on us. We received a message from her, requesting that we would if possible, obtain her admittance into some workhouse where, if we could furnish her with a little tea and sugar, she should be much happier than now, for she was miserable at the idea of diminishing *that fund* which might be the means of rescuing other poor creatures from the state she had herself been in. We got her into a workhouse where she lately died, one of the most peaceful, happy deaths ; the only pain she experienced was from none of us being present that she might have expressed to us her gratitude for the benefit she had derived through our means. Another young woman too, of the same character, is lately dead ; she lived well, and died well.

"We went afterwards through part of the prison, but in a very unsatisfactory manner, owing to the number of persons present. She said that one proof of essential good being done was that, whereas the returns used to be 30 per cent., they are now less than 4."

On June 3rd, 1818, the Marquis of Lansdowne moved an address to the Prince Regent on the state of the prisons of the United Kingdom. In his speech he made this observation in reference to Newgate.

"It was impossible, from the manner in which it was constantly crowded, to apply any general system of regulations. There it was necessary to place several felons in the

same cell, and persons guilty of very different descriptions
of offences were mixed together. The consequences were
such as might be expected, notwithstanding all the efforts
of that very meritorious individual (Mrs. Fry), who had
come like a genius of good into this scene of misery and
vice, and had, by her wonderful influence and exertions,
produced in a short time a most extraordinary reform among
the most abandoned class of prisoners. After this great
example of humanity and benevolence, he would leave it to
their lordships how much good persons similarly disposed,
might effect in other prisons, were the mechanism, if he
might use the expression, of these places of confinement
better adapted to the purposes of reformation. The institution of the great Penitentiary-house was likely to be
attended with great advantages, though he did not approve
of all the regulations. That establishment was a great
step taken in the important work of reformation. He was
aware there were persons who considered all expense of
this kind as useless; who thought that all that could be
done was to provide for the safe custody of prisoners, and
that attempts to reform them were hopeless. Let those
who entertain this notion go and see what had been effected
by Mrs. Fry and other benevolent persons in Newgate.
The scenes which passed there would induce them to alter
their opinion. There were moments when the hardest
hearts could be softened and disposed to reform."

After such an expression made in the House of Lords
and published in the journals of the day, it is not surprising that Newgate became an object of interest to people of
all classes.

In addition to English visitors of all ranks, numerous
foreigners were attracted to Newgate;—among others John
Randolph, at that time American Envoy to Great Britain.

who gave a characteristic description of the scene to a friend who thus relates the particulars:

"Suddenly Randolph rose from his chair and in his most imposing manner thus addressed me: 'Mr. Harvey, two days ago I saw the greatest curiosity in London—aye, and in England too, sir—compared to which Westminster Abbey, the Tower, Somerset House, the British Museum, nay Parliament itself, sink into utter insignificance! I have seen, sir, Elizabeth Fry in Newgate, and have witnessed there miraculous effects of true Christianity upon the most depraved of human beings! And yet the wretched outcasts have been tamed and subdued by the Christian eloquence of Mrs. Fry! I have seen them weep repentant tears while she addressed them. I have heard their groans of despair, sir! Nothing but religion can effect this miracle; for what can be a greater miracle than the conversion of a degraded, sinful woman taken from the very dregs of society? Oh, sir, it was a sight worthy the attention of angels! You must also see this wonder.'"

Persons of distinction from the Continent were introduced to Newgate and its noted reformer, and carried back reports to their different countries which were like seeds of a new interest in humanity. Some of the first fruits were seen in Russia, where the Princess Sophia Mestchersky and other ladies formed themselves into an association, with highly satisfactory results, to visit the women confined in the five prisons of the capital. A gentleman named Walter Venning also devoted himself to visiting the prisoners there. Hearing of this Mrs. Fry opened a correspondence on the subject to encourage the good work. In a letter writt by the Russian Princess to Mr. Venning, on the second of August, 1820, is the following passage:—

"Though I acknowledge myself completely unable to write in English, as you wish me to do, for to show your friends in England the state of our prisons, such as the Ladies Committee found it to be, and such as it is now, eight months after the establishment of the society; yet when you told me it would prove a token of our regard and high esteem for Mrs. Fry and her fellow laborers, I readily comply with your request, and shall try to overcome all the difficulties which ignorance of your language and the novelty of the subject present to me. Not I alone, sir, but all the ladies of our committee expressed a hearty wish that something of our public exertions, and of our efforts to follow the example which that lady gives us, might be communicated to her, as a proof that her labors are blessed from above, and that a spark of that love which animates her generous heart has also reached our distant country, and influenced many hearts with the same Christian feeling for suffering humanity. May this prove a comfort to her soul, and a new encouragement for her to continue her labors in that large and important field of usefulness in which she is called to serve our Lord. We will all endeavor to follow her according to the strength and abilities granted us, looking for help and hoping for success to and from Him from whom we receive every blessing, and whose 'strength is made perfect in weakness.'"

Extract of a letter from Elizabeth Fry to Walter Venning.

"RESPECTED FRIEND:

Though personally unknown to thee I am confident, from the interest we both feel in one cause, thou wilt excuse the liberty I take in writing to thee to express my heart-felt satisfaction at the interesting and important accounts thou hast given my brother Hoare of the proceedings of the Gentlemen and Ladies' Prison Associations of Petersburg. Most warmly do I desire their encouragement

In this work of charity and utility; for the more I am acquainted with the subject, and the more extensive my observation of the effects of prison discipline is, the more confident I feel of its importance; and that, although the work will be gradual, yet through the Divine blessing its results will be sure. Not only that many will be stopped in their career of vice, but some truly turned from their evil ways, and the security and comfort of the community at large in-increased by our prisons which have been too generally the nurseries of vice, and scenes of idleness, filth and debauchery, being so arranged and attended to that they may become schools where the most reprobate may be instructed in their duty towards their Creator and their fellow mortals, and where the very habits of their lives may be changed.

"It will be found in this, as in every other good work, that some trials and discouragements will attend it; but the great end in view must induce those engaged in it to persevere and use increased diligence to overcome them, doing what we do to the Lord and not unto man, and then we shall do it well.

"We continue to have much satisfaction with the results of our efforts in Newgate—good order appears increasingly established, there is much cleanliness amongst our poor women, and some very encouraging proofs of reformation in habit, and what is much more, in heart. This, in a prison so ill-arranged, with no classification, except tried from untried, no good inspection and many other great disadvantages, is more than the most zealous advocates of prison discipline could look for.

"I lately had the pleasure of seeing the Duchess of Gloucester, who is our Patroness; she desired me to express how much gratified she was with thy account of what you are doing in Petersburg, and her wish that the ladies may be encouraged in their good work.

"How delightful it is to hear of the interest that the Emperor Alexander, Prince Galitzin, and ladies of high rank take in the cause of the poor prisoners. May the best of blessings rest upon them for thus manifesting their care over the destitute of the earth.

"We also feel gratefully sensible of the kindness to our friends William Allen and Stephen Grellet. I hope thou wilt let us know before long how you go on. I am much obliged for the book thou kindly sent me; and believe me, with much regard and esteem,　Thy friend

"ELIZABETH FRY."

After the death of Walter Venning the correspondence and the work in Russia were continued by his brother John Venning, who states that the letters which he received from Elizabeth Fry were "invaluable, as regarded the treatment and management of both prisoners and insane persons. It was the fruit of her own rich practical experience, communicated with touching simplicity, and it produced lasting benefit to those institutions in Russia."

"After he had presented to the Emperor Nicholas a statement of the defects of the Government lunatic asylum, the Dowager Empress and her son visited the asylum together, and, being convinced of the necessity of a complete reform in the management of the insane, the Emperor requested his mother to take it under her own care and to appoint John Venning the governor of it. An order was soon given to purchase, of one of the princes, a palace-like house, having above two miles of garden, and a fine stream of water running through the grounds. A plan of this great building was sent to Elizabeth Fry for her inspection and hints for improvements. Two extensive wings were recommended for dormitories. The wings cost 15,000 pounds. In addition to this sum from the Government, the Emperor gave 3000 pounds for cast-iron window frames recommended by Elizabeth Fry; as the clumsy iron bars in the old institution had drawn from many a poor inmate a sigh, with 'Sir, prison! prison!'

"Elizabeth Fry recommended that all, except the violent lunatics, should dine together at a table covered with a cloth and furnished with plates and spoons. The Empress was delighted with this plan, and when the arrangements were completed requested John Venning to invite them to dinner. Sixteen came and took their seats. The Empress approached the table, ordering one of the upper servants to sit at the head of it and ask a blessing. When he arose to do this they all stood up. The soup, with small pieces of meat was then served, and as soon as they had dined they all rose up spontaneously, and thanked her for her motherly kindness. She was deeply moved, and turning to John Venning, said, 'My friend this is one of the happiest days of my life.' The next day the number at table was increased, and the day following was still greater.

"A letter from Elizabeth Fry on 'the great importance of supplying the lunatics with the Scriptures,' which John Venning said 'deserved to be written in letters of gold,' and which he sent to the imperial family, was received with marked approbation. The court-physician, Dr. Richl, a devoted philanthropist requested a copy of it. This letter removed all difficulties on the subject and John Venning was requested to furnish them in their various languages. It was considered by some 'a wild and dangerous proceeding;' but he soon found them collected in groups and quietly listening, while one of their number was reading the New Testament; and instead of disturbing their minds it produced a soothing influence. A Russian priest, a lunatic, collected a number together and read to them. And John Venning found a poor Frenchman in his bed-room, during a lucid interval reading the New Testament, with tears rolling down his cheeks.

"Whenever John Venning received a letter from Elizabeth Fry he would write it out in French for the Empress,

and was pleased to see, as soon as she had read it, with
what alacrity she ordered one of her secretaries to translate
it into Russian, to be entered into the journal of the asylum
for immediate adoption. One contained a list of fourteen
rules which were all confirmed by the Empress the same
day. And they introduced very important arrangements,
viz.: 'treating the inmates, as far as possible, as the sane
persons, both in conversation and manners towards them; to
allow them as much liberty as possible; to engage them
daily to take exercise in the open air; to allow them to wear
their own clothes, and no uniform prison dress; most
strictly to fulfil whatever was promised them; to exercise
patience, gentleness, kindness, and *love* towards them; and
to be exceedingly careful as to the characters of the keepers
appointed to watch over them.

"Petersburg was not the only continental city with which
communication on the subject of ladies visiting prisoners
had now been opened.

"At Turin, La Marquise de Barol née Colbert was assidu-
ously occupied in this important work. This lady was a
Roman Catholic and had entered upon it from a sense of
duty. Francis Cunningham, when traveling through that
place had obtained permission to see the prison, had there
become acquainted with her, and opened a correspondence
for her with his sister-in-law, Elizabeth Fry, which was
maintained for many years. Letters were also received from
Amsterdam, where those interested in the cause were endeavoring to form a Prison Discipline Society and Committee to visit the prisoners." *

In 1822 the Prince and Princess Royal of Denmark visited England, on which occasion the Princess called and
took breakfast with Mrs. Fry. This was the commencement of a life-long association and friendship between these

_____
* Life by S. Corder.

excellent ladies. In November of this year, the following letter was addressed to the Princess.

"DEAR AND RESPECTED FRIEND,

Allow me to call thee so, for such I feel thee, as thou art truly both loved and respected by me. According to thy kind and condescending wish, expressed when here, I take up my pen to inform thee that upon the first of this month through the tender mercy of my God, I was safely delivered of a sweet boy, and to add to our cause of joy and thanksgiving, my dear daughter had also one born on the same day, so that twenty-four hours added a son and a grandson to our already numerous family. (This was her eleventh and last child.) We have both of us with our infants been going on well, and with the exception of some illness that I passed through in the early part of my confinement, and my habitual delicacy at such times, I am as well now as I can expect to be.

"I have often thought of thy kind visit with deep interest, and strong desires are raised in my heart for thy welfare and preservation every way, that the God of Peace may be with thee continually, guiding thee by His counsel, helping thee by His Spirit, comforting thee by His love, during thy continuance here; and afterwards, when He may be pleased to take thee hence, to be seen of men no more, through His mercy in Christ Jesus, receiving thee into glory. I also feel real interest and best desires for the Prince Royal,—may you both be encouraged in every good word and work. I remember the words of Paul in the 15th chapter of the 1st of Corinthians, 58th verse: 'Be ye steadfast, unmovable, always abounding in the work of the Lord, for as much as ye know that your labor is not in vain in the Lord.".

"It would give me great pleasure and satisfaction to hear from thee, or if that be asking too much, perhaps the lady whom we had the pleasure of seeing here, will let us know many particulars respecting your welfare, and how you go on in Denmark, as it respects the prisons, schools, and other works of charity and love. I should also be pleased to know whether the books and the other things which we sent to Count Moltke, and also some of the work of the prisoners, ever came safely to thy hand, as we were prevented sending them quite so soon as we hoped to have done. I should be glad to be very respectfully and affectionately remembered to the Queen, and also to the Prince Royal, thy consort: and believe me, with much respect and regard

"Thy attached and obliged friend,

"ELIZABETH FRY."

The nobility of her nature, so thoroughly redeemed and irradiated by heavenly grace, brought Mrs. Fry naturally into association with the finest spirits of the age in which she lived. She was acquainted with Dr. Chalmers, and to some extent a co-laborer with him; but no particulars are recorded. "They mutually helped each other in their plans of benevolence."

When in Bristol attending religious meetings and visiting the prisons, she called on Hannah More, from whom she had previously received a copy of her "Practical Piety" containing this inscription:

TO MRS. FRY.

Presented by Hannah More,
As a token of veneration
Of her heroic zeal,
Christian charity,
And persevering kindness.
To the most forlorn
Of human beings.
They were naked and she

Clothed them;
In prison and she visited them;
Ignorant and she taught them,
For *His* sake,
In *His* name, and by *His* word,
Who went about doing good.

Barley Wood, June 17th, 1818.

It will be seen by the date that this beautiful tribute was given soon after the commencement of the Newgate reform. In 1825 in reply to a slight request from Elizabeth Fry, Hannah More wrote her the following letter.

"MY DEAR FRIEND,

Any request of yours, if within my very limited power, cannot fail to be immediately complied with. In your kind note I wish you had mentioned something of your own health, and that of your family.

"I look back with no small pleasure to the too short visit with which you once indulged me; a repetition of it would be no little gratification to me. Whether Divine Providence may grant it or not, I trust, through Him who loved us and gave Himself for us, that we may hereafter meet in that blessed country where there is neither sin, sorrow, nor separation.

"Believe me, my dear friend, with true esteem and warm affection to remain your's, sincerely,,

"H. MORE.

"Barley Wood, 15th, April.

The affection and esteem expressed with such Christian grace was fully reciprocated by Mrs. Fry who " entertained a high appreciation of the character of Hannah More and of the benefits which she had conferred upon her contempora‑ ries, especially upon her country-women. She always re‑

ferred with great pleasure to her visit to Barley Wood, and the impression made upon her by the mingled sweetness and dignity of Hannah More's countenance and manner."

Could anything be more charming than the meeting of two such women, and the sisterly love and admiration they felt for each other. Only the great can fully appreciate the greatness of others, and none can be truly great who are not truly good.

With Wilberforce Mrs. Fry was not unfrequently associated in benevolent labors. One of these occasions is thus described:

"The return of the season had brought with it the interest of the annual transportation of convicts. During this year, five ships had been employed for that purpose. A young lady—the daughter of an Admiral—has often recurred to a farewell visit to a convict-ship, on the point of sailing, in which she accompanied Elizabeth Fry. In allusion to this visit she says:—

"I could scarcely look upon her as any other than an angel of mercy, calmly passing from one to another of the poor wretched beings around her with the word of counsel, comfort, or reproof that seemed suited to each individual case, as it presented itself to her notice. With several kind assistants she was arranging work for them during the voyage; in itself no trifling matter. But many a point of deepest interest and anxiety brought to her ready ear, met with such response as could only be looked for from a devoted follower of Him who went about doing good."

"On the mind of this young person the circumstance was strongly impressed of accompanying her father, on another occasion, to the female convict-ships lying off Woolwich, to meet William Wilberforce and Elizabeth Fry.

"On board one of them between two and three hundred

women were assembled in order to listen to the exhortation and prayers of perhaps the two brightest personifications of Christian philanthropy that the age could boast. Scarcely could two voices, so distinguished for beauty and power, be imagined united in a more touching engagement—as indeed was testified by the breathless attention, the tears, and the suppressed sobs, of the gathered listeners. All of man's word, however, there heard, heart-stirring as it was at that time, has faded from memory; but no lapse of time can ever efface the impression of the 107th Psalm, as read by Mrs. Fry, with such extraordinary emphasis and intonation that it seemed to make the simple reading a commentary; and, as she passed on from passage to passage, it struck my youthful mind as if the whole series of allusions might have been written by the pen of inspiration, in view of such a scene as was then before us. At an interval of twenty years it is recalled to me as often as that Psalm is brought to my notice.—Never in this world can it be known to how many hearts its solemn appeals were that day carried home by that potent voice.'"

An interesting incident, in connection with these visits to the convict ships, is related by a boat-captain, afterwards Harbor Master at Ramsgate.

"It was on a fine sultry day in the summer of 1821 that I was racing up the Thames, in command of the Ramsgate Steam Packet, *Eagle*, hoping to overtake our Margate competitors, the *Victory* and *Favorite* steamers, and bring them nearer to view as we rounded the points of the Reach of the river. It was in the midst of this excitement that we encountered one of those sudden thunder squalls so common in this country, and which, passing off with heavy rain, leave behind them a strong and increasing northerly gale. I was looking out ahead, pleasing myself with the reflection that we were the fastest vessel against a head wind, and should certainly overtake our Margate friends; when upon entering Long Reach about two miles below Purfleet, I saw a boat laboring with very little effect against the gale, and with a whole ebb tide just making, to add to their difficulties. In this boat were two ladies in the close habit of the Society of Friends, evidently drenched with the heavy shower that had overtaken them. I was then a dashing, high-spirited sailor; but I had always a secret admiration of the quiet demeanor of that Society, and occasionally had some of them passengers with me, always intelligent and inquiring, and always pleased with any information a sailor could extend to them. Well, here was a dilemma! To stop would spoil my chase, in which most of my passengers were as eager as myself; but to go on and pass two ladies in such a situation! I passed the word softly to the engineer, desired the mate to sheer alongside the boat carefully, threw the delighted rowers a rope, and, before the passengers were fully aware that we had stopped the engines, the ladies were on board, the boat made fast astern, and the *Eagle* again flying up the Thames. I have those two persons strongly, nay, indelibly, stamped upon my mind's eye. The one I had last assisted on board still held my hand as she thanked me, with dignified, but beautiful expression: 'It is kind of thee captain, and we thank thee. We made no sign to thee; having held up our handkerchiefs to the other packets, we did not think we should succeed with thee.' I assured them that I could not have passed them under such circumstances, and called the stewardess to take them below into the ladies' cabin and see to their comfort. They had been well cloaked, and had not suffered so much as I had anticipated.

"The gale had cleared away the rain, and in a very short time they came upon deck again. One of them was Mrs. Fry, and she never lost an opportunity of doing good. I saw her speaking to some of my crew, who were looking very serious as she offered them tracts, and some of them cast a side glance at me, for my approval or otherwise. I had some little dislike to sects then, which I thank God left me in riper years,—but who could resist this beautiful, persuasive, and heavenly-minded woman? To see her was to love her; to hear her was to feel as if a guardian angel had bid you follow that teaching which could alone subdue the temptations . and evils of this life, and secure a Redeemer's love in eternity. In her you saw all that was attractive in woman lit up by the bright beams of philanthropy, devoting the prime of life and health and personal grace to her Divine Master's service; and I feel assured that much of the success which attended her missions of mercy, was based upon that awe which such a presence inspired. It was something to possess a countenance which portrayed in every look the overflowing of such a heart; and thus, as a humble instrument in the hands of Divine Providence, she was indeed highly favored among women.

"She told me that her companion, Mrs. Prior, and herself had been down to Gravesend to take leave of the unfortunate women (convicts) on board a ship bound to the settlements, and gave me so touching a description of their behaviour, that I volunteered to take charge of anything for her at any time, or render her any service in my power, in my voyages. When about to land her anxiety to make some pecuniary recompense was very great, but I would not allow her to do so. Mrs. Fry never forgot me when she came near our locality. I saw her from time to time, the earthly tabernacle failing, but the same spirit lighting up with animation her untiring energies. It was an honor to know her in this world; may we follow her to the society of the accepted and blessed in that which is to come.

K. B. MARTIN."

"Ramsgate, February, 1847."

CHAPTER SIXTH.

Elizabeth Fry's first considerable journey was made in the autumn of 1818, shortly after the commencement of her prison-reform labors. It was directed to the northern part of England and to Scotland, with a view both to religious visits among the Friends, and to an examination of the prisons in those parts of the Kingdom. She was accompanied by her brother John Joseph Gurney, his wife, and one of her own daughters. The commencement of the trip is thus described in her Journal.

"*Bedford, Northumberland, Eighth Month, 25th.*—For some months I have looked to attending the General Meeting in Scotland, but it appeared almost impossible, my home claims being so very strong. Indeed the Monthly Meeting before the last it came with great weight, so as to frighten me; but I neither saw outward way for it, nor did I feel the heart made willing; but as I have so often found when there is a real 'putting forth,' way is made within and without; so it has been now, all my sweet flock are, I trust, carefully provided for; not only outward way has been made, but the willing heart also granted, and I had remarkably sweet peace and relief in being willing to give up to it; such an evidence that I think it remains undoubted in my mind. Friends appeared to feel much unity with me which was a help. My beloved brother Joseph, and sister Jane joining me has been much cause for humble thankfulness; it has made what would have been very hard to flesh and blood comparatively sweet and easy; we are a united band in spirit and in nature; Joseph a very great help in the ministry. I think he is, and will yet be more abundantly, an instrument of honor in his Master's hand. We have sat four Meetings, visited several families of Friends, and inspected many prisons, which is one of our objects. In our religious services our gracious Helper has appeared very near; we have gone on in them with much nearness and unity; we know the blessed truth that, as we abide in Christ, we are one in Him. I have felt at seasons as leaving all for my Master's sake, and setting out without much of purse or scrip; but how bountifully I am provided for, both internally and externally. The great Shepherd of the sheep has been near to me in spirit, as strength in my weakness, riches in my poverty and a present helper in the needful time. I may say,

> 'Are these Thy favors day by day,
> To me above the rest?
> Then let me love Thee more than they,
> And try to serve Thee best.'

Conflicts have attended, and no doubt will attend me; but I look upon it as an honor, a favor and a blessing, even to suffer in the Lamb's army, if we may but be of the number of the soldiers who fight the good fight of faith, and are in any degree permitted to promote the cause of truth and righteousness upon earth.

"*Aberdeen, 29th.*—I have felt low upon arriving here, five hundred miles from my beloved husband and children; but a good account of them is cause for thankfulness: still it is a deeply weighty thing, and I have to try my ground again and again. In almost every new place the language of my spirit is, Why am I here? At this place we find several other Friends also traveling in the ministry, which makes me feel it the more; but as my coming is not of my own choice, or my own ordering, I desire to leave it, and to commit myself, my spirit and body, and all that is dear to me, absent and present, to Christ my Redeemer. We visited the old Barclay seat at Ury where our mother's forefathers once lived. How great the change from what it once was!

"*Stonehaven, Ninth Month, 2nd.*—We left Aberdeen this afternoon, having finished our services there, and at Kinmuck where several Friends reside. Other Friends besides ourselves being at Aberdeen certainly tended to increase my exercise, for fear of the ministry not going on well, or by not keeping in our ranks; but I think we were enabled to do so, and although much passed yet we had cause for thankfulness, inasmuch as there appeared to br harmonious labor for the advancement of truth and the spreading thereof. Our General Meeting at Aberdeen was ended under a feeling of quiet peace; but fears crept in for myself that I had fallen away a little as to life in the truth, and power in the ministry, for I did not experience that overflowing power which I have sometimes done at such seasons. Still gracious help was granted me from season to season. The day after the General Meeting we went to Kinmuck, about fifteen miles north of Aberdeen. A short time after our arrival there, before I went to meeting, such a feeling of suffering came over me as I can hardly express. It appeared only nervous, as I was so well in body that I could not attribute it to that. It continued exceedingly upon sitting down in Meeting, and led me into deep strong supplication that the enemy might by no means deceive us, or cause our ministry to be affected by anything but the holy anointing. I feared, if this awful state had to do with those present, that I should have something very close to express; if only with myself I considered that it might be a refining trial. However Joseph knelt down in the beginning of the meeting, as well as myself, and afterwards he spoke as if he felt it necessary to warn some to flee from their evil ways and from the bondage of Satan. This tended to my relief; but it appeared as if I must follow him and rise with these words, 'The sorrows of death compassed me about, the pains of hell gat hold upon me;' then enlarging upon the feeling I had of the power of the enemy, and the absolute need there is to watch, to pray, and to flee unto Christ as our only sure refuge and deliverer. I had to show that we might be tried and buffeted by Satan as a further trial of faith and of patience, but that if we did not yield to him, it would only tend to refinement. After a time I felt greatly relieved, but what seemed remarkable was that neither Joseph nor I dared to leave the Meeting without once more bowing the knee for these dear Friends. But after all this very deep and remarkable exercise a solemn silence prevailed, really as if truth had risen into dominion; and after my making some such acknowledgment in testimony, that our low estate had been regarded, that our souls could then magnify the Lord, and our spirits rejoice in God our Saviour, that light had risen in obscurity, and darkness had, in measure, become as the noon-day, and the encouragement it was for us to run with patience the race that was set before us, &c., the Meeting concluded, and I think upon shaking hands with the Friends there hardly appeared an eye that had not been weeping, amongst those that were grown up. This whole exercise was very remarkable in a nice little country meeting, and the external so fair; but afterwards we heard of one or two painful things, one in particular. We visited nearly all the families, were pleased with some of them: their mode of living truly humble like our cottagers. The next day we had a Meeting with a few Friends at Aberdeen where the exercise was not very great and the flow in the ministry sweet, and I trust powerful. We parted from our beloved friends, John and Elizabeth Wigham, their children, and children's children, and are now on our way to Edinburgh.

"*Hawick*, 13*th*.—I may thankfully acknowledge being so far on our way, but our journey through life is a little like a common journey; we may, after a day's traveling, lie down and rest, but we have on the morrow to set off again upon our travels: so I find my journey in life. I am not unfrequently permitted to come for a short time to a sweet, quiet resting-place; but I find that I soon have to set forth again. I was glad and relieved in leaving Aberdeen, and then a fresh work began in Edinburgh. On Seventh day we visited the prisons, accompanied by some gentlemen, the Lord Provost and others. Here we were much interested. On First-day we went in the morning to Meeting, and were favored to do well; many were not Friends; and what were my feelings in the evening to find a considerable number of people, quite a Public Meeting. It gave me a great deal of alarm, but we had a good Meeting and I trust the cause was exalted. The morning before we came away about eighteen gentlemen and ladies came to breakfast with us, amongst them Sir George and Lady Grey, good people whom I have long wished to know; we had, after breakfast, a solemn time. Alexander Cruickshank read, and afterwards I knelt down, and I think we were drawn together in love and unity of spirit. We arrived at Glasgow that evening and the next day visited the prisons, and formed a Ladies Committee. We visited some families the next day, and, accompanied by several gentlemen, magistrates and others, we again went to the Bridewell and Prison, where I had to start the Committee in their proceedings; it was awful to me, having to bow the knee for a blessing, before so many who were strangers to our ways, but blessed be the Lord, the power of truth appeared to be over all, so that I remembered these words, 'Rejoice not that the spirits are made subject unto you, but rather rejoice that your names are written in Heaven.' We had two meetings, one in the morning for Friends, but many others came, and one to my deep humiliation in the evening for the public. Awful work it was: we were favored to get through well, and to leave Glasgow with clear minds. We have since traveled through great part of Cumberland, attended many meetings there, some very important ones, and some highly favored by the Presence and Power of the Most High;—thence to Kendal.

" At Liverpool was the next meeting we attended; it was a large public one, and so it has been in many places. I deeply felt it, I hardly dared to raise my eyes because of the feathers and ribbons before me. However best help was afforded, to my very great relief and consolation; truth appeared to be in great dominion. After a sweet uniting time with the Benson family, we left Liverpool for Knowsley, the seat of the Earl of Derby, as we had a pressing invitation from Lady Derby. We were received with the utmost kindness and openness by all this very large household. A palace was now our allotment; a cottage has been so during our journey. My internal feeling was humiliation and self-abasement.

" *Knowsley*, 24th.—Here we are, all the family about to be collected for a religious opportunity. Lord, be pleased to be with us, to own us by Thy life-giving presence, and help us by Thy Spirit, for it is a very awful time. Make us, Thy unworthy children, fit for Thy service, and touch our lips as with a live coal from Thy altar, for we are unworthy to take Thy great and ever-excellent name into our mouths. Thou, Lord, only knowest the state of Thy unworthy servant; help her infirmities, blot out her transgressions, and enable her to show forth Thy praise, if consistent with Thy holy will, that all may be more abundantly converted unto Thee, and brought into the knowledge of Thy beloved Son, Christ Jesus our Lord.

" *Sheffield*, 26th.—After writing the above I was summoned into the dining-room, where the family were assembled—I should think in all nearly a hundred. My beloved brother read the third chapter of John; there was then a solemn pause, and I found it my place to kneel down, praying for a blessing upon the house and family, and giving thanks for the mercies bestowed upon them; particularly in the time of their affliction, in having been supported by the everlasting Arm; and prayer arose for its being sanctified unto them. The large party appeared humbled and tendered. Then dearest Joseph arose and was greatly helped by the power of the Spirit. I followed him with a few words. Many of the party were in tears; some exceedingly affected. Joseph then knelt down, greatly helped; the service principally fell upon him. After he rose I reminded them of the words of our blessed Redeemer, that 'whosoever giveth a disciple a cup of cold water in the name of a disciple, shall receive a disciple's reward.' This, I said, I humbly trusted would be their case. I also alluded to their servant's kindness in the same way. Thus ended this memorable occasion. It was like what we read of in Friends' journals formerly, when the power appeared to be over all in a very extraordinary manner. I remember in John Richardson's journal some such account. So it is,— and this is not, and cannot be, our own work; surely it is the Lord's doing, and marvelous in our eyes.

"*Earlham, Tenth Month,* 6*th.*—Once more arrived at this interesting place that has so long been a home to me. I will go back to where I left off. Our visit to Sheffield was an important one; I had so deeply to feel for a beloved Friend who has long been a mother in Israel, under heavy family affliction. Oh! what I felt for her in meeting and out of meeting I cannot describe; my spirit was in strong intercession for her preservation and support under these deep tribulations. We had a favored meeting in the morning, though I had indeed to go through the depths before I ascended the heights. By the desire of my dear brother we had a Public Meeting in the evening, which was well got through, but not without suffering. We then proceeded to York; I can hardly express how deeply I felt entering that Quarterly Meeting; 'fears got hold upon me,' still hope arose underneath that this one of our services, as to our northern journey, would crown all, and so I think it proved. Not only, from service to service, and from meeting to meeting, did the holy, blessed, anointing Power appear to be abundantly poured forth upon the speakers, but upon the hearers also. Where I feared most, I found least to fear; such unity of spirit, such a flow of love and life, as quite refreshed, encouraged and comforted my soul. I was much rejoiced to find so many fathers and mothers amongst them. 'Bless the Lord, O my soul! and all that is within me bless His holy name!—Praise and exalt Him above all forever!' might then have been the language of my soul.

"We traveled on to Lynn, and there my brother with his dear Jane left me. At the meetings there I felt as if I had to minister almost without the power, and yet that I must yield to the service; but I was so fearful and weak at both meetings that truth did not appear in dominion. Perhaps I found the change after York, and missed my dear brother Joseph. I often minister as if in bonds; this is very humbling—so many fears, so many doubts arising; this was the case in nearly all my services during the day."

"In the course of this northern journey, J. J. Gurney and his sister had visited the prisons of the several towns through which they passed. They found them to be generally in a condition of the most disgraceful neglect—and the hardships, and even cruelty endured by the inmates were harrowing in the extreme to the tender nature of Elizabeth Fry.

"But the cases of the poor lunatics confined in some of those abodes of misery, made, above all, a most powerful impression on her heart, and induced a sympathy with such as were afflicted with this heaviest of physical maladies, that continued deeply to influence her feelings through life.

"The results of their observations were published in a pamphlet—'Notes on a Visit to Prisons, &c., by J. J. Gurney and Elizabeth Fry.'

"To such persons as were interested in Prison Reform, this book afforded much matter for reflection. Whilst they deplored the evils described, they rejoiced that they should be brought to light—as the first step towards their being remedied.

"The voice of Elizabeth Fry was heard and her appeals were promptly responded to. Her brother, in writing of this northern journey says: 'she exhibited a perfect tact and propriety in her transactions, and well knew, when in pursuit of such objects how to soothe all asperities, influence all parties, and overcome the greatest difficulties.' In confirmation of which some passages may be quoted from a letter written by a Scotch lady who accompanied her when she visited the prisons at Glasgow.

"'She found our prisons very badly managed,' &c., and 'has left a letter for the magistrates.' She had an interview with them, and this evening a number of ladies met at the Bridewell. She told them with much simplicity what had been done at Newgate. She entered into pleasant conversation with every one and all were delighted when she offered to speak a little to the poor women. But the keeper of the Bridewell said he feared it was a dangerous experiment; that they never, but by compulsion listened to reading, and were generally disposed to turn anything of the kind into ridicule. She said that she was not without fears of this happening, but she thought it right to attempt it. The women, about a hundred, were then assembled in a large room, and we went in, misdoubting and anxious. She took off her bonnet and sat down on a low seat, fronting the women; then looking at them with a kind, conciliating eye, yet an eye that met every eye there, she said, 'I had better just tell you what we are come about.' She told them she had to deal with a great number of poor women, sadly wicked, and in what manner they were recovered from evil. Her language was scriptural, always referring to our Saviour's promises, and cheering with holy hope these dissolute beings. 'Would not you like to turn from that which is wrong? Would not you like for ladies to visit you, and speak comfort to you, and help you to become better? Surely you would tell them your griefs; they who have done evil have many sorrows.' As she read to them the '*Rules*,' asking them, if approved to hold up their hands, all hands were upraised, and as soon as she spoke tears began to flow. One very beautiful girl near me had her eyes swimming with tears, and her lips moved as if following Mrs. Fry. One old woman who held her Bible we saw clasping it with emotion as she became more and more impressed. The hands were ready to rise at every pause, and these callous and obdurate offenders were with one consent bowed before her. Then she took the Bible and read the parables of the *lost sheep*, the *piece of silver*, and the *prodigal son*.

'It is impossible for me to express to you the effect of her saintly voice, while speaking such blessed words. She often paused and looked at the poor women with a sweetness that won their confidence, applying, with beauty and taste all the parts of the story to them, and in a manner I never before heard,—and particularly the words, 'His father saw him when he was yet afar off.' A solemn pause succeeded the reading. Then resting the large Bible on the ground we saw her on her knees before them. Her prayer was devout and soothing, and her musical voice, in the peculiar, sweet tones of the Quakers, seemed like the voice of a mother to her suffering child.

'In the prison of Glasgow, the emotions were much more varied than at Bridewell—astonishing repugnance, and in some instances obstinate resistance to listen; in others anxious desire to accept her aid. She read and conversed with them, and the proposal of work was in general greedily received. How different were the impressions in the various figures before her! One old woman, with the appearance of a menial servant, and hardened features, said

'No! no use work!' But these rugged lines were at
length relaxed, and I saw a tear fall over the brown visage.
But it was not the prisoners alone; for there was not a man
in the room unmoved.'".

Many letters were received after the publication of the
"Notes;" among them the following from the Countess
Harcourt.

"MY DEAR AND MOST RESPECTED FRIEND:

It is impossible to have read the excellent publication
giving an account of your tour with Mr. Gurney, without
being most anxious to express the satisfaction Lord Harcourt and I received from the work.   He read it to me, and
there was scarcely a page at which we did not stop to ex-
claim our admiration of the justness of the remarks, and
our earnest wishes that they might prove the means of
ameliorating the system of our prisons.   We felt that
each word gave conviction to our minds, and the beauty of
the style certainly added to the gratification of reading it.
Oh! my good friend, what a blessed tour you have made,
and may Heaven reward your wonderful exertions, by
making them effectual to the purpose intended.

"I ought not to use the word envy, but I cannot help
feeling the great difference between the manner in which
your life is spent and my own.   You ought indeed to be
thankful that it has pleased God 'to put into your mind
good desires,' and to have given you health to go through
such arduous undertakings."

Early in the following year, however, the reaction came
from her " great and varied exertions," and she was obliged
to spend several weeks in recruiting her health at Brighton.

Also the secret troubles of her heart were becoming enlarged from the growing cloud of differences in her home;

of which she is compelled very rarely to speak in her Journal. After visiting her sister Priscilla in a dangerous illness, she writes:

"Since I have left her sick room sorrow and deep discouragement have been my portion from the extreme difficulty of doing right toward those most near; it does appear at times impossible for me, but most likely this arises from want of more watchfulness, and more close abiding in the Light and Life of our Lord. When I exercise a watchful care from seeing the dangers that attend some, it seems to give the greatest pain, and so causes me the deepest discouragement. Still, yesterday, in the great and bitter sorrow of my heart, I found in a remarkable manner the power of my Redeemer near, even helping by His own good Spirit and presence. When I felt almost ready to sink, and my footsteps indeed ready to slip—then the Lord held me up. In the first place, after a very little while from having been deeply wounded, my heart overflowed with love and forgiveness towards the one who had pained me, and I felt, what would I not do for the individual? and a most anxious desire if I had missed it to make it up by every means in my power. Thus when I had feared discouragements would have almost overwhelmed my spirit, there was such a calming, blessed and cheering influence came over my heart that it was like the sick coming to the Saviour formerly, and being immediately healed; so that I was not even able to mourn over my calamity. It appeared as if 'the Holy One who inhabiteth Eternity,' would not give me over to the will of my enemies."

We are nowhere informed as to the particular nature of this skeleton in the house of Elizabeth Fry. It is but just, however, that we should know that her path was not all sunshine, that she often carried a heavy heart on missions of love to the sorrowing, and that in ministering consolation to others she referred them to a Fountain of which she was in the habit of herself drinking largely. Perhaps something of this kind was needful to her, like the thorn in the flesh which kept Paul weighted down for his work. After the passage given above, Mrs. Corder remarks:

"Perhaps few will read the preceding extract without perceiving something of the deep and hidden sorrow which often weighed down the spirit, and preyed also on the bodily frame of this precious follower of the Lamb. It is not needful to attempt to penetrate the veil that conceals from the eye of the stranger the circumstances that rendered her path of life a tribulated one: it is enough to know that her perplexities and distresses were endured with meek submission, and a degree of forbearance that could only be the effect of that state of watching unto prayer with all perseverance in which she was so remarkably preserved; and by which she was kept, through all her mental vicissitudes as in a region of love."

In deference to this judgment we may well repress our curiosity while giving increased love and admiration to one who could thus, out of her own heart's experience, comfort the poor and the afflicted.

I again quote from Mrs. Corder's notes, which sometimes supplement the information contained in the original memoir.

"The weighty responsibilities of Newgate did not preclude other objects of public interest, to some of which Elizabeth Fry devoted much attention. Among these was a 'nightly shelter for the houseless.' During the rigorous winter of 1819-20, the sufferings of houseless wanderers called for prompt relief. The heart of this Christian philanthropist was deeply touched by some affecting cases. In one instance a little boy who had in vain begged at many houses for the few half-pence required to procure admittance to some passage or cellar, was found frozen to death on the step of a door! An asylum was immediately provided. It was well warmed, nutritious soup was prepared night and morning, with a ration of bread for each of the inmates, who were also furnished with beds. Employment in various ways was procured; and the bounty of the public flowed in to encourage the hearts and strengthen the efforts of the benevolent persons who united in laboring for the management and success of the establishment. Many hundreds were, night after night, admitted—great numbers who could not be accommodated at the 'Shelter,' were supplied with food, clothing and the means of procuring lodgings elsewhere. The females were placed under the care of a 'Ladies' Committee,' with Elizabeth Fry at their head."

The following brief review, bears date August 1820.

"19th.—I have this day been married twenty years; my heart feels much overwhelmed at the remembrance of it—it has been an eventful time. I trust that I have not gone really backwards spiritually, as I think I have, in mercy, certainly increased in the knowledge of God and Christ Jesus our Lord; but this has been through much suffering. I doubt my being in so lively a state as ten years ago, when first coming forth in the ministry; but I believe I may say that I love my Lord above all—as far as I know—far above every natural tie; although in His infinite wisdom and mercy He has been pleased, at times, to look upon me with a frowning Providence. If I have lately grown at all, it has been in the root, not in the branch, as there is but little appearance of good, or fruit, as far as I can see. In the course of these twenty years my abode has often been in the valley of deep humiliation; still the Lord has been my stay, and I may say through all has dealt bountifully with me. Assuredly He has raised me up from season to season, enabled me to speak well of His name and led me to plead the cause of the poor and those that are in bonds, naturally and spiritually."

After a visit to the Monthly Meeting of Essex in the fall of 1820, she writes:

"4th.—I returned yesterday from finishing visiting the Monthly and Quarterly Meetings in Essex. I was carried through the service to my own surprise; I felt so remarkably low, so unworthy, so unfit, and as if I had little or nothing to communicate to them; but I was marvelously helped from meeting to meeting; strength so arose with the occasion that the fear of man was taken from me, and I was enabled to declare gospel truths boldly. This is to me wonderful; and unbelievers may say what they will, it must be the Lord's doing, and it is marvelous in our eyes—how He strengtheneth them that have no might, and helpeth them that have no power. The peace I felt after these services seemed to flow like a river, for a time covering all my cares and sorrows, so that I might truly say, 'There is even here a rest for the people of God.' I am sure, from my own experience, there is nothing brings the same satisfying, heart-consoling feeling. It is to me a powerful internal evidence of the truth of revealed religion, that it is indeed a substantial truth, not a cunningly devised fable. My skeptical doubting mind has been convinced of the truth of religion, not by the hearing of the ear, but by what I have actually handled and tasted and known for myself, of the word of life, may I not say of the power of God unto salvation."

Another milestone on this eventful journey reads as follows:

"*Eighth Month,* 20*th,* 1822.—Yesterday was our wedding-day; we have been married twenty-two years. How many dispensations have I passed through since that time! how have I been raised up and cast down! How has a way been made in the depths and a path in the mighty waters! I have known much of good health and real sickness; great bodily suffering, and deep depression of spirits.

"I have known the ease of abundance of riches and the sorrow and perplexity of comparative deprivation. I have known to the full I think the enjoyment of domestic life— even what might be called the fullness of blessing, and also some of its most sorrowful and most painful reverses. I have known the abounding of the unspeakable and soul-satisfying joy of the Lord; and I have been brought into states when the depths had well-nigh swallowed me up. I have known great exaltation amongst my fellow mortals, and also deep humiliation. I have known the sorrow of some most tenderly beloved being taken from me by death. and others given me—hitherto more given than taken.

"What is the result of all this experience? It is even that the Lord is gracious and very merciful; that His compassions fail not, but are renewed every morning. And may I not say that His goodness and mercy have followed me all the days of my life? Though He has at times permitted me, amidst many unspeakable blessings, to pass through unutterable sorrows, known only to the full extent by Him and my own soul, yet hath He been an all-sufficient Helper. His right hand hath sustained me and held me up, blessed be His name forever. He hath never forgotten to be gracious, nor hath He shut up His tender mercies from me. May I not indeed raise up my Ebenezer and acknowledge that there is 'no God like our God,' and that it is a most blessed thing to serve Him, even if it be by way of the cross; for He is indeed worthy to be served, worshipped and obeyed now and forever. Above all I pray for myself, that whatever dispensations I may yet pass nothing may separate me from His love or hinder me from His service; but that I may be increasingly and entirely devoted to Him in heart, mind and spirit, through the help of my most dear and blessed Redeemer.

"*Twelfth Month,* 2nd (1822).—Yesterday, at Meeting, the truth rose into much dominion, blessed be the name of the Lord. I was enabled to supplicate and minister, to my own relief, and I trust to the refreshment of others; also my dearest brother Joseph, Rebecca Christy, and my sister, Elizabeth Fry, in prayer. It appeared a solemn time; the day, generally speaking, a favored one; but in the night I was deeply brought to a sense of my own weakness. If the beautiful garments spiritually were put on in the morning, surely they were taken off at night. What are we, but instruments, however, for a season decorated with the Lord's ornaments? Self cannot boast when left to ourselves, and our ornaments taken off. How wonderful is the work of the Spirit!—how it heals and raises up body and soul when they are brought into service! None can tell, but those who have experienced something of it, how the anointing is poured forth from on high. It is an honor I am unworthy of, to be thus helped spiritually, particularly in the ministry. But how deeply doth my spirit crave that I may also be aided in all the practical duties of life."

During this period Elizabeth Fry was earnestly engaged with her Newgate readings, and it is remarkable how rapidly her intellectual powers developed under the influence of this powerful stimulus. She was about thirty-seven years of age when this work began which brought her at once into a notoriety that placed an immense strain on her whole being. Had she not been well endowed with natural force of mind she would soon have shrunk, with her accidental fame, into retirement. And, beyond this, had she not had strong religious faith, which brought her inward

support, and a stimulus equally powerful, the same result
must have followed. But between the inward and the outward fires her mental and moral being blossomed out with
a tropical luxuriance most admirable to witness, and worthy
of the reverent applause so freely bestowed upon it. So
far from exciting vanity, this only increased her modesty
and her humble dependence on what she well knew to be
the real Source of her strength. There was not the slight-
est cant in her humility or her ascriptions of praise. God
was *known* in her heart for a refuge and a very present
help; and pure love and gratitude, no less than her sense
of justice, made it the crown of her joy to glorify her Lord
for the grace and wisdom so evidently bestowed. She
says:

"In nothing has the work of grace been so marvelous to
me as in the ministry. It surely is not my work;—I know
enough of myself to believe it to be quite impossible. Oh,
what an unction I now and then feel! It is as much to be
felt strengthening the soul, as the body is felt to be refreshed after wholesome good food. The work of the Spirit
is a wonderful work; and to my naturally doubting and
skeptical mind astonishing."

"*Plashet, Second Month,* 13th.—I attended Tottenham
Meeting on the 2nd. I went low, and under deep exercise
of mind; I returned in measure relieved, though naturally
upset with many fears. I hardly ever remember being engaged in a service where doubts and fears beset me to an
equal extent. On First-day, the 9th, we were at Devonshire
House; it was an extraordinary meeting. I desire in more
simplicity of faith to attend the other meetings. I think I
have been too anxious, too fearful. If the work be not ours
why worry and perplex myself about it?

"19th.—Since writing the above I attended the Peel

Meeting on First-day, which was to the great relief of my mind. Since that time my bonds have appeared wonderfully broken, my spirit has had to rejoice and be glad, and my fears have been removed, so that I can indeed say, how marvelous is the work of the Spirit!

"On Second-day I dined at the Mansion House, with my husband; a change of atmosphere, spiritually, but if we are enabled to abide in Christ, and stand our ground, we may, by our lives and conversation, glorify God, even at a dinner visit, as well as in more important callings. Generally speaking, I believe it best to avoid such occasions, for they take up time and are apt to dissipate the mind; although it may occasionally be the right and proper calling for Christians thus to enter life; but they must then keep the eye very single to Him who, having placed them in the world can alone keep them from the evil.

" *Third Month*, 5th.—I have lately been remarkably full of occupations, and yet they have appeared right and almost unavoidable. On First-day I attended Southwark Meeting; mercy and peace eventually accompanied it. On Fifth-day I went to town to meet the Secretary of State, (Sir Robert Peel,) and the Speaker of the House of Commons, at Newgate, with my brother, Fowell Buxton, and my husband; I trust the time was blessed to the good of the cause.

"Sixth-day in town again to Newgate; one of the bishops, and many others there. It was a solemn time—a power better than ourselves seemed remarkably over us. I visited another prison and then returned home. Besides these out of door objects I am much engaged in nursing my babe which is a sweet employment but takes time; the rest of the childern, are comfortably settled in with dear Mary Ann Davis who is now once more with us. Upon sitting down to write, and looking round me, surrounded as I am with my family, supplied with so many temporal comforts, spiritual blessings not withheld—for I trust there

is rather an increase than decrease of the best things
amongst us—I thought, as the query arose in my heart,
'Lackest thou anything?' I might indeed say, 'Nothing,
Lord,' except a further establishment for us all in the ever
blessed truth as it is in Jesus: What can I render to Thee
for all Thy benefits? Grant, dearest Lord! in Thy child
and servant, a heart fully and entirely devoted unto Thee
and Thy service. Amen.

"29th.—Since I last wrote I have attended Winchmore
Hill Meeting to satisfaction, together with my dear sister
Elizabeth, William Allen, and my brother Samuel, whose
company I enjoyed. My husband has engaged Leslie, the
painter to come and take likenesses of him and me, to which,
from peculiar circumstances, I have appeared obliged to
yield; but the thing and its effect on my mind are unsatisfactory to me; it is not altogether what I like, or approve;
it is making too much of this poor tabernacle, and rather ex-
alting that part in us which should be laid low and kept
low. I believe I could not have yielded the point had not
so many likenesses of me already appeared, and it would be
a trial to my family only to have these disagreeable ones to
remain. However, from one cause or another, this has not
been a satisfactory week—too much in the earth and the
things of it, too little in the spirit; though not without
seeking to take up my cross, deny myself, and follow my
Lord and Master. I feel particularly unfit and unworthy
to enter again upon my religious engagement: we propose
going to Uxbridge this evening. My only hope is in Him
who can alone cleanse, fit, strengthen and prepare for His
own work. Under a deep feeling of my short-comings
may I not say, dearest Lord, undertake for me.

"*Fourth Month 7th.*—We went to Uxbridge, though
naturally rather a low time, yet it ended to my real comfort.
The Morning Meeting was a very solemn one, a deep feeling of good, and the anointing of the Spirit appeared freely
poured forth. The Evening Meeting was satisfactory; and

in several religious opportunities in the families my heart was enlarged in much love to the dear Friends there, whom, I think I may say, I love in the Lord."

Her next religious visit is thus briefly recorded. It was in the autumn of 1823.

"*Earlham, Tenth Month*, 1st.—My beloved husband left me this morning for London, and I am here, with nine children and my little grandson. Since I last wrote the face of things has brightened. I went to Bristol to attend the Quarterly Meeting there, accompanied by my brother Joseph John Gurney, and my sister E. F.; we left home on Sixth-day, the 11th of last month, and returned on Fifth-day, the 17th. In this short time we traveled about 280 miles, visited the meeting at Bath and the Bristol Quarterly Meeting, held two Public Meetings, visited the prison, attended to the magistrates and the committee; visited Hannah More, my cousin Priscilla H. Gurney, and several others. The last few days my husband and I have been at Cromer and paid an interesting visit to my much loved brothers and sisters there. I was at different times engaged religiously amongst them, and help was granted me in these services. I feel unworthy and unfit, and find that there is need of close, cleansing baptisms of the Spirit to make me in any degree ready thus to espouse the best of causes. I am much struck in having all my children but one now here, several of them grown up. What marvelous changes have I witnessed since I first knew this place! Wonders indeed have been done for me, spiritually and naturally.. How have I been raised up as out of the dust! I am surrounded by a numerous fine and healthy offspring; one only taken from me, and that one with a peculiar evidence of going to an everlasting and blessed inheritance. Spiritually also how has mercy been shown me! Has not the Beloved of my soul said 'live?'—and how has He been with me in many tribulations and sanctified many blessings. Indeed I have found that my Lord is a wonder-working God, and has manifested Himself to be to my soul 'Wonderful, Counsellor, the Mighty God, the Everlasting Father and the Prince of Peace.' What can I render for His unspeakable benefits?"

Early in 1824, she visited the Midland Counties accompanied by her brother Samuel Gurney; but returned in feeble health.

"*Plashet, Third Month,* 29*th.*—We reached home last Fifth-day, having accomplished the duty we had in prospect, to our own peace, and I trust to the edification of those amongst whom our lot has been cast. I continued very unwell during the whole journey, and what with exercise of mind, and real illness of body I think I have seldom known such a time; nor do I ever remember being so helped through the different services that I was brought into. Visiting gaols, attending two Quarterly Meetings and many not Friends there; once in Worcester gaol, one large Public Meeting, the first I ever appointed of that description; and many other meetings. But the way I was raised up, as from the dust, was wonderful to myself; enabled to speak with power; and in the Quarterly Meetings to go from service to service. It was indeed a remarkable evidence that there is in man something beyond the natural part which, when that is in its lowest, weakest state, helps and strengthens. None can tell what its power is but those who submit to it. I now feel fully called to rest. I gratefully remember the abundant kindness shown me upon my journey. Greater enlargement of my heart in love do I never remember, or to have met more from others. I have been permitted to feel, throughout this illness, at times, very sweet consolation,—a state of rest as if the sense of pain and sorrow was taken away from body and mind, and now and then almost like a peep into the joys of the Kingdom."

During this period in addition to her labors at Newgate the need of asylums for the reception of discharged female prisoners claimed the attention of Elizabeth Fry and her fellow-laborers.

"In 1822 a small house for receiving some of the most hopeful of the discharged prisoners was opened at Westminster under the name of Tothill Fields Asylum. It owed its existence to the Christian benevolence of one lady—Miss Neave. She has consecrated her time and purse to this important object which was first suggested to her mind during a drive with Mrs. Fry, thus related by herself:— 'A morning's expedition with dear Mrs. Fry made me at once resolve to add my help, if ever so feebly to the good cause. I distinctly remember the one observation made. I can call to mind at this moment the look and tone, so peculiar, so exclusively her's who spoke—'Often have I known the career of a promising young woman, charged with the first offence, to end in a condemned cell! Was there but a Refuge for the young offender my work would be less painful.' That one day's conversation upon these subjects, and in this strain laid the foundation of our prisoners' home.'

"The inmates at first were only four in number; in 1824 they had increased to nine; after a few years under the name of the 'The Royal Manor Hall Asylum,' it contained fifty young women. Since its first establishment 667 have been received within its walls.*

"There was another class of persons who claimed the attention of the ladies of the British Society at this meeting —the vicious and neglected little girls, so numerous in

---

* "In addition to this excellent Institution which continues very

London, early hardened in crime, who, whether they had, or had not been imprisoned had no chance of reformation at home; yet were too young to be placed with advantage in any existing asylum. Before the next anniversary a School of Discipline for the reception of such children was opened at Chelsea, where, withdrawn from their former associates, they might be trained to orderly and virtuous habits. The idea first occurred to Mrs. Fry when conversing, in the yard at Newgate, with her friend, Mrs. Benjamin Shaw, on the extreme difficulty of disposing of some very juvenile prisoners about to be discharged. She then begged Mrs. Shaw to consider the subject and draw up some plan for the purpose. This lady immediately applied herself to the important work; nor did she relax her exertions until she had seen the school of discipline firmly established, and its value tested by the experience of years.

"Mrs. Fry was anxious that the Government should adopt this Institution for receiving abandoned female children, and addressed Sir Robert Peel, then Secretary of State, on the subject. He warmly encouraged the design as one 'capable of effecting much good.' He recommended its being supported by the subscriptions of individuals, unconnected with public establishments, and enclosed a liberal donation from himself.

"Both these Institutions continue to be very important auxiliaries of the British Ladies Society, receiving considerable pecuniary assistance from its funds, in consideration of the many individuals placed in them, by its sub-committee, for the Patronage of Discharged Female Prisoners.

---

prosperous, a similar one for the reception of discharged female prisoners who appear likely to prove themselves to be reformed characters is now established at Hackney, and, under the designation of the 'ELIZABETH FRY REFUGE,' is effecting much good. Both these Asylums are liberally patronized by our beloved Queen, and they have a very strong claim on the benevolence of the public.—S. CORDER."

"But neither these nor any existing establishments adequately meet the needs of many applicants discharged from the London prisons; and until some further refuge for such is established the labor bestowed upon them during imprisonment must remain, in too many instances, an incomplete work; whether begun by the chaplain, the officers of the gaol, or the ladies of the Visiting Association. Earnestly and unflinchingly did Mrs. Fry urge this topic. She grieved to know that persons not utterly hardened, not wholly given over to depravity, who desired to retrace the downward road along which they had travelled, continually found themselves without resource, without encouragement, exposed to the condemnation of the world, or renewed temptations to vice. She felt that until every unhappy fallen one, without exception had the opportunity afforded her of repentance and amendment of life, England as a Christian country had not fulfilled the injunction of our blessed Lord—'*As* I have loved you that ye also love one another.'" *

The British Ladies' Society Meeting referred to above is thus spoken of in the Journal:

"*First-day*, 15*th*.—Yesterday, after a very weak and faint morning, I attended our 'Ladies' British Society' Meeting. It was surprising, even to myself to find what had been accomplished. How many prisons are now visited by ladies, and how much is done for the inhabitants of the prison-house, and what a way is made for their return from evil. It is marvelous in my eyes that a poor instrument should have been the apparent cause of settling forward such a work."

Mrs. Fry's health continuing delicate she was induced to

---

visit Brighton, in May, 1824, where she remained a little over two months. While here, being much distressed by the multitude of applicants for relief, and the impossibility of determining who among them were deserving, she organized, after much labor and discouragement, a District Visiting Society, composed of persons belonging to different religious denominations, with the Earl of Chichester as its President. Its objects were, "the encouragement of industry and frugality among the poor, by visits at their own habitations; the relief of real distress whether arising from sickness or other causes; and the prevention of mendicity and imposture, together with a system of small deposits, upon the plan of a Savings' Bank." This proved a very useful institution.

Being subject during her illness to attacks of faintness which required her often to be taken to an open window looking toward the sea; her eyes invariably rested, in the grey dawn, or through the gathering storm, on the one living object, "the solitary Blockade-man, pacing the shingly beach." Her sympathy was soon excited by his desolate condition, and she applied to the Bible Society for a grant of Bibles to distribute among this ill-provided class of men. Fifty Bibles, and twenty-five New Testaments were immediately placed at her disposal. She thus reviews this period of recreation at Brighton :

"*Dagenham, Seventh Month, 30th.*—We left Brighton last Sixth-day, the 23rd, and after what I passed through in suffering, and afterwards in doing, in various ways, I may acknowledge that I have no adequate expression to convey the gratitude due to my merciful and gracious Lord. I left it after a stay of nearly ten weeks, with a comparatively healthy body, and above all a remarkably clear and easy mind: with a portion of that overflowing peace that made all things, natural and spiritual appear sweet, and in near love and unity, not only with Friends there, but *many, many* others. I felt as if, although an unworthy instrument, my labors there had not been in vain in the Lord, whether in suffering or doing. It has not been without a good deal of anxiety, fatigue and discouragement that this state of sweet peace has been obtained, as I am apt to suffer so much from many fears and doubts, particularly when in a weak state of health. The District Society in which I was interested, I left, I trust, in a way for establishment, and likely to be very useful to the poor and to the rich. Also an arrangement to supply the Blockade-men on the coast (afterwards called Coast Guard) with Bibles and other books: and I hope they will be put in the way of reading them instead of losing their time. Some of the Blockade-men seemed much affected by the attention paid them, as also did their officers; and I am ready to hope that a little seed is scattered there. In Meetings I passed through much, at times going when I feared I should faint from weakness; but I found that help was laid on One who is Mighty, and I may indeed say, in my ministerial services, that out of weakness I was made strong. The Meetings were generally largely attended by those not Friends, of course without invitation, but I trust that they were good ones, and that we were edified together. This was through deep humiliation and many, many fears. It certainly calls for great care and watchfulness in all things that we enter, to find that they be not of ourselves, but of our Master whose servants we are; for He alone should point out the work. The end, in an uncommon manner, appeared to crown all.

"*26th.*—I returned from a short expedition to Brighton last evening—a very interesting and I trust, not unimportant one. My object was the District Society that I was enabled to form there, when I was so ill, or recovering from that state. Much good appears done, much more likely to be done; a fine arrangement made if it be but followed up; and I humbly trust that a blessing will attend the work, and has already attended it. I feel that I have not time to relate our interesting history; but I should say that the short time we spent there was a mark of the features of the present day. A poor unworthy woman, nothing extraordinary in point of power, simply seeking to follow a crucified Lord, and to co-operate with His grace in the heart, yet followed after by almost every rank in society, with the greatest openness for any communications of a religious nature; numbers at Meeting of different denominations, also at our own house—noblemen, ladies in numbers, clergy, dissenters, and Friends. We had most satisfactory religious opportunities together, where the power of an endless life appeared to be in great dominion—our dear Lord and Master Himself appearing remarkably to own us together.

"*Plashet, Fourth Month,* 21st.—My occupations are are just now multitudinous. The British Society and all that is attached to it; Newgate as usual. Forming with much fear and some misgivings, a Servants' Society, yet with a hope, and something of a trust, that it will be for the good of this class of persons for generations to come. I have felt so much for such, for so many years, that I am willing to sacrifice some time and strength for their sakes. It is, however, with real fear that I do it, because I am sensible of being, at times, pressed beyond my strength of body and mind. But the day is short, and I know not how to reject the work that comes to hand to do.

"*Plashet,* 25th.—I have had some true encouragement in my objects since I last wrote. The British Society Meeting was got through to much satisfaction. To myself (the poor humble instrument among women in this country) it is really wonderful what has has been accomplished in the prisons during the last few years. How the cause has spread, and what good has been done, how much evil prevented, how much sorrow alleviated, how many plucked like brands from the burning! What a cause for deep thanksgiving, and still deeper humiliation to have been, in any degree, one of the instruments made use of to bring about these results. I have also received a delightful account of the effects of my labors for the poor at Brighton; it appears that the arrangements made have greatly prospered amongst both rich and poor; also for the Blockade-men on the coast. This is cause for fresh thankfulness of heart. I may say that I there sowed in tears, and I now reap in joy.

"The Servants' Society appears gradually opening, as if it would be established according to my desires. No one knows what I go through in forming these Institutions,—it is always in fear.

"*Fifth Month*, 23rd.—I think that I am under the deepest exercise of mind that I ever experienced, in the prospect of a meeting to be held this evening for all the young people assembled at the Yearly Meeting. It is held at my request, my brother Joseph uniting in it. In a remarkable degree it has plunged me into the depths, into real distress; I feel so unfit, so unworthy, so perplexed, so fearful, even so sorrowful, so tempted to mistrustful thoughts, ready to say, 'Can such an one be called to such a service?' I do believe that 'this is my infirmity;' and I have a humble hope and confidence that out of this great weakness I shall be made strong. As far as I know, it has been in simple obedience to manifested duty, that I gave up to this service and went through the ordeal of the Yearly Meeting. If I know my own deceitful heart it has been done in love to my Master and to His cause. Lord, preserve me through this depth; through this stripping season! If it should please Thee to grant me the garments of Thy salvation, and the help of Thy Spirit, further enable me wholly to give unto Thee the glory which is due unto Thy name. If Thou makest use of Thy handmaid to speak in Thy name, be

Thou Thyself her help and her strength, her glory and the lifter up of her head. Enable her to rely on Thee, on Thy might and Thy mercy; to commit her whole case unto Thee, and keep in the remembrance of Thy handmaid that the blessed cause of truth and righteousness is not *hers* but *Thine*.

"*Plashet, Sixth Month, 2nd.*—The awful and buffeted state of my mind was, in degree, calmed as the day advanced. I went to town with my beloved brother Joseph, who appeared to have been in something of a similar depth of unusual suffering. We went into the meeting together. The large Meeting-house was soon so crowded that no more could get in; I suppose from eighteen hundred to two thousand persons, principally youth. All my children were there except little Harry. I heard hundreds went away who could not get in. After going in and taking my seat my mind was soon calmed, and the fear of man greatly, if not quite, taken away. My beloved brother Joseph bowed the knee and poured forth prayer for us. I soon after rose and expressed what was on my mind towards the assembly: First, that all were acceptable who worked righteousness and served the Lord. Secondly, that the mercies of our God should induce this service as a debt due to Him. Thirdly, that it must be done by following a crucified Lord and faithfully taking up the cross. Fourthly, how important therefore to the church generally, and to our religious society, for us so to do, individually and collectively; so that if this were done there would be, from amongst that company, those who would be as lights in the world, or as a city set on a hill that cannot be hid. I had to conclude with a desire that an entrance might be abundantly ministered unto them into the everlasting kingdom of our Lord and Saviour Jesus Christ. I then sat down but did not feel to have fully relieved my mind. Joseph rose and stood more than an hour. He preached a very instructive and striking sermon on faith and doctrine. Then my dear sister Elizabeth Fry, and my uncle Joseph said something. Afterwards I knelt down in prayer and thought I found no common access to the Fountain of all our sure mercies. I was enabled to cast my burden for the youth and my own beloved offspring with the rest, upon Him who is mighty to save and to deliver. I had to ask for a blessing upon our labors of love towards them, and that our deficiencies might be made up: that the blessing of the Most High might rest on them, from generation to generation, and that cross-bearers and standard-bearers might not be wanting from amongst them. I felt helped in every way; the very spirit and power appeared near, and when I rose from my knees I could in faith leave it all to Him who can alone prosper His own work. A few hints that impressed me, I afterwards expressed, which were to encourage the youth in the good works of the present day; but to entreat them when engaged in them, to maintain the watch, lest they should build up with one hand and pull down with the other. Secondly, that it was never too soon to begin to serve the Lord, and that there was nothing too small to please Him in. Then, commending them to His grace and bidding them farewell, the Meeting concluded in a very solemn manner. It lasted about two hours and a half, and general satisfaction appears to have been felt. When it was over, I may say we rejoiced together, I hope, in the Lord; so that my soul did magnify the Lord, and my spirit rejoiced in God my Saviour."

In 1827 she visited Ireland, accompanied by her brother Joseph John Gurney and her sister-in-law Elizabeth Fry Arrived at Dublin "a great variety of weighty engagements occupied them closely. They inspected several asylums, four jails, the Bridewell, House of Industry; also a Nunnery; formed Prison Committees, had important interviews with persons in authority, visited many members of their own religious Society, and attended several large meetings for worship, some of them peculiarly favored ones."

They then pursued their journey from place to place visiting all the principal towns in the island and numerous smaller ones,—went to see the Giant's Causeway, calling at a Moravian settlement on the route, and ended with the Yearly Meeting at Dublin. They were detained a week at Waterford, by the serious illness of Mrs. Fry. The sickness was caused by exhaustion and malaria. After arriving home she wrote:—

" The great numbers that followed us, almost everywhere we went, was one of those things I believe was too much for me. No one can tell, but those who have been brought into similiar circumstances, what it is to feel as I did at such times; often weak and fagged in body, exhausted in mind, having things of importance to direct my attention to, and not less than a multitude around me, each expecting a word, or some mark of attention. For instance, or one occasion a General on one side, a Bishop on the other, and perhaps sixty other persons all expecting something from me. Visiting Prisons, Lunatic Asylums, and Infirmaries; each institution exciting feeling and requiring judgment. I endeavored to seek for help from above, and for a quiet mind, and my desire was that such times should not be lost upon those persons. They ended frequently in religious opportunities, and many came in consequence to our Public Meetings. However these things proved too much for me, and tired me more than any part of our service.

"There were some I believe who feared my exaltation, and if they judged from outward appearance I do not wonder at it; but a deep conviction of my unworthiness and infirmity was so living with me that these things appeared more likely to cast me into the dust than to raise me up on high. We went on thus, from place to place, until we reached Waterford. We had visited Limerick, Cork and other places. I felt completely sinking—hardly able to hold up my head, and by degrees became seriously ill. Fever came on and ran very high, and I found myself in one of my distressing faint states; indeed a few hours were most conflicting. I never remember to have known a more painful time; tried without, distressed within, feeling such fears lest my being thus stopped by illness should try the faith of others and lest my own faith should fail. My pain too, in being from home was great. We were obliged to stop all the Meetings, that we had appointed for days to come. However, much as I suffered for a short time, I had most sweet peace afterwards. My blessed Saviour arose with 'healing in His wings,' delivered me from my fears, poured balm into my wounds, and granted me such a sense of having obtained full reconciliation with my God as I can hardly describe. All was peace. I no longer hankered after home, but was able to commit myself, and those nearest, to this unslumbering, all-merciful, and all-powerful Shepherd. By degrees I was sufficiently raised up to attend Meetings, visit some prisons, and see many persons; and we concluded our general visit to Ireland to my relief, peace and satisfaction. The Yearly Meeting crowned all, as to our ministerial services in our own Society. We left Waterford on the 11th of Fifth Month, after visiting Wicklow and Wexford, at that time remaining in Waterford a few hours only. We entered the steam-packet, slept on board, and left the harbor about three o'clock in the morning."

CHAPTER SEVENTH.

It has already appeared that the home life of Elizabeth Fry, though favored with perhaps its full share of blessings, was not without its peculiar and deep trials. Without striving to unveil the source of the secret sorrow which caused the severest pain, and which apparently lay between herself and her husband, there is no occasion to conceal the fact that as their children grew up they generally inclined away from the peculiar views and customs of the religious Society to which they belonged by right of birth, and to which their mother was devotedly attached from sincere conviction of its worth. It is easy to see what ever-recurring pain this fact must have caused, in the maternal heart, as well as constant practical difficulties in the household. Every deviation, every inclination toward the customs of the world, and even toward those of other good people seemed a turning away from herself, and also from Him who had called her into a path of self-denial, and so signally blessed her faithfulness in bearing her allotted cross. How could she believe that the same cross was not equally adapted to her dear offspring, or that in declining it they were not giving evidence of an unconcerted state. However correct or erroneous her judgment may have been, the motherly solicitude she felt was most touching and commendable. Her position was indeed a most trying one.

"22nd (August 1827).—It is hard, very hard, a most diffi-cult matter, to help those whose welfare and salvation are past expression near to us. We can only go to Him who is willing and able, not only to hear our prayers on our own account, but on account of those most tenderly beloved, and who does, in His tender mercy, so bear our griefs and carry our sorrows that our souls can rest on Him. Oh! may I ever have the encouragement of seeing those nearest to me walking closely with God; not doing their own pleas-ure, nor walking in their own ways, but doing His pleasure, and walking in His ways. I believe it would bring unspeak-able joy, refreshment and consolation to my soul; and may I never cease to commend them to Him who can work with or without human instrumentality."

The discretion and care which she exercised to avoid un-pleasant differences, and to show forth moderation, in the midst of difficulties, are finely illustrated in the following note and comment.

"*Third Month*, 3rd, 1825.—I hope I am thankful for being really better though delicate in health. I wish I did not dread illness so much; it is a real infirmity in me; may grace be granted to overcome it. I think, strange to say, I felt, and I fear appeared to those about me, to be irritable. Certainly I had some cause to be so; but after what I have known of the power that is able indeed to help us, I never ought to give way to anything of the kind; all should be meekness, gentleness and love. Perhaps I said too much about some pictures and various ornaments that have been brought from France for us. Much as I love true Christian simplicity, yet if I show a wrong spirit in my desire to maintain it in our house and furniture, I do wrong and harm the best of causes. I far prefer moderation, both from principle and taste, although my experience in life proves two things: first, that it is greatly for the good of the community to live according to the situation in which we have been placed by a kind Providence if it be done unto the Lord, and therefore done properly; then I believe that by so doing we should help others and not injure ourselves. Second, I have so much seen the extreme importance of occupation to the well-being of mankind, as to be convinced that many works of art which tend to our accommodation, and even the gratification of our taste, may be innocently partaken of, may be used and not abused, and kept in their proper places; as by so doing we encourage that sort of employment which prevents the active powers of man from being spent in things that are evil."

In reference to the above, and other occasional confessions of irritability by Mrs. Fry, her daughters bear the following testimony:—

" The contrition so frequently expressed in the course of Mrs. Fry's journal for *irritability of temper* is calculated to *mislead* a stranger who would naturally suppose that it must occasionally *have betrayed itself in conduct*. To those who intimately knew the never-failing gentleness, forbearance and Christian meekness of her deportment, that *such* feelings ever ruffled her mind is almost *inexplicable*. Those most closely connected with her, in the nearest and most familiar relations of life, can unhesitatingly bear their testimony to the fact that they *never* saw her in what is called a pet, or heard an angry, or passionate expression of displeasure pass from her lips. Her tender conscience, and fear of offence towards God and man can alone account for these outpourings of the hidden evils of her heart."

Even this last clause, is considered by her friend and biographer, Mrs. Corder, as too great an admission. "Surely," she says, "they can scarcely be termed *evils.* Sin does not consist in being *tempted.* The Apostle says, 'Blessed is the man who endureth temptation, for when he is tried he shall receive a crown of life.' There is abundant evidence that if a temptation to any feeling of irritability of temper ever presented itself to the mind of this meek servant of Christ, it was resisted and overcome through His grace. Her husband has recently given the Compiler a full assurance of this in the following words:—'I never knew her do an act, and never heard her utter a word that, in her most solemn moments, she could have wished to recall.'"

I am not sure that Mrs. Fry can be so fully vindicated on another point; unless it be lawful to throw the responsibility for our conduct upon those who have made us rules and exacted obedience by penalties too hard to be borne. That point is where she declined, in obedience to the rules of her religious Society, to witness the marriage of such of her children as chose companions of another persuasion, and accepted the aid of a "hireling priest" at the marriage ceremony. If these children manifested no irritability on these occasions, or afterwards, I think it is proof that they inherited some of their mother's virtue.

There is no evidence that she dissented from the narrow rule of her over-scrupulous sect in this matter, and she must therefore bear the reproach of what looks very much like bigotry in her thus sitting apart in sackcloth and ashes while her children were joining hands for life with partners of their own choice and in the manner that best pleased their companions or themselves. Still we shall find ourselves unable to judge her severely when we read her careful records of these sore trials.

"*Plashet, Eighth Month,* 29*th.*—My beloved daughter Rachel was married last Fifth-day, the 23rd, at Runcton, by my brother-in-law Francis Cunningham.

"*Plashet, Ninth Month,* 3*rd.*—I doubt not but that my late tendency to depression of spirits is caused not only by the sorrow which I certainly feel, and great disappointment from a child not keeping to principles that I have brought her up in, and also from the deep sense I have of their intrinsic value; but, moreover, that I have to bear my conduct in the affair being misconstrued by others. Yet I have certainly met with much kindness, great love and sympathy, and from quarters where I should least have expected it, also particularly from the Friends of my own Monthly Meeting.

"I am very much absorbed at home where many things deeply occupy my heart and head. To do right in my many relative duties is very difficult. How deeply I feel my shortcomings in them! and yet I fervently desire to do my best."

"*Dagenham, Tenth Month,* 3*rd,* 1833.—Here I am, sitting in solitude, keeping silence before the Lord; on the wedding-day of my beloved son William. As I could not conscientiously attend the marriage I believe it right to withdraw for the day. Words appear very inadequate to express the earnestness, the depth of my supplication for him and his—that the blessing of the Most High may rest upon them. As for myself, I sit solitary, in many things, but I thought to day (from this wedding bringing these things home to me).—Have I not my Lord as my friend and my comforter? and is He not a husband to all the members of His church? and am I not often satisfied and refreshed by His love?"

How different is the picture, and certainly a very pleasing one, when her daughter Richenda, like a good girl, marries in the Society and agreeably to its truly beautiful order.

"21st, (*May*, 1828).—The day before yesterday the wedding was accomplished. The Meeting was solemn and satisfactory. Our bride and bridegroom spoke well and with feeling.* My dearest brother Joseph prayed for them, and ministered to them; as did others. I prayed at the close of the Meeting most earnestly for them, for the other young people, and ourselves further advanced in life. After a short, solemn silence the certificate was read and signed. In the morning we had a satisfactory reading with our children.

"Thanks be to our Heavenly Father there was, I think, throughout the day, a great mixture of real solemnity with true cheerfulness. It was certainly no common day. Through everything, order, quietness, and cheerfulness were remarkably maintained. After dinner I returned thanks for our many blessings, and could, with a few present, feel how many outward deliverances we had experienced; that we had had our heads kept above the waters, spiritually and temporally, and were able to have such a day of rejoicing. Our dear bride and bridegoom left us in the afternoon. The evening was fine and our lawn looked really beautiful, covered with the large and interesting party. In the evening we assembled together and had a solemn religious time, giving, I trust, the praise that was due alone to Him from whom all good and blessings flow."

The closing scene above referred to is thus described in

---

*Quakers marry without the aid of a minister, mutually taking each other as wife and husband, and pledging love and fidelity until death. A certificate is then signed by the parties, and others present.

the Memoir—perhaps by the hand of the daughter whose marriage had caused a very different feeling:

"This marriage was hailed by Elizabeth Fry with sincere pleasure: not only was the connexion highly acceptable to her, and one that she believed likely to promote the happiness of her child, but it also possessed what was, in her estimation, the peculiar advantage of being with a member of the Society of Friends. Whilst her hospitable and affectionate nature was gratified with the prospect of receiving the bridal party at Plashet, she craved spiritual blessings for the two most interested, and that the occasion, like the marriage at Cana in Gallilee, might be owned by the presence of the Lord. It was a beautiful summer day; the sun shone brilliantly; Plashet was arrayed in all its verdure, gay with bright flowers, and sprinkled with groups of happy young people. After the bride was gone, one of the sisters crossed the lawn to speak to her mother. She said something of the scene before them and the outward prosperity which seemed to surround that beloved parent. The reply was remarkable; for after expressing a strong feeling of gratification and enjoyment she added in words which have riveted themselves on the memory of her to whom they were addressed—'But I have remarked that when great outward prosperity is granted, it is often permitted to precede great trials.' There is an an old rhyme which says,

'When joy seemeth highest
Then sorrow is nighest!'

Surely this was verified in the contrast between that day and the events which so shortly followed."

"*Plashet, Eleventh Month, 4th,* 1828.—I have been favored to partake of very sweet feelings of peace and refreshment of soul—that which I am ready to believe, in the most unmerited mercy, is something of the 'Well of water

springing up unto eternal life.'   But I find outwardly, and
about me there are storms: not, at present, so much in my
very own borders as close to them.

"15th.—The storm has now entered my own borders—
once more we are brought into perplexity and trial—but I
have this consolation, 'He will regard the prayer of the
destitute, and not despise their prayer.'   To whom can I
go in this time of emergency but to Him who hitherto has
helped me, and provided for me and mine in a marvelous
manner—made darkness light before me, and crooked
things straight?   Lord! Thou who remainest to be the
God of my life, above all things in this, our sorrow and
perplexity, cast us not out of Thy presence, and take not
Thy Holy Spirit from us; keep us from evil and from the
appearance of it, that through the help of Thy spirit our
conduct may be kept upright, circumspect, and clean in
Thy sight, and amongst men! that in all things, at all
times, and under all circumstances, we may show forth Thy
praise.   Keep us in love and unity with those with whom
we have to act even if they do contrary to our wishes and
judgment.   But oh, dearest Lord, if it be Thy holy will,
make a way of escape for us from the calamity we so much
dread, and continue, in Thy unmerited mercy, to provide
for Thy unworthy servant, her family, and all concerned
in this trial, that we may not want what is good and needful for us, and that others may be kept from suffering
through us.   If it be possible remove this bitter cup from
us; yet if it be Thy will that we drink it, enable us through
the grace and spirit of Him who suffered for us to drink it
without repining,—yet trusting in Thy love, Thy mercy,
and Thy judgment."

This time the cup was not removed, though the prayer
was granted.   During a severe financial crisis which occurred
at this time, 1828, in England, one of the business houses
in which Joseph Fry was a partner, though not that which

be personally conducted, failed in a manner that "involved Elizabeth Fry and her family in a train of sorrows and perplexities which tinged the remaining years of her life. Nature staggered beneath the blow—but the staff on which she leaned could not fail her and she fell not."

"*Eleventh Month,* 25th.—I have been brought at times into little less than anguish of spirit; not I think so much for what we must suffer ourselves, as for what others may suffer. The whole thing appears fraught with distress. When I look at this mysterious dispensation, permitted by Almighty Wisdom, I am ready to say, How is it Lord, Thou dealest thus with Thy servant who loves Thee, trusts Thee, and fears Thy name?—and then I say, this is my infirmity thus to query. Need I not chastisement? Do I not deserve it? May it not be a mysterious dispensation of deep and sore affliction laid not only upon us, but upon others, to draw us all more from the things of time, and to set us more on the enduring riches of Eternity? I cannot reason upon it; I must bow, and only bow, and say in my heart, which I believe I do, 'Not as I will, but as Thou wilt.' Well, if it be of the Lord, let Him do as seemeth Him good. · Lord, let Thy grace be found sufficient for us in this most awful time; and grant that we faint not when Thou rebukest us."

· The circumstances which caused this misfortune to be so peculiarly distressing are not stated. We are left to conjecture the meaning of that "if it be of the Lord," and why, "on the following Sunday the question was much debated as to whether she, and her family generally, should attend their meeting for worship, or not." But "*she* felt it right to go, and of course she was accompanied by her husband and children. She took her usual seat, bowed down and overwhelmed, with the bitter tears rolling down her

cheeks—no common thing with her. After a very solemn
pause, she rose with these words, her voice trembling with
emotion; 'Though He slay me yet will I trust in Him;'
and testified, in a short and beautiful discourse, that her
faith and love were as strong in the hour of adversity as
they had been in the time of prosperity. Her friends were
deeply affected, marking by their manner, their sympathy
and love."

To her only absent child she wrote:

"*Plashet, Eleventh Month, 27th.* 1828.

"MY DEAREST R.:

I have at last taken up my pen to write to thee; but to
one so near, and so much one with myself, it is difficult. I
do not like to pour out my sorrows too heavily upon thee,
nor do I like to keep thee in the dark as to our real state.
This is, I consider, one of the deepest trials to which we are
liable; its perplexities are so great and numerous, its mortifications and humiliation so abounding, and its sorrows so
deep. None can tell, but those who have passed through
it, the anguish of heart at times felt; but thanks be to our
God this extreme state of distress has not been very frequent, nor its continuance very long. I frequently find my
mind, in degree, sheathed to the deep sorrows, and am enabled not to look so much at them—but there are also times
when secondary things arise—parting with servants, the
poor around us, schools, and our dear Place. These things
overwhelm me; indeed I think naturally I have a very acute
sense of sorrow. Then the bright side of the picture rises.
I have found such help and strength in prayer to God; and,
highly mysterious as, in some points of view, this dispensation may be, yet I think I have frequently, if not generally,
come to be able to say, 'Not as I will, but as Thou wilt,'
and to bow under it. All our children, and children-in-law,
my brothers and sisters, our many friends and servants,

have been a strong consolation to me; and above all a little refreshment to my tribulated spirit has been granted me at times from what I trust are the well-springs from on High."

"The tide of sympathy flowed marvelously in from all quarters. The mass of letters that exist attest by how many, and how well she was loved, how highly she was valued, and upon how many hearts she and her sorrows were borne."

FROM WILLIAM WILBERFORCE.

"Farnham Castle, 29th. Nov. 1828.

"MY DEAR FRIEND :

Though my eyes are just now weaker than usual, I must claim a short exercise of their powers for the purpose of expressing to you the warm sympathy which Mrs. Wilberforce, and indeed all of my family that have the pleasure of knowing you, as well as myself, are feeling on your account. Yet you, I doubt not will be enabled to *feel* as well as to *know*, that even this event will be one of those which in your instance are working for good. You have been enabled to exhibit a bright specimen of Christian excellence in *doing* the will of God, and I doubt not you will manifest a similar specimen in the harder and more difficult exercise of *suffering* it. I have often thought that we are sometimes apt to forget that key for unlocking what we deem a very mysterious dispensation of Providence, in the misfortunes and afflictions of eminent servants of God that is afforded by a passage in St. Paul's Epistle to his beloved Philippians. ' Unto you it is given not only to believe on Him, but also to suffer for His sake.' It is the strong only that will be selected for exhibiting those graces which require peculiar strength. May you, my dear friend (indeed I doubt not you will) be enabled to bear the whole will of God, with cheerful confidence in His unerring wisdom and unfailing goodness. May every loss of this world's wealth be more than compensated by a larger measure of the unsearchable riches of Christ. You will not forget that the time is short; but there will be no end to that eternity of happiness and glory which I doubt not will in your instance follow it. Meanwhile you are richly provided with relatives and friends whom you love so well as to relish receiving kindnesses from them, as well as the far easier office of doing them. That you may be blessed with a long continuance of usefulness and comfort in this world, to be followed by a still better portion in a better, is the cordial wish and shall be the prayer also of (begging from you a frequent performance of the last named office of friendship for myself and mine),

My dear Mrs. Fry,
Your sincere and affectionate Friend,
W. WILBERFORCE."

FROM THE REV. JOHN W. CUNNINGHAM.

"*Harrow, November, 26th,* 1828.

"MY VERY DEAR FRIEND :—

I need not tell you with what sorrow I have received the most unexpected intelligence which reached me yesterday. It is but a short time since I was called to sympathize with a near relative in similar circumstances, and now again I am called to mourn as for a brother and a friend. My experience in the former case has enabled me to take a more hopeful and cheerful view of your heavy trial. Perhaps, dear friend, this event may be made a blessing to every member of your family; and we must not complain of a little rough handling when the jewels are to be polished for the treasury of God. All that drives us home to Him and to the power of His Spirit for grace and strength and joy is beyond all price to the soul. Is it not a comfort to you, dear friend at this moment, that you have spent so much of your time and property for God and His creatures?

is not money given to the poor lent to the Lord, and to be returned again, in some form or other 'with usury?' I beg
my very kind remembrances to Mr. Fry and your dear children. I have already been led to pray for them more than
once that this affliction may be sanctified to them, and that
thoy may more and more seek the durable riches of the
kingdom of Christ.

"My wife unites with me in very kind regards, and I am
very affectionately yours.

J. W. CUNNINGHAM."

FROM T. FOWELL BUXTON.

"Northrepps, December, 1st, 1828.

"MY DEAREST SISTER :—

I have hitherto, I confess, shrunk from writing to you.
Not surely, however, from any want of feeling for you, and
with you; but from so deep a sense of your calamity as to
make all attemps at comfort appear almost idle. A very
quiet day yesterday, and a long time spent over the 69th
Psalm from the 13th to the 17th verse, with peculiar reference to you, have given me more encouragement. I am
more able to feel that we may confidently commit you and
yours to that most merciful Lord from whom the dispensation has come; and I have been comforted by the reflection, strange comfort as it may seem, that you and all of
us have not long to live; that in truth it signifies little
how we fare here for a few years, provided we are safe in
that long and endless journey upon which we shall soon
enter. I think, however, I have in some degree followed
you in the little mortifications, as well as the great ones, of
this trial. I am not sure that the great and lasting disas-
ter is so galling to my mind at the moment, as some of
the little provoking and humbling attendauts on it. But
since the time I spent in heart with you yesterday I have
been able in some measure to get rid of these intruders, and
to took upon you under the aspect of one beloved of God,

honored of men, and more than ever loved, cherished and delighted in by a large brotherhood. I never felt so keenly as now the privilege of belonging to you, or so conscious of the honor and benefit of such a sister; and I feel no distrust about your future lot. I cannot doubt that years of contentment and happiness await you. I expect that your light will shine forth more brightly than ever. You have ever been a teacher to the whole family, and now I am confidently persuaded you will instruct us with what humility, with what submission, and with what faith, we ought to bear our deepest trials. What comes from above cannot be bad for us; and under the sense of this I adopt David's words, 'Why art thou cast down, oh my soul! and why art thou disquieted within me? Hope thou in God, for I shall yet praise Him.' Ever, my dearest Betsey,

Your most affectionate brother

T. F. Buxton."

From. Mrs. Opie.

" *Twelfth Month*, 17th. (*First-day Morning*) 1828.

"Though I have not hitherto felt free in mind to write to thee, my very dear friend, under thy present most severe trial, thou hast been continually, I may say, in my thoughts, brought feelingly and solemnly before me, both day and night. But I am now desired by thy sister Catherine to tell thee that she will be with thee to-morrow evening. I must also tell thee, to please myself, that two nights ago I had a pleasing, cheering dream of thee!

"I saw thee looking thy best, drest with peculiar care and neatness, and smiling so brightly that I could not help stroking thy cheek and saying, 'Dear friend! it is quite delightful to me to see thee looking thus again, so like the Betsey Fry of former days;' and then I awoke. But this sweet image of thee lives with me still, and I trust that when this dark cloud has passed away from you (as it has passed away from so many, many others) I shall not only see thee in a dream, but in reality, as those who love thee desire to see thee always.

"Since your trials were known I have rarely, if ever, opened a page of Scripture without finding some promise applicable to thee and thine. I do not believe that I was looking for them, but they presented themselves unsought, and gave me comfort and confidence. Do not suppose, dear friend, that I am not fully aware of the peculiar bitterness and suffering which attends this trial, in thy situation, to thy own individual feelings; but then, how precious and how cheering to thee must be the evidence it has called forth of the love and respect of those who are near and dear to thee, and of the public at large! Adversity is indeed the time to try the hearts of our friends, and it must be now, or will be in future, a cordial to thee to remember that thou hast proved how truly and generally thou art beloved and reverenced."

We may add the testimony of Mrs. Corder to the spirit manifested by Elizabeth Fry during this period.

"Whilst this precious servant of God was thus passing through the furnace of adversity, the Compiler of this volume was privileged to belong to the meeting (that of Gracechurch-street) which, when her state of health permitted, Elizabeth Fry constantly attended. The opportunities of public worship, as well as many of a more private character, at which this afflicted handmaid of th. Lord was united in worship with her endeared friends, were often favored with a solemnity of which perhaps no adequate idea could be conveyed in words; and the offerings of prayer as well as, at seasons, of devout thanksgiving which she was enabled to dedicate to her Almighty Sustainer, were accompanied by a heavenly power and unction that cannot even now be remembered without a reverent and affecting sense of that

mercy and Fatherly loving-kindness which thus strengthened her to glorify God in this furnace of affliction. The
sweetness of her disposition and the remarkable wisdom
with which she was endowed shone, in this time of trial,
with increased brightness."

Her daughters observe:

"She had a quality difficult to describe, but marked to
those who knew her well, the power of rapidly, and by a
process of thought which she could herself hardly have explained, arriving at the truth, striking the balance, and finding the just weight of a question; no natural gift could be
of more value under such circumstances.

"Mr. and Mrs. Fry resolved upon at once leaving Plashet
and seeking a temporary home in Mildred's Court, then
the residence of their eldest son. One great mitigation attended this calamity, that the mercantile business, formerly
their grandfather's, and conducted by their father, remained
to the young men of the family who were thus enabled with
the important assistance of their mother's brothers, to re-
establish their parents in comfort. With leaving Plashet
came much that was sad uprooting habits, long-formed
tastes and local associations, parting with servants, and
leaving many old pensioners and dependents.

"Mrs. Fry had, for many years, displayed singular wisdom and economy in her household arrangements, as well
as in her charities and benevolent objects, varying according
to the circumstances in which she had been placed. To 'be
just before generous,' was a maxim often expressed to
those around her. On this occasion these powers were
called into full action.

"As winter advanced her health greatly failed. Circumstances occurred to weaken her husband's and children's
attachment to the Society of Friends. Truly the sorrows

of her heart were enlarged. She exclaims in her journal, (which was very irregularly kept) that her 'soul was bowed down within her, and her eyes were red with weeping.' Yet she was enabled to adopt the language 'I will hope continually and yet praise Thee more and more;' and also to acknowledge that she was much sustained inwardly, and that at times her heart was kept in almost perfect peace. In addition to domestic trials, her tender feelings were at times grievously and unnecessarily wounded; from without, there was much of bitterness infused into her daily cup, which can only be appreciated by those who have had to bear the brunt of a similar calamity." *

"*Plashet, Twelfth Month*, 16th.—I have had some quiet, peaceful hours, but I continue in the low valley, and naturally feel too much leaving this sweet home, but not being well makes my spirits more weak than usual. I desire not only to be resigned, but cheerfully, willing to give up whatever is required of me, and in all things patiently to submit to the will of God, and to estimate my many remaining blessings. I am sorry to find how much I cleave to some earthly things—health, ease, places, possessions. Lord, Thou alone canst enable me to estimate them justly, and to keep them in their right places. In Thine own way, dearest Lord, accomplish Thine own work in me, to Thine own praise! grant that out of weakness I may yet be made strong, and through Thy power wax valiant in fight, and may yet, if consistent with Thy holy will, see of the travail of my soul and be satisfied, as it respects myself and my most tenderly beloved family. Amen!

"*Mildred's Court, First Month*, 19th, 1829.—My first journal in this year! What an eventful one was the last! prosperity and adversity were peculiarly our portion. It has been in no common degree a picture of life comprised in a small compass. However, through all, in prosperity

---

* Memoir Vol. 2, page 95.

and in adversity, however bright, or cloudy my present
position or prospects may be, my desire for myself and all
whom I love is this, so strongly expressed by the Psalmist,
'I will hope continually and will yet praise Thee more and
more!' So be it, saith my soul, and if it be the Lord's
will, may light rise in our present obscurity, and our darkness become as the noonday, both as to temporal and spiritual prospects!"

That she suffered an undue sense of humiliation, from
the failure of her husband and the mortifying incidents attending it, of the nature of which we are not informed, is
shown by a letter from her faithful friend and co-laborer
Mr. Wilberforce, dated one day after the above entry.

"*Highwood Hill, Middlesex, 30th January,* 1829.
"MY DEAR FRIEND:

Though my eyes are just now so indifferent that I must
be extremely sparing in the use of my pen, yet I cannot forbear or delay assuring you, that I do not see how it is possible for any reasonable being to doubt the propriety, (that
is a very inadequate way of speaking—let me rather say
absolute duty,) of your renewing your prison visitations.
A gracious Providence has blessed you with success in your
endeavors to impress a set of miserables whose character
and circumstances might almost have extinguished hope;
and you will return to them, if with diminished pecuniary
powers, yet we may trust, through the mercy and goodness
of our Heavenly Father, with powers of a far higher order
unimpaired, and with the augmented respect and regard of
every sound judgment, not merely of every Christian mind,
for having borne, with becoming dispositions, a far harder
trial, (for such it is,) certainly than any stroke which proceeds immediately from the hand of God. May you continue, my dear madam, to be the honored instrument of
great and rare benefits to almost the most pitiable of your
fellow-creatures.

"Mrs. Wilberforce desires to join with me in saying that we hope we shall again have the pleasure of seeing you, by and by, at this place. Meanwhile, with every kind regard, and friendly remembrances to Mr. Fry, and your family circle, I remain, with cordial esteem and regard,

My dear friend, very sincerely yours,

W. WILBERFORCE."

For our instruction it is well to note that the dark shadow of misfortune was not suddenly or miraculously, lifted from the heart and home of this devoted Christian. When relief came, it came, as we should say naturally—that is by God's regular appointment—through her again entering, after months of painful waiting, upon the active duties of her various callings.

"During that mournful winter in London," write her daughters, "there were periods of peculiar suffering and anxiety. Mrs. Fry's own health being so shaken by her severe mental distresses, as nearly to confine her to her room, with a bad cough. Her beloved son William was on the bed of sickness from oppression of the brain, the result of an overstrained and exhausted mind. Shortly afterwards her daughter-in-law was, in the same house, in an alarming state of illness, and a friend who came to assist in nursing, was taken ill with the measles. The measles in a grown up family becomes a serious disease. They were driven from London in consequence, though too late to escape infection, and took shelter in the vacant house at Plashet, which for many weeks became a scene of anxious nursing. Thence they removed, early in June, to a small but commodious dwelling in Upton Lane, immediately adjoining the

Ham House grounds, the residence of her beloved brother Samuel Gurney, Esq."

"*Mildred's Court, Third Month.*—It appears late to begin the journal of a year; but the constant press of engagements to which I am liable in this place prevent my having time for much writing. We are remaining here with our son and daughter and their children uutil there is some opening for having a settled home. However my desire is that we may in faith and humility entirely bow. I have of late not visited the prisons and been much occupied at home; but I trust that I may be permitted to enter this interesting work again, clothed as with fresh armor, both to defend me and qualify me for fresh service; that my hands may be taught to war, and my fingers to fight; and that, if consistent with the will of my God, I may, through the help of the Captain of my salvation, yet do valiantly.

"*Upton*, 10*th.*—We are now nearly settled in this our new abode; and I may say, although the house and garden are small, it is pleasant and convenient, and I am fully satisfied, and I am thankful for such a home. I have at times been favored to feel great peace, and I may say joy, in the Lord—a sort of seal to the important step taken; though at others the extreme disorder into which things have been brought by all these changes, and the difficulty of making new arrangements has harassed and tried me. But I trust it will please a kind Providence to bless my endeavor to have and keep my house in order. Place is a matter of small importance if that peace which the world cannot give be our portion—even at times—as a brook by the way—to the refreshment of our weary and heavy laden souls. Although a large garden is not now my allotment, I feel pleasure in having even a small one, and my acute relish for the beautiful in nature and art is, on a clear day, almost constantly gratified by a delightful view of Greenwich Hospital and Park, and other parts of Kent, the shipping on the river as well as the cattle in the meadows. So that in

small things and great, spiritual and temporal, I have yet
reason to raise up my Ebenezer, and praise, bless and magnify the name of my Lord.

"*Sixth Month,* 23rd.—I little expected to attend the
Yearly Meeting, having of late appeared to be so much
taken out of such things and such services; but, contrary
to my expectation, way opened for me to attend every sitting, and to take rather an active part in it, to my real consolation, refreshment and help. The unity of Friends was
remarkable. I certainly felt very low at the commencement.
After having, for so many years, received dear friends at
my house, and that with heartfelt pleasure, it tried—not to
say puzzled me, why such a change was permitted me.
But I rest in the weighty import of the words, 'That which
I do thou knowest not now, but thou shalt know hereafter.'"

Can anything exceed the admirable temper and disposition thus exhibited during a great trial. Mitigated indeed
the trial was, in many respects by the ability and generosity
of her friends; and a beautiful picture the whole presents
of a Christian family and society closing round the falling
member, with quick and tender care, and not only breaking
the fall as much as love could do it, but as soon as might
be, again establishing the broken home in peace and comfort, and continuing such aid so long as necessary. The
graceful manner in which this was done may be seen from
the following extracts of letters to Elizabeth Fry from her
brother Joseph John Gurney, both before and after these
events, during which all needful aid was given by her
brothers and some other friends in the most delicate and
hearty manner.

"*Earlham, First Month,* 19th, 1819.
"MY DEAREST BETSEY:
'He that giveth let him do it with simplicity.' In the

desire to fulfil this precept, I may state that I have on the settlement of my accounts, five hundred pounds to spare; and after some consideration, believe it my duty to apply it to the oiling of thy wheels. I therefore put it into Samuel's hands to whom thou mayst apply for the money, as wanted. My intention is that it should be a little stock in hand, to meet thy private and personal exigencies. My condition is that thou wilt not say a word about it to any one. Of course I take no refusal and can admit but very little gratitude."

"*Norwich, First Month,* 19*th,* 1836.

"I have a surplus fund which I think I ought to dispose of at the winding up of the year 1835, and I had been thinking of sending thee a portion of it, to which thou art perfectly welcome. I order Barclay and Co., to pay the draft for the amount. Pray do not allow thyself any compunction or hesitation on this point. I shall always depend on thy being perfectly free in mentioning thy needs to me. In fact it is a kindness, as I do not consider that my circumstances justify much, if any, accumulation.

"In haste thy very affectionate brother

———　　　　J. J. GURNEY."

"P. S.—I shall consider myself very ill-used if thou art ever detected in walking when it is better for thy health thou shouldst ride, or if thou art ever denying thyself any of the comforts of life which are needful for thee."

It is pleasant to add a tribute from this excellent and accomplished man, to his sister's worth, and her rare personal qualities, found in his journal, bearing date about the time we have now reached in her history.

"*Ninth Month,* 17*th.* (1828).—The time which has passed since I last wrote has been fraught with lively interests. My dear sister Fry's satisfactory and comforting visit, from fourth to seventh day last, was perhaps the principal. I never saw her, that I remember, in a more favored condition, and she was the means of raising me considerably in the scale of spiritual feeling, wherein I am so very apt to find a low place. Greatly gifted she assuredly is, both by nature and grace, and is enabled to exercise a gentle and unseen, yet powerful influence over all about her. She was present at our large and highly favored Monthly Meeting, last fifth-day, and was memorably engaged amongst us as a daughter of consolation."

"*Eighth Month*, 29*th*, 1829.—Our wedding-day! twenty-nine years since we were married! My texts for the morning are applicable:—'Our light affliction, which is but for a moment worketh for us a far more exceeding and eternal weight of glory.'—'We walk by faith, not by sight.' As far as we can judge from external appearances, mine has not been a common life. He who seeth in secret only knows the unutterable depths and sorrows I have had to pass through, as well as, at other times, I may almost say, joys 'inexpressible and full of glory.' I have now had so many disappointments in life that my hopes, which have so long lived strong that I should see much brighter days in it, begin a little to subside, and my desire is more entirely to look beyond the world for that which can alone satisfy me; and not to have my heart so much set upon the things of this life; or even on those persons nearest me; but more set upon the life to come, and upon Him who is faithful and will be *all in all* to His dependent ones. At the same time I desire faithfully to perform all my relative duties; and may my heart be kept in tender love to all near me.

"*Upton, Tenth Month*, 21*st*.—Something has occurred which has brought me into conflict of mind; how far to restrain young persons in their pleasures, and how far to leave them at liberty. The longer I live the more difficult do I see education to be; more particularly as it respects the religious restraints that we put upon our children. To do enough and not too much is a most delicate and important point. I begin seriously to doubt whether as it respects the peculiar scruples of Friends, it is not better quite to leave sober-minded young persons to judge for themselves. Then the question arises, When does this age arrive? I have such a fear that in so much mixing religion with those things which are not delectable we may turn them from the thing itself. I see, feel, and know that where these scruples are adopted from principle they bring a blessing with them; but where they are only adopted out of conformity to the views of others I have very serious doubts whether they are not a stumbling-block.

"On First-day we were rather suddenly summoned to Plashet House to attend Anna Golder (aunt to my faithful Chrissy) who had charge of the house. She was one of the lowly, retired, humble walkers before the Lord; she was suddenly taken very ill, and died in half an hour after her niece got there. It was apparently a departure without sting to mind or body; as far, therefore, as it respected her, all was peace. But to myself it was different. I arrived there after dark, drove once more to the dear old place,— no one to meet me but the poor man who lived in the house, no dog to bark, nor any life, nor sound, as used to be. Death seemed over the place, such was the silence—until I found myself upstairs in the large and once cheerful and full house. When I entered the bed-room there lay the corpse. Circumstances combined to touch some very tender feelings, and the inclination of my heart was to bow down upon my knees before the Lord, thankful, surely, for the release of the valued departed—but deeply and affectingly impressed with such a change!—that once lively, cheerful home left desolate—the abode of death—and two or three watchers. It brought, as my visits to Plashet often have done, the hymn to my mind,—

'Lord, why is this? I trembling cried!'

Then again I find I can do nothing but bow, trust, and depend upon that Power that has, I believe, thus seen meet to visit us in judgment, as well as in mercy.

"31st.—Since I last wrote I have been called to another death-bed scene; our old and valued Roman Catholic friends, the Pitchfords, have lost their eldest son, a sweet, good boy. I felt drawn in love, I trust I may say Christian love, to be much with them during their trial; I felt it right to leave my family and spend First-day evening with them, when all hope of the child's life was given up. I had not only to sympathize with them in their deep sorrow, but to pour forth my prayer in their behalf. The next day I was with the poor child when he died, and was nearly the whole day devoted to them. We had a deeply interesting time after his death—my dear friends themselves, all their children, their mother, sister and old nurse. My mouth was remarkably opened in prayer and praises, indeed all day at their house something of a holy influence appeared to be over us: a fresh, living proof that what God has cleansed we are not to call or feel common or unclean. It surely matters not by what name we call ourselves, or what outward *means* we may think right to use, if our hearts are but influenced by the love of Christ, and cleansed by His baptism, and strengthened by His spirit to prove our faith by love and good works. With ceremonies, or without ceremonies, if there be but an establishment upon the Rock of Ages, all will be well. Although I am of opinion the more our religion is pure, simple, and devoid of these outward forms, the better and safer for us, at the same time I do earnestly desire a more full union amongst all Christians, less judging one another, and a general acknowledgement in heart, judgment, and word of the universality of the love of God in Christ Jesus our Lord."

"Amidst Elizabeth Fry's numerous avocations, she found time to select a passage of Scripture for every day in the year. She endeavored to combine in it that which is 'profitable for doctrine, for reproof, for correction, for instruction in righteousness ;' and in a little preface she urged the importance of so seeking to appropriate the truths contained in it, with a heart uplifted, that the blessed Spirit might apply the word; and concludes, 'The rapid and ceaseless passing away of the days and weeks, as well as the months of the year, as numbered at the head of each day's text, it is hoped may prove a memento of the speed with which time is hastening on, and remind the reader of the importance of passing it as a preparation for eternity, in the service of God and for the benefit of mankind.' As soon as her little work was finished and printed she began its distribution; many thousands of copies did she give away, being amply supplied from the stores of affluence, with the right means of dispersing them. Great numbers were otherwise circulated. Where have not these little Text-books penetrated, from the monarch's gilded hall to the felon's dungeon?"

Among the numerous instances of their usefulness which came to light the following is related.

"Two or three years after their publication a text-book bound in red leather, which she had given to a little grandson, fell out of his pocket at the Lynn Mart, where he had gone to visit the lions. He was a very little boy, and much disconcerted at the loss of his book for his name was in it, and it was 'the gift of his grandmother' written by herself. The transaction was almost forgotten, when, nearly a year afterwards, Richard Coxe, the clergyman of Watlington, a parish about eight miles from Lynn, gave the following history of the lost book. He had been sent for to the wife of a man living on a wild common, on the outskirts of his parish, a notorious character, between poacher and rat-catcher. The message was brought to the clergyman by the medical man who attended her, and who, after describing her as being most strangely altered, added 'you will find the lion become a lamb,'—and so it proved. She who had been wild and rough, whose language had been violent and her conduct untamed, lay on a bed of exceeding suffering, humble, patient, and resigned..

"Her child had picked up the text-book and carried it home as lawful spoil. Curiosity, or some feeling put into her heart by Him without whom a sparrow falleth not to the ground, had induced her to read it; the word had been blessed to her and her understanding opened to receive the gospel of truth. She could not describe the process, but the results were there. Sin had in her sight become hateful; blasphemy was no longer heard from her lips. She drew from under her pillow her 'precious book,' her 'dear little book,' which had been the means of leading her soul to Him who 'taketh away sin.' She soon afterwards died in peace and joyful hope."

In 1830 Mrs. Fry paid a religious visit to parts of Suffolk and Norfolk and attended the Quarterly Meeting at Ipswich. In·the fall of the same year she went to Sussex to attend the Quarterly Meeting there, and some of its particular Meetings. The Yearly Meeting is thus described:

"*Sixth Month, 7th.*—I had a difficult path to tread during the Yearly Meeting. I did not of course receive Friends, but went, as I was kindly asked to various houses. I could not but at times naturally feel it, after having for so many years, delighted to entertain my friends and those whom I believe to be disciples of Christ; and now, in considerable degree, to be deprived of it. But after relating my sorrows I must say that through the tender mercy of my God I have many blessings, and what is more, at times such a sweet feeling of peace that I am enabled to hope and trust that through the unbounded and unmerited mercy of God in Christ Jesus, my husband, my children, and myself will eventually be made partakers of that salvation which comes by Christ. The state of our Society as it appeared in the Yearly Meeting, was satisfactory, and really very comforting to me; so much less stress laid upon little things, more upon matters of great importance; so much unity, good-will, and what I felt, *Christian* liberty amongst us—love appeared truly to abound, to my real refreshment. I am certainly a thorough Friend, and have inexpressible unity with the principle, but I also see room for real improvement amongst us; may it take place; I want to see less love of money, less judging others, less tattling, less dependence upon external appearance. I want to see more fruit of the Spirit in all things, more devotion of heart, more spirit of prayer, more real cultivation of mind, more enlargement of heart towards all; more tenderness towards delinquents, and above all, more of the rest, peace and liberty of the children of God!

Among the frequent testimonials received during this period was a letter accompanied by an elaborately embroidered counterpane.

"*Liverpool, Sixth Month,* 23rd, 1830.

"The Ladies Committee who visit the House of Correction at Yorkdale, near Liverpool, beg Elizabeth Fry's acceptance of a counterpane worked by the female prisoners, and trimmed with a fringe of their own making. This memorial of a class of her unhappy fellow-creatures so eminently benefited and tenderly felt for by Elizabeth Fry, will, the Committee believe, be peculiarly grateful to her, as well as being a proof of their own affectionate regard.

"Signed on behalf of the Committee by,
REBECCA CHARLEY. *Secretary.*"

From Hamburg she received an application that a copy of her likeness might be engraved for an Almanac published by Beyerink, entitled, "For that which is Beautiful and

Good." The Almanac, when published contained this passage:

"1830.—Though faithful to her duty as a wife and mother, into the night of the prison Elizabeth Fry brings the radiance of love—brings comfort to the sufferers, dries the tear of repentance, and causes a ray of hope to descend into the heart of the sinner. She teaches her that has strayed again to find the path of virtue, comes as an angel of God unto the abode of crime, and preserves for Jesus' kingdom that which appeared to be lost. Is not this indeed what may be called loving our neighbor more than one's self?"

In September of this year she made a brief religious visit in Sussex county.

From Brighton she addressed a letter to Queen Adelaide expressing her "desire that, for the good of the community, she might promote the education of the poor, the general distribution of the Scriptures, and the keeping of the Sabbath seriously, by discouraging parties &c., &c., on that day amongst the higher ranks, as the tendency of them was very injurious to the lower classes, and to the community at large."

At this fashionable resort several of the higher classes were invited to attend the mid-week meeting, which is thus described:

"To my own feelings, a remarkable time we surely had. It appeared as if we were overshadowed by the love and mercy of God our Saviour. The ministry flowed in beautiful harmony. I deeply felt the want of vocal prayer being offered, but I did not see it my place upon our Meeting assembling together, when, to my inexpressible relief, a friend powerfully and beautifully offered up thanksgiving and prayer, which appeared to rise as incense and as an acceptable sacrifice. After a time of silence I rose with this text: 'There are diversities of gifts, but the same spirit; differences of administration, but the same Lord; diversities of operations, but it is the same God who worketh all in all.' In a way that it never did before the subject opened to my view whilst speaking. How did I see and endeavor to express the lively bond of union existing in the Christian church, and that the humbling, tendering influence of the love and power of Christ must lead us not to condemn our neighbors but to love all. I had to end the Meeting by praying for the King, Queen and all their subjects everywhere; for the advancement of that day when the knowledge of God and His glory would cover the earth, as the waters cover the sea; for those countries in Europe that are in a disturbed state, and that these shakings might eventually be for good. After a most solemn feeling of union the Meeting broke up."

In the spring of 1831 this most industrious and faithful messenger of love made a visit to the Quarterly Meeting of Kent. She writes—

"I was much engaged, from Meeting to Meeting; labored to encourage the low, the poor and the sorrowful, to lead to practical religion, and to shake from all outward dependencies, and to show that our principles and testimonies of a peculiar nature should not be maintained simply as a regulation amongst us, but unto the Lord, and in deep humility, in the true Christian spirit; particularly as to tithes, war, &c. I felt much peace afterwards, and in going from house to house, breaking, I trust, a little bread, spiritually, and giving thanks. It appeared *very* seasonable, though long delayed, as I have had it on my mind many months, but hitherto have been prevented by various things; yet this appeared to be the right time; and I take the lesson home, quietly to wait for the openings of Providence, particularly in all religious services, and not to attempt to plan them too much myself.

"The kindness of Friends was great, and I received much *real* encouragement from them; some from the humble ones that did my heart good. Indeed I cannot but acknowledge, in humiliation of spirit, however any may reason on these things, and however strange that women should be sent out to preach the gospel, yet I have, in these services, partaken of joy and peace that I think I never felt, in the same degree, in any other."

"*Fifth Month*, 14th, (1831).—About three weeks ago I paid a very satisfactory visit to the Duchess of Kent and her very pleasing daughter, the Princess Victoria. William Allen went with me. We took some books on the subject of slavery, with the hope of influencing the young Princess in that important cause. We were received with much kindness and cordiality, and I felt my way open to express not only my desire that the best blessing might rest upon them, but that the young Princess might follow the example of our blessed Lord, that as she 'grew in stature she might grow in favor with God and man.' I also ventured to remind her of King Josiah who began to reign at eight years old, and did that which was right in the sight of the Lord, turning neither to the right hand nor to the left— which seemed to be well received. Since that I thought it right to send the Duke of Gloucester my brother Joseph's work on the Sabbath, and a rather serious letter, and had a very valuable answer from him, full of feeling. I have an invitation to visit the Duchess of Gloucester next Fourthday; may good result to them, and no harm to myself; but I feel these openings rather a weighty responsibility, and desire to be faithful, not forward. I had long felt an inclination to see the young Princess and to endeavor to throw a little weight in the right scale, seeing the very important place that she is likely to fill. I was much pleased with her, and think her a sweet, lovely and hopeful child," (then 12 years of age.)

"*Sixth Month, 3rd.*—The Yearly Meeting has concluded this week. I was highly comforted by the good spirit manifested in it by numbers. I think I never was so much satisfied with the ground taken by Friends, leading us to maintain what we consider our testimonies upon a Scriptural and Christian ground, rather than because our forefathers maintained them. My opinion is that nothing is so likely to cause our Society to remain a living and spiritual body as its being willing *to stand open to improvement;* because it is to be supposed that as the Church generally emerges out of the dark state it was brought into, its light will shine brighter and brighter, and we, as a part of it, shall partake of this dispensation. My belief is that neither individuals, nor collective bodies should *stand still* in grace, but their light should shine brighter unto perfect day."

During this season she held some meetings among the lower classes around Barking and Dagenham, some ten miles east of London—where she spent the summer.

"*Eighth Month, 1st.*—Last evening we finished our Public Meetings in barns. I passed a humbling night. Even in our acts of obedience and devotion how evident is the mixture of infirmity, (at least so it appears to me,) and we need to look to the great offering for sin and iniquity to bear even these transactions for us. I apprehend that all would not understand me, but many who are much engaged in what we call works of righteousness will understand the reason that in the Jewish dispensation there was an offering made 'for the iniquity of their holy things.' Humiliation is my portion, though I may also say peace, in thus having given up to a service much against my inclination; and I hope thankfulness for the measure of power at times granted in them.

"*Dagenham, Eighth Month,* 24*th.*—Upon my return home to Dagenham this day week, in the pony chair, with little Edmund Gurney, there was a severe thunder-storm the greater part of the way, but I felt quite easy to persevere through it. But when I arrived at the Chequers Inn I thought another storm was coming and went in. We had been there but a few minutes when we saw a bright flash of lightning, followed instantaneously by a tremendous clap of thunder. Upon being asked if I was alarmed I said that I certainly was, and did not doubt that an accident had happened near to us. My dear husband who was out in the tempest arrived safely, but in a few minutes a young man was carried in dead, struck by the lightning in a field close at hand. I felt our escape—yet still more the awful situation of the young man, who was a sad character; he had been at our meeting at Beacontree Heath. This awful event produced a very serious effect in the neighborhood; so much so that we believed it right to invite all the relations of the young man, (a bad set,) and the other young men of the neighborhood to meet us in the little Methodist Meeting House which ended in one more rather large Public Meeting. The event and circumstances altogether made it very solemn: it appeared to set a seal to what had passed before, in our other meetings. My belief is they have had a stirring effect in this neighborhood, but they have been very humbling to me; the whole event of this young man's awful death has much confirmed me in the belief that our concern was a right one, and tended to prepare the minds of the people to profit by such a lesson. My dear brother and sister Buxton and their Pricilla were with us at many of our Meetings.

"27*th.*—We are just about leaving this place. I have endeavored to promote the moral and religious good of the people since the Meetings by establishing libraries of tracts and books at different places, and my belief is that my humble labors have not been in vain, nor I trust will they be.

I have felt so strikingly the manner in which the kindness and love of the neighborhood has been shown to me, after thus publicly preaching amongst them; and as a poor frail woman, advocating boldly the cause of Christ, I expected rather to be despised; whereas, it is apparently just the reverse,—the clergyman and his wife almost loading us with kindness, the farmers and their wives very kind and attentive, the poor the same. I felt how sweet it is to be on good terms with them all—one day drinking tea at the parsonage, abounding with plate, elegancies and luxuries, the next day at a humble Methodist shoemaker's, they having procured a little fresh butter, that I might take tea under their roof. The contrast was great, but I can indeed see the same kind Lord over all, rich to all, and filling the hearts of His servants of very different descriptions with love to each other."

Elizabeth Fry's character, and the effects of her ministry are beautifully illustrated in the following extract from her journal while at home in Upton Lane.

"*Twelfth Month*, 20*th*.—I am once more favored, after being far from well, with a renewal of health and power to enter my usual engagements, public and private. Yesterday I went to town,—first attended the Newgate Committee, then the British Society, which was encouraging to me. There were many present of different denominations of Christians, and a sweet feeling of love and unity pervaded the whole. Elizabeth Dudley spoke in a lively manner, and I had to pray. There is still much ground for encouragement in the prison cause; I believe a seed is sown in it that *will* grow and flourish, I trust when some of us are laid low. It is a work that brings with it a peculiar feeling of blessing and peace; may the Most High continue to prosper it! Afterwards I went to Clapham to visit a poor, dying, converted Jew who had sent a letter to beg me to go and see him. My visit was highly interesting. I often wish for the pen of a ready writer and the pencil of an artist to picture some of the scenes that I am brought into. A man of pleasing countenance, greatly emaciated, lying on a little white bed, all clean and in order, his Bible by his side, and animated, almost beyond description, at seeing me. He kissed my hand, the tears came into his eyes, his poor face flushed, and he was ready almost to raise himself out of his bed. I sat down and tried to quiet him, and by degrees succeeded. We had a very interesting conversation. He had been in the practice of frequently attending my readings at Newgate, apparently with great attention. Latterly I had not seen him, and was ready to suppose that, like many others, his zeal was of short duration; but I had lately heard that he had been ill. He is one of those Jews who have felt perfectly liberated from keeping any part of the Law of Moses, which some other converted Jews yet consider themselves bound to observe. I found, when he used to come so often to Newgate that he was a man of good moral character, seeking the truth. But to go on with my story. In our conversation he said that he felt great peace, no fear of death, and a full reliance upon his Saviour for salvation. He said that his visits to Newgate had been to him beyond going to any church—indeed I little knew how much was going on in his heart. He requested me to read a Psalm that I had read one day in Newgate, the 107th. This I did and he appeared deeply to feel it, particularly as my dear friends and I made our little remarks in Christian freedom as we went along, truly, I believe, in the life. The poor Jew prayed very strikingly; I followed him and returned thanks. What a solemn, uniting time it was. The poor Jew said 'God is a Spirit and they that worship Him, must worship in spirit and in truth,' as if he felt the spirituality of the Christian administration. His countenance lightened with apparent joy when he expressed his undoubted belief that he should soon enter

the Kingdom, and that I should, before long, follow him.
Then he gave me his blessing and took leave in much tenderness, showing every mark he could of gratitude and
love. He did not accept any gift of money, saying that he
wanted no good thing, as he was most kindly provided for
by serious persons in the neighborhood. After about two
weeks I received an account of the peaceful end of this
poor Jew.

"*First Month*, 2nd, 1832.—I think I have seldom entered
a year with more feeling of weight than this. As the clock
was striking twelve, the last year closing and this beginning, I found myself on my knees by my bedside, looking
up to Him who had carried me and mine through the last
year, and could only really be our Helper in this. We have
had the subject of marriage much before us this last year;
it has brought us to some test of our feelings and principles respecting it. That it is highly desirable and important to have young persons settle in marriage, particularly
young men, I cannot doubt; and that it is one of the most
likely means of their preservation, religiously, morally and
temporally. Moreover it is highly desirable to settle with
one of the same religious views, habits and education as
themselves; more particularly for those who have been
brought up as Friends, because their mode of education is
peculiar. But if any young persons, upon arriving at an
age of discretion, do not feel themselves really attached to
our peculiar views and habits, then I think their parents
have no right to use undue influence with them, as to the
connexions they may incline to form; provided they be with
persons of religious lives and conversation. I am of opinion that parents are apt to exercise too much authority upon
the subject of marriage, and that there would be more really
happy unions, if young persons were left more to their own
feelings and discretion. Marriage is too much treated like
a business concern, and love, that essential ingredient, too
little respected in it. I disapprove the rule of our Society

that disowns persons for allowing a child to marry one not
a Friend—it is a most undue and unchristian restraint, as
far as I can judge of it."

The regulations of the Society in respect to marriages
have been greatly modified since that time.

In 1832 Mrs. Fry together with her sister-in-law of the
same name visited the Half-Year's Meeting in Wales, and
some places in Ireland, with the usual happy reusults.

In the autumn of this year a son and also a daughter
were married—both out of the Society—which left the little
band at Upton Lane much reduced. Soon afterward with
her husband and two remaining daughters she visited her
sister Mrs. Cunningham at Lowestoft. The latter lady,
wife of an able and pious clergyman, gave a long account of
this visit, from which I cannot forbear making a few extracts showing the wonderful charm and power of Elizabeth Fry's personality on all who could appreciate spiritual
beauty.

" *November, 22nd.*—We had the treat and great advantage of a visit from our dearest sister. She was encouraged
to come and assist us in the formation of our District Society which in this large place we find to be essential for the
right working of the parish. We are most thankful for the
assistance of our dear sister, (our brother and two of our
nieces accompanied her) it is almost like having an angel
visitor, so full of loveliness and grace is she. On Sunday
my dearest sister being at Pakefield with the Friends induced my remaining all day there. She drank tea with me
at the Hawtreys. Mr. Hawtrey and she had some animated
and delightful conversation before we went down to the
lecture in the school-room; dearest Betsey accompanied us,
and some of the other friends joined us. After the usual
singing and prayer Mr. Hawtrey read very impressively

the latter part of the third of Ephesians; we then had silence, after which she arose and beautifully addressed the meeting on the necessity of domestic and private religion, and enlarged a good deal on the duty, spirit and manner in which scripture should be read and studied; it would not do to hear it only in public service. After the powerful outward means which had been granted to the people of Pakefield how were they called upon to examine and digest for themselves the written *word* of God. Then in a full and beautiful prayer she seemed to bring the blessing of Heaven upon us. I hardly know any scriptural treat so great as uniting with her in *prayer!* it is such a heavenly song—so spiritual, so elevating, enjoying glimpses, as it were, of the eternal world. Oh! may we long retain the power and the blessing of it!

"On Monday we were all in movement, in preparation for our District Society Meeting; this was held at our house and well attended. Our dear sister displayed much of her tact and power, and gave us the *greatest* assistance. How marvelously gifted she is! Through her influence all parties were brought together, and the District Society begun under the most favorable auspices; the town was divided and every arrangement made according to her advice. Our meeting was highly satisfactory and promised the most favorable results; every one seemed willing to yield to her wisdom and eloquence. What a power of communicating good she possesses! what a faithful steward in that which is committed to her!

"Surely these times do leave a peculiar savor which is not to be forgotten; it adds to the precious seasons which are foretastes of Heaven. Her mind appears to me in more lively exercise and more gifted than ever; rich both in grace and gifts. She is indeed beloved of the Lord, and dwells in safety by Him. . . Nothing can be more benevolent and beautiful than her spirit, overflowing with love and tenderness."

Leaving this sister, they visited the old home at Earlham, and went thence to North Repps Hall, the home of her brother-in-law, Thomas Fowell Buxton, who was now in the midst of his great struggle for the emancipation of slaves in the British Colonies. Her warm interest and sympathy in his heroic efforts were a timely encouragement as he was confronting the influence of a selfish Government in the House of Commons, supported without by the stirring eloquence of Wilberforce, to effect what has honored England more than any other national act.

In 1833 Mrs. Fry spent several months at a quiet retreat in the island of Jersey, with her family, in order to rest and recruit her health. She enjoyed the retirement as only those can do who have accomplished their appointed tasks. But idleness was not rest to a spirit like hers. The hand and heart did not forget their congenial employment. It was her meat and drink to do the will of Him that sent her. When the happy party went out for a picnic, or to spend the day amongst the secluded and romantic bays of the island, "the tract bag was not forgotten—whilst the rest of the party were sketching or walking, she would visit the cottagers, and, making herself as well understood as their antique Norman dialect permitted, would give her little French books and offer the kind word of sympathy or exhortation." At first she held meetings in private houses with poor accommodations, but at length a room was fitted up in the town and large congregations assembled, including many of the gentry and principal inhabitants. "Philanthropic objects also presented themselves to her notice, especially the state of the Hospital, including the Workhouse and Lunatic Asylum, and the Prison."

"*Eighth Month*, 12th.—We feel much at home in this lovely island, and in rather a remarkable manner our way opens in the hearts of those amongst whom we are residing. A very extensive field of service appears before us, in many ways. To try thoroughly to attend to the prisoners, to strive to correct the evils in the Hospital, to assist in various ways the Friends and those who attend Meeting, to visit several in Christian love and try to draw them nearer together—oh! gracious Lord, grant Thy poor unworthy servant the help of Thy Spirit, to do Thy will, and let not her labor be in vain in Thee, her Lord and her God! but through Thy unmerited mercy in Christ Jesus grant that her way may be made *very* clear before her, and ability given her to walk in it to Thy praise, her own peace, and the real edification of those among whom her lot may be cast. Amen!

"*Jersey, Ninth Month*, 10th.—I have much enjoyed and valued the pleasant retreat we have here. I desire, in deep gratitude, to acknowledge the renewed capacity to delight in the wonderful works of God. The scenery, and feeling fully at liberty to spend part of many days in the enjoyment of this beautiful country and weather, and my beloved husband and children, has been very sweet to me! What has not religion been to me? How wonderful in its operation? None but Him who knows the heart can tell. Surely it has brought me into some deep humiliations; but how has it raised me up, healed my at times wounded spirit, given me power to enjoy my blessings, in what I believe an unusual degree, and wonderfully sustained me under deep tribulations! To me it is anything but bondage, since it has brought me into a delightful freedom; although I had narrow places to pass through before my boundaries were thus enlarged; so that from experience I wish to be very tender over those still in bonds."

In the spring of 1834 she made a brief religious visit in

Dorset and Hants, accompanied by two of her nieces, one of whom, the daughter of Sir Fowell Buxton, made the following statements, illustrative of Elizabeth Fry's character and methods of doing good.

"There was no weakness or trouble of mind or body which might not safely be unveiled to her. Whatever various or opposite views, feelings or wishes might be confided to her, all came out again, tinged with her own loving, hopeful spirit. Bitterness of every kind died when entrusted to her; it never re-appeared. The most favorable construction possible was always put upon every transaction. No doubt her failing lay this way; but did it not give her and her example a wonderful influence? Was it not the very secret of her power with the wretched and degraded prisoners? She always could see hope for every one; she invariably found, or made, some point of light. The most abandoned must have felt that she did not despair for them, either for this world, or another, and this it was that made her irresistible.

"At Southampton time and opportunity were rather unexpectedly afforded for an excursion to the Isle of Wight. I think she undertook it chiefly for the sake of pleasing Priscilla Gurney and myself; but it had important consequences. We traveled round by Shanklin, Bonchurch and Undercliff. She was zealous in the enjoyment of the scenery and the wild flowers; but the next day, on reaching Freshwater, she was fatigued and remained to rest, whilst we went to see Alum Bay. On our return we were told she had walked out, and we soon received a message desiring us to join her at the Coast Guard Station. We found her in her element, pleased and giving pleasure to a large group who were assembled around her. She entered with the greatest sympathy into their somewhat dreary position, inquired into their resources for education for their children, and religious improvement for themselves—found them

much in want of books; and from this visit originated that
great undertaking of providing libraries for all the Coast
Guard Stations in Great Britain—an undertaking full of
difficulties, but in which her perseverance never relaxed till
it was accomplished."

This is perhaps a suitable place to mention the work of
Christian philanthropy above referred to, which consisted
in furnishing the five hundred Coast Guard Stations of
Great Britain with libraries of suitable reading for the men
and their families. That such a task required, not only
great labor and perseverance, but a large outlay of personal
influence for its successful accomplishment, is obvious.
The results are concisely stated in the Report of the Committee acting under the sanction of the Government for
carrying out the object. It is as follows:—

"The Committee acting under the sanction of His Majesty's Government for furnishing the Coast Guard of the
United Kingdom with libraries of religious and instructive
books and also with school books for the families of the
men employed in that service, having, by the blessing of
Divine Providence completed that object, it becomes their
pleasing duty to lay before the subscribers a Report of their
proceedings.

"In the commencement of this duty it is proper gratefully to acknowledge that the idea of furnishing these libraries first suggested itself to the benevolent mind of Mrs.
Fry, whose active and charitable exertions, on all occasions
affecting the benefit of mankind, are too well known and too
highly estimated to need further remark on the present occasion, and who, having previously succeeded in inducing
His Majesty's Government to establish libraries for the use
of the patients in the naval hospitals, was induced by the
observations she had made on the subject, to endeavor to

extend the same beneficial measure to the Coast Guard Service, and after several unsuccessful efforts arising from the expense which it would occasion, a sum of 500 pounds was obtained in 1835, from the First Lord of the Treasury (Sir Robert Peel) for this purpose, which munificent donation has since been followed by subscriptions from charitable individuals, and grants from several book societies, but as the whole of these funds were not sufficient to meet the object in view, the present Chancellor of the Exchequer (Mr. Spring Rice) kindly granted two further sums amounting together to 460 pounds to effect its completion.

"The means thus so liberally afforded have enabled the committee to provide and forward to the coast,—

498 libraries for Stations on shore, containing		25,896	vols
74	Ditto	Districts	12,880	"
48	Ditto	Cruisers	1,867	"
School books for the children of crews of Stations		6,464	"
Pamphlets, Tracts, &c.,		5,357	in nos

Making a total of   52,464 vols.

and thereby to furnish a body of deserving and useful men and their wives and families, (amounting to upwards of 21,000 persons,) with the means of moral and religious instruction, as well as profitable amusement, most of whom, from their situation in life, have not the means of procuring such benefits from their own resources, and who in many instances, are so far removed from places of public worship and schools as to prevent the possibility of themselves or their families deriving advantage from either."

Mrs. Fry's only note on the journey last referred to is as follows :—

"*Upton, Fourth Month.*—At Portsmouth we paid an interesting visit to Hasler Hospital, the Hulks Hospital Ship, and some prisons; we also paid a delightful little visit to the Isle of Wight. I felt more able to enjoy the great beauties of nature, from having been owned by my Lord and Master in my religious services. What a relish does true religion give for our temporal as well as spiritual blessings! I have still much to feel respecting the offer of marriage made to my dear L———. It is a very serious thing, my children thus leaving Friends; and I have my great fears that in so doing they are leaving that which would be a blessing and preservation to them. At the same time I see there is no respect of persons with God; nor in reality is there the difference some would make out of the different administrations of religion, if there be but a true, sincere love of our Lord, and endeavor to serve Him. What is above all to me I have felt peace in it rather peculiarly: still we at present are exceedingly feeling the weight of the affairs. It is also a considerable pain to me to go through the discipline of the Society respecting it—but in bearing it patiently and humbly I may in that way be enabled to preach Christ. Lord, be it so—Help me Thyself through all these rather intricate paths, and make a way for Thy servant in all these things; that she may do right in Thy sight, and not offend even the weakest of her brethren and sisters in religious connection with herself—help, Lord, or we perish!

"21st.—Yesterday (First-day) I attended Meeting rather oppressed in body and mind. Ministered to by dear Elizabeth Dudley, but had such heaviness of body as to hinder spiritual revival. In the afternoon I went, accompanied by Elizabeth Dudley, Rebecca Sturges, and some others, to visit the female convict ship; the sun shone brightly, the day delightful, the poor women rejoiced to see us, but my spirit was in heaviness from the difficulty of leaving my family, even for a few hours on that day. It was a fine sight to see about one hundred and fifty poor female convicts, and some sailors, standing, sitting and leaning round us, whilst

we read the Scriptures to them. I spoke to them and Elizabeth Dudley prayed. Surely to witness the solemn effect,
the tears rolling down many cheeks, we must acknowledge
it to be the Lord's doing. Still I fell flat, though the others
thought it a very satisfactory time; but in the evening I
became more revived, and comforted, and thankful that it
has pleased the Lord to send me to the poor outcasts, although at times feeling as if I went more as a machine
moved by springs, than in the lively state I desire; but at
other times it is different, and there is much sense of life,
light, love and power. To-day I expect to go to the Duchess of Gloucester, and amongst some of the high in this life.
May the Lord be with me that my intercourse with these
may not be in vain in Him. I feel it no light responsibility
having the door so open with the Government of our country, and those filling high places; I am often surprised to
find how much so; and yet the Lord only knows the depth
of my humiliations, and how it has been out of the depths
that I have been raised up for these services. At the Ad-
miralty I have lately had important requests granted; at
the Home Office they are always ready to attend to what I
ask; and at the Colonial Office I expect that they will soon
make some alterations in the arrangements for the female
convicts in New South Wales.

"Who has thus turned the hearts of those in authority?
Surely it is the Lord. May He grant me wisdom and sound
discretion rightly to use the influence He has given me.
Be near to Thy servant, this day, gracious Lord, in every
place; and so help her by Thy Spirit that she may do Thy
will, and not bow to man, *but alone to Thee her God;* doing
all to Thy glory. We made several other calls and dined at
my Brother Buxton's where we met some gentlemen. I
felt, as I mostly do after such days, fearful and anxious,
lest I had done any discredit to the vocation wherewith I
am called; or in any degree, in my own heart or conduct towards God, done amiss. It caused me rather a watchful

fearful night. I see it much easier, and in many respects safer, in the religious life to be quiet, and much at home; yet I also feel that in a more general association there are great advantages—enlarging our spiritual borders and removing our prejudices; and if we are really enabled to stand our ground as Christians, in the meekness of wisdom, and so adorn the doctrine of God our Saviour it may be the means of promoting the good of others.

"24th.—We dined at Lord Bexley's and met Captain Mangles the great traveler, several clergyman, and others. I desired to maintain the watch, but the company of serious, intellectual and refined persons is apt to draw me a good deal forth in conversation and mind, and often leads me to many fears afterwards, lest there should imperceptibly be anything of showing off, and being exalted by man; but I may truly say, inwardly I mostly feel reduced and humbled after such times, and fearful lest I should have a cloud over me so as to hinder my near communion with my Lord.

"A few words in the Proverbs rather encouraged me: 'Reproofs of instruction are the way of life.' I see it well to be reproved; may I profit by it. I often fear for myself lest I am forsaking my first love, or becoming lax, because I certainly feel far more liberty than I used to do in uniting with others in their prayers, grace, &c., &c., and less in bonds generally: in short my borders are greatly enlarged. May this arise not from my love becoming cold, but from experiencing the service of my Lord to be already to me perfect freedom. Oh dearest Lord! make manifest in Thy own light, if this be in me laxity, that I may be reproved, and amend my ways; if, on the contrary, it be the liberty wherewith Thou hast made me free, cause me in Thine own power firmly and fixedly to stand in it, even if some of my fellow-mortals whom I love and esteem appear to remain under a different dispensation.

"A few days ago I visited Plashet: it was almost too much for my natural spirits. When I saw our weedy walks that once were made and kept so neatly—our summer-houses falling down—our beautiful wild flowers that I had cultivated with so much care, and no one to admire them—the place that had cost us so much, and been at times so enjoyed by us, the birth-place of so many of my children, the scene of so many deep and near interests—the tears trickled down my face, and I felt ready to enumerate my sorrows and say, 'Why is this?' But I felt the check within and desired and endeavored to look on the bright side of the picture, and acknowledge the tender and unmerited mercy of my God in Christ Jesus. Mine has been, I fully believe, a very unusual course in many particulars; in some things known, in some hidden from the eye of man. Oh! may all end in good and blessing.*

"*Fifth Month, 5th.*—Yesterday was the Sabbath. I can hardly say how deeply I feel these days as they come: first as it respects the ministry of the Word. Its wholly resting on two or three women in our rather large assembly is an exercise of my faith, and a real trial to my natural feelings. Then to believe, as I do, that some of our congregations are in an unregenerate state; how must their silent meetings be passed?—and for the babes in Christ I have great fears, inasmuch as true, solemn, silent worship is a very high administration of spiritual worship. I frequently fear for such that more external aid is wanted, though I see not how it is to be given. I also feel the want of each one openly uniting in some external act of worship; for there is much in taking an absolute part in what is doing,

---

* I might here state that I have recently been informed by one well acquainted with all the circumstances, that the loss of their property is believed to have been blessed to Joseph Fry, who after several years of separation from the Society of Friends was again united in fellowship with them, to the great satisfaction of his most patient and loving wife, who could thus finally see the hand of her Lord in subduing the natural growth of vine, that the better fruits of the spirit might be brought forth.

to feel a full interest in it; but I see not with our views (in which I unite) how this can be remedied. Then for myself as a minister of the Gospel I desire to be very faithful, and give the portion of meat in due season to the household; but even here deep humiliation is my portion, in its appearing that though I preach to others I cannot manage my own; my children, one after another, leaving a Society and principles that I love, value, and try to build up. My Lord only knows the exercise of my spirit on those days. Then for my home hours: not having space as we had at Plashet, in which my boys can recreate in the way I consider advisable during a part of this day, now I have anxiously to watch where they go, and what they are about, so that I am not often favored to know the Sabbath a delight, or day of rest. Yet through all these things, and my too anxious nature help is wonderfully granted to me: I find the spring within that helps, keeps, revives, sustains, and heals; but I feel that I am bound to seek and to pray not to be so exquisitely anxious."

The above is a very suggestive passage, showing the gradual expansion of a broad and liberal mind, under the influence of free association with other enlightened minds, toward the perfect freedom which we have in Christ to adapt our principles and practices to the existing wants of society. It is a very great pity that the Society of Friends so utterly failed to recognize this practical law of expediency, though it is abundantly illustrated in the Bible and elsewhere as God's method of education and government for a progressive state. The effects of this narrowness of conception in matters of doctrine, and its contrast with a spirit which was becoming more and more catholic through enlarged sympathy and acquaintance with humanity, are further exhibited in the next entry of this richly instructive

Journal; and yet it will be seen from its last sentence that she was herself but just emerging from the entangling traditions of a puritanical age. To an enlightened mind at the present time it seems an absurdity that a Christian should be excommunicated for marrying a person of a somewhat different persuasion.

"*Sixth Month*, 10*th.*—Since I last wrote I have got through the Yearly Meeting, which I attended nearly throughout. There appeared to be much more love and unity than last year; still it is a shaking time, and some of the Leaders of our Tribes think they differ in some points of doctrine *; but I believe it is more in word than in reality; and as they love the Lord Jesus, if they have wandered a little they will be brought back. I was a good deal engaged, having to take a quiet view, neither on one side nor the other, but seeing the good of both. But I have a very great fear of ever being too forward, a thing I very much dislike and disapprove. May my Lord preserve me from it.

"I was favored to get well through the British Society Meeting, and could but return thanks that our Holy Head had so blessed this work.—With respect to my dear L——'s engagement of marriage I have apprehended that the hand of the Lord is in it; and oh! saith my soul, may it prove so. The pain of her leaving our Society, and the steps attending it have begun, to the wounding of my spirit; for though I do not set much value on outward membership in any visible church, yet it has its pains, at times great pains, to me, and I am ready to say in my heart, How is it? When I have one after another of my family thus brought before our Meeting, it has its trials and humiliations. It would be to me a pleasanter, and I think a more satisfac-

* This was a wave from the conflict which caused the division of Friends in America, in 1827-8.

tory thing, if the discipline of our Society had not so much of the inquisitorial in it, and did not interfere in some things that I believe no religious body has a right to take a part in; it leads I think to undesirable results. Though I approve persons being disowned for marrying out of our Society, I had rather the act of marriage in itself forfeited membership."

"*Upton, Seventh Month 25th.*—To-morrow I expect to set off on a journey to Scotland. I have taken an affecting leave of my family, praying that we might again (if the will of God) be refreshed together; and my way was satisfactorily opened to go.

"*By Loch Fay, Eighth Month, 9th, First-day.*—Not having a Meeting to go to, and not believing it right for me to attend any other place of worship, I desire to spend a time in solemn searching of heart before the Lord; and may I be enabled to hold communion with Him in spirit. On the morning of the 1st, the day appointed for the liberation of all the slaves in the British dominions, (August 1st, 1834) and on which my dear niece, Priscilla Buxton was to be married, I poured forth my soul in deep supplication before my Heavenly Father, on behalf of the poor slaves, that a quiet spirit might be granted them—that their *spiritual* bonds might also be broken—that the liberty prepared for the children of God might be their portion. I also prayed for my beloved niece and her companion in life, that the Lord would be with them, keep them, and bless them.

"*Edinburgh, Eighth Month, 28th.*—I left my dearest husband and two daughters in the Highlands, as I wished to accompany my boy on his way to England, and above all to attend the Meetings, see the Friends and visit the prisons here." . . .

Of her engagements at Edinburgh she writes :

"I had much to be thankful for in the help granted to

me in such religious services as I believe I was called into, in Meetings, families, and Institutions. I had very solemn religious times in the Gaol and large Refuge, also shorter ones in the Bridewell and another Refuge. The hearts of many appeared to be peculiarly opened to me, and entire strangers wonderfully ministered to my wants and upheld my hands, particularly the Mackenzie family. Our dear friends who knew me before were abundantly kind to me. May the Lord in His love and mercy, reward them for their great kindness to me, His very unworthy servant, and may He still soften and enlarge their hearts towards me until the work that He gives me to do amongst them be accomplished. I find a field for much important service for the poor, and to make more arrangements, for the ladies who visit the prisons. I desire and earnestly pray to be preserved from an over-active spirit in these things; and on the other hand faithfully, diligently, humbly and watchfully, to do whatever my Lord gives me to do that may be to His glory, or the good of my fellow-creatures.

"We have passed through a very lovely country; but the sun has not shone much upon us, and the atmosphere of my mind has partaken of the same hue, which is not so pleasant as more lively coloring of the mind, but I am ready to think more profitable, and perhaps more likely to qualify me for the weighty duties before me."

"From Loch Katrine the party passed to Balloch, and Luss, and thence to Inverary and Loch Awe, from whence Mrs. Fry returned to Edinburgh, her time and energies being devoted to the completion of those objects begun on a former visit.

"But whilst many institutions of great importance, owe their existence, either directly, or indirectly, to her skill and exertions—and she sowed the seed of many a noble tree—she did not omit the smallest opportunities of benefiting others that are presented in the occurrences of each passing hour. It was her unvarying practice, both at private dwellings and at the inns where they passed their First-days, to invite the servants to attend the evening Scripture readings; many of the visitors who like themselves were only sojourners for a short time, also joined them on these solemn and interesting occasions. Hers was a constant endeavor to leave some savor of good on all with whom she had any communication. The chambermaid and the waiter received the word of kindness and counsel, and a little tract, or text-book to impress it upon their memories. The postillion at the carriage window, and the cotter at the roadside, met with appropriate notice, and this mingled with the most unaffected enjoyment of the country and spirit in all the incidents of traveling.

"The results of her observations on the state of the Scotch prisons she forwarded to the proper authorities after her return."*

During the year 1835 she accompanied her husband to the South of England, calling at the Coast Guard Stations, Hospitals, etc., made a brief visit to the Isle of Wight, and to Guernsey, thence to Weymouth, Plymouth and Falmouth, where she arranged to have the packets continually sailing from the latter port supplied with Bibles, Testaments, tracts, &c. She returned by way of North Devon, and Amesbury where she paused long enough to arrange for the establishment of a library for the use of the Shepherds of Salisbury Plain. All these movements were successful in the objects aimed at, and resulted in no small amount of good to the poor who were thus provided with means of improvement.

* Memoir Vol. 2, page 210.

During a visit to Sussex and Kent, in March 1836, occurred the following incident.

"At Hastings several of the Coast Guard men and officers were at the Meeting. I had many proofs of the use and value of the libraries sent them to my comfort and satisfaction, proving it not to have been labor 'in vain in the Lord.' Real kindness, almost affection, as well as gratitude was shown to me by several of the men and officers and their families. We hope a Bible Society will be formed at Rye in consequence of our visit, and a Prison Society at Dover. But to come to one of the most interesting parts of our expedition, we went to Sheerness to visit the women and children in the ship in ordinary. Captain Kennedy had them collected at my request; it was a fine sight, in a large man-of-war, instead of bloodshed and fightings to see many naval officers, two chaplains, sailors, soldiers, ladies, numbers of women and children, all met to hear what two Quakers had to say, more particularly a woman, and to listen to any advice given by them. We examined the children as to their knowledge, then gave them advice, afterwards we addressed their parents, and lastly those present generally—we were received with great cordiality by Captain Kennedy, and his wife."

In April and May of the same year she spent a month in Ireland. The description of the setting out and the return has a touching personal interest, and perhaps illustrates the power of prayer.

"*Fourth Month*, 14*th.*—Just about leaving home for Ireland—oh dearest Lord! bless, I entreat Thee, this act of faith, to my family, myself, and those amongst whom I go, and be, I most humbly pray Thee, my Keeper, and their Keeper; my Helper, and their Helper; my Strength, and their Strength; my Joy and Peace, and their Joy and Peace,

Amen! Grant this for Thine own name's sake, O most gracious Lord God! cause also that we may again meet in love, joy, peace and safety.

"*Upton Lane, Fifth Month*, 13*th*.—I returned home safely, yesterday afternoon. I think I never had so happy and so prosperous an arrival. I wept with joy: the stream appears to be turned for awhile: my tears have often flowed for sorrow, and now my beloved husband and children have caused them to flow for joy. I found not only all going on well, and having done so in my absence, but, to please, comfort and surprise me, my dearest husband had had my rooms altered and made most comfortable, and my children had sent me nice presents to make them more complete. Their offerings of love quite gladdened my heart, though far too good for me; I felt utterly unworthy of them; I may say peculiarly so. I have seldom returned home more sensible of the hidden evils of my heart. Circumstances have unusually made me feel this. I fully believe in this going out much help has been granted me in various ways. My understanding has appeared to be enlightened more fully to see and comprehend gospel truth, and power has been given me to utter it boldly, beyond what I could have supposed."

Referring to the above, Mrs. Corder remarks: "The preceding extract depicts what was, under all circumstances, the striking characteristic of this remarkable woman—her deep humility and low estimate of herself. She who was continually devoting every energy of mind and body to promote the happiness of the human family, and whose self-sacrificing love assumed a concentrated form of tenderest attachment towards each member of her own immediate circle, calling forth, in every hour of need, the most assiduous exertions in their service, is yet found to be so acutely affected by tokens of kind attention from her husband and children—

tokens which might naturally be expected by every affectionate wife and mother—that the tears of grateful joy are shed, and *her heart is gladdened* by offerings of love which *she feels herself 'utterly unworthy' to receive.* This incident portrays her mind in lines more vividly defined than pen can describe."

"*Sixth Month,* 18*th.*—I have felt a good deal pressed in spirit during these last few days. The day before yesterday I counted twenty-nine persons who came here on various accounts, principally to see me. There are times when the tide of life is almost overpowering. It makes me doubtful as to our remaining much longer in this place which from its situation brings so many here. I have several things which rather weightily press me just now. I desire to lay my case before the Lord, trusting in Him, and casting myself and my whole care upon Him. Dearest Lord, help: supply all our needs through Thy riches of grace in Christ Jesus! Amen."

July 27th she set out for another visit to the islands of Jersey and Guernsey, to further the work previously inaugurated and minister the Gospel to such as were in need. She felt constrained to remain until her task was completed, notwithstanding that one of her sisters, the wife of Samuel Hoare, was at the time rapidly approaching her end. She finished her public work in time to attend at the bedside of her dying sister. She had gone on this mission under a sense of duty notwithstanding her sister's low state. She writes:

"I had the inexpressible comfort of being permitted a few days with her, and she evidently liked my company. I particularly observed how gently I was dealt with, by her reviving after I arrived, so that I had not the bitterness of seeing her at once sinking. The affliction was thus mitigated to me; I was enabled to show her some marks of my deep and true love, and to be with and earnestly pray for her in the hour of death. I was helped to be some comfort to many of her family, and (utterly unworthy as I know I am of it) I believe in my various ministrations I was enabled to prove the power of the Spirit to qualify for his own work; and amongst them all, particularly with my dear nephew who has just entered the 'Church,' deeply to impress the necessity of the work of the Spirit being carried on in the heart, and of having Christian charity towards others of every denomination. My beloved sister Hoare's death has made a deep impression on me. I do not like to enter life or its cares, or to see many, or to be seen. I like to withdraw from the world and to be very quiet."

Soon after this her husband and one of their daughters met with serious injuries in France, by the falling of their carriage over a precipice twelve feet in perpendicular height. The father was severely shocked and the daughter barely escaped with her life. While watching this daughter, accounts came from another daughter who, with her little boy and his nurse, was sick with scarlet fever. All these recovered; but about three months later, a beloved and amiable sister-in-law, Lady Harriet Gurney, wife of her brother Daniel, died very suddenly, leaving a family of eight young children. On the day of the funeral she writes:

"What a scene of unutterable sorrow at Runcton, where a few days ago all was, in no common degree, joy, peace and great prosperity. Oh! what occasions are these where families meet together for the affecting and solemn purpose

of committing the remains of a beloved one to the silent
grave. May the Lord Himself lift up the light of His countenance upon them and bless them, and keep them in a
sound mind and sound faith. Be pleased, O gracious
Lord! to help, pity, and comfort these afflicted ones this
day."

"*Sixth Month*, (1837)—The King died last Third-day,
the 20th. Our young Queen was proclaimed yesterday.
My prayers have arisen for her that our Heavenly Father
would pour forth His Spirit upon her, guide her by His
counsel, and grant her that wisdom which is from above. I
have received a long letter from the Duchess of —— giving
a very interesting account of her, and the death of the late
King.

"*Seventh Month*, 20*th*.—I returned home yesterday evening from Lowestoft, after having accompanied my brother
Joseph to Liverpool on his way to America. Our time at
Earlham was very interesting; I believe I was helpful to my
brother in a large Meeting that he held to take leave of the
citizens of Norwich. It was a highly interesting occasion
and I trust edifying to many. I am very sorry to say that
my mind has too much the habit of anxiety and fearfulness.
I believe this little journey would have been much more useful to me, but from an almost constant cloud over me, from
the fear of being wanted by some of my family. I think it
would be better for myself and for them, if they did not
always cling so closely round my heart so as to become too
much a weight upon me.

"My beloved brother's taking leave of Earlham and the
family there, [his wife was deceased] was very affecting;
still there was peace in it, and joy in the Lord, inasmuch as
there is delight in doing what we believe to be His will.
We went from Earlham to Runcton; there we dined. Shall
I ever dine with my three brothers again? The Lord only
knows—my heart was tendered in being with them."

This parting visit to her brother was concluded at Liverpool, and is thus graphically described:

"We made all things comfortable for him; I attended to the books, and that a proper library should go out for the crew, passengers and steerage passengers. However occupied or interested, I desire never to forget anything that may be of service to others. We had a delightful morning with Joseph, but the tears often rose to my eyes; still I desire to be thankful more than sorrowful, that I have a brother so fitted for his Lord's service, and willing to give up all for His name's sake.

"That evening again we had an interesting religious time in prayer. The next morning there was a solemn calm over us—the day of parting was come. After breakfast we all assembled, with some of our friends. We read the 4th of Philippians, our spirits were much bowed and broken, but the chapter encouraged us to stand fast in the Lord, to help one another in Christ—even the women who labored in the gospel—and to be careful for nothing, for that the Lord would supply all our need.

"Soon afterwards we went to the ship. I saw the library arranged, with some others to help me; then devoted myself to my beloved brother, put sweet flowers in his cabin which was made most comfortable for him. It was announced that the ship was going—we assembled in the ladies cabin—I believe all wept. William Forster said the language had powerfully impressed him—'I will be with you always, even to the end of the world;' therefore we might trust our beloved ones to Him who had promised. I then knelt down with these words—'Now, Lord, what wait we for, our hope is in Thee,' and entirely committed him and his companions in the ship to the most holy and powerful keeping of Israel's Shepherd; that even the voyage might be blessed to him and to others. In short our souls

were poured forth before and unto the Lord in deep prayer
and supplication. Joseph almost sobbed; still a solemn
quiet and peace reigned over us. I believe the Lord was
with us and owned us at this solemn time. We left the
ship and walked by the side of the Pier, until they were
towed out; then we went away and wept bitterly—but not
the tears of deep sorrow; far from it; how different from
the grief for sin, or even disease, or the perplexities of life.'

Soon after this Mrs. Fry proposed a plan for securing
more intercourse on religious subjects with her children,
who had, in different ways, and by various means, been
brought to acknowledge their Saviour's claims—thus affording an answer to her motherly travail and prayers, though
not in the manner of her own choosing. She thus speaks
of it immediately before the experiment was tried.

"*Ninth Month*, 2*nd*, 1837.—I have for many months
past deeply felt the wish for more religious intercourse with
my children, and more uniting with them upon important
and interesting subjects. I have turned it in my mind
again and again, and at last have proposed making the experiment, and meeting this evening, first to consider different subjects of usefulness in charities, and then to close
with serious reading, and such religious communication as
way may open for.

"Thou, Lord, only knowest the depth of my desire for
the everlasting welfare of my children. If it be Thy holy
and blessed will, grant that we may be truly united to
Thee, as members of thy Militant Church on earth, and
spiritually united amongst ourselves, as members of one
body, each filling his different office faithfully unto Thee.
Grant that this little effort may be blessed to promote this
end, and cause that in making it we may experience the

sweet influence of Thy love shed abroad in each of our hearts, to our real help, comfort, edification and unity."

The proposal was made as follows:

" *Upton Lane, Eighth Month,* 15*th,* 1837.

"MY DEAREST CHILDREN,

Many of you know that for some time I have felt and expressed the want of our social intercourse at times leading to religious union and communion amongst us. It has pleased the Almighty to permit that by far the larger number of you no longer walk with me in my religious course. Except very occasionally, we do not meet together for the solemn purpose of worship, and upon some other points we do not see eye to eye; and whilst I feel deeply sensible that notwithstanding this diversity we are truly united in our Holy Head, there are times when, in my declining years I seriously feel the loss of not having more of the spiritual help and encouragement of those I have brought up, and truly sought to nurture in the Lord. This has led me to many serious considerations how the case may, under present circumstances, be in any way met.

"My conclusion is that believing as we do in one Lord as our Saviour, one Holy Spirit as our Sanctifier, and one God and Father of us all, our points of union are surely strong; and if we are members of one living Church, and expect to be such forever, we may profitably unite in some religious engagements here below.

"The world and the things of it occupy us too much and they are rapidly passing away; it would be well if we occasionally set apart a time for unitedly attending to the things of Eternity. I therefore propose that we try the following plan; if it answer, continue it; if not, by no means feel bound to it.—That our party, in the first instance, should consist of no others than our children, and such grandchildren as may be old enough to attend. That our object in meeting be for the strengthening of our faith, for our advancement in a devoted, religious, and holy life, and for the promotion of Christian love and fellowship.

"That we read the Scriptures unitedly, in an easy, familiar manner, each being at perfect liberty to make any remark or ask any question; that it should be a time of religious instruction by seeking to understand the mind of the Lord, for doctrine and practice in searching the Scriptures, and bringing ourselves and our deeds to the light, that it may be made manifest if they are wrought in God. That either before or after the Scriptures are read, we should consider how far we are really engaged for the good of our fellow-men, and what, as far as we can judge, most conduces to this object. All the members of this little community are advised to communicate anything they may have found useful or interesting in religious books, and to bring forward anything that is doing for the good of mankind in the world generally.

"I hope that thus meeting together may stimulate the family to more devotion of heart to the service of their God, at home and abroad, to mind their different callings, however varied, and to be active in helping others. It is proposed that this meeting should take place once a month, at each house in rotation.

"I have now drawn some little outline of what I desire, and if any of you like to unite with me in making the experiment it would be very gratifying to me; still I hope that all will feel at liberty to do as they think best themselves.

I am indeed your nearly attached mother,

ELIZABETH FRY."

In refe nce to this proposal and its results the daughters state, in her Memoir, that "The plan was tried and found to answer exceedingly well. Some of the collateral branches of the family afterwards joined these little reunions: they proved occasions of stimulus in 'every good word and work.' Some important good has resulted from the combined exertions consequent upon them, and they continue to this day under the name of 'philanthropic evenings;' and they are always concluded by a Scripture reading, and occasionally by prayer." Thus do her works follow her.

CHAPTER NINTH.

In 1838 Elizabeth Fry began the remarkable series of visits to the Continent of Europe which rendered her name almost as familiar there as it was in England. The subject is thus briefly opened in her Journal:

"*Twelfth Month, 20th.*—I have laid before my Monthly Meeting my prospect of visiting France, and obtained the concurrence of Friends. Oh! for help, daily, hourly,—and may a sound mind, love and power be granted to me and to others, to our own peace and the glory of God.

"*Upton Lane, First Month, 6th,* 1838.—I yesterday returned from a visit to Norfolk. Before going there I laid my concern to go to France before our large Quarterly Meeting, and had the very great encouragement of such a flow of unity as I have seldom heard expressed on any occasion.

"*24th.*—I expect to leave home to-morrow for France. My spirit has been very much brought down before the Lord; some causes of anxiety have arisen; still in this my going out love abounds in no common degree, and a portion of soul-sustaining peace underneath. These words comforted me this morning, 2 Timothy, i. 12: 'I know whom I have believed, and am persuaded that He is able to keep that which I have committed unto Him against that day.' I therefore, in this my going out commit myself and my all to my most blessed and holy Keeper, even to the Lord God of my salvation, my only hope of real help and defence, and of eternal glory."

She was accompanied in this journey by her husband, their friend Josiah Forster, and Lydia Irving. In keeping with the plan I have in view I shall give only the most important incidents of these journeys, leaving those who wish a more detailed account to find it in the fuller memorials from which these selections are made.

The travelers found but little to do in Bologne, but visited the prison, convent and hospital and then went directly to Paris where "comfortable and commodious apartments were prepared for them at the Hotel de Castile by the kind attentions of M. Francois Delessert. They arrived there very tired and very cold on the 30th of January. The morning of the 31st was opened with solemn united prayer, offered for wisdom from on High to direct, and strength to perform, whatever might be called for at their hands. Then came a visit from Madame Delessert, two notes from Lord Granville, the English Ambassador at Paris, a call at the Embassy, and in the evening the company of M. de Pressensé, the Secretary of the Bible Society, with his wife.

"*Feb.* 1st, they attended a small Friends' Meeting held in the Faubourg du Roule, and afterwards called on La Baronne Pelet de la Lozere. In her Elizabeth Fry found a friend and sister in Christ. They then paid a visit to Count Montalivet, Minister of the Interior, by whom they were most kindly received and promised all needful admissions to the different prisons."

A summary of her engagements in Paris is given in a letter to her children written from St. Germains.

" *Third Month*, 5th, 1838.

"We arrived here last evening after quitting the most deeply interesting field of service I think I was ever engaged in. My first feeling is peace and true thankfulness for the extraordinary help granted to us; my next feeling an earnest desire to communicate to you, my most tenderly beloved children, and others nearest to me, the sense I have of the kindness, and goodness, and mercy, of my Heavenly Father who has dealt so bountifully with me, that it may lead all to serve Him fully, love Him more, and follow more simply the guidance of the Spirit.

"I mean now to tell you a little of my reflections upon this important period, the last month in Paris. I was at first very poorly, very low, and saw little opening for religious usefulness, though some for charity and benevolent objects. Soon my health revived and we had full occupation in visiting prisons and other institutions, and saw many influential persons. This opened a door in various ways for close communication with a deeply interesting variety of both philanthropic and religious people, and thus introduced into a more intimate acquaintance with the state of general society. Religiously, we find some, indeed we may say a great many, who appear much broken off from the bonds of Roman Catholic superstition; but with it, I fear have been ready to give up religion itself, though feeling the need of it for themselves and others. To these I think we have been helpful by upholding religion in its simplicity and most strongly expressing our sense of the necessity of it, and that nothing can alter or improve the moral character, or bring real peace, but true Christian principles. To this we have very faithfully borne testimony, and most strongly encouraged all to promote a more free circulation of the Scriptures, particularly the New Testament, and a more diligent reading of the Bible in institutions and families. I have in private circles introduced (frequently by describing what poor criminals wanted in prisons) the simple truths of the Gospel, illustrated sometimes by interesting facts respecting the conversion of these poor woman prisoners; and have been thus enabled in numerous parties to show the *broad*, *clear*, and *simple* way of salvation, through our Lord and Saviour for *all*. It has been striking to me in our dinner visits, some of them splendid occasions, how curiously way has opened, without the least formality, or even difficulty, in conversation, to ' speak the truth in love' —especially one day as to how far balls and theatres were Christian and right; the way in which Roman Catholic priests appeared to hinder the spread of the Gospel; the importance of circulating good books (this has been a very common subject) and above all the New Testament. At our Ambassador's, Lord Granville's several were in tears during the conversation. I think our dinner visits have been an important part of our service, so much has been done by these communications after and at them. In many instances numbers have joined us in the evening, particularly the youth. With these it has pleased my Heavenly Father to give me some influence. Last First-day evening I had a very large party of them to a reading, which appears to have given much satisfaction. It has been a most curious opening with persons of many nations. Many have lately flocked to our little meetings. I wonder how I could feel easy to go away from such a field of service, but I did, and therefore went. On Third-day went to the King and Queen, and therefore could not attend our little week day Meeting: they said eighty persons came to it who went away. I have found unusual help at these times to speak the truth with power; my belief is that there are many unsettled and seeking minds in this country.

" We have had much intercourse with the Minister of Instruction, and he gives me leave to send him a large number of books from England to be translated into French. My full belief is that many Testaments and valuable books will circulate in consequence of our visit.

"The efforts made to form a Ladies Society to visit the prisons of France, and particularly Paris, (whether they succeed or not) have been important. First, by my taking many ladies to visit the great Female Prison of St. Lazare and there reading, or having read, small portions of Scripture, and my few words through an interpreter producing (far beyond what I could have expected) such a wonderful effect upon these poor sinners. The glad tidings of the Gospel appeared to touch their hearts; many wept exceedingly, and it was a fresh and striking proof of the power of truth, when simply told. In the next place the large number of ladies that have met at our house upon the subject has afforded so remarkable an opportunity to express to them my views of salvation by Christ alone, of the unity that should exist among Christians, and must do so, if sanctified by the Spirit; and deeply to impress the simplicity and spirituality of true religion. I think something important in the prison cause will eventually come of it, but it will take time.

"We have had very large parties of English and Americans, and some French, at the houses of the Methodist minister, the American minister, and at another serious person's. Also we joined the French Wesleyan Methodists in their chapel, and had a precious meeting with them. Of the highly evangelical Episcopalians and Independents, we had large parties at different houses. In all these we have had solemn religious service. The Episcopalians have been brought into very close union with us. In our own house we have had two large parties of a philanthropic and religious nature, attended by many. Lady Olivia Sparrow has often been quite a comfort to me; and many others I may say have proved true helpers—French and Americans, and more than these—the Chargé d'Affaires of the Hanse Towns and his wife, also Russians and Swiss. The Greek Ambassador Coletti came to me for advice on some points in the state of Greece, in which I believe I shall be enabled to

assist him. A Captain B—— thinks of having my sister
Hoare's 'Hints for the Laboring Classes' translated for
the parents of the children who attend the schools upon
the mountains in India. We have also seen many of the
medical students, English and American, and are anxious
to have some efforts made for their moral and religious
good, in Paris where so many come.

"Our visit to the King and Queen was interesting; but
alas! what, in reality is rank? The King I think in person
like the late Lord Torrington, the Queen a very agreeable
and even interesting woman. I expressed my religious
interest and concern for them, which was well received, and
we had much conversation with the Queen and the Princess
Adelaide before the King came into the room. We strongly
expressed to the Queen our desire to have the Sabbath better kept, and the Scriptures more read. She is a sweet-
minded, merciful woman. There were present Madame
Adelaide, the King's sister, one of the young Princesses,
the Marchioness of D——, principal Lady of Honor to the
Queen.

"We then proceeded to the Duchess of Orleans; there
we had a delightful visit, and the sweetest religious communication with her, and other interesting conversation.
We found her an uncommon person; my belief is that she
is a very valuable young woman.

"The Queen appeared much pleased with my Text-book;
and the Princess Adelaide said she should keep it in her
pocket and read it daily. Indeed no books have given the
same pleasure as the Text-books, both in French and English. I think we have given many hundreds of them, and
next in number my sister Louisa's books on Education;
they delight the people; also a great many of Joseph's letters to Dr. A——, of which we have a beautiful edition in
French, and his Sabbath; of these we expect to give many
hundreds; and one or two other tracts on Christian Duties,
and the offices of the Holy Spirit. Our various books and

tracts have had a very open reception, but we have been very careful when, where, and what to give; although in some of the newspapers it was stated that I distributed controversial tracts, which is not true.

"I began in my letter to say what a variety we have seen, but I did not say what interesting and delightful persons we have met with; amongst the Protestants particularly some first rate ladies who have been as sisters to me, so abundant in kindness and love. One has truly reminded me of my sister Rachel in her person, her mind, and her excessive care over me; she has felt me I believe like her own. We have indeed increased our dear and near friends by this visit, much as it was in Jersey and Guernsey, only in far greater numbers. I think nothing could be more seasonable than our visit, as it respected the prisons; and I believe the influence of our advice has been very decided, with many persons of consideration. The schools we have also attended to, and I have encouraged a more Scriptural education; some schools of great consequence, kept by serious Protestants in a district of Paris, want much help. There are seven hundred children, and we hear that the Head of the Police in that neighborhood says the people generally are improved in consequence.

"The want of the language I have now and then much felt, but not very often, so many speak English well, and many understand it who cannot speak it. Also I blunder out a little French.

"The entreaties for us to stop longer in Paris have been very great, but my inclination draws homeward; I am a very great friend to not stopping too long in a place. And as I believed I saw a little light on our departure, we thought it best to leave all for the present, if we even have, before many months more, to return for a short time. We have been a united and often a cheerful little party. At times I have carried a great weight, never hardly having my home party out of mind for long together, however full and occupied.   At other times our business has been so great as almost to overwhelm us—callers almost innumerable, and most of them on important business, and out and in almost constantly ourselves, so that I have sometimes felt as if I could not long bear it, particularly when I could not obtain some rest in the afternoon.   Through all I must say He who I believe put me forth has, from season to season, restored my soul and body and helped me from hour to hour.   This day week I sat down upon my chair and wept; but I was soon helped and revived.   I long for every child, brother, sister, and all near to me, to be sensible how very near my Holy Helper has been to me; and yet I have exceedingly and deeply felt my utter unworthiness and short-coming, and that all is from the fulness and freeness of unmerited mercy and love in Christ Jesus.   I can hardly express the very near love I have felt for you all.   My prayers very often have arisen for you; and if any labor I have been engaged in has been accepted *through the Beloved*, may you, my most tenderly beloved ones partake of the blessing attendant upon it.   My dearest husband has been a true helper; and Josiah Foster and Lydia Irving, very kind and useful companions.

"I forgot to say, I think the few friends in Paris have been greatly comforted and stimulated by our visit.

"I end my account by saying what I trust is true, 'The Lord is my Shepherd, I shall not want.'   We are now quietly at St. Germains.   We hear most interesting accounts of the state of Normandy, and have many letters of introduction to the places where we propose to go: if not wanted home I shall be glad to go there.   We propose going to Rouen to-morrow.

I am your most devotedly attached

ELIZABETH FRY."

The remainder of the account is from the pen of her daughters.

"At Rouen they were much interested by meeting with a respectable woman in humble life who had lived nurse fifteen years in a gentleman's family, a Roman Catholic, but his wife a Protestant. There she had been so much impressed by religious truth, (though still a Roman Catholic herself) that she felt it her duty where she resided to circulate the Scriptures and religious tracts. Her master told them it was surprising the great influence she had obtained in the neighborhood. Mrs. Fry supplied her with six Testaments and a Bible, from the Bible Society Depot. From the same society she obtained a number of copies for the school in the prison, where the Testament was habitually read but the supply was very inadequate. This school was under the care of the Abbé Gossier, M. Du Harnel, and other religious gentlemen who themselves daily instructed the young prisoners.

" At Caen they found some excellent and devoted Methodists amongst the French, and learned that through the efforts of one young English lady, (an orphan residing in a gentleman's family as governess,) many copies of the Scriptures had been purchased; and at the shop of a Roman Catholic more than a hundred of de Lacy's Testaments sold since the beginning of the year.

"The prison of Beaulieu, near Caen, was visited by them with much satisfaction; nearly a thousand prisoners were confined there. They found it admirably regulated and a serious Roman Catholic clergyman devoted to the good of those under his care. He gladly welcomed the gift of fifty Testaments.

" At Havre the Ladies' Bible Society had sold during the former year, four hundred and twenty-six Testaments, and thirty-three Bibles, and had given fifty Testaments to soldiers who were in the habit of reading them every evening to their comrades in the barracks.

" At Bologne they made arrangements for the sale of the Holy Scriptures, and took a lively interest in the District

Society, thence crossed to Dover, and on the following day Mrs. Fry had the comfort of finding herself again with her family at home.

"The effect on her mind of this, her first introduction to France, was very powerful. She was greatly attracted by the life and facility of the French character. In a letter she speaks of them as 'such a nation—such a numerous people—filling such a place in the world—and Satan appearing in no common degree to be seeking to destroy them; first by infidelity and so-called philosophy; secondly, by superstition, and the priesthood rising with fresh power; thirdly, by an extreme love of the world and its pleasures; fourthly by an unsettled, restless and warlike spirit : yet under all this a hidden power of good at work amongst them, many very extraordinary Christian characters, bright, sober, zealous Catholics and Protestants ; education increasing; the Holy Scriptures more read and valued; a general stirring to improve the prisons of France—the Government making fresh regulations for that purpose—but great fear of the priests prevailing, from the palace downwards; and they, alas! resisting all good wherever or however it may arise."

The Journal continues:

"*Upton Lane, Fourth Month*, 27*th*.—Yesterday was the largest British Society meeting I ever remember, partly collected to hear my account of our French journey; there must have been some hundreds of ladies present, many of them of rank. In the desire not to say too much perhaps I said too little upon some points. Although I do not feel condemned, yet I am ready to think if I had watched and prayed more I should have done better. My prayers have arisen that, however imperfectly or unworthily sown the seed scattered yesterday may be so prospered by His own free power, life and grace that it may bear a full crop to His praise!"

"20th.—To-morrow I am fifty-eight, an advanced period of what I apprehend to be not a very common pilgrimage. I now very earnestly desire and pray that my Lord may guide me continually, cause me to know more of the day of His power, that I may have my will wholly subjected to His will. What He would have me to do that may I do, where He would have me to go, there may I go—what He may call me to suffer for His name's sake may I be willing to suffer. Further may He keep me from all false fears and imaginations, and ever preserve me from putting my hand to any work not called for by Him, even if my fellow-creatures press me into it; as I think some are disposed to do about America. Be pleased to grant these my desires and prayers for Thine own Holy and Blessed name's sake."

In reference to what called forth the above prayer her daughters remark: "There was a subject at this time weighing heavily upon the mind of Elizabeth Fry which she turned again and again before she dare dismiss it; and then it was more that other calls of duty appeared immediately required of her, than that she deliberately abandoned the idea. Her brother Joseph John Gurney was pursuing his labors in America as a minister of the Gospel; and she doubted whether it might not be her duty to cross the Atlantic, in order to join him for a time in his visits in the United States, and to accompany him to the West Indies. There were those who thought she ought to go;* but on

---

* This was urged from the belief that her remarkable power as a peace maker might aid in closing the breach which had recently occurred in the Society of Friends in America. But some who were acquainted with the case were convinced that the effort would have been unavailing, partly from the extent and intensity of the discord, and partly from the failure of British Friends fully to understand all the

the other hand she knew how entirely it would be against, not only the wishes, but the judgment of her own family. She had learned to trust very little to the opinions of any of her fellow-mortals, and these conflicting views only served to bring her in deeper dependence and more entire self-resignation, to the footstool of her great Master to learn His will, that she might fulfil it. Whilst she pondered these things a strong conviction arose in her heart that there was a present duty for her to fulfil—once more to visit Friends and their Meetings in North Britain, again to inspect the prisons there, and to communicate with the magistrates and men in authority, whilst the Bill was still pending which had been brought before the House the preceding Session of Parliament, to improve prisons and prison discipline in Scotland."

This expedition occupied something more than a month and resulted in much benefit to the cause of Prison Reform, her recommendations being received with great consideration by the authorities, and often speedily put into practice. The following passage exhibits her method of dealing with difficult points, and shows the discriminating character of her mind.

"Mrs. Fry was at this time extremely anxious as to the extent to which Prison Discipline was carried in Scotland. She greatly feared the enforcement of solitary confinement, and felt it her duty to make a sort of appeal against its possible abuses.

---

causes of the division, which embraced not merely points of doctrine but the principles of liberty in religious association. One party stood for Orthodoxy in doctrine, the other for the right of Christians to differ in opinion, and each was on too strong ground to be easily convinced.

"She had therefore invited this large number of influential gentlemen whose attention had been given to the subject—magistrates, lawyers, members of the Prison Discipline Society, and others, to meet her on this occasion (at the Royal Hotel Edinburgh,)—an appalling audience, as they sat all round, to the number of fifty. She gently engaged in conversation with some who were seated at the most distant part of the room, and by degrees fell into an account of her experience, and a full exposition of her mind on the subject.

"As an abstract principle she doubted the right of man to place a fellow-creature under circumstances of such misery, if his offences were not of a very heinous or aggravated nature. She could not believe that it was accordant with reason or religion thus to isolate a being intended by his Creator for social life, unless necessary for the safety of the community, at large; nor did she consider continued solitude as the best method of reforming the offender. Very many hours, she thought, might be passed alone with advantage, and the night always; but she recognized a vast difference between useful and improving reflection, and the imagination dwelling upon past guilt or prospective evil. Her conviction was that with the greater number of criminals left to feed upon their own mental resources, the latter state of mind was highly probable, the former very unlikely. Confinement that secluded from the vicious but allowed of frequent intercourse with sober, well-conducted persons would have been in her view perfect. But where could funds be obtained to raise the prison, or maintain its discipline on such a system? Some intercourse for a few hours daily among prisoners carefully classed, diligently employed, judiciously instructed, and under most vigilant and unceasing superintendence, with the remaining hours of the twenty-four passed in separate, but not gloomy seclusion, was, in her opinion, the best and most likely method of benefiting the criminal and thus eventually diminishing crime. She shrank from the abuses to which the solitary system is liable. How soon might the cell become an oubliette; how short the transition from kind and constant attention to cruelty and neglect; how entirely the comfort, nay, the existence of a prisoner, must depend upon his keeper's will; and what was human nature to be trusted with such responsibility? With an active magistracy, a zealous clergyman, and careful medical attendant, all might be well; but who could ensure the continuance of these advantages? and were the activity and benevolence of the present day to pass away why might not the slumber of indifference again cover the land?"

A few interesting extracts from the Journal of Mrs. Fry after her return from Scotland, will give an idea of how her time was employed between her visits abroad.

Upton, Ninth Month, 26th.—We arrived at home last Seventh-day, and to my great comfort I found all my family going on well and comfortably. I ventured to ask, or at least to desire, if my goings out were acceptable to the Lord, and if I were to be called to further, and perhaps to still more weighty service, that I might find the blessing of preservation extended to those most dear to me at home, as well as to myself in going. Through mercy this sign has been rather unusually granted me. What can I render unto my Lord for His tender and unmerited mercies?

" *Tenth Month,* 28th.—I have been on a satisfactory visit with my husband, and partly accompanied by Peter Bedford and John Hodgskin, to Croydon and Ifield. Our Meeting in Sussex was a very satisfactory one, and a reading we had next morning at a cottage on the common, belonging to a dear Friend where we had been before. The libraries we established appear to have been much read and valued. It is cause for much thankfulness to find that our labor has not been in vain in the Lord. How sweet are His mercies! May all become His servants saith my soul!

"I have also left home, accompanied by my beloved husband, and my sister Elizabeth to visit a few meetings in Essex.

"*Twelfth Month*, 6th.—This morning I deeply feel the seriousness of laying before my Monthly Meeting my belief that it may be my duty again to visit France and some other parts of the Continent of Europe. It is after much weighty consideration that I have come to the conclusion that it is right to do this. I have long thought that this summer my course might be either to my dearest brother Joseph in America, or to the Continent of Europe; after much weighing it I have believed the latter to be the right opening for me.

"28th.—Yesterday, excepting our dear F—— and R—— C——, all our beloved children dined with us. It really was to me a beautiful sight. Sixteen round our table, happy in each other, a strong tie of love amidst the brothers and sisters, and much united to us, their father and mother. I felt the occasion serious as well as sweet, and very earnestly prayed to the Lord, that I might be very faithful if He called me to any religious service amongst them, whether it were to pray for them or speak to them of His goodness. When the cloth was removed after dinner, I believed it my duty to kneel down and very fervently to pray and to return thanks to my God for all these most tenderly beloved ones. Great help and deliverance has been granted to some of our circle; the Lord has been very gracious; He has added to our number and not diminished them. . . .

"After this solemn time thirteen of our sweet dear grandchildren came in. We passed an evening of uncommon enjoyment, cheerful, yet sober, lively yet sensible of the blessing and peace of our Lord being with us. I seldom if ever remember so bright a family meeting; it reminded me of our Earlham days; but I could not but feel it a blessing when a mother as well as a father is spared to watch their

family grow up and prosper, and to see and enjoy their children's children.

"When I remember all that I have passed through on
their account; above all the exquisite anxiety about their
spiritual welfare, and now so far to see what the Lord has
done for me and for them, what can I say? What can I
do? Ought I not to leave them all to His most holy keeping, and no longer 'toil and spin' so much for them?

"*First Month,* 12th.—I returned from Lynn last evening.
I was a good deal with my beloved sister Catherine who
was there. Before parting we had a deeply interesting
time together, when the spirit of prayer was remarkably
poured forth upon us. I prayed for them each separately,
and I believe that access was in mercy granted to the
Throne of Grace. My dearest sister offered a solemn prayer
for us before we rose from our knees. I felt as I have often
done, an earnest desire that we may none be in spiritual
bonds. I think Satan in hardly any way mars the Lord's
work more than in putting persons in the stiff bonds of
high-churchism. He attacks all professors in this way, and
leads them to rest in their sectarianism rather than their
Christianity. I do not mean that this was the case with
those I was amongst, but I see in it a frightful bait thrown
out to all professors of all denominations. Few things I
more earnestly desire than unity in the Church of Christ,
and that all partition walls may be broken down. Lord,
hasten the coming of that day, for Thine own name's sake!"

In order to raise money for the numerous demands on
the British Society, Mrs. Fry resolved, with the consent of
her friends, upon having a public sale—or what we call a
Fair. It is thus spoken of.

"*Paris, Third Month,* 17th.—Before leaving home we
were much occupied by a very large sale for the British

Society held in Crosby Hall. I felt it an exercising time
lest any should be exposed to temptation by it, and I see
that there are two sides to the question respecting these
sales, as there is an exposure in it that may prove injurious
to some. However, I think I saw in this instance many
favorable results, and particularly in the kind and capital
help my children gave me in it, and the way in which it occupied them. One day I had fifteen children and several
grandchildren helping me to sell. A sweet and Christian
spirit appeared to reign in the room. There were more
than a thousand pounds obtained by it, clear of all expenses,
which will be a great help to the British Society. The
marks of kindness shown me by numbers, in the things sent
to the sale, were very encouraging to me. My brothers
and sisters, my nephews and nieces were also very kind
in aiding me in many ways."

The second journey to the Continent was commenced on
the 11th of March, 1839. She was accompanied by Josiah
Forster, as on the previous visit, and also by her husband
and one of her daughters; the youngest son was to join
them in Paris.

The former visit had been a kind of seed-sowing. This time
on her arrival at Boulogne, many came to seek her and to
welcome her to their shores, and she was soon besieged by
persons in the humbler ranks of society asking to be supplied with Testaments, tracts, &c. Some had lent what
they had received before to friends going into the country
and could not get them again. At the Hotel at Abbeville
"those to whom she had given them on her previous visit,
begged for more, and came creeping up to her apartments
to prefer their request. Her Text-books were the favorites.
In the morning the people of the Hotel gathered round

her.   The First-day that she had spent there on her former
visit to Paris—the reading they had in the evening—the
prayer she had offered for them, had made a deep impression.   They beguiled her into the kitchen where she told
them, in broken French—which, however, they contrived to
understand—a little of her wishes for them as to faith and
practice.   Then all would shake hands with her."

Another month was spent in Paris revisiting the places
previously inspected and holding philanthrophic and religious meetings.   The former of these appear to have been
held as a kind of weekly Reception.

"Last evening about a hundred persons spent the evening with us.   The subject of prisons was brought forward—
Newgate, &c.   I endeavored to show the state of prisons
formerly, and many of their improvements.   But above all
to inculcate Christian principle as the only sure means of
improving practice.   I sought in every way, in the cases
brought forward, to uphold the value of the Scriptures, and
to show the blessed results of faith and repentance.   We
finished by reading in a solemn manner the 15th of Luke
as the chapter so greatly blessed to poor prisoners.   I made
little comment, there was very great solemnity over us.
There were Catholics and Protestants and I believe some of
the Greek Church.   There were Greeks, Ionians, Spaniards,
a Pole, Italians, Germans, English, Americans and French
—several of the English and French, persons of rank; the
Marquis de Brignolles, Sardinian Minister, and Prince
Czartorinsky.   Thus the week has run away! may it have
been for the real good of others, and the glory of God."

" *Paris*, 21*st*.—I feel that under a lively sense of peace and
rest of soul, I may record the mercies of the Lord this week.

" Our First-day was very satisfactory, a large Meeting;
five of our children with us.   (Several of her family spent a
few days in Paris at this time.)

"I had a very serious, interesting, and intimate conversation with the Duchess of Orleans.

"I visited and attended to some prisons, formed a Ladies' Society to visit Protestants in prisons and hospitals, met a very influential company at dinner at Lord Granville's, much interesting conversation in the evening; the same twice at Baron Pelet's, and we had an agreeable dinner at Lord William Bentincks. I have paid some very interesting private calls, spent one morning with my children; our great philanthropic evening largely attended—about about a hundred and forty present. Josiah Forster gave a concentrated account of our former evenings, and added other things very agreeably. I strongly impressed upon them the extreme importance of the influence of the higher upon the lower classes of society, by their example and precept; mentioned late hours, theatres, and other evils. Then advised—giving the poor, Christian education; reading the Holy Scriptures in their families; lending Libraries; District Societies, and other objects. We finished with a very solemn Scripture reading, the greater part of the third chapter of Colossians and the 20th and 21st verses of the last chapter of the Epistle to the Hebrews, 'Now the God of peace that brought again from the dead our Lord Jesus, that great Shepherd of the sheep, through the blood of the everlasting covenant, make you perfect in every good work to do His will, working in you that which is well pleasing in His sight, through Jesus Christ, to whom be glory forever and ever. Amen."

"Previous to reading this I had expressed some solemn parting truths and our party broke up in much love and peace.

"On Fifth-day we dined with some sweet, spiritual and delightful people, the de Presensés and de Valcours; in the evening to Mark Wilke's to meet a very large party of ministers from different parts of France come to attend the Meetings of the various Societies.

"*Fontainbleau*, 28*th*. The day before our departure

from Paris we visited the Prefét de Police, took in our report of the state of the prisons, and obtained leave for the
Protestant ladies to visit the Protestant prisoners; we had
much interesting conversation.   We have the great satisfaction of hearing that a law is likely to pass for women prisoners throughout France to be under the care of women.

"In the evening, and during the day, numbers came to
take leave of us; a good many Greeks who appeared to feel
much interest in and for us, as if our labors with them had
not been in vain."

Before leaving Paris Mrs. Fry was furnished with a letter
from the Minister of the Interior, granting her, Josiah Forster and her husband, permission to visit all the prisons in
France.   This insured them every respect and attention
on their further journey.   They proceeded, with a few stops
to Lyons where "there was a great press of engagements
—prisons and refuges to inspect, besides many schools of
which I had time to visit only one, a woman's adult school."

In a letter to her children written from Nismes, May 12th,
she says:—

"We paid a very interesting visit to Lyons and found a
good deal new in the prisons and Refuges.   An order or
Catholics, called the 'Brethren and Sisters of St. Joseph,'
believe it their duty to take care of prisoners and criminals
generally.   They do not visit as we do, but take the entire
part of turnkeys and prison-officers, and live with the prisoners night and day, constantly caring for them.   I thought
the effect on the female prisoners surprisingly good, as far
as their influence extended.   But the mixture of gross superstition is curious, the image of the Virgin dressed up in
the finest manner in their different wards.   I feared that their
religion lay so much in form and ceremonies that it led from
heart work and from that great change which would proba-

bly be produced did these sisters simply teach them Christianity. Their books appeared to be mostly about the Virgin; not a sign of Scripture to be found in either prison or refuge. I felt it laid upon me as a weighty, yet humbling duty, before I left Lyons, to invite Roman Catholics and Protestants who had influence in the prisons, to come to our Hotel, and there, in Christian love, to tell them the *truth*, to the best of my belief, as the *only* real ground of reformation of heart, and the means likely to conduce to this end. It was the more fearful, as I had to be entirely interpreted for. My heart almost sank within me as the time approached. It was about three o'clock in the day; about sixty people came of the very influential Catholics and Protestants and I was enabled, through a most excellent interpreter, to show them that nothing but the pure simple truth, as revealed in Scripture, through the power of the Holy Spirit, could really enlighten the understanding, or change the heart. My husband and Josiah Forster als > took a very useful and valuable part. *Much* satisfaction was expressed. We afterwards dined at a gentleman's who lived in a lovely situation on the top of a hill near Lyons. Our invitations began to flow in, and we should, I doubt not, had we staid longer, soon have been in as great a current as at Paris, or greater. We met with some very interesting, devoted Christian characters—a cousin of the Baroness Pelét's, almost like herself; her notes and flowers coming in every morning. The last day was most fatiguing; we had to rise soon after three in the morning for Avignon, to go a hundred and fifty miles down the Rhone.

"We have passed through the most delightful country I ever saw. Lyons, with the Rhone and Saone, is, in its environs, beautiful, and the passage from Lyons to Avignon really lovely; mountains in the distance, (parts of the Alps,) their tops covered with snow; vegetation in perfection, the flowers of spring and summer in bloom at once, grass just ready to be cut, barley in the ear, lilacs, laburnums, syr-

ingas, roses, pinks, carnations, acacias in full bloom, yellow
jessamine wild in the hedges.   It is a sudden burst of the
finest summer combined with the freshness of spring.   The
olive groves intermixed with abundant vineyards and mul-
berry groves, all beautiful from their freshness.   The ancient buildings of Avignon, the ruins on the banks of the
Rhone, the very fine and wonderful remains of the Roman
aqueduct, called the Pont du Gard, really exceed description."

The travelers found at Nismes, and in the neighboring
villages a scattered body of people professing the principles
of the Society of Friends.   "This simple, but interesting
body of people are the descendants of the Camisards, who
took refuge in the mountains of the Cevennes during the
persecutions subsequent to the revocation of the Edict of
Nantes."   At Congenies the inhabitants were almost all
Friends—a kind and religious people.   They regularly attended meetings with them, and the last meeting was
crowded, the people clustering "to the top of the doors, in
all the open windows, and on the walls outside, yet in perfect quietude and order."

After visiting Marseilles, Toulon, and Aix, where many
important objects called for attention, including the galley-
slaves, the travelers returned in June to Nismes.

"*Sixth Month.*—Our First-day at Nismes was deeply
weighty in prospect, so that I rested little that night, as I
had ventured to propose our holding one Meeting in the
morning in the Methodist chapel, that whosoever liked might
attend it ; and in the evening to do the same in a very large
school-room, that all classes might attend, as I believed
that all would not come to a Methodist Meeting-house.   I

went prostrated before the Lord to this Meeting in the morning, hardly knowing how to hold up my head. I could only apply for help to the inexhaustible Source of our sure mercies, feeling that I could not do it either on account of myself, or because it was the work in which I was engaged; but I could do it for the sake of my Lord, and that His kingdom might spread. Utterly unworthy did I feel myself; but my Lord was gracious. My dear interpreter, Christine Majolier, was there to help me in a very large Meeting, and I felt power wonderfully given me to proclaim the truths of the Gospel, and to press the point of the Lord Himself being our teacher, immediately by His Spirit, and through the Holy Scriptures, and by His providences and works, and to show that no teaching so much conduced to growth in grace as the Lord's teaching. There was much attention; at the close I felt the spirit of prayer much over us, longed for its vocal expression, and felt a desire that some one might pray, when a Methodist minister, in a feeling manner expressed a wish to offer something in prayer, to which we, of course, assented. It proved solemn and satisfactory.

"We dined at our dear friend, the Pasteur Emilien Frossard's; he and his wife have been like a brother and sister to us. We were also joined by a Roman Catholic gentleman who has, I think, been seriously impressed by our visit, and it has led him to have the Scriptures read to his workmen. There were also Louis Majolier, his daughter, and a young English friend. I think I have very seldom in my life felt a more lively sense of the love of God than at this table. I may say our souls were animated under its sweetness; I think we rejoiced together, and magnified the name of our God.

"In the evening we met in a large school-room that would contain some hundreds, where numbers assembled, principally the French protestants and some of their pastors. There again I was greatly helped, I really believe, by the

Holy Spirit to speak to them upon their important situations in the Church of Christ, and the extreme consequence of their being sound both in faith and practice. I also felt it my duty to show them, as Protestants, the infinite importance, not only in France, but in the surrounding nations, of their being 'as a city set upon a hill that cannot be hid.' I showed them how the truth is spreading and how important to promote it, being preachers of righteousness in life and conversation, as well as in word and doctrine. There was here also much attention; and our dear and valued friend and brother in Christ, Emilien Frossard, prayed beautifully that the word spoken might profit the people, and particularly that the blessing of the Lord might rest upon me. It was no common prayer on my behalf. Thanks to my Heavenly Father, the Meeting broke up in much love, life and peace."

Another meeting was held the next morning at the village of Codognan. Her account then continues:

"After this we proceeded to Montpelier where important service opened for us. A Protestant Ladies Committee was formed to visit the great Female Prison there; much important advice offered to the Governor, upon the charges now being made in the prison, and female officers being appointed. We appeared to go in the very time wanted, and obtained the liberation of several poor women from their very sad cells. The Préfét was most kind to us, and thus our way was easily made: the Mayor and all with us. Help was given me to speak religiously to the poor women before all these gentlemen."

"We proceeded from place to place until we arrived at Toulouse, on Seventh-day evening, the 16th of the Sixth Month. On First-day evening we met a large number of Protestants at one of their Scripture readings. We took part in the service. At the close a solemn prayer was offered for us by Francis Courtois, one of a very remarkable trio of brothers, (bankers there,) all three of whom are given up to the service of their Lord, and appear to have been instruments greatly blessed. Their kindness to us was very great. In Toulouse we visited two prisons, had one important prison Meeting and one exceedingly solemn and satisfactory Scripture reading and time of prayer with the Courtois family, one or two pasteurs, and other relig. ious persons."

She next went to Montauban, the place where the minis- ters of the Protestant Church of France were educated. Here "without expressing any other wish than to have an evening party at one of their houses, to meet some of the professors and students of the College, (the only one in France for educating pasteurs of the Reformed Church,) we found, to our dismay, all arranged to receive us in the Col- lege; and on arriving there imagine how I felt when the Dean of the College offered me his arm to take me into the chapel. There I believe the whole of the collegians were assembled, in all at least a hundred. It was fearful work. There were also numbers of the people of the town, we thought about three hundred. Josiah Forster spoke first, explaining our views at some length. Then I rose with an excellent interpreter, one of their pasteurs. I first told them something of my prison experience, and the power of Chris- tian principle and kindness; then I related a little of the state of their prisons in France; then my ideas as to the general state of France; and afterwards endeavored to bring home to them the extreme importance of their calling as pasteurs in their Church. I reminded them of that passage of Scripture ' the leaders of the people caused them to err.

I endeavored to show them how awful such a state of things must be, and the extreme importance of their being sound in doctrine and practice."

"Simple duty led me to Montauban.   We were united in much Christian love to many there.   I forgot to say that at the close of the occasion the pasteur who interpreted for me prayed beautifully and spiritually that the words spoken might profit the people; he also prayed for us.   This has frequently occurred at the close of some of our interesting Meetings ; a pouring forth of the spirit of prayer has been granted.   My not knowing the language has obstructed my offering it, and it has appeared laid upon others instead.   I have seldom felt sweeter peace in leaving a place than Montauban."

Constant exertion, together with the heat of the climate, had now affected Mrs. Fry's health so that her husband strongly urged their turning aside for a brief rest in the cooler atmosphere of the Pyrenees.   But wherever she went she scattered the seeds of the Kingdom, in words of kindness, and in Bibles, text-books and tracts.   Having some Scripture extracts in Spanish, when they went over the line, she gave them to the peasants, or left them at the cottages, and even in the manger of a cow-house—having heard that the Spaniards, including the priests, were eager for books, and carefully preserved them.

She also employed her *rest* in preparing a "memorial of considerable length, with the aid of her companions, for the Minister of the Interior, and a shorter one for the Prefect of Police, embodying her observations on the state of the prisons which she had inspected and her recommendations for their improvement."

Thus refreshed the little party hastened backward through the south of France and turned their steps toward Switzerland. At Bonigen, near Interlachen, she writes, August, 11th.

"I believe that my gracious Lord has guided our steps to this place; blessed be His name. At Grenoble, where I felt rather pressed in spirit to spend a First-day, I had a curious opening for religious service, and I believe an important one, with several enlightened Roman Catholics, several Protestants, and a school of girls. It was a time of spiritual refreshment by which many appeared helped and comforted. The next day was occupied in important prison visits, and in the evening a Meeting with influential Roman Catholics.

"Josiah Forster having left us to go by diligence to Geneva, we traveled alone through Savoy, and had a pleasant journey through a lovely country; but the darkness of the Roman Catholic religion, and the arbitrary laws, not allowing even a tract to be given away, were painful; we found that a Swiss gentlemen had lately been imprisoned for doing it, and confined with a thief. We arrived at Geneva the 25th of the seventh month in the evening. Here we passed a very interesting time, from various and important openings for religious service in large parties, in prisons, &c. My belief is that we were sent to that place, and amidst some trials from different causes, there was a pouring forth of spiritual help and spiritual peace. Many of the pasteurs came to us and not a few expressed their refreshment and satisfaction with our visit. Before we left, several of the most spiritual in a very striking and beautiful manner preached to us, particularly to myself, and prayed for us all; a time I think never to be forgotten by us. We had one of the most beautiful entertainments I ever saw, given by Colonel Tronchin at a lovely place a few miles from Geneva, the fine snowy mountains about us, the lake within sight. In an avenue in the midst of a fine wood we had a handsome repast to which about a hundred persons sat down. The gentleman who gave it is a devoted Christian, a man of large property and this blessing sanctified by grace. I visited a delightful institution for the sick of his establishment on his grounds. To return to our entertainment, grace was very solemnly said before our meal, and very beautiful hymn-singing afterwards. Then withdrew· into the house where I believe the anointing was poured forth upon me to speak the truth in love and power. I had an excellent, spiritually-minded interpreter, (Professor La Harpe): many apparently felt this occasion. A young English gentleman came up to me afterwards and expressed his belief that it would influence him for life; and a lady came to me and said how remarkably her state had been spoken to. Much love was also shown to us, and unity. Indeed 1 felt how our Lord permits his servants to rejoice together in love; and even to partake of the good things of this life in His love and fear, with a subjected spirit rejoicing in His mercies, temporal and spiritual. We had very great kindness also shown to us by many, amongst others by our dear friend Mary Ann Vernet and her family, including her daughter, the Baroness de Stael, with whom we dined at Cappet. The Duke de Broglie and his family were with her; we had a very interesting visit. We went from Geneva to our dear friend Sophia Delesserts; her husband was out; they have a beautiful place on the banks of the Lake of Geneva, near Rolle; here we had the warmest reception, and were refreshed and comforted together; she is truly loved by me."

The following description of an evening at the beautiful residence of Colonel Tronchin, at Beseinge, where more than a hundred persons were gathered, is from the pen of a young student, afterwards Secretary of the "Belgian Société Evangélique."

"We had half expected a philosophical discourse upon subjects of philanthropic and general interest, but everything that fell from her lips was characterized by delicacy, extreme simplicity, and an ardent desire to draw our attention to our own happiness, in being permitted the opportunity for meditation on the one subject which seemed always present in her thoughts, Christ Jesus, crucified for the expiation of our sins. At this distance of time I have an actual realization of the opening of her exhortation. 'I think,' said she, 'it is impossible for us to be more profitably employed than by occupying the next few moments with the contemplation of the love which the Lord Jesus has for us.' The rooms were full to overflowing; my fellow-students and I took up our places in the passage, on the stair-case, crowded round the open door, eagerly hanging on such parts of the beautiful exhortation as we could catch by the most breathless attention; after she had concluded she kindly came out amongst us and expressed her regret that we should have been so inconvenienced. I can see her now, her tall figure leaning on Colonel Tronchin's arm, M. La Harpe at her side, her dignified, animated, yet softened countenance bending towards us. I can never forget it. Such occasions are rare in life, they are very green spots in the garden of memory—more, they are opportunities given for improvement, solemnly increasing the responsibility of each who participate in them. May I never lose the impression of that day at Beseinge, nor the holy lessons I there heard and learnt."

After leaving Geneva the travelers went to Lausanne, Berne, Thun, Grindel, Brienz, Bonigen, and Zurich, in Switzerland, scattering everywhere the seeds of peace, kindness and reform. The following incident, is illustrative of Mrs. Fry's peculiar gifts as a peacemaker.

"Whilst at Bonigen, Herr Mitchell, the landlord of the

little inn, and his family, attended their First-day evening readings. On one of these occasions a peasant girl was with them who appeared pious and afflicted; her name was Madelina Kauss. She came from a neighboring village to seek counsel of Elizabeth Fry. Madelina and her mother had joined themselves to a little body of serious people, Pietists, somewhat resembling Methodists, seceders from the National Church. The father, a coarse, ignorant man, vehemently threatened his wife, and turned his daughter out of doors to earn her own livelihood, which she did by weaving for nine French sous a day. Pious people from Berne had interfered on their behalf, but had only made matters worse. It so fell out that about this time a certain small old-fashioned black-letter German newspaper reached the little inn at Bonigen; the host and his household were startled on finding in it a long account of his guests,—'a history of Mrs. Fry, her work and labors of love;' concluding with her visit to the Oberland of Berne and residence at Herr Mitchell's country inn. After careful perusal it occurred to the worthy host that in his inmates he had found the very people to rectify the wrongs of poor Madelina and restore peace in her parents' dwelling; persons in his opinion not to be resisted by Heurich Kauss, the peasant of Wildersewyl, to whom he advised that a visit should forthwith be made. When the carriage came to convey the party he insisted on driving it himself arrayed in his holiday costume. The interview with the family was quite pathetic. The father laid the fault of his violence and severity on the grandfather, and he on the schoolmaster; but a little kind and wise conciliation sufficed to bring them all to tears; they wept and kissed, and Herr Mitchell wept for sympathy. After which Elizabeth Fry had a religious time with Madelina, her mother, and a few of their neighbors; leaving them with the thankful belief that they had been permitted to act the part of peacemakers." *

* Life by S. Corder. page 540.

"*Zurich, Eighth Month*, 25*th*.—We left our sweet little home at Bonigen, on the banks of Lake Brienz, last Fourth-day. I felt refreshed by our visit to this country. I think my prayers have been heard and answered in its being a very uniting time with those most tenderly beloved by me. We have had some interesting communications with serious persons in the humble walks of life who reside in that neighborhood. We have desired to aid them spiritually and temporally, but the difficulty of communication has been very great, from want of suitable interpreters; still I trust that some were edified and comforted. I also hope our circulation of books and tracts has been useful, and the establishment of at least one library at Brienz for the laboring classes. We have traveled along gently and agreeably by Lucerne, and through a delightful country."

"On the morning of their departure from Zurich the venerable pastor Gesner, and many others, called to take leave. This apostolic old man pronounced a striking bless-ing on Elizabeth Fry to which she replied in terms that caused the bystanders to weep aloud."

"*Ludwigsburg, (a few miles from Stuttgard,) Ninth Month*, 1*st*.—On the evening of the day that I wrote at Zurich, we went with our dear friend the Baroness Pelet, afterwards joined by the Baron, to the house of an ancient devoted pasteur, Gesner. His wife was the daughter of that excellent servant of the Lord, Lavater. We met a large number of persons, I believe generally serious. I had proposed to myself speaking on the prison subject; but my way opened differently—to enlarge upon the state of the Protestant Church in France, to encourage all its members to devotedness; and particularly in that place where deep trials have been their portion from their Government up-holding infidelity and infidel men. At the close of the Meeting our venerable friend Gesner spoke in a lively, pow-erful manner, and avowed his belief that the Lord Himself had enabled me to express what I had done, it was so remarkably 'the word in season.' I paid also a satisfactory religious visit to the female prisoners in the afternoon The next morning I visited the head magistrate, represented the evils I had observed, and saw some ladies about visiting prisons. We afterwards went a sweet expedition on the Lake with our beloved friends, the Baron and Baroness Pelet. Early in the evening I set off with a dear girl— great grand-daughter to Lavater and grand-daughter to Pasteur Gesner—Barbara Usteri, in a curious little carriage to pay some visits, and to spend an evening at the house of the aunt of Matilda Escher, another interesting young woman with whom I had become acquainted, I believe providentially, at an inn near Interlachen. I had no one with me but strangers as my dear family stayed with the Baron and Baroness Pelet at my desire; but I feel not among strangers; because those who love the Lord Jesus are dear to me, and in our holy Head we are one. I can hardly express how much I have found this to be the case on this journey—the love, the unity and the home feeling I have had with those I never saw before! and I have also found how little it matters where we are, for 'where the God of peace is there is home.'"

After visiting the Prison and Orphan Asylum at Ludwigsburg the travelers proceeded to Frankfort where they had a stall opened for the sale of Bibles and tracts, and then hastened home by way of Ostend and Dover, arriving in peace and health September 13th, 1839. The journey through France and Switzerland occupied about six months.

The following shows some of the results of Elizabeth Fry's extensive observation and deep experience, regarding different religious persuasions.

"*Upton, First-day Twelfth Month, 8th.*—I yesterday had some intimate conversation with Captain ——, who has just joined, or is about to join, the Plymouth Brethren; with a young lady, a follower of Edward Irving; with another lady, a high Church woman; and with Josiah Forster, an elder in our portion of the church. I cannot say but that it is at times an exercise of my religious faith to find the diversities of opinions existing amongst the professors of Christianity, and not only the professors, but those who I believe really love their Lord; but my better judgment tells me that there must be a wise purpose in its being so. These divisions into families and tribes may tend to the life and growth of religion, which, if we were all of one mind, might not be the case. But whilst I perceive these differences, I perceive that there is but one Christianity, one Body, one Spirit, one hope of our calling; one Lord, one faith, and one baptism; one God and Father of all. All true members of the Church of Christ are, and must be, one in Him, and the results we see the same everywhere. Love to God and love to man manifested in life and conduct; and how strikingly proved in death, as well as life, that victory is obtained through the same Saviour; that in the dying hour death loses its sting and the grave its victory. Therefore if we believe and know our hearts to be cleansed by the blood of Christ, and through the power of the Holy Spirit live to His glory, bearing the fruits of faith, it matters little, in my estimation, to what religious denomination we belong, so that we mind our calling and fill the place our Lord would have us to fill in His Militant Church on earth."

CHAPTER TENTH.

Previous to her first tour in Belgium, Holland, and Germany Elizabeth Fry paid her respects to her own Sovereign whose marriage is thus referred to :

"*First Month*, 1840.—An eventful time in public and private life. Our young Queen is to be married to Prince Albert. She has sent me a present of fifty pounds for our Refuge at Chelsea by Lord Normanby. Political commotions about the country—riots in Wales—much religious stir in the 'Church of England,' numbers of persons becoming much the same as Roman Catholics—Popish doctrines preached openly in many of the churches—infidel principles in the form of Socialism gaining ground."

"*Upton, Second Month*, 1st.—I am called to visit our young Queen to-day, in company with William Allen, and I hope my brother Samuel also.

"Went to Buckingham Palace and saw the Queen. Our interview was short. Lord Normanby, the Home Secretary, presented us. The Queen asked us where we were going on the Continent. She said it was some years since she saw me. She asked about Caroline Neave's Refuge for which she had lately sent the fifty pounds. This gave me an opportunity of thanking her. I ventured to express my satisfaction that she encourged various works of charity; and I said it reminded me of the words of Scripture, 'with the

merciful Thou wilt show Thyself merciful.' Before we
withdrew I stopped and said I hoped the Queen would allow me to assure her that it was our prayer that the blessing of God night rest upon the Queen and her Consort.

"I have for some time believed that duty would call me
to have a meeting in London or the neighborhood previous
to leaving.   I see many difficulties attached to it, and perhaps none so much as my great fear of women becoming
too forward in these things, beyond what the Scripture dictates; but I am sure the Scripture most clearly and forcibly
lays down the principle that the Spirit is not to be grieved,
or quenched, or vexed, or resisted; and on this principle I
act, under the earnest desire that whatever the Lord leads
me into by His Spirit may be done faithfully to Him and
in His name; and I am of opinion that nothing Paul said
to discourage women's speaking in the churches alluded to
their speaking through the help of the Spirit, as he clearly
gave directions how they should conduct themselves under
such circumstances, when they prayed or prophesied."

The Meeting is thus described by one who was present :

"It was really a most impressive occasion,—the large,
fine, circular building filled—not less I should think than
fifteen hundred present.   She began by entreating the sympathy and supplications of those present.   I cannot tell you
how mine flowed forth on her behalf.   After her prayer we
sat still for some time; then William Allen spoke; and then
she rose, giving as text, 'Yield yourselves unto God as those
that are alive from the dead;' and uncommonly fine was
her animated, yet tender exhortation to all present, but
more especially to the young, to present themselves as living sacrifices to the Lord, to be made of Him new creatures
in Christ—the old things passed away and all things become new, as those alive from the dead.   This change she
dwelt and enlarged on much ; its character and the Power

that alone can effect it ; the duty demanded of us—'Yield yourselves;' and its infinite and eternal blessedness. I was astonished and deeply impressed; the feeling was, 'surely God is amongst us of a truth.'"

Mrs. Fry and her companions—William Allen, her brother Samuel Gurney and his daughter Elizabeth, Lucy Bradshaw and Josiah Forster, arrived at Ostend, Feb. 27th, whence she wrote to her family.

"We are favored with a bright morning and we may thankfully say that our spirits are permitted to partake of the same brightness. I have a sweet feeling of being in the right place. An order is come from the Belgian Govern·ment for us to visit their prisons. So the way opens before us; and though I give up much to enter these services, and feel leaving my most tenderly beloved ones, yet there is such a sense of blessedness in the service, and the honor of doing the least thing for my Lord, unworthy as I am, that it often brings a peculiar feeling of health, (if I may so say) as well as peace, to my body, soul and spirit.

"My brother Samuel is a capital traveling companion, so zealous, so able, so willing, so generous; and I find dear Elizabeth sweet, pleasant and cheering. Bruges is a beauti·ful old town; such exquisite buildings—they delighted my eye. Here we visited the English Convent where to our surprise, we could only speak through a grating. We had a good deal of conversation with dear S. P——'s sister and the Superior. They appeared very interesting women. We talked about their shutting-in system. I expressed my dis·approbation of it, as a general practice, and one liable to great abuse. I sent them some books and mean to send more. We also visited a large school; and to the great pleasure and amusement of the children your uncle gave them all a present. They could not in the least understand our language as they speak Flemish.

"We have been much interested this morning in visiting the Maison de Force; it is a very excellent prison of considerable size, but wants some things very much. We have since been occupied with the numerous English here. They are without pasteur, or school, and quite in a deplorable state. We propose having a meeting with them of a religious and philanthropic nature, and hope to establish some schools, &c., amongst them."

"*Brussels, Third Month,* 1st.

"We left Ghent on Seventh-day, about half-past two o'clock, after visiting a most deplorable prison where we found a cell with the floor and sides formed of angular pieces of wood, so that no prisoner could stand, lie down, or lean against the wall without suffering. We also visited a Lunatic asylum so beautifully conducted that I more took the impression how happy such persons may be made than I ever did before. They are cared for by the 'Sisters of St. Vincent de Paul.' After rather a slow journey we arrived here to dinner at six o'clock.

"*Ghent, Third Month,* 3rd.—Here we are once more— we have visited another large prison for the military, and had a very interesting Meeting with the English workmen, their wives and children. I am glad to say they conclude for us to send them schoolmasters. We had flocks after us last evening, English and Belgians—I suppose about seventy; they appeared to be touched by our reading. I observe how much the English appear impressed on these occasions. Our little party are very comfortable and each has plenty to do.

"*Antwerp, Third Month,* 6th.

"Upon our return to Brussels from Ghent we visited the great prison of Vilorde. We gave many of our little Scripture extracts to the prisoners. We got home to dinner and spent the evening at the Baron de Bois' where we met several pleasant persons. A considerable number of Belgians, poor and rich came to an evening meeting at our Hotel. The next

day was one of no common interest. After some engagements in the morning, breakfasting out, &c., we visited the
King. Our party were William Allen, my brother Samuel, J.
Forster and myself; and before we left Lucy Bradshaw and
dear Elizabeth were admitted to see him. We first had a
very interesting conversation on the state of the prisons, and
your uncle read the King our address to him upon the subject,
When the part was read expressing our desire for him the
Queen and his family, he appeared to feel it much. We had
open, interesting communication on many subjects. We
remained nearly an hour. The Queen was unwell and the
children asleep, therefore I did not see them. We gave the
King several books for himself and the Queen. We were
invited by Count Arrivabene to dine with one of the first
Belgian families. I felt it rather fearful when, to my surprise, after dinner I was seated by the Dean of Brussels,
surrounded by the company and told that I was permitted
to speak openly upon my religious views. Indeed I think
the wish was that I should preach to them. This was
curious, because I was warned on going, to say nothing
about religion. Preach I did not, as I do not feel that at
my command; but I spoke very seriously about the Scriptures not being read in the prisons, and endeavored to show
in few words, what alone can produce change of heart, life
and conduct, and the danger of resting in forms. We
parted in much good-will, and we sent the Dean and the
ladies some books. In the evening we had a philanthropic
party at our hotel. The next morning a large, very solemn
and interesting, religious meeting at the hotel. We left
Brussels in much peace—*rejoicing* would not be too strong
a word. In nearest love. E. F."

The interview with the Dean of Brussels is thus described by her niece, Elizabeth Gurney.

"*Brussels, March 6th.*—We expect to end our very interesting visit in this place to-day. Had I a hundred times

more power of writing I could not initiate you into our life here. A great Meeting is now assembling in the Table de Hote salon, fitted up by our landlord for the occasion. This is to be our farewell meeting. We have had a very full morning, partly employed in distributing books. The servants at the palace sent an entreaty that they might not be overlooked. I wish you could have seen us looking out a good variety for about sixty of them.

"Yesterday began with a full tide of business. They were to see the King at twelve o'clock. My aunt looked beautifully. He is a particularly pleasing-looking man, rather older than I expected. The Duchess of Kent had kindly written to the King to say that my aunt was likely to visit Brussels.

"I must tell you about our dinner at M. le Comte de ——'s the first Roman Catholic family here. The party consisted of fifteen persons, only two speaking English. Amongst them was the Dean, the head of the Church here, under the Bishop of Malines. Much that was interesting passed. The Dean and our aunt seated themselves in a corner of the room, and by degrees the whole party gathered round,— the Count and Josiah Forster, interpreting by turns. It was a critical thing to know what to say, as the conversation became more and more of a religious nature. She began on the prisons—prevention of crime—how much the upper classes are often the cause, by example, of the sins of the lower, related a few of her prison facts as proofs, and finally ended by saying, 'Will the Dean allow me to speak my mind candidly?' His permission being granted, and that of the Count and Countess, she began by expressing the sincere interest that she felt for the inhabitants of the city, and how much she had been desiring for them, 'that, as a people, they might each place less confidence in men, and in the forms of religion, and look to Christ with an entire and simple faith.' The priest said nothing, but turned the subject and asked what the views of the Quakers were;

upon which Josiah Forster gave them a short account in French which appeared to interest them all."

Leaving Brussels they spent about two weeks in visiting Rotterdam, Amsterdam, and Twolle. A letter from Dr. Bosworth, whose acquaintance was formed at Rotterdam, shows the kind of fruit borne in those places. In it he says:

"Before answering your questions let me discharge a debt of gratitude which I and my wife owe to you and your friends, for your benevolent exertions in Rotterdam. You have excited amongst us, and have left, I trust, an abiding Christian affection. We feel we are brethren, united in the same good cause of our adorable Saviour, that of promoting 'peace on earth and good-will to men.' How soon will the wood, hay and stubble of party be burnt up, and what is built on the Rock of Ages remain, &c., &c. We are here in a parched wilderness, but your visit has brought a refreshing dew, and may it abide with us."

"Amsterdam, Third Month, 19*th.*

"MY DEAREST H——,

We find this a very interesting place. How much amused you would all be at some of our curious meetings. The other evening we went to drink tea at the house of a converted Jew, where we met a member of the Pietists; he read the 14th chapter of John in French; I spoke and gave a little advice on Christian love and unity; then the Jew spoke, and another Jew prayed, and afterwards William Allen. The serious, the sweet, the good and the ludicrous were curiously mixed up together. Yesterday was very full; first company, breakfast and reading; then preparation for two meetings, one for prisoners in the afternoon, and one in the evening for philanthropic objects, &c. At three o'clock about twenty gentlemen came to discuss with us the state of the prisoners of Holland—an excellent meeting. A gentleman named Surengar was present who has followed us from Rotterdam, and has kindly invited us to his house in the North of Holland. Your uncle is very clever in his speeches and real knowledge of the subject. I received blessing and thanks from many, far too much; our visit appears most seasonable here, so much wanting to be done in the prisons and other things.

"*Fifth-day morning.*—We went to our Friends' Meeting; when we arrived the numbers round the door were so great that we doubted whether we could get in; however way was soon made for us and we found a large and highly respectable congregation needing no interpreter. We had certainly a flowing Meeting in every sense, I think the cup flowed over with Christian love. I believe it has been a most unusual thing the way in which hearts have been opened towards us. I then went off to the prison to launch the Committee of Ladies in visiting it, several gentlemen also with me. I had just time to come home, rest and dress, and set off to a dinner at our friend Van der Hope's where there are the most exquisite paintings by the Dutch masters. I think I never saw any so much to my taste.

"I can assure thee, my dearest H——, when I see how ripe the fields are unto harvest everywhere, I long and pray that more laborers may be brought into this most interesting, important, and, may I not say delightful service; but there must be a preparation for it, by yielding to the cross of Christ, and often deep humiliations and much self-abasement are needful, before the Lord makes much use of us: but above all we must yield ourselves to God, as 'those that are alive from the dead;' He will then fit for His own work in His own way.

Dearest love to all of you,

I am thy most tenderly attached mother

ELIZABETH FRY."

The party now turned eastward toward Hanover to visit a small colony of Friends at Minden and Pyrmont. From these places Mrs. Fry writes to her family:

"*Minden, Third Month*, 28*th*.—We left Twolle on Second-day the 23rd and slept at a true German inn— neither carpet nor curtain. Our night was disturbed, still we did well. The next day we set off in good time and traveled until twelve o'clock; we did not settle till two in the morning. I think I have not yet recovered the fatigue, not having slept well one night since. We have been interested by the Friends, who are much like those of Congenies, but more entirely Friends. We have visited them in almost all their families and had two Meetings with them. We have been brought into much sympathy with them, for they are a tried, and I believe a Christian people. We have this evening had three pastors with us, two of them I think spiritual men. Our meeting was largely attended this afternoon, and I can assure you my heart almost failed me, being interpreted for in German is so difficult; but we have, in Auguste Mundbenck, a well educated young Friend, a capital interpreter. The meeting ended well. In my wakeful nights I feel solitary, and have you very present with me; but I humbly trust He that sleepeth not is watching over you with tender care.

"*Pyrmont*, 29*th*.—In our way here we visited at Hameln a large prison, under the King of Hanover, almost all the poor prisoners, upwards of four hundred in number, heavily chained. I told them a little of my deep interest for their present and eternal welfare; they appeared to feel it very much; one poor man, a tall fine figure with heavy chains on both legs, sat weeping like a child. I am just come in from visiting some families of Friends; they are really a very valuable set. I longed to take a picture for you of an old Friend with a plain scull-cap, either quilted or knitted, a purple handkerchief, a striped apron, and the whole ap-

pearance truly curious; but she was a sweet old woman, full
of love. I am really amused; the old and young are as
fond of me as if I could fully speak to them; the little ones
sitting on my lap as if I were their mother, and leaning
their little heads upon me. A little child about four or five
said, what happy days they should have when we went to
see them. We expect a large party this evening.

"30th.—We had our party and understand there were
present some of the first persons of the town, besides the
master of the hotel, his wife, the doctor, the post-master,
the book-binder, the shoemaker, &c., &c., &c.! We discussed the state of their poor, their not visiting them or
attending to them; for it appears that visiting the poor is
not thought of here. I hope and expect our coming will be
useful in this respect.

"*Hameln—ended Hanover, Fourth Month, 2nd.*

"While stopping at a small inn I mean to finish my account of our visit to Pyrmont. After I wrote we went
shaking on over such bad roads from house to house to see
Friends, that I almost feared we must break down. We
twice dined with them in their beautiful spot at Friedensthal, (or the valley of peace,) surrounded with hills and a
river flowing through it; roebucks wild from the woods
abounding. We were very pleasantly received. Our visits
were very satisfactory to these very valuable and agreeable
people. Tears and kisses abounded at our departure. I
must tell you of an interesting event. I went to buy something for little John at a shop where a very agreeable lady
spoke to me in English, and I was so much attracted by her
that I requested her to accept a book, and sent a work on
the rites and ceremonies of the Jews. I asked her to attend
our Meeting on Second-day morning. She proved to be a
Jewish lady of some importance; she came to the Meeting
with several other Jews, and truly I believe her heart was
touched. I invited her to come to see us the next evening,
when we expected several persons to join our party. The

following day we agreed to form a District Society to attend
to the deplorable state of the poor. The Jewish lady capitally helped us; she then appeared in a feeling state; but
this morning when the ladies met to finish our arrangements, and I felt it my place to give them a little advice,
and my blessing in the name of the Lord, the tears poured
down her face. I then felt it my absolute duty to take her
into my room to give her such books as I thought right
and to tell her how earnest my desires were that she should
come to the knowledge of our Saviour. I think in our
whole journey no person has appeared to be so affected
or so deeply impressed; may it be lasting and may she
become a Christian indeed!

"*Hildesheim, Fourth Month, 6th.*

"We left Hanover to-day about five o'clock, after rather a
singular visit. We arrived there on Fifth-day evening.
On Sixth and Seventh-day our way did not open quite so
brightly as sometimes. We saw a deplorable prison,—poor
untried prisoners chained to the ground until they would
confess their crimes, whether they had committed them or
not, and some other sad evils. Several interesting persons
came to see us. Seventh-day evening we spent at a gentleman's house where we met some very clever and superior
persons, and had much important communication upon
their prisons, &c., &c. On First-day we had our little
Meetings; such a tide on the Sabbath I think I hardly ever
had; it was like being driven down a mighty stream; we
had allowed persons to come to us, supposing it would be
the last day there. I made some calls of Christian love.
The principal magistrate came for an hour about the prisons,
and very many other persons. In the evening we had also
a party of a select nature to our Scripture-reading, and after
a very solemn time we represented many things wanted
in Hanover. I forgot to tell you, amongst other visitors
the Queen's Chamberlin came to say that the Queen wished
to see our whole party on Second-day at one o'clock. We

had proposed going that morning early, but put it off on
this account. I think I never paid a more interesting visit
to royalty—my brother Samuel, William Allen and myself.
In the first place we were received with ceremonious respect,
shown through many rooms into a drawing-room where
were the Queen's Chamberlain and three ladies-in-waiting
to receive us. . . After some little time we were sent
for by the Queen; the King was too ill to see us. She is a
stately woman, tall, large, and rather a fine countenance.
We very soon began to speak of her afflictions, and I gave
a little encouragement and exhortation. She was much
affected, and after a little requested us to sit down. We
had very interesting and important subjects brought forward; the difficulties and temptations to which rank is subject, the importance of their influence, the objects incumbent upon them to attend to and help in—Bible Societies,
Prisons, &c. We then read our address to the Queen, wishing her to patronize ladies visiting the prisons; it contained
serious advice, and our desires for her, the King, and the
Prince; then I gave the Queen several books which she accepted in the kindest manner."

The travelers then proceeded to Berlin where they met
with a warm welcome from all classes and found an ample
field of labor. In the Princess William, sister of the late
King Frederick William III., Mrs. Fry found a zealous
supporter of her efforts for the improvement of the prisons.
Their first public reception is thus described by her niece:
also a meeting at the palace of the Princess William.

"*Hotel de Russie, Berlin.*

"Our dear aunt's first evening for philanthropic purposes
took place on the 13th. There is a splendid room in the
Hotel capable of containing two hundred persons, where
we have our reunions. (At one end of this large room was

a platform on which the company were seated, with Professor Tholuck, as interpreter.) It would be impossible to describe the intense interest and eagerness which prevailed when our aunt rose. The attention of the whole assembly seemed completely riveted by her address. William Allen had previously told them the object of their mission, and a little of what they had been doing since our arrival in Berlin.

"The Princess William h_s been desirous to give her sanction, as far as possible, to the Ladies' Committee for visiting the prisons that my aunt has been forming; and to show her full approbation had invited the Committee to meet her at her palace. The Princess had also asked some of her friends; so we must have been about forty. Such a party of ladies and only our friend Count Groben to interpret. The Princess received us most kindly. The Crown Princess arrived. The Princess Charles was also there; and the Crown Prince himself soon afterwards entered. Our aunt sat in the middle of the sofa, the Crown Prince and Princess, and the Princess Charles on her right, the Princess William, Princess Marie, and Princess Czartoryski on the left; Count Groben sitting near her to interpret; the Countesses Bohlen and Dernath by her—I was sitting by the Countess Schlieffen, a delightful person who is much interested in all our proceedings. A table was placed before our aunt, with pens, ink and paper, like other Committees, with the various rules that she and I had drawn up, and the Countess Bohlen had translated into German, and which she read to the assembly. Our aunt then gave a clever, concise account of the Societies in England. When business was over my aunt mentioned some texts which she asked leave to read. A German Bible was handed to Count Groben, the text in Isaiah having been pointed out, that our aunt had wished for, 'Is not this the fast that I have chosen,' &c. The count read it, after which our aunt said, 'Will the Prince and Princesses allow a short time for

prayer?' They all bowed assent and stood, while she knelt
down and offered one of her touching heartfelt prayers for
them—that a blessing might rest on the whole place, from
the King on his throne to the poor prisoner in the dungeon;
and she prayed especially for the Royal Family; then for
the ladies, that the works of their hands might be prospered in what they had now undertaken to perform.
Many of the ladies now withdrew, and we were soon left
with the Royal Family. They all invited us to see them
again before we left Berlin, and took leave of us in the
kindest manner."

How admirably did this meek and trustful woman maintain the simple dignity of her apostolic office. Like Paul
she was polite to the high as well as to the low in position,
remembering the words "Ye have one Master, even Christ,
and all ye are brethren." She was not captivated by the
glitter of court-life, even when it was sustained by true
nobility of mind and character, as was the case in Prussia.
Her sympathies were with the people, and she felt their
sufferings and bonds, as bound with them, using her
divinely given influence to ameliorate sorrow wherever
found. She seized on this favorable moment to present to
the Crown Prince a concern which weighed upon her spirit.
Having learned by inquiry that members of the Lutheran
church still suffered great oppression, in various ways, she
opened the subject to the heir to the throne. He gave her
an attentive hearing and encouraged her to act as she believed to be right. Thereupon an address was drawn up
by William Allen and officially presented to the King.
"On the following day the King's chaplain was the bearer
of the delightful intelligence that the address had been

graciously received, and that the King had said that, 'He thought the Spirit of God must have helped them to express themselves as they had done.'"

"*Leipzig, Fourth Month,* 30th.

"My dearest L——,

The deeply weighty exercises at Berlin had so much expended all my powers, that I concluded to remain here alone with my maid and our young friend Beyerhaus whilst the rest of our little company went to Dresden. I have had a quiet time and am much refreshed. I enjoy this fine weather. How beautiful is the breaking forth of spring!

"We have been particularly interested in visiting Luther's abode at Wittemberg, being where he was, and sitting where he sat by his table. Though in an old monastery he appears to have had very comfortable apartments. We saw a beautiful painted ceiling in his sitting-room, though now much defaced. I hope you have all read Merle D'Aubigné's History of the Reformation, we have found it so very interesting; we expect to visit many of the places mentioned in it, and see the castle in which Luther was confined."

"*Frankfort, Fifth Month,* 4th.—I felt very unwell yesterday and low in spirits. My dearest brother and sweet niece were most kind to me; all that I required I had; so 'the Lord doth provide.' I almost dreaded my night; but through tender mercy the Comforter was near to comfort and help my great infirmity, so that I rested in my Lord and feel revived in body and soul this morning. This text has been present with me, 'I am the Lord that healeth thee.'—Exodus xv., 26. Such fears presented themselves— How could I get home? How could I bear the sea? Should I not feel much burdened, not having finished what I thought I ought to do? and so on; but now my most gracious and holy Helper delivers me from my fears. Thanks to His most blessed and holy name."

From Dusseldorf they visited "the establishment of Kaiserwerth, under the care of Pastor Fliedner, for training Deaconesses to tend and nurse the sick and to aid their spiritual necessities whilst providing for their temporal wants. At that time this admirable institution had existed only four years, but its utility was generally acknowledged, and information upon the subject earnestly desired. Pastor Fliedner, in furnishing his recollections of the visit says: "

"The 8th of May 1840 was a great holiday to us; Elizabeth Fry of London visited our institution. Of all my contemporaries none has exercised a like influence on my heart and life: truly her friendship was one of the 'all things' which God in sovereign mercy has worked for my good.

"In January 1824, I had had the privilege of witnessing the effects of Mrs. Fry's wonder-working visits among the miserable prisoners of Newgate. On my return to my fatherland my object was to found a society entitled the 'Rhenish Westphalian Prison Association,' having ramifications in all the provinces of Germany. In this I was greatly assisted by the advice and experience afforded me by this eminent servant of God. During my second stay in England, in 1834, I had the happiness, in common with Dr. Steinkopff, of spending a day with Mrs. Fry at her own home, and also of accompanying her in one of her visits of mercy to Newgate. By this means I was enabled to see and admire her in her domestic as well as public character.

"Thus may my happiness be estimated when, in 1840, Mrs. Fry, accompanied by her brother, her young niece, William Allen, and Lucy Bradshaw, came in person to see and rejoice over the growing establishment of Kaiserwerth. She saw the whole house, going into every room, and minutely examining each in detail, and then delivered to the inmates a deeply interesting discourse. Many were the tears shed, and I have a bright hope not in vain. . . . Truly God was in the midst of us, and the remembrance of that spirit of active, self-denying love is one of the sweetest consolations I possess amid the trials and difficulties which every such institution must afford.

May, 26, 1848.   THOMAS FLIEDNER."

Her own account of their engagements at Dusseldorf bears date May 10th.

"Here we are, and, thanks to my Heavenly Father, I am much revived : my cough better; unfavorable symptoms subsided ; sufficient strength given me for the various duties as they arise. I feel my prospect weighty; first going to the prison to visit some prisoners whom I did not see yesterday; and then we expect a large party in the evening to read the Scriptures and for worship,—and this amongst strangers who know little or nothing of us, or our ways, and our interpreter not accustomed to us. But our holy Helper can, through his own unmerited mercy and almighty power, really so help us to touch the hearts of those who come to us, to their true edification. O gracious Lord! be with us, help us and bless us. Thy servants have come in much fear, much weakness, and under a belief that it is Thy call that has brought them here. Now be Thyself present with us, in this, our last occasion of the kind, to our help, consolations and edification! I can only cast myself on Thy love, mercy and pity.

"In the afternoon I visited the prison, accompanied by my dear brother, William Allen and Lucy Bradshaw. We first collected a large number of men in a yard, and I was, in my low state of body strengthened to speak to them in the open air. Unexpectedly a valuable man, the Pastor Fliedner, met us, who interpreted beautifully for me. We then visited several wards, and the prisoners appeared to feel a great deal. May its effects long remain. I also visited a very valuable lady, a Roman Catholic, who has visited

the prison many years. We partook of Christian love, and
I believe of Christian unity. In the evening wo had a very
large party to our reading and worship; I should think
nearly a hundred persons. My Lord and Master only
knows what such occasions are to me, weak in body, rather
low in spirits—amongst perfect strangers to us—not able
to speak to them in their own language. To whom could
I go? I could say, 'With God all things are possible;'
and so I found it. My brother Samuel read the 7th chapter of Matthew. One of the pastors read it in German. I
soon spoke, and unexpectedly had to enlarge much on the
present state of Germany; how it was that more fruit had
not been produced, considering the remarkable seed sown
in years past; the query what hindered its growth? I expressed my belief—first that it arose from a lukewarm and
indifferent spirit; secondly, from infidel principles creeping
in under a specious form; thirdly, from too much superstition yet remaining; fourthly, and above all, from the love
of the world and the things of it, beyond the love of Christ.
After showing the evil and its results—the seed obstructed,
as in the parable of the Sower, bringing no fruit to perfection.
I endeavored to find out the remedy—to look at home and
not judge one another; to ask for help, protection and
direction to walk in the narrow way; to be doers and not
hearers of the word; and to devote themselves to His service who had done so much for us. William Allen followed
with a satisfactory sermon. I then prayed very earnestly
for them and afterwards exhorted on reading the Scriptures.
family worship, keeping the Sabbath, &c., and ended with a
blessing. The attention was excessive; the interpretation
excellent by my dear friend the Pastor Fliedner; hearts
much melted, and great unity expressed by numbers. It
was a solemn seal set to our labors in this land, and one
not to be forgotten. So our Lord helped us and regarded
me, His poor servant, in my low estate; afterwards peace
was in no common degree my portion. Blessed be the name

of the Lord. All my dear companions, William Allen, my brother, and the younger of the party, my dear niece and Lucy Bradshaw, appeared happy and cheerful. I returned thanks on sitting down to a refreshing meal, after the labors of the day; and I think I may say we ate our 'meat with gladness and singleness of heart.'"

The return to England was made in time for the Yearly Meeting of Friends which was held in May, so that the journey lasted about two months and a half.

" *Upton*, 19th.—I attended the first sitting of the Select Meeting yesterday. My lot was to sit in silence. I saw many much loved by me. May my most gracious Lord help me, by His own Spirit, at this Yearly Meeting fully, simply and clearly to lay what I think and feel before this people—that which is right for the aged and more experienced before them, and that which is for the youth before them. Gracious Lord help me to do it in faithfulness, in love, in truth, in deep humility and godly sincerity. Amen.

"We have, altogether, a favorable reply to our letter from the King of Prussia. He justifies the measures pursued towards the Lutherans, but I believe our address will not be in vain. We have had satisfactory reports of the Government already acting on our suggestions respecting the prisons in Prussia. The prisoners are to have more religious instruction and more inspection. I have also had a very interesting letter from the Queen of Denmark expressing regret at our not going there, and not only great desire to see me there, but much unity with my views on many subjects."

The Yearly Meeting proved satisfactory, but no particular account is preserved.

" *Eighth Month*, 6th.—There has been some fear of a war

with France, which has been really sorrowful to me; I could have wept at the thought; so dear are the people of that country to my heart, and so awful is it to think of the horrors of war, whichever way we look at the subject, religiously, morally, or physically. The longer I live and the greater my experience of life, the more decided are my objections to war, as wholly inconsisted with the Christian calling. Oh! may the Almighty grant that through His omnipotence and unutterable love and mercy in Christ our Saviour, the day may not be very far distant when the people shall learn war no more,—when peace and righteousness shall reign in the earth."

"*Earlham, Eighth Month,* 21st.—My dearest brother Joseph is safely returned home after his absence of three years in America and the West India Islands. I think I never saw any person in so perfectly peaceful a state; he says unalloyed peace, like a sky without a cloud, and above all enabled thankfully to enjoy his many blessings.

"*Twelfth Month,* 31st.—I deeply feel coming to the close of this year, rather unusually so: it finds me in a rather low estate, and from circumstances my spirit is rather overwhelmed although I am sensible that blessings abound, through unmerited mercy. I think the prison cause, at home and abroad, much prospering, many happy results from our foreign expedition, and much doing at home. Among other things the establishment of a Patronage Society for prisoners, by which many poor wanderers appear to be helped and protected, and a Society for the Sisters of Charity to visit and attend the sick."

The last named institution, the management of which, from the urgency of her numerous engagements was entrusted largely to her sister Elizabeth Gurney, and her daughters, was constituted somewhat in imitation of Pastor Fliedner's Kaiserwerth, and was finally called the "Nursing

Sisters." Of this Society the Queen Dowager became Patroness and Lady Inglis President, and with an effective committee to conduct the management, it has steadily advanced and prospered. "Their aid in sickness has been sought and greatly valued by persons of all classes, from Royalty to the most destitute."

Notwithstanding the abundance of home interests and cares, and that her health already began seriously to yield to the constant drain upon her strength, this great-hearted philanthropist, and devoted servant of the Lord, still felt that more work remained for her abroad, whence appeals for aid continued to be received. She "shrank from the great effort of leaving home, and encountering the fatigue of traveling, from the shaken state of her health; her life of exertion and effort had told irremediably upon her vital powers; but it was not because the shades of evening were gathering around her that she would slacken her labors for the good of others. Whilst it was yet day, she desired to work and finish all that her great Master might have for her to do, before the night should come when no man can work." In view of this new prospect she writes :—

"*Sixth Month.*—I most earnestly desire the direction of my Lord and Master, through the immediate teaching of His Holy Spirit, that I may really know and do His will, and His will only. For Thy name's sake, O Lord! lead me, and teach me. . .

"*27th, First-day.*—After most deeply weighing the subject, and after very earnest prayer for direction, I felt best satisfied to inform my friends of my belief that it might be right for me to accompany my dearest brother Joseph to the Continent and to visit some of the more northern countries of Europe. I had very decided encouragement from Friends, particularly the most spiritual amongst them, which I felt helpful to me; but I was surprised at the degree of relief and peace that I felt afterwards, as from a voice before me saying 'This is the way, walk in it.'

"*Seventh Month*, 28*th*, *Second-day.*—I had, on Seventh-day, letters from the Queen of Prussia and the Princess William—the first expressing much satisfaction at our proposed visit; our way is clearly open in her heart, and that of the King."

The company on this fourth tour consisted of her brother Joseph John Gurney, his daughter Anna, Elizabeth, daughter of Samuel Gurney, and Mrs. Fry's maid. The prospect embraced portions of Holland, Germany, Prussia and Denmark.

The first stop was made at Rotterdam where they had a large party in the evening, and the next day visited the prisons. She remarks, "I find a second visit to a place much better than a first."

They then went to the Hague, and sent their letters to the King from Prince Albert. "On Sixth-day a message came to desire that we would wait upon the King and Queen the next day, at half-past one o'clock, accompanied by Lady Disbrowe, (wife of the British Minister.)

"We remained with the King and Queen and their daughter, the Princess Sophia, about an hour. As rather an interesting event in my life, I mean to tell you (the home circle) particulars of this interview. Before we went we had a solemn, short meeting for worship with our dear and valued friends of this town: afterwards we prepared to go. "I was decorated in my best garments outwardly, (a neat brown silk dress presented by a son, and a drab silk shawl, the gift of another of her family,) and I desired so to be clothed with better ornaments spiritually as to render attractive that which I had to recommend. We all felt very weightily our serious engagement, as we had much to represent to the King respecting the West Indies, prisons, and religious education for the people of his own country. The King, a lively, clever, perfect gentleman, not a large man, in regimentals; the Queen, (sister to the Emperor of Russia,) a fine, stately person, in full and rather beautiful morning dress of white; the Princess much the same. After our presentation the King began easy and pleasant conversation with me about my visiting prisons. I told him in a short, lively manner, the history of it. He said he heard I had so many children, how could I do it? This I explained, and mentioned how one of my daughters now helped me in the Patronage Society. He appeared much interested, as did the Queen. I then said my brother had visited the West Indies and would be glad to tell the King and Queen the result of his observations in those islands. This he did capitally, showing the excellency of freedom and its most happy results. He represented also the sad effects of the Dutch enlisting soldiers on the Gold Coast, and how it led to the evil of slavery, which so touched the King that he said he meant to put a stop to it. I then began again and most seriously laid before the King the sad defect of having no religious education in their Government schools, and the Bible not introduced. He said he really felt it, but what could he do when there was a law against it. We then endeavored to explain how we thought it might be obtained. Our very serious conversation was mixed with much cheerfulness. I felt helped to speak very boldly, yet respectfully; so did my brother. I concluded by expressing my most earnest desire that the King's reign might be marked by the prisoners being so reformed that punishment might become the means of the reformation of criminals; by the lower classes being religiously educated; and by the slaves in their colonies being liberated. The King then took me by the hand and said he hoped God would bless me. I expressed my desire that the blessing of the Almighty might rest on the King, Queen, their children, and their children's children. We gave them books which they accepted kindly. It certainly was a very pleasant and satisfactory interview that I humbly trust will not prove in vain in the Lord."

"On Sixth-day, with my brother, I visited the Princess of Orange. We had open, free, pleasant communication on many important points. The same morning I visited the Princess Frederick, sister to the King of Prussia just out of her confinement. I found her like the other members of that superior family. My brother also had very satisfactory intercourse with the Princess of Orange. The Ministers of the Interior and of Finance have been very kind, and we hope and expect that real good will result. The Princess of Orange has a lovely little boy about two months older than our Princess. The girls went to see him; they accompanied me to the Princess Frederick who wished to see them, from her knowledge of us through the Prussian Court."

On the 7th of August the party reached Amsterdam where they inspected all the public institutions and held philanthropic and religious meetings in the usual manner. On the 14th they arrived at Bremen where a large meeting was held in the Museum at which several of the pasteurs were present. One of these said to Mrs. Fry, "Your name has long been to us *a word of beauty;*" and a Christian gentleman wrote to them afterwards, "Now I am more than convinced that you are sent to us by the Lord to be

and to become a great blessing, and a salt to our city."
"An address, embodying subjects of great importance, was
afterwards prepared by Elizabeth Fry and her brother and
forwarded to the municipal authorities of the place."
"When the carriage came to the Hotel door for their departure crowds of the lower classes surrounded it, wishing
them a prosperous journey, 'bon voyage,' thanking them
for the good Meeting they had had the evening before, and
begging for tracts; whilst numbers could not be persuaded
to move till Elizabeth Fry had shaken hands with them.
Their little transit across the Elbe would have been delightful, with a splendid setting sun, but for a mob of persons
returning from Hamburg market, who, having discovered
Elizabeth Fry and her tract bag, so pressed upon her that
she was glad to take refuge in a carriage."

After various engagements and a large meeting at Hamburg, they embarked on the Baltic for Copenhagen, where
they remained a week. The following is Mrs. Fry's description of this part of the mission, written to her family on
board the packet, August 30th, 1841.

"We have been favored to leave Denmark with peaceful
minds, having endeavored to fulfil our mission as ability
has been granted us: a more important one, or a more interesting one, I think I never was called into. On First-
day morning when we arrived in the harbor we were met
by Peter Browne the Secretary to the English Legation, to
inform us that the Queen had engaged apartments for us in
the Hotel Royal. The appearance of the Hotel was I
should think like the arrangements of one of our first rate
hotels about a hundred years ago.

"The next morning the Queen came to town and we had
a very pleasant and satisfactory interview with her. She

certainly is a most delightful woman, as well as a truly Christian and devoted character; lovely in person and quite the Queen in appearance. She took me in her carriage to her infant school: it really was beautiful to see her surrounded by the little children and to hear her translating what I wished to say to them. After staying with her about two hours, we returned to our Hotel, and that evening took a drive to see the beautiful Palace of Fredericksburgh, in a most lovely situation, the beauties of land and sea combined, with fine forest trees around it. The following morning we regularly began our prison visiting. Very sad scenes we witnessed in some of them. We saw hundreds of persons confined for life in melancholy places; but what occupied our most particular attention was the state of the persecuted Christians. We found Baptist ministers, excellent men, in one of the prisons, and that many others of this sect suffered much in this country, for there is hardly any religious tolerance. It produces the most flattening religious influence, I think more marked than in Roman Catholic countries. We were most devoted to the service of visiting prisons. Third and Fourth-days we received various persons in the evening, but saw as yet but few Danes.

"On Fourth-day we dined at Sir Henry Watkyn Wynn's, our ambassador, and here we became acquainted with several persons. They live quite in the country and we saw the true Danish country-house and gardens. The King and Queen were kind enough to invite us all to dine at their palace in the country on Fifth-day. This was a most serious occasion, as we had so much to lay before the King;— slavery in the West Indies, the condition of the persecuted Christians here, and the sad state of the prisons. I was in spirit so weighed down with the importance of the occasion that I hardly could enjoy the beautiful scene. We arrived about a quarter past three o'clock; the Queen met us with the utmost kindness and condescension and took us a walk in their lovely grounds which are open to the public. We had much interesting conversation, between French and English, and made ourselves understood. When our walk was finished we were shown into the drawing room to the King who met us very courteously; several were there in attendance. Dinner was soon announced: imagine me, the King on one side and the Queen on the other, and only my poor French to depend upon; but I did my best to turn the time to account. . . When dinner was over we all went out together. The afternoon was very entertaining; the King and Queen took us to the drawing-room window where we were to see a large school of orphans, proteges of the Queen. I took advantage of this opportunity and laid the state of the prisons before the King, telling him at the same time that I had a petition for him which I meant to make before leaving the palace. After an amusing time with the children my brother Joseph withdrew with the King into a private room, where, for about an hour he gave him attention whilst he thoroughly enlarged upon the state of their West India Islands. I staid with the Queen, but after awhile went to them and did entreat the King for the poor Baptists in prison, and for religious toleration. I did my best, in few words, to express my mind, and very strongly I did it. I also gave Luther's sentiments upon the subject. . . . . On Seventh-day (one of our fullest days) we drove out into the country to visit the King's sister, the Land-gravine of Hesse Cassel, the Prince her husband, brother to the Duchess of Cambridge, and the lovely Princesses, her daughters. We endeavored to turn these visits to account by our conversation. In the evening we held one of our very large Meetings. I trust that we were both so helped to speak the truth in love on various and very important subjects as to assist the causes nearest our hearts, for our poor fellow-mortals. It did not appear desirable to allude to the persecuted Christians: as we had laid their case before the King we might have done harm by it. But I feel the way in which Protestant Europe is persecuting to be a subject that cannot and must not be allowed to rest. Where we now are, the same old Lutherans whom we found persecuted in Prussia are persecuting others.

"The way in which ceremonies are depended upon is wonderful. No person is allowed to fill any office, civil or religious, until confirmed,—not even to marry! and when once confirmed we hear that it leads to a feeling of such security spiritually that they think themselves at liberty to do as they like. Sadly numerous are the instances of moral fall.

"These very weighty subjects so deeply occupying my attention, and being separated from so many beloved ones prevent the lively enjoyment I should otherwise feel in some of the scenes we pass through; but I see this to be well, and in the right ordering of Providence. I have the kindest attendants and everything to make me comfortable.

"On First-day morning we had a very interesting meeting with the poor Baptists. We then again went into the country to lay all our statements before the King and Queen. I read the one about the prisons and the persecuted Christians, and my brother read the one about the West Indies; we had them translated into Danish for the King to read at the same time. After pressing these as strongly as we felt right, we expressed our religious concern and desires for the King and Queen. I read a little to them in one of Paul's epistles; after that I felt that I must commit them and these important causes to Him who alone can touch the heart. We had a very handsome luncheon, when I was again seated between the King and Queen. I may say their kindness to me was very great.

"On Second-day morning we formed a Society for attending to poor prisoners—gentlemen and ladies; and then paid a most delightful farewell visit to the Queen and Princess. I forgot to mention a very interesting visit to the Queen Dowager."

They returned, by Lubeck, to Hamburg, whence Mrs. Fry wrote to her family :

"*Hamburg, Ninth Month,* 3rd.

. . . . . .

"We last night finished our labors in these Hanse Towns. We have labored in them in various ways, particularly in this large and important town. We have boldly set our faces against religious persecution, and upheld religious tolerance and Christian unity in the Church of Christ. We have also labored about their prisons, and expect to have many evils mitigated. It is extraordinary the good fellow-ship and love we have enjoyed with numbers. In a spirit-ual sense, fathers, mothers, brothers and sisters given to us, and helpers most curiously and constantly raised up from place to place."

From Hamburg they proceeded towards Hanover by way of Minden and Pyrmont, again visiting the Friends in these places. The visit is described in a letter to her youngest daughter.

"*Hanover, Ninth Month,* 9*th,* 1841.

"I cannot express the fulness of my love and interest for my children, in their different allotments, and how often I think of you and your families before the Lord, in my quiet meditations. We arrived here after finishing our interest-ing and satisfactory visits to our dear Friends at Minden and Pyrmont. I felt it refreshing being again with these dear, simple-hearted people, and I do think they are useful in their allotments. How much I should like you to have seen us dining with them at Friedensthal; such a numerous family, grandmother, children, grandchildren, in a large room, and a beautiful and most hospitable German dinner. We not only were favored with outward refreshment but it

reminded me of the disciples formerly who went from house
to house breaking bread and giving thanks; and I desired
that we might do as they did, 'eat our meat with gladness
and singleness of heart.' I hope there was something of
this spirit. The country is lovely. I retired for rest on a
little German bed whilst my companions took a ride on
horseback over the beautiful hills. We had a very interesting Meeting, largely attended by the company who come
here to drink the waters and by the Pyrmontese. At Minden the Friends are in more humble life. I could not but
be struck with the peculiar contrast of my circumstances;
in the morning traversing the bad pavement of a street in
Minden with a poor old Friend, in a sort of knitted cap
close to her head, in the evening surrounded by the Prince
and Princesses of a German court; for to our surprise Dr.
Julius's sister followed us to Minden to inform us that in
the town of Bukeburg which we had passed through there
was a desire expressed that we should hold a meeting, and
that the reigning Princess wished us to go to the palace.
After some consideration we agreed to go, and upon our
arrival in the town found a large meeting of the gentry assembling. Sometime afterwards the Prince and Princesses
and their family came in. They rule the state of Lippe
Schouenburg, one of the small, rich German states. I endeavored to speak the truth boldly in love, drawing results
from my experience in prisons, and seeking, as ability was
granted me, to bring it home to the hearts of those present. Your uncle also spoke to the same purpose. Afterwards we had a very agreeable visit to the palace where we
were most cordially received and had tea at five o'clock;
there were many to meet us. After this singular visit we
proceeded here, but did not arrive until twelve o'clock at
night, having had two meetings at Minden and one at Bukeburg. We were completely tired; almost too much so.
To-day we are busy here, and I am delighted to find the
dear late Queen really had the chains knocked off the poor

prisoners at Hameln. It was delightful to see their happy, grateful faces. They looked as if they knew that we had pleaded for them. I think it was one of the pleasantest visits I ever paid, and to find that the prisoners had behaved so well since, and that the kindness shown them had had so good an effect. We are now much occupied in answering an interesting letter from the King of Hanover to me, and as I have many weighty things to say to him, I fear I must leave off, being very tired and expecting a large party this evening."

The evening proved particulary satisfactory, and after meeting the prison committees the following day, they set out for Berlin by way of Magdensburg, diverging on the second day to visit Wittemberg.

After examining the prisons in Berlin, and presenting their recommendations to the proper authorities, the party, by special invitation, followed the Royal Family to their summer retreat in Silesia. No record of this visit was preserved by Mrs. Fry, except in a letter to her grandchildren; but the following extracts from an account by one of her companions give a lively picture of her work. After describing the various locations of different members of the House of Brandenberg, many of whom were estimable Christians, the writer says:

"To many of the Royal Family, Elizabeth Fry had been introduced in the previous year at Berlin, and the Princess Frederick of the Netherlands had been visited by her at her own beautiful home near the Hague sometime before. It was a lovely spot in which Elizabeth Fry now found her tent pitched for awhile. To a mere passing traveler there was much to delight and to please; but still more of deep interest to those who could in any degree enter into the

Royal domestic circles there assembled, and this Elizabeth
Fry was privileged to do, with much enjoyment, and with
an earnest desire to be permitted to be useful and faithful
in all her intercourse with them.   The morning was
usually passed in writing and preparing important docu-
ments on the Prison, Slavery, and other questions, and the
afternoon in some visit to one of the palaces, which had
been previously arranged. The First-day was replete with
interest.   In the early part of it it was necessary to finish
an address to the King on Religious Toleration, and on
matters connected with the Prisons.

"Elizabeth Fry was at that time suffering from great
debility and fatigue; but a power not her own seemed
granted her to rise above her infirmities, and to meet the
various duties which on that day were given her to fulfil.
It is only those who held intimate communication with her
at these times who can, in any measure, understand the extreme nervousness of her constitution on the one hand, or,
on the other, the amount of strength granted her in every
time of need.   She prayed that in nothing might she seek
herself, in all, Christ Jesus; and that all which He laid
upon her for His glory and the good of her fellow-creatures
she might rightly and faithfully perform.   The long and
interesting papers which had been prepared for the King
were again perused during the drive to Princess William's
Palace which was reached about one o'clock, she having
called on the way at Buchwald for the excellent Countess
(Reden) whose ever ready aid was given to support and
help her, and who, in the present instance, interpreted Elizabeth Fry's words for the Princess.   Many other ladies were
assembled at the Palace, and after some conversation of a
general nature every one remained in silence to listen to
what she might have to say to them.   This opportunity of
addressing Gospel truth to such a company she dared not
pass by.   Every word appeared to be listened to with the
deepest attention by all present.   She spoke of the impor-

tance of upholding a religious standard in the world; of making a final and decisive choice in these matters; of taking Christ as the only portion and rejecting all besides. She impressed upon her hearers the duties incumbent on persons of a higher class, of using their influence with others for good, and not for evil. She spoke of the privilege of possessing such means of usefulness. Very solemnly she urged upon all heads of large establishments the vast amount of responsibility entrusted to them; the prevention of crime, and the good to be derived even by silent example, and by the daily reading of the Holy Scriptures to the assembled family. She added an account of the experiences of many prisoners, as to the blessing of being placed in professedly religious families, and the awful temptations presented to the servants of those who take no care for their souls, and are neglecting their eternal interests. Many tears were shed on this occasion and all seemed anxious to share her sympathy and love.

"During her stay in Silesia Elizabeth Fry had opportunities of intercourse with the poor Tyrolese who, having fled from their native Zillerthal, on account of the religious persecution which they endured from the Austrian Government, had thrown themselves under the protection of the late King of Prussia, and by him had been placed under the care of the Countess Reden who had proved herself indeed a nursing mother to them. . . . She had cottages built for them in true Swiss style, with large balconies and long roofs, and established for them schools, and in every possible way employed and instructed them. Ever thoughtful of their interest, the Countess invited them to come to Buchwald on that evening to receive encouragement and comfort from Elizabeth Fry; she having expressed her anxious wish to hold some communication with them in Christian love. A meeting was appointed for them on this First-day evening. The King and Queen and other members of the Royal Family arrived to attend it. At length came the exiles from Zillerthal, forming a curious and picturesque group dressed in the costume of their country; both men and women in dark green clothes and high-pointed hats, many of the latter ornamented with garlands and nosegays of flowers. A long table was placed at one end of the room, at which the Zillerthalians sat, and in front of it was a Moravian brother, for whom the good Countess had sent forty miles, to act as interpreter. On the right hand of the table were seated the Royal family and others, and many stood crowding round the door. It would be scarcely possible to describe the deep interest of that whole group, or the solemn silence which prevailed when Elizabeth Fry began to speak.

"After J. J. Gurney had in a few words, prepared the way for her, she rose with much solemnity and earnestness.*ʳ Never did she address any assembly more beautifully, with more unction, or more truly from the depths of her heart, and no audience could have given more profound attention to every word she uttered. She invited them all to a close dependence upon Jesus Christ, and urged a full, firm, constant trust in Him as their Lord and their Saviour, their King and their God.

" With her usual clearness and power each individual, each class present, seemed included in her address. It was the first occasion on which she had seen the King† since his accession to the throne, and she knew too that it was the first time of his meeting many there present as their sovereign. Her words of sympathy to him on the death of

---

* J. J. Gurney states in his Journal that by request of the King, who wished to save her fatigue, she spoke from her seat—probably after the commencement. But this is noteworthy as an instance where two perfectly candid, and probably entirely truthful eye-witnesses make statements which seem diametrically opposed to each other, and yet are not so, each statement being in itself incomplete.

† Frederick William IV, brother of the Emperor William I.

his father, and her estimate of his present important posi
tion in Europe, which she spoke for herself as well as for
those about her, were beautifully adapted to the occasion.
Joseph John Gurney added a few words; afterwards a hymn
was sung led by the Moravian brethren; and then the Tyrolese departed. Every one flocked around her with a word
of love or kindness, but none expressed more interest, or
more gratitude, than the King himself."

Mrs. Fry's own brief account to her grandchildren will
not be found tedious, even where it treats of the same subject as the preceding.

"Fischbach.

"My MUCH-LOVED GRANDCHILDREN:
Instead of my private Journal I am disposed to write
you from this very lovely and interesting place. I am not
very well in health but I may thankfully acknowledge, that
although tried by it for awhile, such sweet peace was granted
me that I was permitted to feel it sleeping as well as waking; so that I may say, my Lord restored my soul, and I
fully expect is healing, and will heal, my body. I think a
more interesting neighborhood I never heard of, than the
one we are in. These lovely mountains have beautiful palaces scattered about them; one belonging to the King,
others to Prince William, Prince Frederick, and other Princes and Princesses, not royal; besides several to the nobility.
But what delights my heart is that almost all these palaces
are inhabited by Christian families—some of most remarkable brightness. Then we find a large establishment with
numerous cottages in the Swiss style, inhabited by a little
colony of Tyrolese. They fled from Zillerthal because they
suffered so much on account of their religious principles,
being Protestants. The late King of Prussia allowed them
to take refuge in these mountains, and built them these
beautiful cottages. We therefore rejoice in the belief that

in the cottages as well as the palaces there are many faithful servants of the Lord Jesus Christ. This evening we are to hold a meeting for such as can attend at the mansion of the Countess Reden who is like a mother in Israel to rich and poor. We dined at her castle yesterday. I think the palaces for simple country beauty exceed anything I ever saw. The drawing-rooms are so filled with flowers that they are like green-houses, beautifully built, and with the finest views of the mountains. We dined at the Princes William's with several of the Royal Family; the Queen came afterwards. She appeared much pleased with my delight on hearing that the King had stopped religious persecutions in the country, and that several other things had been improved since our last visit. It is a very great comfort to believe that our efforts for the good of others have been blessed—may we be thankful enough for it. Yesterday we paid a very interesting visit to the Queen, then to Prince Frederick of Holland and his Princess, sister to the King of Prussia; with her we had much serious conversation on many important subjects, as we had also with the Queen. Dined early at the Countess Reden's. The Princess William and her daughter, the Princess Mary, joined us in the afternoon, with several others. How delighted you would be with the Countess and her sister; they show the beauty of holiness. Although looked up to by all they appear so humble, so moderate in everthing. I think the Christian ladies on the Continent dress far more simply than those in England. The Countess appeared very liberal, but extravagant in nothing. A handsome dinner, but only one sort of wine, and all accordingly. To please us she had apple-dumplings which were thought quite a curiosity, and they really were very nice. The company stood still before and after dinner instead of saying grace.

"*Afternoon.*—We are just returned from Prince William's where we have had a Meeting of a very interesting nature. Many ladies were assembled to meet us that I might give them some account of my experience in prisons. Your uncle added some account of his journey to the West Indies. We expressed our desire that the blessing of God might be with them. Great love was shown us: indeed they treat me more like a sister than a poor humble individual as I feel myself to be. On our return we met the King: we rather expect he will be at our meeting at the Countess Reden's this evening.

"*Second-day Morning.*—We returned from our interesting Meeting at the Countess's about eleven in the evening. The Royal Family were assembled, and numbers of the nobility; after awhile the King and Queen arrived. The poor Tyrolese flocked in numbers. I doubt such a meeting ever having been held before anywhere—the curious mixture of all ranks and conditions. My poor heart almost failed me. Most earnestly did I pray for best help, and not unduly to fear man. The Royal Family sat together, or nearly so; the King and Queen, Princess William, Princess Frederick, Princess Mary, Prince William, Prince Charles, brother to the King, Prince Frederick of the Netherlands, young Prince William, beside many other Princes and Princesses not royal. They began with a hymn in German. Your uncle Joseph spoke for a little while, explaining our views on worship. Then I enlarged upon the changes that had taken place since I was last in Prussia, mentioned the late King's kindness to those poor Tyrolese in their affliction and distress: afterwards addressed these poor people, and then those of high rank, and felt greatly helped to speak the truth to them in love. They appeared very attentive and feeling. I also, at the close of my exhortation, expressed my prayer for them. Then your uncle Joseph spoke fully on the great truths of the Gospel, and showed that the prince as well as the peasant would have to give an account of himself to God. In conclusion he expressed his prayer for them. They finished with another hymn. It was a solemn time. We afterwards had interesting con-

versation for about an hour. When the King and Queen
were gone we were enabled to pray with the Countess for
herself and her sister that all their labors in the Lord's service might be blessed. Now, my much-loved grandchildren,
let me remind you that we must be humbled and take up
the Cross of Christ if we desire to be made use of by the
Lord. 'Him that honoreth me will I honor.' May you
confess your Lord before men, and He will then assuredly
confess and honor you. I can assure you when surrounded
by so many who are willing to hear me, I feel greatly
humbled.

"I wish dear Frank to read this as my eldest grandchild
and one in whom I take so tender an interest. Indeed, my
beloved grandchildren you dwell very near my heart; may
the same Holy Spirit who has helped and guided your
grandmother, help and guide you!

"May the Lord bless and keep you and raise you up for
His own service; for it is a most blessed service. Dearest
love to your fathers and mothers: I am

Your most loving grandmother,

E. F."

"It was on this occasion the Princess William gave an
account of the great prison at Jauer, and the King expressed a strong wish that Elizabeth Fry should see it,
though considerably out of her route. This visit was afterwards accomplished. It proved one of mournful interest.
In one cell was a murderer, in another a man of well-known
desperate character; they were both most cruelly fettered
to prevent their escape through the window. Each was
fastened to an iron staple in the floor, with a heavy iron
bar across the shoulder, to make any movement irksome.
Their condition was afterwards represented by Elizabeth
Fry to the King who ordered their chains to be lightened,
and commanded that immediate attention should be paid
to their health, &c.

"Many of the prisoners on this occasion were assembled in the chapel, when both J. J. Gurney and Elizabeth Fry spoke to them at considerable length. Their addresses were interpreted by the Moravian brother from Buchwald, whose attendance at the prison had been commanded for that purpose." *

"*Ermansdorf, Ninth Month*, 20th.

"This morning we visited the King and Queen after our very interesting Meeting last evening which they attended, at the Countess Reden's; a meeting never to be forgotten. We went with a long document to the King and Queen about the prisoners, and various other subjects. We were received with the utmost kindness and remained with them nearly two hours and a half. We also had a reading of the Holy Scriptures and I prayed for them. We parted in love. . . . . I wish I could fully describe the deep interest we have had in this journey, and how marked has been the kindness of Providence towards us in many ways, and how blessed is His service. I certainly think the inhabitants of the mountains of Silesia the most interesting and curious assemblage of persons I ever met with. We, from this place, see those beautiful mountains, the Reisenburg, in their splendor, the morning being very fine and bright; probably the last time I shall ever see them— though the King and Queen begged me to return; but this I never expect to do, for I find the roughs of the journey are, with all my numerous indulgences, far too much for me, and I often feel very nearly ill. I think through all I have seldom had more reason to believe that I have been called to any service."

It soon became evident to both Elizabeth Fry and friends that her lease of strength for this journey was about ex-

* Life by S. Corder.

hausted, and they turned their steps homeward, arriving at
Dover on the 2nd of October, where she was met by her
husband "who was little prepared for the debilitated state
in which she was brought back to him." Two or three
months of rest, however, enabled her again to appear cau-
tiously in public. During this interval of rest she carried
on an extensive correspondence and received heart-cheering
reports of the results of her labors.

On the 14th of January she records a visit from the distinguished Baron Bunsen, whose son Earnest afterwards
married her niece Elizabeth, daughter of Samuel Gurney,
who had twice accompanied her aunt to the continent.

"We had an interesting visit from the Chevalier Bunsen,
(the Prussian Minister,) and his wife, in which I was enabled to relieve my mind, by speaking to him on some
weighty subjects, after a solemn Scripture reading and
prayer. I felt relieved by it, as I had borne him much in
mind, believing him to be a sincere and Christian man."

On the 17th of January, 1842, she attended a dinner at
the Lord Mayor's house in London, specially arranged by
the Lord Mayor's wife, who was one of her co-adjutors in
prison reform, that she might meet Prince Albert and
others whose influence would further their objects. Honors and successes had not blinded her eyes to the Source
whence all good comes, and as usual she entered upon the
work with earnest prayer.

"*First Month*, 17th.—Be pleased, O Lord, to be very near
to us this day, and help us to adorn Thy doctrine, and to
speak the right thing in the right way, that the Cause of
truth, righteousness and mercy may be promoted!
"18th.—Through condescending mercy I may say I

found this prayer answered. I had an important conversation on a female prison being built with Sir James Graham, our present Secretary of State; upon the Patronage Society, &c. I think it was a very important beginning with him for our British Society. With Lord Aberdeen, Foreign Secretary, I spoke on some matters connected with the present state of the Continent. With Lord Stanley, our Colonial Secretary, upon the state of our penal colonies, and the condition of the women in them, hoping to open the door for further communication with him on those subjects. Nearly the whole dinner was occupied in deeply interesting conversation with Prince Albert and Sir Robert Peel. With the Prince I spoke very seriously on the Christian education of their children, the management of the nursery, the infinite importance of a holy and religious life; how I had seen it in all ranks of life—no real peace or prosperity without it. Then the state of Europe; the advancement of religion in the Continental courts. Then prisons; their present state in this country—my fear that our punishments were becoming too severe—my wish that the Queen should be informed of some particulars respecting separate confinement, &c., &c. We also had much interesting conversation about my journey, the state of Europe, habits of countries, mode of living, &c., &c. With Sir Robert Peel I dwelt much more on the prison subject. I expressed my fears that gaolers had too much power, that punishment was rendered uncertain and often too severe—pressed upon him the need of mercy, and begged him to see the New Prison, and to have the dark cells a little altered."

A few days after this event the King of Prussia visited London to stand as sponsor to the infant Prince of Wales. During this visit he requested Elizabeth Fry to meet him at the Mansion House where they partook of lunch, provided by the Lord Mayor, who, at her special request, arranged to have no toasts. At this time the King planned to meet her the following morning at Newgate and afterwards take lunch with her at her home in Upton Lane. Her account of these incidents presents one of the finest episodes in human history.

"*First Month*, 29*th*, (1842.)—To-morrow the King of Prussia has appointed me to meet him to luncheon at the Mansion House. I have rather felt its being the Sabbath; but as all is to be conducted in a quiet, suitable and most orderly manner, consistent with the day, I am quite easy to go. May my most holy, merciful Lord be near to me as my Helper, my Keeper, and my Counsellor. My dearest husband and K—— are to go with me. Oh! may my way be made plain before me as to what to do, what to leave undone; when to speak, and when to be silent.

"30*th*, *First-day*.—I felt low and far from well when I set off this morning for London; but through the tender mercy of my God, soon after sitting down in Meeting I partook of much peace. I was humbled before my Lord in remembrance of days that are past, when I used to attend that meeting (Gracechurch Street) almost heart-broken from sorrow upon sorrow; and I remembered how my Lord sustained me, and made my way in the deep waters. He also raised me up, and then He forsook me not. I was enabled very earnestly to pray to my God for help, direction and preservation.

"After this solemn and refreshing Meeting we went to the Mansion House. We waited sometime in the drawing-room before the King arrived from St. Paul's Cathedral. I have seldom seen any person more faithfully kind and friendly than he is. The Duke of Cambridge was also there, and many others who accompanied the King. We had much deeply important conversation on various impor-

tant subjects of mutual interest. We spoke of the christen-
ing. I dwelt on its pomp as undesirable, &c.; then upon
Episcopacy and its dangers; on prisons; on the marriage
of the Princess Mary of Prussia; on the Sabbath. I entreated the Lord Mayor to have no toasts, to which he
acceded, and the King approved; but it was no light or
easy matter. I rejoice to believe my efforts were right. I
told the King my objection to anything of the kind being
allowed by the Lord Mayor on that day; indeed I expressed
my disapprobation of them altogether. I may at the end
of this weighty day return thanks to my most gracious Lord
and Master who has granted me His help and the sweet
feeling of His love.

"*Second Month*, 1st.—Yesterday was a day never to be
forgotten while memory lasts. We set off about eleven
o'clock, my sister Gurney and myself, to meet the King of
Prussia at Newgate. I proceeded with the Lady Mayoress
to Newgate where we were met by many gentlemen. My
dear brother and sister Gurney, and Susanna Corder being
with me was a great comfort. We waited so long for the
King that I feared he would not come, however at last he
arrived and the Lady Mayoress and I, accompanied by the
Sheriffs, went to meet the King at the door of the prison.
He appeared much pleased to meet our little party and
after taking a little refreshment he gave me his arm and we
proceeded into the prison and up to one of the long wards
where everything was prepared; the poor women round the
table, about sixty of them, many of our Ladies Committee
and some others; also numbers of gentlemen following the
King, Sheriffs, &c. I felt deeply, but quiet in spirit—fear
of man much removed. After we were seated, the King on
my right hand, the Lady Mayoress on the left, I expressed
my desire that the attention of none, particularly the poor
prisoners, might be diverted from attending to our reading
by the company there, however interesting, but that we
should remember that the King of Kings and Lord of Lords

was present, in whose fear we should abide and seek to profit by what we heard. I then read the 12th chapter of Romans. I dwelt on the mercies of God being the strong inducement to serve Him, and no longer to be conformed to this world. Then I finished the chapter, afterwards impressing our all being members of one body, poor and rich, high and low, all one in Christ, and members one of another. I then related the case of a poor prisoner who appeared truly converted, aud who became such a holy example; then I enlarged on love and forgiving one another, showing how Christians must love their enemies, &c., &c. After a solemn pause, to my deep humiliation, and in the cross, I believed it my duty to kneel down before this most curious, interesting and mixed company, for I felt that my God must be served the same everywhere, and among all people, whatever reproach it brought me into. I fiist prayed for the conversion of prisoners and sinners generally, that a blessing might rest on the labors of those in authority, as well as the more humble laborers for their conversion; next I prayed for the King of Prussia, his Queen, his kingdom, that it might be more and more as a city set on the hill that could not be hid; that true religion in its purity, simplicity and power might more and more break forth, and that every cloud that obscured it might be removed; then for us all that we might be of the number of the redeemed, and eventually unite with them in heaven in a never-ending song of praise. I only mention the subject, but, by no means the words. The King then gave me his arm and we walked down together. There were difficulties raised about his going to Upton, but he chose to persevere. I went with the Lady Mayoress and the Sheriffs, the King with his own people. We arrived first: I had to hasten to take off my cloak and then went down to meet him at his carriage door, with my husband and seven of our sons and sons-in-law. I then walked with him into the drawing-room where all was in beautiful order—neat and adorned with flowers. I presented to the King our eight daughters and daughters-in-law, (Rachel only away,) our seven sons and eldest grand-son, my brother and sister Buxton, Sir Henry and Lady Pelly, and my sister Elizabeth Fry—my brother and sister Gurney he had known before—and afterwards presented twenty-five of our grandchildren. We had a solemn silence before our meal which was handsome and fit for a King, yet not extravagant—everything most complete and nice. I sat by the King who appeared to enjoy his dinner, perfectly at his ease, and very happy with us. We went into the drawing-room after another solemn silence and a few words which I uttered in prayer for the King and Queen. We found a deputation of Friends with an address to read to him! This was done—the King appeared to feel it much. We then had to part. The King expressed his desire that blessings might continue to rest on our home."

"*Fourth Month*, 17th.—This week we have a very large sale at the Mansion House for the British Society. Although on the whole I approve these sales there are many difficulties attached to them. I earnestly desire and pray that through the tender mercy of God no harm may come of it; but in whatever we do the cause of truth and righteousness may be exalted.

"24th.—On Third, Fourth and Fifth-day we were fully occupied by the sale. It was very largely attended; quantities of things given and sent to us; extraordinary kindness shown to us by numbers, and the Lord Mayor and Lady Mayoress treating us with almost unbounded hospitality and kindness. One day they gave dinner and lucheon to three hundred persons, and I should think nearly as many another day or days. We sold things to the amount of about thirteen hundred pounds; still many things were left on hand. When I consider the great trouble, the enormous expense, the time taken up, the obligation we put ourselves under to so many persons, and the fatigue of body, I think

I can never patronise another sale. However in mercy I was carried through without much suffering.

"*Upton, Fifth Month, 8th.*—On Third-day the Lady Mayoress and I paid interesting and satisfactory visits to the Queen Dowager, the Duchess of Kent and the Duchess of Gloucester. I went with my heart lifted up for help and strength and direction, that the visits might prove useful, that I might drop the word in season, and that I might myself be kept humble, watchful and faithful to my Lord. I have fears for myself in visiting palaces rather than prisons, and going after the rich rather than the poor; lest my eyes should become blinded, or I should fall away in anything from the simple pure standard of truth and righteousness. We first called on the Duchess of Kent and had interesting conversation about our dear young Queen, Prince Albert, and their little ones. We spoke of my foreign journey—the King of the Belgians, and other matters. I desired whenever I could to throw in a hint of a spiritual kind, and was enabled to do it. I gave the Duchess some papers with a note to Prince Albert, requesting him to lay the suffering state of the Waldenses, from their fresh persecutions, before the Queen. We next visited the Queen Dowager and her sister, and the Duchess of Saxe Weimar and her children. We had a very satisfactory time, much lively and edifying conversation upon the state of religion in Europe particularly amongst the higher classes, and the great advancement, of late years, in the conduct and conversation of the great of this world."

Her health continuing very infirm, Mrs. Fry spent four months near the sea shore at Cromer, in the company of several of her brothers and sisters, commencing in July. Doubtless her improvement was facilitated by the spirit shown in this entry of her Journal:

"*Cromer, Seventh Month, 6th.*—Here I am, in what was

my dearest sister Hoare's little room, looking on the sea, but poorly after my journey; feeling the air almost too cold for me: but I am favored to be quiet and restful in spirit, and desire to leave all things to Him who only knows what is best for me. My sister Catherine being with us, and my brother Joseph and his Eliza, and my dear Anna, near to us, is very pleasant, and our dear brother and sister Buxton and Richenda being still at Northrepps."

Every week was marked by slow but sure increase of strength. But her amendment was retarded by anxiety on account of a daughter, then very ill in the Isle of Wight. To this daughter who was under much trial she wrote:—

"I am not very well to-day, but have not, by any means lost the ground I had gained, though your trials appear to have brought me some steps back. If, in the ordering of Providence things shall be brighter, I think I shall rally again; but I desire to have my will given up to the will of Him who knows best what is best for us all, and earnestly desire to be very thankful that our trials are not of a deeper dye; and being as far as I know, brought on us by Infinite Wisdom, I do not feel them like those produced by the exquisite suffering of sin.

"I am thy loving, sympathizing and yet hopeful mother,
E. F."

"*Seventh Month*, 14th, (First-day.)—I have deeply and sorrowfully felt our grandson Frank's going into the army. I truly have tried to prevent it but must now leave it all to my Lord, who can, if He sees meet, bring good out of that which I feel to be evil.*

"*Eighth Month*, 14th.—I have felt the weight of undertaking to establish a library and room for the fishermen,

---

* This young man, being of a serious mind, soon retired from the army.

and something of a friendly society, as in my tender state the grasshopper becomes a burden. I was encouraged, however, in the night by these words, 'Steadfast, immovable, always abounding in the work of the Lord.' In weakness and in strength we must, as ability is granted, always abound in the work of the Lord. May our labor not be in vain in Him! I have had very comforting accounts from Denmark—our representations attended to respecting the prisons, and likely to have much good done in them: also from Prussia. Surely our Lord has greatly blessed some of our poor efforts for the good of our fellow-mortals.

" *Upton Lane, First Month,* 1st, 1843.—Another year is closed and passed never to return. It appears to me that mine is rather a rapid descent into the valley of old age.

" *Second Month,* 6th.—I am just now much devoted to my children and all my family, and attend very little to public service of any kind. May my God grant that I may not hide my talents in a napkin; and on the other hand that I may not step into services uncalled for at my hands. May my feeble labors at home be blessed. Gracious Lord, heal help, and strengthen Thy poor servant for Thine own service, public or private.

" *Third Month,* 19th.—Met Lord Ashley at dinner at Manor House (my dear son William's) to consider the subject of China and the Opium Trade. Lord Ashley is a very interesting man, devoted to promoting the good of mankind and suppressing evil—quite a Wilberforce I think.

" *Fourth Month,* 2nd.—I entered the last week very low in my condition, bodily and mentally, so much so that some of my family could hardly be reconciled to my attending the Quarterly Meeting. In the Select Meeting of Ministers and Elders the subject of Unity was much brought forward; several spoke to it, and I had to express, rather strongly, my belief that there is a great work going forward in the earth, and Satan desires to mar it by separating the Lord's servants. I warned Friends upon this point; because there are diversities of gifts, difference of operation and administration, they should not sit in judgment one on another, or condemn one another, or suppose they are not of the same spirit, and one in the same lord, and the same God."

How the ripening tint of that wisdom which is from above shines in these utterances, reaching far beyond the narrow bounds of sect, toward the day of the Lord's coming.

The fifth and last visit of Elizabeth Fry to the Continent was made in the spring of 1843, commencing the latter part of April and ending about the last of May. She felt that there was still important work for her to do in Paris in confirming what had been begun, and strengthening the hands to which it must soon be left. She was accompanied by Joseph John Gurney, who with his new American wife, also a minister, contemplated a more extended journey; and by their faithful friend and co-laborer Josiah Forster. Her eldest daughter Katherine also attended as her mother's especial companion and care-taker. The latter office had now become quite essential, as the veteran apostle and reformer, though but sixty-three years old, had so nearly spent her allotted measure of strength that it was doubted after the voyage to Bologne, whether she would be able to proceed on the journey. However by using the best medicine, prudence, patience and faith, she revived and slowly advanced by way of Amiens, where they held a Meeting for worship in a room used by the few Protestants as their chapel. Their pastor was eighty years of age.

"At Clemont-en-Oise the ladies were permitted to inspect the Great Central Prison for women, calculated to contain twelve hundred, although nine hundred only were in confinement when they were there. It was under the charge of a Supérieure and twenty-two nuns, no men being allowed to enter.

"On first arriving Mrs. Fry had expressed a great wish to see all the nuns, but the Supérieure considered it impossible, as they never leave the women; however just before quitting the prison, she was conducted into an apartment around which sat, some on chairs, some on extremely low seats, some apparently on the floor, the twenty-two nuns in their grey dresses, and the lay sisters in black; placed in the middle were Mrs. Fry and her sister Mrs. Joseph John Gurney, the Supérieure between them, holding Mrs. Fry by the hand, whose daughter was requested by the Supérieure to interpret for them. It was no light or easy task to convey exactly her mother's address on the deep importance of not only maintaining good discipline amongst the prisoners, but endeavoring to lead them in living faith to Christ as the only Mediator between God and man, through whom alone they could be cleansed from the guilt and power of sin. At His name every head bowed. She then went on to tell them of Newgate, and the effects of the Gospel there. Many tears were shed at this recital. She concluded by a lively exhortation to these devoted nuns whom she could 'salute as sisters in Christ,' to go forward in their work, but in no way to rest upon it as in itself meritorious. Here the Supérieure interposed 'Oh non mais il y a un peu de mérite, l'homme a quelque mérite pour ce qu 'il fait:' an old nun who understood English rejoined, ' Ma mère, Madame thinks that if the love of God does not sufficiently animate the heart to do it without feeling it a merit, or desiring reward, it falls short.' 'Ah c'est bien! comme elle est bonne!' replied the Supérieure. Mrs. Fry concluded by a short blessing and prayer in French. It was a striking scene and a solemn feeling pervaded the whole."*

* Memoir—Vol. 2, page 471.

Arriving in Paris Elizabeth Fry felt much depressed by her weakness, but was met with warm welcome and encouragement from her friends, especially the Countess Pelet who assured her that her visit was most timely. They attended the little Friends' Meeting in the Faubourg du Roule, made some social visits, and called on the Duchess of Orleans and her pious stepmother the Grand Duchess of Mecklenburgh. The second Sabbath they held a large public meeting in the Methodist chapel, and on Monday evening met a party of "about thirty persons of color, chiefly from Hayti, the Island of France, and Guadaloupe, principally students of law or medicine; one a painter who had some good pictures in the exhibition. . . Wednesday was a dinner at Count Pelet de la Lozère's; Thursday at M. Guizot's. Seated by their celebrated host, the dinner was felt by Mrs. Fry to be an occasion of great responsibility. She was encouraged by his courteous attention unreservedly to speak to him on the subjects which had so long been near to her heart. It was no common ordeal for woman weak even in her strength to encounter reasoning powers and capabilities such as his: their motives of action arising probably from far different sources, but curiously meeting at the same point; hers from deep-rooted benevolence directed by piety in its most spiritual form; his from reflection, observation, and statesman-like policy guided by philanthropy, based on philosophy and established conviction—yet in the aggregate the results the same; an intense desire to benefit and exalt human nature, and arrest the progress of moral and social evil, and an equal interest in ascertaining the most likely methods of effecting the de-

sired end. They spoke of crime in its origin, its consequences, and the measures to be adopted for its prevention;. of the treatment of criminals; of education, and of
Scriptural instruction. Here Mrs. Fry unhesitatingly
urged the diffusion of Scriptural truth, and the universal
circulation of the Scriptures, as the one means alone capable of controlling the power of sin, and shedding light upon
the darkness of superstition and infidelity.

"The following morning Mrs. Fry and her brother
received at their hotel a large party of Greeks; amongst
others their Ambassador, M. Coletti. The Duke de Broglie
was kind enough to interpret for Mrs. Fry. Before the
party separated Mr. Gurney read an account of St. Paul's
visit to Athens: his comments on this portion of Holy Writ
were *luminous*, *powerful*, and appropriate.

"When in Paris in 1839, Mrs. Fry had become interested
in a large party of Greeks who met her at her hotel one
evening. On the present occasion that interest was confirmed. The want of books in Greece, even those of elementary instruction, was fully discussed, and it was decided
to form some regular plan to supply this want. That this
might be done effectually a second evening was appointed
for the purpose. There were assembled on this occasion
several very superior men, among others M. de Commène,
who, though not 'born in the purple,' was one of a family
recognized as lineally descended from the Emperors of
Constantinople. A committee of Greeks, French and English was formed to draw up rules and endeavor to raise
subscriptions, though not till after much animated discussion,—the young Greek students in Paris undertaking to

translate some works of elementary instruction. A spelling book with pictures was to be the first work attempted— something not existing in that country. There was reason to expect that through influence with the Government at Athens these books would be dispersed into every Commune for the use of the schools and poor. Mrs. Fry had before been interested on the subject of female education in Greece, and in this important movement for supplying that country with elemental literature, she believed that the women also would eventually partake of the benefit.

"It being the period of the annual religious Meetings many pasteurs were assembled in Paris: about thirty of them were invited by Mr. Gurney to breakfast at the Hotel Meurice." (Memoir.)

"*Paris, Fifth Month*, 14*th.*—On Second-day about thirty pasteurs came to breakfast: they are from different parts of France; a very interesting set of men. First we had a Scripture reading; Joseph and myself had much to express to them at the time; a most weighty concern it was. My brother prayed and one of the pasteurs spoke. We then breakfasted, and had really a delightful meal. I remember that our Lord condescended to attend feasts, and this was a feast offered to His servants, of which we partook in love and peace. The pasteurs afterwards gave us an account of the religious state of the people around them, a good work certainly appears going on, amidst many obstructions. We then spoke to them. I particularly recommended *religious unity with all who love the Lord*, as a valuable body of Christians."

Observe how "UNITY WITH ALL WHO LOVE THE LORD," is becoming the key-note of her exhortations.

"*Paris, Fifth Month*, 21*st, (First-day.)*—My birth-day—

sixty-three! My God hath not forgotten to be gracious, nor hath He shut up His tender mercies from me.

"The last week has been an interesting one. We were sent for by the King. My brother, sister and I paid rather a remarkable visit to him, the Queen, and Princess Adelaide. To my surprise and pleasure yesterday there arrived from the Queen a most beautiful Bible with fine engravings, without note or comment; given me as a mark of her satisfaction in our visit."

"One evening the Prime Minister, M. Guizot, dined with Mrs. Fry's party. The topics before discussed were then resumed:—the state of Protestants in France, La liberté de culte, and Negro Slavery. Elizabeth Fry entreated M. Guizot's attention to the state of the Sandwich Islands. She had a few months before received from Kamehameha III., the King of those islands, a letter entreating her good offices to second his endeavors to prohibit the importation and use of spirituous liquors in his kingdom, the baneful and demoralizing effects of which he stated to be lamentable.

"Much had been done for the improvement of prisons since Mrs. Fry was last at Paris. The importance of the subject had been fully recognized, and a bill brought before the chamber of Deputies."

The concluding memoranda of the farewell visit will enable us to see her very pleasantly in her favorite occupations. Nearly all of her own minutes in this connection have been given.

"*Boulogne*, 28*th* —Through the condescending mercy of of our Heavenly Father we are safely and peacefully arrived here, after a quiet journey with my dearest Katherine. We were near meeting with a serious accident, but through mercy we escaped without injury. Our leaving Paris was no common occasion. The morning before, several of our beloved friends were with us,; they literally loaded us with presents; indeed it appeared as if they did not know how to show their love to us enough. Before we parted from each other we had a most solemn time in prayer, little knowing whether we should see each other's faces more. I hardly knew how to accept all their generous kindness. What can we say but that their hearts being thus turned to us must be 'the Lord's doing and is marvelous in our eyes.'

"The previous evening many of our dear friends, English and. French, came to take leave of us; we read together the 121st Psalm. In the morning I visited a Roman Catholic Refuge, and finished well with the Greeks in the afternoon.

"On Third-day we visited the great military prison at St. Germain, accompanied by a French general, an English colonel, our excellent friend Count Pelet, and Moreau Christophe. We were received very kindly by the Colonel, Governor of the Prison, and his wife, and took our déjeuné with them.

"In the evening we went to a large Meeting in one of the Faubourgs with the French Methodists in humble life. How curious the changes of my daily life!—what a picture they would make!—in the morning surrounded by the high military, and the soldier prisoners—in the evening in a Methodist Meeting-house, with the people and their pasteurs, and afterwards by poor little French children hearing them read.

"Another day I was at a large Prison Committee of Protestant ladies. I think they have been greatly prospered in their work of Christian love, in which they have persevered ever since my first visit to Paris; there have been many instances of great improvement in the prisoners under their care. After prayer for them I left them.

"The afternoon of the Sabbath I paid a distressing visit to the St. Lazare Prison; such a scene of disorder, and deep evil I have seldom witnessed—gambling, romping,

screaming. With much difficulty we collected four protestant prisoners and read with them. I·spoke to those poor
disorderly women, who appeared attentive and showed some
feeling. I have represented to many in authority the sad
evils of this prison, and have pleaded with them for reform,
for religious care, and for Scriptural instruction.

"In the evening the dear Countess Pe'et was with us and
we had a large assembly, mostly of English; it was thought
ninety, or a hundred. I was tired and poorly, my flesh and
my heart ready to fail; but the Lord strengthened me, and
I felt really helped by a power quite above myself. With
this company I had a most satisfactory parting time, and a
sweet feeling of love and unity with these servants of the
Lord."

Thus ended the missionary labors, abroad, of this devoted minister of Mercy, the fruit of whose sowing has continued to yield its increase all over Europe. The party returned home in season to attend the Yearly Meeting of
Friends in London and for a short time Mrs. Fry was able
"to encounter the current of life better than she had done
before her journey."

During these five visits to the Continent what an expen-
diture of the highest moral force had Elizabeth Fry made:
and it is easy to believe that little or none of the good seed
sown, even when the ground seemed least propitious, failed
to bring forth fruit; while in many instances it not only
sprang up quickly, but yielded its thirty, sixty, or hundred
fold in time for the sower and reaper to rejoice together,
and praise the Lord of the harvest who alone "giveth the
increase." And beyond the more immediate effects who
can compute the compound results, as each generation has
taken up and added to the work, and to the area where

these influences have operated to redeem the fallen, to ameliorate the consequences of evil, and to add courage and strength to human efforts for the elevation of the race?

CHAPTER ELEVENTH.

We can see the ripening toward Heaven in many of the later entries of Elizabeth Fry's journal.

"*Sixth Month,* 25th.—A week of considerable occupation: Second-day the British Society Committee; an interesting meeting with those beloved ladies; so much oneness of heart and purpose, a delightful evidence of the sweetness of Christian unity, and how those who differ in secondary points may agree in the essential one, and be one in Christ. We have cause for thankfulness in the excellent arrangements made by Lord Stanley for our poor prisoners in Van Diemen's Land; he appears so carefully to have attended to the representations we made respecting the evils existing there and to have proposed good measures to remedy them."

During this week she attended the Quarterly Meeting of Friends at Hertford. This was the last time that she left home expressly on religious service. But wherever she went, she was the same wise counselor and loving comforter. In July she wrote:—

"Last First-day was one not to be forgotten; much of the morning without clouds. My dear brother and sister Buxton were at meeting. I felt it my duty to encourage the weary, and enlarged upon our foolishness, yet now the

Lord is made unto His people wisdom, righteousness, sanctification and redemption. There were some who appeared much impressed. Through the whole of that day, and into the next renewed peace rested upon my spirit.

"As the month passed on," says her biographer, "Elizabeth Fry showed increasing symptoms of illness, the consequence, doubtless, of bodily fatigue and mental exertion, the effects of which were severely aggravated by a chill from sitting one evening in the garden at Upton Lane."

This induced her to visit Sandgate, in company with her sister-in-law, of the same name, also in declining health, to obtain the benefit of sea air. While here she wrote:

"I have at times passed through a good deal of conflict and humiliation in this indisposition, and it is a real exercise of faith to me—the way in which I am tried by my illness. I suppose it arises from my extremely susceptible nerves that are so affected when the body is out of order as to cast quite a veil over the mind. I am apt to query whether I am not deceiving myself in supposing I am a servant of the Lord, so ill to endure suffering, and to be so anxious to get rid of it; but it has been my earnest prayer that I might truly say, 'Not as I will, but as Thou wilt.' Lord, help me! I pray that I may be enabled to cast all my burthen and all my care upon Thee, that I may rest in the full assurance of faith in Thy love, pity, mercy and grace."

"After several distressing weeks she was moved to Tonbridge Wells, closely and faithfully nursed by her two youngest daughters." But the change was unavailing, and she returned to Upton near the end of September, and remained confined to her sick chamber during the winter of 1842 and '43. Her bodily sufferings were very great, but her soul had its hiding-place.

"*Upton, Tenth Month,* 10th.—My God hath not forgotten to be gracious, or shut up His tender mercies from me. It appears to me that all of nature is to be brought low, for what is of the Lord only can stand the day of humiliation. I may thankfully say, I am quiet and sustained in spirit, but do not often know peace to flow as a river, as at some former times. Still help is constantly near from the sanctuary, though I abide under a sense of deep unworthiness before the Lord; but what can I do but wait in faith until He be pleased fully to clothe me with the garments of His righteousness and His salvation? I feel I can do nothing for myself."

"One afternoon when some members of her family were reading with her, she was unable to attend to a very interesting religious biography, saying 'it is too touching to me,—too affecting.' She added, after a pause, 'How I feel for the poor when very ill; in a state like my own, for instance, when 'good' ladies go to see them.—Religious truths so strongly brought forward, often injudiciously.' She went on speaking on this subject and then dwelt on 'the exquisite tenderness of the Saviour's ministrations;' 'His tone and manner to sinners.'

"Soon afterwards she resumed, in the most impressive manner, saying that 'religious truth' was opened to her and supplied to her, 'inwardly, not by man's ministration but according to her need,' adding, 'if I may so say, it is my life.'

"She frequently spoke of not being called to active service now, and that she had no desire as to recovery; on the contrary she was 'able quite to leave it.' Frequently she repeated to those about her, '*I feel the foundation underneath me sure.*'

"One evening she opened her heart on her deep and earnest desires for the good of her children: of her 'great sufferings'—'greater than any one knows'—that if they were to last no one could wish for her life; but soon added 'there is one thing I would willingly live for—the good of my husband and children and my fellow-creatures.'.

"On the night of October the 25th, her spirit was remarkably strengthened to declare her faith and hope in God. She quoted many passages of Scripture to prove that faith must work by love, and that faith, if true, must produce works. She said, with the text, ' He that keepeth my saying shall never see death,' take this one also 'He that believeth on me shall never die.' She afterwards expressed, in a tone of deepest feeling, her 'perfect confidence,' her 'full assurance that neither life nor death, nor angels, nor principalities, nor powers, nor things present, nor things to come, nor height, nor depth, nor any other creature, should be able to separate her from the love of God which is in Jesus Christ, our Lord,' adding, 'my whole trust is in Him, my entire confidence.'—' I *know* in whom I have believed, and can commit all to Him who has loved me and given Himself for me; whether for life or death. sickness or health, time or eternity.'

"In the course of the same day she said very emphatically to one of her daughters, 'I can say one thing—since my heart was touched at seventeen years old I believe I never have awakened from sleep, in sickness or in health, by day, or by night, without my first waking thought being how best I might serve my Lord.'"

This prayer is among the few remaining entries in her Journal:

"Lord! undertake Thyself for me; Thy arm of power can alone heal, help, and deliver ; and in Thee do I trust and hope, though at times deeply tried and cast down before Thee; yet, O Lord! Thou art my hope, and be therefore entreated of Thy poor, sorrowful, and often afflicted servant, and arise for my help. Leave not my poor soul destitute, but through the fulness of Thine own power, mercy

and love keep me alive unto Thyself unto the end! that
nothing may separate me from Thy love, that I may endure
unto the end; and when the end comes that I may be altogether Thine, and dwell with Thee, if it be but the lowest
place within the gate, where I may behold Thy glory and
Thy holiness, and forever rest in Thee. I do earnestly entreat Thee that to the very last I may never deny Thee, or
in any way have my life or conversation inconsistent with
my love to Thee, and most earnest desire to live for Thy
glory; for I have loved Thee, O Lord, and desire to serve
Thee without reserve. Be entreated that through Thy
faithfulness and the power of Thy own Spirit I may serve
Thee unto the end. Amen."

The following notes are from the Journal of her son William who, notwithstanding he was now anxiously caring for
his mother, and watching for the " veiled ferryman," pre-
ceded her, by more than a year, in the final crossing.

"The evening of the 29th was one of the greatest suffering and distress; such as I never remember to have witnessed. But through all her faith was triumphant and her
confidence unshaken. I endeavored to remember a few of
her expressions and have succeeded in calling to mind the
following:—

"'I believe this is not death, but it is as passing through
the valley of the shadow of death, and perhaps with more
suffering, from more sensitiveness; but the Rock is here;
the distress is awful, but He has been with me.'

"'I feel that He is with me, and will be with me, even to
the end. David says 'why hast Thou forsaken me?' I do
not feel that I am forsaken. In my judgment I believe this
is not death, but it is as death: it is nigh unto death.'
She frequently expressed fears of being impatient. 'May
none of you be called to pass through such a furnace; but

still my sufferings have been mitigated through mercy and grace—fulness of grace! Now my dear William be stead-fast, immovable, always abounding in the work of the Lord, and then Thy labor shall not be in vain in the Lord. Oh the blessedness of having desired to be on the Lord's side! (not that I have any merit of my own.) I cannot express even in my greatest trials and tribulations the blessedness of His service! My life has been a remarkable one; much have I had to go through—more than mortal knows, or even can know; my sorrows at times have been bitter, but my consolations sweet! In my lowest estates, through grace my love to my Master has never failed, nor to my family, nor to my fellow-mortals. This illness may be for death, or it may not, according to His will; but He will never forsake me even should He be pleased to take me this night.'"

To one of the "nursing sisters" who was attending her at one time she said, "I am of the same mind as Paul, 'for me to live is Christ, and to die is gain.' What a grand thought it is! everlasting to everlasting, without trouble and without pain; to meet there and together be forever with Christ.'"

Reviewing her history she said to an intimate friend; "My life has been one of great vicissitudes; mine has been a hidden path, hidden from every *human* eye. I have had deep humiliations and sorrows to pass through. I can truly say I have "wandered in the wilderness in a solitary way, and found no city to dwell in;' and yet how wonder-fully have I been sustained. I have passed through many and great dangers, many ways;—I have been tried with the applause of the world, and none know how great a trial *that* has been, and the deep *humiliations* of it; and yet I fully believe that it is not nearly so *dangerous* as being made much of in religious society. There is a snare even in religious unity, if we are not on the watch. I have sometimes felt that it is not so dangerous to be made much of by the world, as by those whom we think highly of in our own Society. The more I have been made much of by the world the more I have been inwardly humbled. I could often adopt the words of Sir Francis Bacon, 'When I have ascended before men, I have descended in humiliation before God.'"

In physical suffering it would seem that little could be added to what she was called to bear during this terrible winter, and though usually clear, the inward sky was occasionally darkened that, like her beloved Master she might be tried in all things, for the encouragement of those who seem to themselves forsaken. The friend last mentioned visiting her a month later and perceiving that she was much depressed, remarked: "I believe there is an open door set before thee, although thou mayst not always be able to *perceive* it open." "The precious invalid wept much, and after a time said, 'Oh yes: it *is* an open door.' Presently she continued, 'The Lord is gracious and full of compassion, I believe He will never leave me nor forsake me;' and after a solemn pause she added, 'I have passed through deep baptisms of spirit in this illness,—I may say, unworthy as I am to say it, that I have had to drink, in my small measure, of the Saviour's cup when He said, 'My God, my God, why hast Thou forsaken me?' Some of my friends have thought there was a danger of my being exalted, but I believe the danger has been on the opposite side of my being too low.'"

As the spring of 1844 advanced, the conflict became less severe so that she was able to be taken to Bath for a short time, and returned somewhat improved. But afflictions of still another kind now awaited her, and she for whose departure others had watched and for whom all had felt such intense solicitude, was to be herself sorely bereaved before her own place became vacant. First her beloved sister-in-law, fellow minister and frequent traveling companion, Elizabeth Fry, who had long sat beside her in the home Meeting at Plaistow, entered into rest on the second of July. This was but a beginning, and something of the approaching changes seemed to weigh on the invalid's spirit which now "dwelt much and often on the invisible world." She even dreamed that there were graves opened all around her. On the 18th of the same month, July, a favorite little grandson was taken; August 15th, a lovely grand-daughter followed, "one of the sweetest blossoms that could gladden the heart of a parent." This was by scarlet fever in the family of her beloved son William; and before the fearful malady finished its work the father and two of his daughters lay together in one grave.

This was a heavy blow for the great motherly heart of Elizabeth Fry. Some said "can she hear this and live?" But she met it as she had met the pains of the flesh, and the fear of man, by putting on the whole armor of God. "She wept abundantly, almost unceasingly, but she dwelt constantly on the unseen world, and on those passages in the Bible which speak of the happy state of the righteous." Her journal, written before the last grand-daughter's death, describes her feelings.

" *Walmar, Eighth Month,* 29th.—Sorrow upon sorrow! Since I last wrote we have lost by death first, my beloved sister, Elizabeth Fry ; second, Gurney Reynolds, our sweet, good grandson ; third, Juliana Fry, my dearest William and Julia's second daughter; and fourth, above all, our most beloved son, William Storrs Fry, who appeared to catch the infection from his little girl, and died on Third-day of scarlet fever, the 27th of this month. A loss inexpressible—such a son, husband, friend and brother ! but I trust that he is forever at rest in Jesus, through the fulness of His love and grace. The trial is almost inexpressible. Oh! may the Lord sustain us in this time of deep distress. Oh, dear Lord! keep Thy unworthy, poor, sick servant, in this time of unutterable trial ; keep me sound in faith and clear in mind, and be very near to us all—the poor widow and children in this time of deepest distress, and grant that this awful dispensation may be blessed to our souls. Amen.

" This tenderly beloved child attended me to meeting the last First-day I was home, and sat beside me on the women's side."

The event last spoken of is thus described by her daughters :—

" A change of scene and air seemed so important for her that her son William's success in obtaining a very suitable house in Walmar was a real matter of gratulation ; but there was another office of love for that beloved one to perform for his mother singularly suited to the bond of love and sympathy which had so long united them, and eminently fitted to be his last.

" She had long and earnestly desired again to attend the meeting for worship at Plaistow. It was proposed, from Sunday to Sunday, but the difficult process of dressing was never accomplished till long after eleven o'clock, the hour when the Meeting assembled. An attempt was made on the 28th of July, but totally failed. Her disappointment was extreme, and the hold it took of her spirits so grievous that it was resolved to make the effort at any cost the following Sunday. Her son William undertook to carry out her wishes. Drawn by himself and a younger son in her wheeled chair, she was taken up to the Meeting a few minutes after Friends had assembled, followed by her husband, her children, and attendants. Her son William seated himself close by her side, and the rest near her. The silence that prevailed was singularly solemn. After some time, in a clear voice, she addressed the Meeting. The prominent topic of her discourse was 'The death of the righteous.' She expressed the deepest thankfulness, alluding to her sister Elizabeth Fry, for the mercies vouchsafed to 'one who having labored long amongst them had been called from time to eternity.' She quoted that text, 'Blessed are the dead who die in the Lord, for they cease from their labors and their works do follow them.' She dwelt on the purposes of affliction, on the utter weakness and infirmity of the flesh; she tenderly exhorted the young, 'The little children amongst us,' referring to the death of little Gurney Reynolds. She urged the need of devotedness of heart and steadiness of purpose; she raised a song of praise for the eternal hope offered to the Christian; and concluded with those words of Isaiah,—'Thine eyes shall see the King in His beauty, they shall behold the Land that is very far off.' Prayer was soon afterwards offered by her in much the same strain. He joined her in that solemn act who never was to worship with her again, till before the Throne and the Lamb they should unite in that ineffable song of praise which stays not, night nor day, for ever.

"About six weeks after the decease of her son," says Mrs. Corder, "she was again favored with strength to attend the meeting at Plaistow. The occasion was a *memo-*

rable one. She was led with great power and solemnity to address the different classes then assembled; and perhaps few could remember a Meeting in which her gift in the ministry had been exercised with greater weight and clearness, or with a more remarkable appropriateness to the varied conditions of those who were present: and she afterwards supplicated with a degree of heavenly power and unction that deeply affected many hearts. From this time she continued frequently to labor amongst her friends in the ministry of the word; and her bodily strength gradually increased, so that, though very feeble, she was able with some assistance, to walk a little."

On the first of November she addressed her last letter to the Committee of the Ladies British Society.

" MY MUCH-LOVED FRIENDS:

Amidst many sorrows that have been permitted for me to pass through and bodily suffering, I still feel a deep and lively interest in the cause of poor prisoners; and earnest is my prayer that the Lord of all grace may be very near to help you to be steadfast in the important Christian work of seeking to win the poor wanderers to return, repent and live; that they may know Christ to be their Saviour, Redeemer, and hope of glory. May the Holy Spirit of God direct your steps, strengthen your hearts, and enable you and me to glorify our Holy Head, in doing and suffering, even unto the end: and when the end comes, through a Saviour's love and merits, may we be received into glory and everlasting peace.

In Christian love and fellowship,

I am affectionately your friend,

ELIZABETH FRY."

The list of near and dear friends that were to pass on

before her and swell the company in waiting to welcome
her spirit to its final rest, was not yet complete. On the
first of December a niece, "daughter of her late beloved
sister Louisa Hoare, died,—a few days after her infant
son." On this occasion Elizabeth Fry wrote:—

"*Eleventh Month*, 2nd.—The accounts of to-day are
deeply affecting—to have the grave once more (and so soon)
opened amongst us. What can we say, but that 'it is the
Lord;' for the flesh is very weak and these things are hard
to our nature. I have felt the pain of this fresh sorrow,
but desire that all most closely concerned may find Him
very near to them who 'healeth the broken in heart and
bindeth up their wounds.' My love and sympathy to all
most nearly interested. We have our poor Julia and her
children here, and very touching it is to be with them. I
am, I think, just now very poorly, and much cast down,
but I remember the Scriptural words, 'cast down, but not
destroyed.'"

The increasing illness of her brother-in-law, Sir Thomas
Fowell Buxton, now enlisted her warm interest and sympathy. To his eldest daughter she wrote:

"*Twelfth Month*, 1844.
"MY DEAREST PRISCILLA:
Thanks for thy kindness in writing to me in this time of
deep sorrow; but, strange to say, before thy note came I
had been so much with you in spirit that I was ready to
believe thy dearest father was sinking. I have felt such
unity with him spiritually. My text for him, in my low
state this morning was, 'The sun shall be no more thy
light by day; neither for brightness shall the moon give
light unto thee: but the Lord shall be unto thee an eve-

lasting light, and thy God thy glory.' I believe this will be his most blessed experience whenever our Lord takes him to Himself. I write with difficulty and in haste, but my heart is so very full towards you that I must express myself. My dear love to every one of your tenderly beloved party, particularly thy mother. I feel as it respects thy dearest father, whether a member of the Church militant or the Church triumphant, all is well—and we may, through all our tribulations return God thanks who giveth us the victory through Jesus Christ our Lord."

This noble man and Christian statesman passed to his inheritance on the 19th of February, 1845.

After this event, and the removal of a son-in-law, on account of his health, with his wife and a portion of their children to Madeira,—which also proved a final parting—Elizabeth Fry felt a strong desire to revisit Norfolk and stay awhile at her childhood home. This was accomplished with great difficulty by the aid of her husband and daughter Louisa; and she remained at Earlham many weeks, "often able to partake of enjoyment, and highly valuing the communion with her endeared brother, Joseph John Gurney, his wife, and her beloved sister Catherine.",

"She went frequently to Meeting at Norwich. She was drawn up to the Meeting seated in her wheeled chair, and thence ministered with extraordinary life and power to those present; her memory in using Scripture in no degree failing her, or her power in applying it."

That wheeled chair ought to be preserved as long as art can keep it. The throne of Queen Elizabeth is not half so honorable. Her brother, speaking of this visit, says:

"My dear sister Fry's visit has been very satisfactory, and very sweet has it been to our feelings to enjoy her company. Her infirmity is indeed great, and her memory a little failing. Yet at times this infirmity subsides and she is much like her own dear and precious self. The Lord's anointing is still upon her, and she has been well engaged in our meeting, which is held at eleven o'clock, on her account, and which she has attended two First-day mornings in succession. The preserving, sustaining hand of the Lord is evidently with her."

From Earlham she went to Northrepps "in order to mingle her sorrows with those of her much beloved and bereaved sister Buxton and other mourners there. The last letter she ever addressed to her husband was from that place, dated Fourth Month, 10th, 1845."

"MY DEAREST HUSBAND:—

I am anxious to express to thee a little of my near love, to tell thee how often I visit thee in spirit, and how very strong are my desires for thy present and everlasting welfare. I feel for thee in my long illness which so much disqualifies me from being all I desire to thee. I desire that thou mayst turn to the Lord for help and consolation under thy trials, and that whilst not depending on the passing pleasures and enjoyments of this world, thou mayst, at the same time be enabled to enjoy our many remaining blessings. I also desire this for myself, in my afflicted state, for I do consider such a state of health a heavy affliction, independent of all other trials. I very earnestly desire for myself that the deep tribulation I have had to pass through for so long a time, may not lead into temptation, but be sanctified to the further refinement of my soul, and preparation for eternal rest, joy and glory. May we, during our stay in time, be more and more sweetly united in the unity of the Spirit, and in the bond of Peace. . . ."

Her health improved sufficiently to enable her to attend two sittings of the Yearly Meeting. The event is thus described by a Friend who was present:—

"She had for many years been regular in her attendance upon these meetings, and had taken a lively interest in their proceedings. After an illness so critical, and still in a state of such great infirmity, to see her again amongst them was scarcely less gratifying to many of the Friends there than it was interesting to herself. On this occasion she spoke of the Saviour's declaration, 'I am the vine, ye are the branches; as the branch cannot bear fruit of itself, except it abide in the vine, no more can ye except ye abide in me.' She alluded in the course of her observations to the day that is 'fast approaching to every one;' but urged the blessed truth on her hearers that those 'who loved, served and obeyed Him who alone is worthy of all glory and praise, would find death deprived of its sting and the grave of its victory.' The second meeting she attended was one when a Friend, Edwin O. Tregelles, gave a relation of his missionary labors in the West Indies. This recital drew from her some account of her own travels on the Continent. She afterwards enlarged upon the various instruments by which God accomplishes His works in the world. She referred to the simile of the different living stones which compose the temple of God. She addressed those of every age who heard her; especially such as might be compared to the hidden stones of the building. She encouraged them to go forward faithfully in the path of righteousness and good works: for though they might not be so much seen and known as the more polished stones in the ornamental parts of the structure—though perhaps not so fitted to shine and occupy a conspicuous station—yet were their places equally ordered, equally important, and equally under the direction and all-seeing eye of the Divine Architect. She expressed doubts as to whether she should again be permitted to meet her beloved friends in that place. She offered prayer, her rich full voice filling the house, and concluded with that sublime passage, 'Great and marvelous are Thy works Lord God Almighty! just and true are Thy ways Thou King of Saints.'"

On the 3rd of June she attended the Annual Meeting of the Ladies British Society which, to spare her fatigue, was held in the Friends Meeting-house at Plaistow. After her death this occasion was referred to in a touching memorial drawn up by the members of this first of the numerous organizations of which she was the founder.

"Contrary to usual custom the place of meeting fixed on was not in London, but at Plaistow, in Essex; and the large number of Friends who gathered round her upon that occasion proved how gladly they came to her, when she could no longer with ease be conveyed to them. The enfeebled state of her bodily frame seemed to have left the powers of her mind unshackled, and she took, though in a sitting posture, almost her usual part in addressing the Meeting. She urged with increased pathos and affection the objects of philanthropy and Christian benevolence with which her life had been identified. After the Meeting, and at her own desire, several members of the Committee and other Friends assembled at her house. They were welcomed by her with the greatest benignity and kindness, and in her intercourse with them strong were the indications of the heavenly teaching through which her subdued and sanctified spirit had been called to pass. Her affectionate salutation in parting unconsciously closed, in regard to most of them, the intercourse which they delighted to hold with her, but which can no more be renewed on this side of the eternal world."

At this time Newgate, Bridewell, the Millbank Prison, the Gillspur Street Compter, White Cross Street Prison, Tothill Fields Prison, and Cold Bath Fields Prison were in good order, and the female convicts all cared for by the Committee. The prisons generally, throughout England were much improved, and in the greater number ladies were encouraged to visit the female convicts, and more than this, Elizabeth Fry had the satisfaction of knowing " that the principles she had so long asserted were universally recognized; that the object of penal legislation is not revenge, but the prevention of crime; in the first place by affording opportunity of reform to the criminal, and in the second by warning others from the consequences of its commission."

As summer advanced her husband took her to Ramsgate, to obtain the benefit of sea air. Before going there to remain she made a large wedding-party, at Upton, for her youngest son whose marriage was particularly pleasing to her, because he chose a Quakeress and friend of hers for his wife. She spoke of it as a "ray of light upon a dark picture."

"She received her guests in a room opening into the flower garden, and thence was wheeled to the end of the terrace; a very large family circle surrounded her, many connections, and others of her friends. It was a beautiful scene,—the last social family meeting at which she presided; and although infirm and broken in health, she looked and seemed herself.

"In an easy chair, under the large marquee, she entered into an animated discourse on various important topics with the group around her, the Chevalier Bunsen, M. Merle D'Aubigne, Sir Henry Pelley, Josiah Forster, her brother

Samuel Gurney, and others of her friends. An event of great interest shortly followed—the marriage of her faithful niece, Elizabeth Gurney, to Ernest Bunsen. This connection was one which her aunt liked, inasmuch as she valued the individual and highly esteemed his excellent and gifted parents, though not unmingled with regret that the children of her brother and sister, as so many of her own had done, should leave the Society of Friends by marriage, and thus separate themselves from that body of Christians to which their parents were so warmly attached. The wedding took place on the 5th of August. She joined the party afterwards at Ham House. It was an occasion of singular interest; Christian love, unity, and good feeling prevailing over 'diversities of administration,' yet all owning 'the same Lord.'"

This occasion was referred to by Madam (afterward Baroness) Bunsen, in a letter written after Mrs. Fry's death, as follows:

"We shall not look upon her like again! and must try to preserve the impression of her majesty of goodness which it is a great privilege to have beheld. I never wished more for the possession of the accurate memory which once was mine, than after hearing her exhort and pray, particularly on the day of Ernest's marriage. When we were at her house on the 3rd of July, on taking leave she said, 'May God bestow upon you His best gifts! the fatness of the earth is good, but the dew of Heaven is better.'"

In a letter of condolence to her daughter-in-law, Madam Bunsen also made this remark which it is pleasant to repeat as the tribute of one gifted and noble woman to another:

"What your blessed Aunt was for those who had the

privilege of approaching her continually, can in some degree be felt, even by us who only occasionally had felt her influence and been aware of the degree in which her whole life seemed to realize the life of God in man. She met everybody in every human sympathy, but of sin seemed to take no cognizance except in compassion." *

. "During the week following she was moved to the house on Mount Albion at Ramsgate which had been prepared for her A spacious bed-chamber adjoining the drawing-room. with pleasant views of the sea, in which she delighted, added to her hourly comfort and enjoyment. She found objects there well suited to her tastes. She distributed tracts when she drove into the country, or went upon the Pier in a Bath chair. Seafaring men have a certain openness of character which renders them more easy of access than others. They would gladly receive her little offerings and listen to her remarks. She was also anxious to ascertain the state of the Coast Guard Libraries—whether they required renewing, and were properly used."

Some of her family and friends were always with her, and did all that love and art could do to make her descent easy; but the bonds of mortality were still very painful. Her account with Nature had been over-drawn, and though it was in the best of causes, the day of reckoning must come. One had before said, speaking prophetically for Another, "The zeal of Thine house hath eaten me up:" and although in a different manner, it was yet true that this pure-souled woman laid down her life prematurely and painfully, that she might reconcile sinners unto God. The earnestness with which she toiled cut short her days in sor-

---

*Life and Letters of Baroness Bunsen.

row. Whether or not it was wise or justifiable to go beyond her strength, whether the Spirit of Highest Love and Wisdom really called for so much, or for only a part, and the momentum of excited feeling gave the extraordinary exertion and incurred the suffering, and whether more good was done during the time she labored than would have been done had she kept the fire from consuming the instrument and lived to work longer, are questions difficult to answer. It is no doubt true that in the disordered condition of the world, where so few will do their part, those willing and best competent must often become martyrs; must freely sacrifice their lives for the safety or improvement of the race. And the three years of daily outpouring, struggle, and combat which Jesus spent in Judea and Gallilee formed a longer span of time, if measured by their fruits, than that of the whole patriarchal age. Still the forfeit must be paid. The laws of nature, physical and moral alike, are inflexible. Atonement cannot be completed without a vicarious sacrifice equivalent to the shedding of blood, in larger or smaller measure, according to the exigency. The sacrifice of Christ was for the whole world; that of His children is for such a part as they stand related to in like manner, as His ministers—heads of nations, families and so on. As we are branches of the one Vine our crosses must also be branches of the one Cross. Having been saved by the one efficient Offering, does not exempt us from sorrow and sacrifice; but it raises these to the same divine order and makes us partakers of the vicarious sorrow of Christ for the sins and wants of others. How it ennobles the sufferings of Elizabeth Fry to know that they were the direct consequence of her earnest zeal to serve her Master in pleading for the lowest class of society and bringing the means of restoration within their reach. How touching becomes this nearly last entry in her Journal, written in an almost illegible hand:—

"*Ramsgate, Eighth Month,* 27*th.*—It still pleases my Heavenly Father that afflictions should abound to me in this tabernacle; as I groan, being burthened. Lord, through the fullness of Thy love and pity and unmerited mercy be pleased to arise for my help. Bind up my broken heart, heal my wounded spirit, and yet enable Thy servant, through the power of Thine own Spirit, in everything to return Thee thanks, and not to faint in the day of trouble, but in humility and godly fear to show forth Thy praise. Keep me Thine own, through Thy power to do this, and pity and help Thy poor servant who trusteth in Thee. Be very near to our dear son and daughter in Madeira. Be with them and all near to us wherever scattered; and grant that Thy peace and blessing may rest upon us all. Amen and amen."

September 14th she wrote to her brother Samuel Gurney—

"I was very low when I wrote to thee yesterday, therefore do not think too much of it. There is One only who sees in secret who knows the conflicts I have to pass through. To Him I commit my body, soul, and spirit; and He only knows the depth of my love and earnestness of my prayers for you all. I have the humble trust that He will be my Keeper even unto the end; and when the end comes, through the fullness of His love, and the abundance of His merits, I shall join those who, after having passed 'through great tribulation,' are forever at rest in Jesus, having 'washed their robes and made them white in the blood of the Lamb.'

"I am, in nearest love,

Thy grateful and tenderly attached sister, E. F."

"Pray remember the books for the poor old women; we must work while it is called 'to-day,' however low the service we may be called to; I desire to do so to the end, through the help that may be granted me."

After this she rode four miles to attend a little meeting, and "preached a most powerful and remarkable sermon on the nearness of death and the necessity of immediate repentance and preparation, for she believed to some of that small congregation it was the eleventh hour of the day."

"Her habits at this time were apparently those of former days. She was a good deal occupied by writing. She arranged and sorted Bibles, Testaments and tracts. She had applied to the Bible Society for a grant of foreign Bibles and Testaments which was liberally acceded to, and in the distribution of which, amongst the sailors of different nations in the harbor, she took great interest."

She attended meeting for worship October 5th, referring to which on her return she said, "We have had a very remarkable meeting, such a peculiarly solemn time;" adding that she had been so impressed by the "need of working whilst it was day, to be ready for the Master's summons, come when He might." Those who were present described the occasion as "a very peculiar one. She had urged the question 'Are we all now ready? If the Master should this day call us, is the work completely finished? Have we anything left to do?' Solemnly, almost awfully reiterating the question, 'Are we prepared?'"

On Friday of the following week she wrote a letter, and copied some texts for a person who desired her autograph. She then brought out some sheets of Scripture selections which she was preparing with a view to eventually publish-ing another Text-book. "With this devout employment, was finished her work below." On riding out later in the morning her mind seemed to be abstracted from surround-ing objects, so that she failed to notice a request for "some reading" from a farmer's boy who was keeping cows, until her grandchildren placed her tract-bag in her hand, and then she made the selections "with a slow and distracted air, as if her thoughts were far away."

The next morning she awoke suffering severely in her head; but received company which she had invited to din-ner, and conversed a little. In the afternoon her strength failed and she was with difficulty removed to her bed; but she answered the physician's questions correctly.

About six o'clock on Sabbath morning she said to her maid, "Oh! Mary, dear Mary, I am very ill!" "I know it, dearest Ma'am, I know it," replied the servant. Soon she added, "Pray for me—it is a strife—but I am safe." Near nine o'clock, while one of her daughters was sitting by her bed side with the Bible opened to a favorite passage in Isa-iah, she roused a little from her comatose state, and in a slow, distinct voice uttered these words:—"Oh! my dear Lord, help and keep Thy servant!" Her daughter then read the passage,—"I the Lord thy God will hold thy right hand, saying unto thee, fear not thou worm Jacob, and ye men of Israel, I will help thee, saith the Lord, and thy Redeemer, the Holy One of Israel." One bright look of recognition passed over her features, and then she sank into a state of unconsciousness from which she did not re-vive. About four o'clock in the morning of October 13th,

1845, the strife of nature ceased, and she entered into that Rest which remaineth for the people of God.

What imagination can picture the scene as her spirit rose to meet the happy company waiting to welcome her to that "City which hath no need of the sun, neither of the moon to shine in it; for the Glory of God doth lighten it, and the Lamb is the light thereof!"

The funeral took place at Barking a few miles from London, where a large company assembled in a spacious tent erected for the occasion, and appropriate services were held in the quiet order of Friends, which admitted of no public demonstration. Her monument had long been erected in the hearts of the people, where it must remain, rising still higher as long as her story is read. If every grateful recollection of Elizabeth Fry were represented by a stone as beautiful as that memory, no material monument of king or hero has ever equaled what these would build. And may not such, in some higher sense, be the nature of the heavenly mansion which her Lord has prepared for her, by the aid of her own faithfulness and industry—a home of joy—built up and adorned not only with gems of human love and esteem, but, crowning all with that Pearl for which she freely gave all that she possessed.

Possibly too that faithful Rewarder of His servants may have ordained as He did in the case of another, who, from the broken alabaster box, poured the precious ointment upon His head and His *feet*—"Wheresoever this gospel shall be preached in the whole world, there also shall this which this woman hath done be told for a memorial of her."

We cannot more fittingly close this account than with

the concluding remarks of her daughters who are her authentic biographers, and who were naturally best qualified to express what remained to be said after she had herself spoken.

"Conclusion.—There may be some who expect a sketch to be here given of the character of Elizabeth Fry—but a little reflection will show that in the present case to attempt doing so would be presumptuous. Neither is it necessary. Her actions and conduct in life have been narrated. Her letters to her family and friends portray her domestic feelings and her power of loving. Her communications to others supply the knowledge of her opinions upon the subjects to which she gave her attention. In her Journal may be found the outpourings of her heart, the communings between God and her own soul.

"But there is a voice from the Dead—and the living are called to proclaim, before their work is concluded and the memory of the departed committed to the stream of time, something of her earnest desires for the well-being of her fellow creatures, especially for that of her own sex. She was willing to spend and be spent in her Master's service. She considered herself called to a peculiar course. She was very young when she first saw a prison; she had an extraordinary desire to visit one, and at last her father yielded to her wishes and took her to see a bridewell—when and where is not exactly known; but not long before her death she narrated the circumstances to a friend, and how powerful an impression it had made upon her mind. It must be a question whether this visit was occasioned by, or led to the peculiar bent of her disposition; that it tended to strengthen it is indubitable, and that it was one link in the chain of Providential circumstances which produced in the end such signal results. But she would have shrunk from urging the same course upon others. She feared her daughters, and young women generally, undertaking questionable or difficult public offices; but she believed that where one erred from over-activity in duty many more omitted that which it behooved them to perform. 'Woman's mission' has become almost a word of the day. Elizabeth Fry was persuaded that every woman has her individual vocation and that in following it she would fulfill her mission. She laid great stress on the outward circumstances of life; how and where providentially placed; the opportunities afforded; the powers given. She considered domestic duties the first and greatest earthly claims in the life of woman; although, in accordance with the tenets of the Society to which she belonged, she believed in some instances, her own amongst others, that under the immediate direction of the Spirit of God, individuals were called to leave for a time their homes and families and devote themselves to the work of the ministry. She did not consider this call to be general, or to apply to persons under an administration different from her own. But it was her conviction that there is a sphere of usefulness open to all. She appreciated to the full the usual charities of gentlewomen—their visits to the sick and aged poor, and their attention to the cottage children; but she grieved to think how few complete the work of mercy by following the widow or disabled when driven by necessity to the workhouse, or caring for the workhouse school, that resort of the orphaned and forsaken, less attractive, perhaps, than the school of the village, but even more requiring oversight and attention.

"A fearful accident, or hereditary disease, consigns the mother of a family, or some frail child to the hospital. In how many cases does she lie there from day to day, watching the rays of the morning sun reflected on the wall opposite, tracing them as they move onward through the day and disappear as it advances—and this, perhaps for weeks and months, without hearing the voice of kindness and sym-

pathy from her own sex, save from the matron, or the hired
nurses of the establishment. What might not, and when
bestowed, what does not, woman's tenderness effect here?

"She heard of thousands and ten-thousands of homeless
and abandoned children, wandering or perishing in our
streets. She knew that attempts were made to rescue them,
and that unflinching men and women labored and toiled to
infuse some portion of moral health into that mass of living
corruption; but she mourned that so few assisted in this
work of mercy, compared to the many who utterly neglect
the call. She saw a vast number of her own sex degraded
and guilty—many a fair young creature, once the light of
her parents' dwelling, fallen and polluted—many who had
filled useful situations in business or domestic service sunk-
en and debased—the downward road open wide before them
but no hand stretched forth to lift them the first step up
the rugged path of repentance, or assist in their hard struggle against sin. She encountered in the prisons every grade
and variety of crime—woman bold and daring and reckless,
reveling in her iniquity and hardened in vice, her only remaining joy to seduce others and make them still more the
children of Hell than herself; the thoughtless culprit, not
lost to good and holy feeling nor dead to impression from
without; and lastly the beginner, she who from poverty
had been driven to theft or drawn by others into temptation. Elizabeth Fry marked all these and *despaired of none
amongst them!* Here again, in her estimation, a crying
need existed for influence, for instruction, for reproof, and
for encouragement. But it was not to all she would have
allotted *this* task, though she could never be persuaded but
that in every instance women well qualified for the office
might be found to care for the interests of the people.

"These were the things which she saw and bitterly deplored. She believed that a mighty power rested with her
own sex to check and control this torrent of evil—a moral

force which the educated and virtuous might bring to bear upon the ignorant and vicious. She desired to have every home duty accomplished, every household affection met; but reason and Scripture taught her that each individual has something to bestow, either of time, talent, or wealth, which, spent in the service of others, would return in blessing on herself and her own family. In the little parlor behind the shop, in the suburban villa, in the perfumed boudoir and the gilded hall, she saw powers unemployed and time unoccupied. She lived to illustrate all that she had advocated. She wore away her life in striving for the good of her fellow-beings.

"Does she now regret those labors? or find any service to have been 'in vain in the Lord?' When our great Redeemer declared that in feeding the hungry and giving the thirsty drink, receiving the stranger, clothing the naked, and visiting the sick, it was done unto Him, He added, 'I was in *prison* and ye came unto me.' She was one who felt the force of this commendation, and took it in its largest sense—not as applicable to those alone who 'suffer for conscience sake,' but to the guilty and the wretched—in the spirit of Him who came to seek and to save that which is lost. Through weariness and painfulness she labored to fulfill it. And now that her conflicts upon earth are ended, and her work done, may it not be confidently believed that for her, and such as her, are those words of marvelous joy—'Come ye blessed of my Father, inherit the Kingdom prepared for you from the foundation of the world.'"

ELIZABETH FRY.

"A Name of Beauty," well hath said
  Admiring love of one whose charms
A pure and saintly radiance shed
  O'er human life—a light which warms

The soul to virtue while it feeds
  Hope with a calm celestial fire,
And confidence in noble deeds.
  · Why hath the rapt heroic lyre

Not sung thee, Earlham's gentle maid,
  Modest and sweet, who taught the poor
And many a grateful offering laid
  By sorrow's couch and penury's door?—

Who bowed thy heart with all its dower
  Of brilliant hopes and love replete,
Like a fresh-opening passion-flower,
  Low at thy waiting Savior's feet,—

Took up a cross so few could bear,
  Unmurmuring; doffed the idle weeds
Of fashion; bade thy feet prepare
  To follow Christ where'er He leads,—

To honor follow, or to shame—
　　It matters not: thy troth is given
Without reserve, only from blame
　　Deliverance asking, and in Heaven

To love and be beloved, to meet,
　　With all thy friends in safety there,
Vast multitudes made pure and sweet
　　By Jesus' love, its bliss share.

Oh great heart motherly! God saw
　　Thy wish, God heard thy noble plea
And sent His angels forth to draw
　　Thy golden net through Galilee.

After a night of toil and strife,
　　Fruitful in trial's needful lore,
And increase fair of thy own life,
　　Thy risen Savior walked the shore,

And taught thee how to drop thy line,—
　　Where in the world's great heaving pool
To cast thy net; *the word divine*
　　Thou kept, and lo! a motley school

Of fishes gathered at His call
　　From the deep shadows of the lake!
And what is wondrous most of all
　　Thy quivering cords did never break!

A dozen fair apostles soon
  With thee grasped oar, and Christ-ward drew
Right womanly, while the strange boon
  Larger with every moment grew,

Until good men, brave, true and strong,
  Seized manfully the lengthening line,
And urged the miracle along,
  Searching for souls in sin's dark brine.

All Britain's coasts and stagnant pools
  Thy love bade search for drowning men,
And many were the dying souls
  Thus taught to love and live again.

Nor thus content, while foreign seas
  And rivers rolled with sorrow's tide,
There flowed thy boundless sympathies,
  O saintliest type of Jesus' Bride!

"Ho! stretch the cords from shore to shore!
  Join all for sweet Humanity!
For God, for Heaven, join rich and poor!
  Join, high and low, and bond and free!"

And kings the noble frenzy caught,
  And queens thy sweet behest obeyed,
Statesmen by thy wise lips were taught,
  And the rude throng their magic swayed.

Light through the dismal dungeon poured,
    With rainbow hues of mercy clothed!
Again the words of Salem's Lord
    The sinful roused, the sorrowing soothed!

March on! march on! admiring France
    Thrills to the music of thy voice!
Not Joan with her virgin lance
    Made gallant pulses more rejoice!

The Christian patriot bids hail
    Mercy's meek angel as she threads
The glittering street or gloomy vale,
    Where most the call of sorrow leads!

And Freedom from her Alpine heights
    Comes forth to kiss the gentle hand
Which to a purer realm invites
    The least and greatest of her band.

March on! the Netherlands give ear
    Gladly to thy mellifluous plea;
Harsh chains relax, the mellowing tear
    Leaps from the rock at Love's decree.

On to the wakening Fatherland,
    Where kings a royal welcome give,
And sister queens uphold the hand
    Which bids the weak and wandering live '

Nor yet alone the poor and blind
   Thou win'st to virtue's upward road,
But princes of the heart and mind
   With thee walk nearer to their God.

Lifting the soul on wings of prayer
   Thou bear'st it to the blossoming skies,
Or gently layest it, weeping, where
   The Lamb of God for sinners dies.

Sweet gift of mother love divine!
   Oh how the thirsting heart of man
Needs thee, ev'n at devotion's shrine,
   To teach as only mother's can—

How the Lord Gracious stooped to bless
   And break for us sin's prison doors,
To smile away life's bitterness,
   And point dead Hope to mercy's shores—

Through light and darkness, praise and blame,
   How like a slave for us He toiled,
Raised us to glory by His shame,
   And by His death our spoiler spoiled.

Such lessons yet may woman teach
   In holy word and graceful deed;
So cheer the struggling soul to reach
   Redemption's gate and faith's bright meed.

Forgetful only that thine arm
    Was mortal, though by Heaven inspired,
Assured that love can work no harm,
    And bear each cross by Love required,

Through storm and sunshine thus thy feet
    Past mount and valley hastened on,
Still scattering Zion's golden wheat
    O'er fertile field and wayside stone,

And founding granaries where the poor,
    And the lone watchman, with his flock,
May feed upon thought's healthful store,
    And find green pastures on the rock.

Nor ceased thy toils when evening fell,
    Fire-winged, upon the harvest plain,
And saw the o'erflowing river swell
    To meet thee with thy goodly train.

Nor did thy loving arms forget,
    With all their load of gathered sheaves,
Ev'n amid Jordan's billows, yet
    To grasp and clasp the falling leaves.

Though burns the fire of wasting pain
    Thy soul with heavenly music flows,
And like the Lamb for sinners slain
    Yields fragrant balm for others' woes.

Oh more than conqueror! thy Lord
   Did well to press such vintage hard,
For sweeter wine was never stored
   In heart of saint or tongue of bard.

In the pearl gate thou fain wouldst turn
   To see if all were pressing on—
Still o'er a dying world to yearn
   Like angel mother o'er her son—

One word of comfort more to give,
   One jewel more to gather up,
Another soul for Christ to live,
   A drop of balm for sorrow's cup!

Seraphic Spirit! saintliest star
   Of England's bright and beauteous train!
So shineth from her throne afar
   The gem that lights the morning main!

Shine on and tell us how to sail,
   Unmoved by fortune's frowns or smiles,
How on time's sea to bide the gale,
   And anchor by Life's golden isles.—

"The Pilot!" aye, we hear thee, mother—
   "With heart and ear attend His word!
"Him love and also one another!
   "Greeting to all who love the Lord!"